FROM WORL[...]

JOHANNESB[...] -
tions were calle[...]
search failed to [...]
who vanished a[...]ing their dome on a
charity mission. Questioning of Outsiders
turned up no clues to the
disappearance. . . .

STOCKHOLM, 05/16/46—Open Sky spokeswoman Ingrid Hibberd was taken into custody today. Ms. Hibberd's organization has
been increasingly vocal in its criticism of
Stockholm's policy toward the local Outsider
population. "Open Sky" refers to the members' conviction that doming is unnatural and
should be done away with as soon as Outside conditions permit. . . .

TUAMATUTETUAMATU 05/15/46—Planters
Assocation President Imre Deeland was overheard by an alert press when he admitted that
he had indeed heard stories about the Conch,
the mythical hero of the local tribes and a symbol of their resistance to the proposed doming
of the island. Mr. Deeland has previously denied
all knowledge of the folk hero, despite tribal
claims that the Conch actually exists and that his
magical powers are being employed in the
service of their cause. . . .

HARMONY

Marjorie Bradley Kellogg

A ROC BOOK

ROC
Published by the Penguin Group
Penguin Books USA Inc., 375 Hudson Street,
New York, New York 10014, U.S.A.
Penguin Books Ltd, 27 Wrights Lane,
London W8 5TZ, England
Penguin Books Australia Ltd, Ringwood,
Victoria, Australia
Penguin Books Canada Ltd, 2801 John Street,
Markham, Ontario, Canada L3R 1B4
Penguin Books (N.Z.) Ltd, 182–190 Wairau Road,
Auckland 10, New Zealand

Penguin Books Ltd, Registered Offices:
Harmondsworth, Middlesex, England

First published by Roc, an imprint of New American Library, a division
of Penguin Books USA Inc.

First Printing, September, 1991
10 9 8 7 6 5 4 3 2 1

"Morning Poem," by Mary Oliver
From the book *Dream Work*, Atlantic Monthly Press, 1986

 Roc is a trademark of New American Library, a division of
Penguin Books USA Inc.

PRINTED IN THE UNITED STATES OF AMERICA

to S. R.
(at last)

For their willingness to read and for their generously offered expertise, heartfelt thank-yous to Diann Duthie, John Kellogg, Lynne Kemen, Ken Frankel, Michael Golder, Mel Marvin, Betsy Munnell, Bill Rossow, Joel Schwartz, Angela Wigan, and of course, my editor, John Silbersack.

And special thanks to Ming, Robin, Tony, Ted, Virginia, and Desmond, the Micahs in my own life.

. . . there is still
somewhere deep within you
a beast shouting that the earth
is exactly what it wanted—

each pond with its blazing lilies
is a prayer heard and answered
lavishly,
every morning,

whether or not
you have ever dared to be happy,
whether or not
you have ever dared to pray

—Mary Oliver

PROLOGUE

GWINN:

I wasn't born in Harmony. I've never been that lucky, except for being born Inside. Chicago's my birth-dome, a sad and sullen place to grow up if ever there was one. But overcoming disadvantage can make you strong. My mom always said that about herself, and my dad swore I took after her.

You could say my story begins with the Dissolution, though I wasn't born 'til ten years after the worst of it, when Famine, War, Plague, and that newer grim horseman, Ecological Collapse, had already reordered life on this earth, and those who were able: the strongest, the richest— in Chicago, we'd have said the most righteous—had holed up twenty years since behind the high-tech walls we post-crisis generations took for granted.

Your history program will have taught you that Chicago was one of the first cities to Enclose by public ballot: October 4, 2002, it was, our only official holiday for decades after. Every liquifiable civic asset was staked on a first-generation field-technology dome. There was pioneer courage in that, to be sure, but there was shame as well. Having sold off the priceless contents of the Art Institute and stripped the sculpture gardens and libraries bare, Chicago's crisis leadership finally delegalized the Arts. Painting, writing, music, sculpture—all declared "societally non-productive." After all, they said, you can't eat Art.

True enough. But these righteous citizens also felt the need to revenge themselves on the "decadents" who had opposed the final measures. Punishment was mass expulsion of all artists but those with a useful skill—my wise painter-mother took up industrial design just in time. People who were neither warriors nor survivalists were thrown out without recourse when the dome was raised, to fend for themselves in what had already come to be called the Outside.

The witch-hunts continued for years. You'd see it on the vid at dinnertime: some poor citizen caught with his life's work stashed away in his vent ducts or inside his mattress. The expulsion ceremony was preceded by a public burning

of the offending work, attendance for children compulsory.
The generation who built those walls intended that we who
had never seen the Outside would fear it as much as they
did. Extreme times require extreme measures, you'll say,
but why, with the food crisis well under control, is it still
illegal to be an artist in Chicago?

The point is, Chicago then or now holds no future for a
would-be artist, and that was me from an early age. Others,
friends of mine, dutifully channeled their creative leanings
into the approved applications. I continued to scribble and
sketch when I should have been learning resource management or the new economic theory. My mother's fault, no
doubt, despite endless bedtime conferences in the glare of
the overhead fluorescents. She meant to help me overcome
my anti-social impulses but never could hide her longing for
the old paints and brushes. Being Inside-born, I took for
granted my right to safety in the dome and thought my
mom's Dissolution-survivor gratitude too slavish for one
who'd been forced to give up her art. The secret hours of
my childhood were enlivened by the struggle to capture the
images rising unbidden behind my eyes—with pencil, paper,
plastic, wood scraps, bits of string, anything available. Nothing else seemed worthwhile, or even interesting.

And so I went to Harmony.

I couldn't just pick up and go. It wasn't as easy as that.
I didn't even know where—or if—Harmony was. Nobody
official in Chicago would admit to the existence of such a
heathen place. But I'd heard rumors and chose to believe
them. I *needed* to believe them. Surely every artist in her
heart believes there is a place like Harmony, where if only
she can find it, she will be left alone to do her work in
peace.

The rumors were forbidden, delicious. I nursed them like
the precious candies my mother made with hoarded sugar
on the sly. They said Harmony was green and spacious, the
food was varied and plentiful. Each citizen owned his own
home. Paintings were exhibited right out in the streets, and
all the studios had north light.

The downside, rumor claimed, was that only artists could
live there and that Harmony's population was by constitutional law fed only by the adoption of promising young talent from *other domes*, as a guard against aesthetic
inbreeding. At the time, I was deeply impressed by such

total commitment to Art and Excellence. Population was always a crisis issue within the domes. Chicago's census was updated daily on the public news channels, alongside the harvest data from our struggling farm domes, and any unlicensed child was put Out as soon as discovered. (Into the Lord's hands, my mother would say, with reflex if compassionate acceptance, the way of a true survivor.) So I didn't wonder what became of the children *born* under Harmony's dome. I saw this Outside Adoption Policy as my escape hatch. I had only to prove I was the sort of promising young talent Harmony was looking for.

Once I'd decided to resist authority, the trick was doing it invisibly. I pondered this late into the night during the long, gray months of my thirteenth year, then buckled down to my math and physics and managed to qualify for a Building and Engineering course at the local technical school, the closest thing to art training you could get in Chicago. My mother watched me narrow-eyed while my father sighed with relief, secure in his delusion that I was at last preparing to assume a citizen's proper responsibility.

They wouldn't teach free-hand drawing at Chi-Tech, but one of the endemic shortages was terminals, so I did learn to draft by hand. Happy to be drawing at all, I produced endless plans, elevations, and orthographics of boring solar collectors and hydroponics plants. I was initiated into the mysteries of the laser knife and the point welder, if only to build hulking models of factories and housing blocks. I absorbed graphics programming, memorized load- and stress-tolerance tables, all critical information for survival in this broken world, but dull stuff for a teenager living on romantic fantasies. It was boredom as profound as starvation. My manna in the wilderness was my dream of an artistic future. Concentrating on technique, I locked my imagination away until it could wing free in Harmony.

By the time my schoolmates threw off their cocoons to flutter about as women and young men, I had metamorphosed into a determined workaholic. Friendships and social life died from neglect. Every credit I could pry loose from basic food and clothing went in secret to buy computer time, literally bit by bit, until I had enough to send formal e-mail application to Harmony. In truth, there was nothing formal about it. I had no forms, no names or addresses. I couldn't save enough to send a real portfolio. I hadn't a single assurance that my painstakingly worded plea would reach the proper hands, or any hands at all outside Chicago.

But months later, when I had nearly given up hope, a foreign signal waltzed through Chicago's electronic blockade like a voice from another planet. What this said about Harmony's power in the post-Dissolution world impressed my parents more than it did me. All I cared was that Harmony's computers, sifting reams of applications from domes everywhere, had spat mine out into the Yes pile.

A miracle.

The acceptance statement made me an instant provisional ward of the Town of Harmony, to avoid complications when I tried to leave Chicago. I was invited for a year of trial apprenticeship in the studio of Micah Cervantes. Harmony, the information file explained, was a dome complex in the upland valleys of what used to be Vermont, USA. It was, as rumor claimed, home to many of the world's most famous painters, sculptors, actors, and musicians, glittering names that meant nothing to me in benighted Chicago.

No matter. After six years of blind faith and sacrifice, there on our living room terminal was proof that while Harmony was not so far from Chicago geographically, it was ideologically at the other end of the universe. Exactly where I wanted to be.

The offer was better than my wildest imaginings. It included transportation, room, and board. My parents would not suffer, at least not materially, from my repudiation of their city and their values. The catch was that if I failed to please in Harmony, I would be put Out, and my birth-dome was in no way required to take me back. My citizenship was forfeit the second I walked out of Chicago. My father called me a fool and a wasteling. My mother wept, but her eyes smiled proudly.

I, in the flush of youth, didn't give the long run an instant's thought. I was sure Harmony would recognize my genius and take me immediately to her long-dreamed-of bosom. I had no idea who this guy Cervantes was or what he did. That he did it in Harmony was enough for me. I accepted the invitation, my every fantasy come true. Or so I thought.

But of course, therein lies my tale.

THE OUTSIDE:

A brief digression:

Do you remember the world twenty years ago?

Of course not. Like me, you were taught very little about it. In straitened isolationist enclaves like Chicago, truth was an unaffordable luxury in those days. Even with order restored Inside, often with an iron fist, the average dome-dweller remained too haunted by memories of plague and collapse to admit that the horrors he'd walled himself away from still lurked Outside, awaiting solution. Inside air was sanitized, water purified, food and materials dome-grown and recycled. Living Inside, you didn't think about the Outside. You only feared it.

Children were raised on horror stories, at home, in church, in school. No one went Outside, at least not willingly. Outside was Ye Forest Darke, Grendel's Cave, the final circle of Hell. Outside was where I'd end up if I didn't behave. My actual experience of it was limited to staring at the ruined suburbs from atop Chicago's encircling generator wall. Broken buildings, dead, littered streets and smoke, always smoke. Something was always burning Out there. We'd nod to each other, wise children: *Outsider work*, we'd say. *Berserkers*. But even those grim visions were softened by the wavering energies of our primitive dome. Field technology has improved a lot since then. Much harder now to pretend that what you see out there isn't quite real.

When it was time to leave for Harmony, I was in a terror about facing the Outside. But domers would never leave a vital transportation system on the surface where Outsiders could get at it. The entire thousand-mile journey was safely underground by high-speed Tube. That is, until I got to Harmony.

Harmony was a mere village of twenty thousand when the Enclosure Movement caught fire, a colony of successful artists hiding out in the cleaner, safer hills from the increasing violence and political polarization of the times. They Enclosed reluctantly and as a last resort, vowing to remain a haven for the inalienable freedoms of speech and belief,

if not of movement. They weren't the only small community
to try doming without big-city resources, but their wealth
and like-mindedness made them one of the few to succeed.
Still, the irony of having to wall themselves in and others
out in order to preserve these freedoms was not lost on
them, for the Founders made sure that to enter Harmony,
one must at least briefly go Outside.

They made their point.

Most domes are like Chicago: urban, fortified, with Tube
transport to the airports accessed from Inside. Not so Harmony. Vacuum tubes bring imported supplies direct from
the transfer network, but Harmony has allowed no passen-
ger-tube connection to her residential dome. Material goods
may travel fast and deep enough to be safe from Outsider
tampering, but a human visitor must board a shuttle at an
overworked air/rail terminal shared with Albany Dome and
the Springfield industrial complex. This lethargic hover is
little more than a rickety frame with windows. It lumbers
between gray and smoking hills, drops sickeningly onto a
broad oval tarmac, and spits you out into the open air.

You huddle among strangers at the bottom of the ramp.
They're mostly tourists on day visas, and you're all stunned
as the hover takes off and leaves you . . . *Outside*. Ahead
the great curve of Harmony's main dome looms like a rising
planet, huge and blue-green and shimmering above a rolling
gray horizon. I'd never seen a dome from the Outside
before. How disconcerting that this dance of energies should
look so fragile, as insubstantial as a soap bubble. And
though its vastness makes it seem close, you must walk an
entire half kilometer down a wide boulevard paved in amber
granite before you reach the arched and columned safety of
Harmony's Gate.

You suffer an eternity walking down that boulevard.

Your dome-bred lungs constrict against air that smells like
smoke and dirt, and leaves an aftertaste of metal on your
tongue. Ingrained terrors of poisoned air catch at your
throat. You wonder should you, could you, hold your
breath until the Gate? You discover agoraphobia, which has
nothing to do with marketplaces at all, but with the gasping
need for a lid, a roof, of any kind, anything to shut out the
vast, unending sky. The tourist brochures suggest it helps
to bring a wide-brimmed hat.

Finally, should you conquer your panic sufficiently to

maintain a dignified pace, or manage even to raise your glance from the solid, blessed ground to peer through the double lines of green-uniformed security guards, stern and anonymous behind their respirators, you come face-to-face, maybe for the first time in your life, with the understanding that there are actual people living outside the domes. Not the blurred shadows I tracked slow-moving beyond Chicago's coarse-tuned force field, but walking, breathing humans camped along the boulevard in tents and board shacks and lean-tos, cuffing their ragged children not five feet away, stirring their pots of gray muck over dying coals, too weak and dispirited to do anything more terrifying than stare. They are short and scrawny and misshapen by filthy layers of domer cast-off clothing. Their masklike faces are too weather-roughened to be anything a domer might recognize as skin. They wear odd hoods and scarves and slant-brimmed hats, and thick gloves with the fingers torn away, but the thing you can't avoid is the reflex hatred in their eyes, so confused with desperation it's like they grab the heart right out of you and squeeze it dry.

But my story is not about the Outside, nor about the lies that are lived beneath the domes, at least not here, not at the beginning. What I need to tell is what Harmony was, since you know better than I what it is now. And so, we move on to my arrival, and one detail that seemed colorful but insignificant at the time.

Would it have made any difference if I had known?

HARMONY:

I gained the Gate without incident and got in line. It was air lock eight, I remember. One lock said CITIZENS ONLY, nine said VISITORS. I wondered at that, as I patted the pockets of my thin shirt for my precious apprentice visa. It was March, cold and raw Outside. The air made me sneeze. Many of the tourists wore coats and even gloves. I did not own a coat. Variable-climate technology was too recent and too expensive for the likes of Chicago.

I distracted myself from my coughing and shivering by studying the imposing facade of the Gate. Three tiers of classical arches connected tapered pillars of polished granite. The air locks were set inside the lower arches. Above the highest tier, a bas-relief crossed smooth salmon-colored stone. Big-boned women with serious eyes danced the width of the Gate, holding aloft thick books and paintbrushes, and playing strange musical instruments.

"Turpsish . . ." I struggled with the block-lettered inscription.

"Terpsichore! Calliope! Euterpe! Music in the very names, child!"

The tall figure beside me was robed and veiled in black, like Arab women in my ancient history video. A braceleted arm curled familiarly around mine. A dark-skinned hand pointed gracefully. "See them up there? Laughing Thalia and Melpomene, always so sad? And Erato . . . well, we know about her. And there's noble Polyhymnia in the center. The Muse of Harmony, you know."

"Of course," I lied. The voice, deep and rhythmic, was a woman's, and full of laughter. Her oval fingernails were bright turquoise-blue. I tried to peer without staring through her veil.

"Well, greet them, child! These poor ladies are so neglected!" She hugged my arm to her side and steered me back into the queue. She jingled and tinkled as she moved, faint melody and dissonance from beneath the soft folds of her robe. "Few visitors take the time with them. Too much haste to scurry back Inside."

She seemed to want to share a laugh with me, but I felt that same haste myself and didn't know why I should mock the tourists for it. She chattered gaily as we approached the airlock. Her energy and volubility made me chatter back. I am not a chatterer by nature, but she had my whole story by the time the six tourists ahead of us had cycled through the lock. Then she was sliding her papers and my own together through the vacuum slot to the green-coated immigration official in his plastic booth.

Her hand guided my shoulder. Her posture was suddenly slower, stooped. An old woman's voice reassured the official from under the opaque black veil: "Delivering this young 'un to be apprentice."

He studied my papers quite carefully. He barely glanced at hers. When I passed muster, he nodded and cycled us through the lock together. I reclaimed my papers on the other side and entered into my new life on the arm of a magical stranger.

My first, relieved gulps of "proper" Inside air were an instant sense memory of my grandfather's bedroom. My beloved grandfather: physically and spiritually broken by the horrors of the Dissolution, he hid himself away to spend every waking hour tending a scavenged zoo of houseplants. He groomed them, crooned to them, rotated them in turns into the light of his tiny window. I was allowed to visit but had to slip in quickly and shut the door, so that Grandpa's precious "green air" did not escape. Because he told wonderful stories of Before, I forgave his obvious insanity. His generation often exhibited such damage. We kids knew that was the way things were.

And now, an entire dome filled with Grandpa's green air, moist and sweet and earthy. How could I help but fall in love with it?

My tall companion drew me away from the Gate, still chattering. I was too bedazzled to answer. We faced a vast plaza, sun-drenched and warm. Outside it was March-gray. The pavement was an intricate floral swirl, yellow flowers chasing green and blue leaves across the square. Public eating places lined opposite sides, wide glass doors open to the square, umbrella-shaded tables spilling into the plaza like children's toys. In Chicago, there might be a cafeteria every eight or ten blocks, but you really had to search for it. Here, the clatter of laughter and glassware was as gay as the flowerboxes trailing fuchsia and nasturtiums from the second-story terraces. Crowds strolled the square, plump with shopping bags, resplendent in bright, strange clothing. Men in ankle-length skirts or thigh-length shorts. Women in saris and kimonos. Clothing I'd seen only in pictures from Before and thought people didn't wear anymore. The riot of color made my eyes brim and my fingers itch for pastel or crayon, as if it might be taken from me at any moment.

Past the blue-tiled café roofs, steep hillsides rose frothed in green. The plaza could be easily defended from above if the Gates were breached (which had surely occurred in the early days: I'd been taught no doming was ever accomplished without violence). At the far end of the square, a half-dozen graceful tiled arches framed the domestic Tube station.

I turned to my companion with a question, and promptly

forgot it. Her black headcloth and veil had vanished. Her black robe had become a breathtaking blue. I stared, and her strong mahogany face glowed with mischief. The glass beads trimming her hundreds of tiny braids chimed and glittered as she laughed. "Now, child! How do I look?"

"Oh! Incredible!"

Her smile was ageless and dazzling. She was the most astonishing creature a poor innocent from Chicago could ever hope to meet on her first day in a new world.

She snatched up my hand and pulled me deeper into the crowd, glancing about as if looking for someone. In the shade of a red and white café awning, she let the front of her blue robe fall open and peeled back her draping sleeves. Rows and rows of bracelets circled her arms. Necklaces layered her dark neck and looped around her waist, bright against the silky black of her undergarment. Hoops and chains of beaten brass and wood and pale white bone, strands of blue glass and threaded opalescent shells, pendants of carved pink stone and semiprecious jewels, loops of dyed fiber and painted wood. I'd never seen such jewelry in all my life.

"Choose which you will have. For bringing me through the Gate."

Had I done that?

She smiled at my puzzlement, that astonishing smile that made me stare again in wonder. "Quick, now. Choose. Before the Greens catch on to me. The merchants aren't happy that the tourists prefer my wares to theirs."

But a child of Chicago has not been taught to make such choices. "You tell me."

She seemed surprised and obscurely pleased. Dancing high on her toes to be away, she didn't just toss me an easy bauble from her visible store. Instead she searched an inner pocket, chittering and jangling with every move, and pulled out a length of braided leather, supple but plain. Three strands of subtly different browns strung with a single dark bead the size of a small walnut. The bead was faceted with tiny carvings. She circled my head with arms of sparkle and flash, and fastened her simple gift around my neck.

The twined leather lay soft against my skin. I touched the bead as it nestled into the hollow of my throat. "Thank you."

"From Tuamatutetuamatu. Wear it honestly, child. There

is power in it." Her head snapped up. "Ah. Here they come."

I turned, saw nothing but the crowds streaming in from the Gate. I turned back and my stranger was gone.

I wore the necklace for a few days, then put it away and forgot it. Three years later, it became very important that I find it again, but on that day, I stood alone and dumb-founded as the tourists elbowed past, giggling none too privately at my provincial astonishment and plain provincial dress. There were no tourists in Chicago. How was I to know that in its dome-centered way, the world was getting back on its feet, that tube systems crossed continents and supersonic air transport was again available to anyone who could afford it? People were traveling, rich people mostly but more and more the not-so-rich, and Harmony's Open Studio policy was world-renowned. Strolling a market square during visiting hours was a lesson in global sociology.

But the greatest wonder of all, and the final irony, was that Harmony and its many farm and support-system domes—water and air, power and recycling—were all sustained through aggressive marketing of exactly what impoverished Chicago had forbidden: the Arts.

Later that night, wide-eyed in my new bed in my new dormitory room, narrow as a coffin but totally mine, I fingered the carved bead at my throat and contemplated what it really means to have one's mind boggled.

But you needn't hear every detail of my adjustment to the strange and giddy freedom of life in Harmony. It was earthshaking enough to me, but much the thing you'd read in any artist's biography. The story that is special, the tale I must tell, begins three years later, after I'd survived the first hurdles of my apprenticeship, the easy first-year cut and the murderous second, when two thirds of each class was winnowed out, or more precisely, winnowed *Out*. My only competition in Chicago had been Chicago itself. In Harmony, I had artistic peers. The competition was stiff and my confidence sorely shaken. But I'd done well enough to be granted an unusual three-year renewal and was ready to relax a little, to believe again in the future I'd dreamed about, my future as an artist.

My story is about that future and what became of it. It

begins quietly, though I thought it an unpardonable interruption at the time. It begins early one sunny morning—early mornings in Harmony were always sunny—in the studio of Micah Cervantes.

PHASE I

Pre-Production

HARMONET/ARTNEWS

EVENTS ABOUT TOWN: 05/13/46—15:30

WELCOME TO HARMONY. Visitors, please note: this
listing for performance and special events only. For
more detailed listings, press D and organization file-
name. For gallery information, press G and enter gallery name.

AMADEUS
Minot's Hill Chamber Ensemble [MHCE]: *Mozart, D.
Scarlatti, Saunders, Verger.* At the Village Odeon.
14:30, 20:00. Tickets available evening only.
Greentree Mews [GTM]: *Program of works by con-
temporary choreographers.* 14:00. Some locations
available.
BARDCLYFFE
Images [IMAG]: *Works by Balanchine, Taylor, Wal-
ley, Takata.* BardClyffe Village. 20:00 Tickets
available.
Theater in the Glade [TIG]: *PHAEDRE, starring Lil-
ian Shu.* 14:30, 20:30. See ARTNEWS/COMMENT
for reviews. Sold out.
Galleria Finzi: The special exhibit, *The Art of the
Glassmaker,* has been held over for another week.
EDEN VILLAGE
The Woodstock [WOOD]: *RUE THE DAY, by
Suzanne Pryor. Directed by Philly Krentzmuller.*
14:30. Tickets available.
The Archive [OLDFILM]: *A BOY AND HIS DOG.*
13:00, 15:30, 18:00.
The Eden Philharmonic [EDEN]: *Rachmaninov,
Faure, Glidden.* Maria Lewis Ricardo, conductor.
14:30.
Museum of the Musical Instrument [MUSE]: *Special
exhibit of pre-Dissolution wind instruments. Some
contemporaneous recordings.* 12:00–17:00 Daily.

FETCHING GREEN

Arkadie Repertory Theatre [ARK]: Theatre One: *LES MISÉRABLES, with Will Egan and Miranda Pilar.* 14:00, 19:30. Sold out.

Theatre Two: *BAGNA.* 20:00 Tickets available at all prices.

Harmony Rare Book Library [BOOK]: Daily by appointment only. Gift Shop open to the public, Daily 12:00–19:00. Special exhibit: *The Marquez Legacy.*

FRANKLIN WELLS

The Beat Street Theatre: Daily around the town. Keep your eyes and hears open!

Interaction [INT]: *Jazzabelle.* 21:00. Some seats available.

The Composer's Group [TCG]: *The Dingo Sonata.*

LORIEN

Windermere Opera Society [WIND]: *Presenting the Cardiff/Bath Interdome Opera production of DER ROSENKAVALIER.* 19:00

SILVERTREE

Willow Street [WILLO]: *SECRET LIVES, by James Carlisle. Directed by William Rand.* 14:30, 20:00. Tickets available.

UNDERHILL

The RoundHall [HALL]: *A MIDSUMMER NIGHT'S DREAM.* 19:00 or after dark. Tickets available.

THE STUDIO:

The studio was best in the early morning. In the mornings we got the real work done, before the rush of calls and visitors that followed the opening of the Public Gates at noon.

Our little stone building was a twelve-minute hike from BardClyffe, the local village, up a narrow dogleg lane, away from the bustle of cafés and shops and galleries on the market square. The humble wooden gate was unmarked by the usual tourist signage. A magnificent copper beech stood just inside, its russet branches shrouding the gate in leaf-shadow. High stucco walls enclosed the cobbled yard, smothered in a chaos of untrimmed vegetation: honeysuckle, ice-white jasmine, vermilion trumpet vine, and purple clematis. Inside, fruit trees: orange and plum, peach and kiwi and vines of luscious grapes. Each day I came to work in a Garden of Eden, actually eating fruit right off the vine.

One year, the Tourist Bureau had the master artists' names leafed in gold on granite plaques, in honor of Harmony's fortieth anniversary, and mounted them outside each studio gate. Micah made us take his down and still the world beat a path to our door, to his supposed irritation and chagrin. Later, I came to suspect that secretly he loved it. For if that many strangers were willing to work so hard to find him, he must be a very great artist indeed. Or well known, at least. Micah often worried this particular distinction into the wee small hours.

On the off chance that the name means nothing to you, Micah Miguel Cervantes was a master scenographer. A profound conceptualist, a sculptor in space and light and time. An opera or ballet designed by him might sell out on his name alone. Mind you, I had never seen a live play before I came to Harmony, never sat in a theatre except to hear boring civic lectures. But Micah's studio was where the computers deemed my skills most appropriate. I could have requested reassignment after a six-month trial. The thought never occurred to me. I was hooked from the beginning.

But about those mornings. Mornings that turn in my mind like crystal in the wind—the early sun sinking soft as milk through the skylight, we apprentices bent like monks over our drawing tables, the Master puttering away in his corner. Micah refused to schedule meetings before noon, so with the tourists at bay and the phone off-line, those few peaceful hours were our sanity and the cornerstone of our productivity. We guarded them with near-religious fervor because they could be, from time to time, purely about making Art.

Still, what's sacred to one is sure to be profane to the next. And so, that crisp sun-flooded May morning, our precious monastic silence was disrupted a mere hour after we'd settled into it. It was only a knock at the door, but in that moment of pure peace, it was the worst kind of sacrilege.

HOWIE:

The evil rapping set Micah's slippers whispering irritably across the slates. In his cavey recess, he shuttled from palette to work table to drawing board, like a chunky, white-frocked badger, humming absently and pretending not to hear.

I glanced at Songh to my left, then past him to Jane, immobile at the cutting table. Both stared at me a little stupidly, their mouths dropped open the same half inch, and I wondered when they were going to learn to think for themselves. Songh Soonh was very young and new to the studio, and so had some excuse. But Jane Kessler was six full years my senior, what we called an "old" apprentice. Still, it was me who'd just been made First Assistant, and along with my very own key to the studio came the responsibility of providing a fully detailed code of studio behavior.

The first rule was: sit tight, maybe whoever it is will go away. I frowned hopefully at the front door, grandly wide and dark against the white plaster walls. It was solid wood, preserved from some pre-Enclosure barn, and the long bank of windows facing the courtyard were too high to allow for any preliminary screening of visitors.

The knocking continued.

"Could be an emergency," whispered Jane. She was tall-ish and worry-thin, with large eyes and a heart-shaped chin set at a watchful angle. She was always the first to jump to the direst conclusion.

I sighed. "Micah, do I go?"

"That Marin bunch is due after lunch," the Master grumbled. "I have roughs to finish."

I slid off my stool. "I'll tell them to come back at five."

"Authority Training 101," intoned Crispin, rising like a swimmer from his numerical daze at far end of the room. The holographic miniature of the Marin site froze on a north/south axis over the computerized model stand. "The Polite-but-Firm Negative."

Crispin Fox was Second Assistant, in charge of programming, and the latest of the affairs I'd fallen into since I'd discovered I could both work and have a social life. Cris had that dark, wild-eyed beauty that turns heads on the street and looks promisingly "artistic." When I was mad at him, I thought him bony and overbearing, but my status among our peers had improved perceptibly since he'd given me the nod. My own looks were more responsible and workmanlike, a source of some career anxiety to me in a Town where style was paramount, never mind the personal woe of wishing to be gorgeous enough to hold on to any man I wanted. I experimented mildly with the cut of my honey-colored hair and didn't delve too deeply into why I'd hooked up with someone who often wasn't very nice to me.

Conscious always of Crispin's judgmental eye, I made my stride to the door look purposeful. On the stoop stood Howie Marr, shifting about with genial impatience.

"Oh," I said, none too brightly. It was going to be hard sending this one away.

"Morning, Gwinn. Know it's early. Is Micah about?"

Howie was producer and sometimes director at the Arka-die, fondly called the Ark, one of Harmony's leading the-atres. With his mop of red-gold curls stealing toward gray and his rich imposing voice, he was just what you'd want on the vid screen selling your product.

"You know how he gets," I warned. Howie was an old friend of Micah's and nearly his contemporary, but his man-ner encouraged far greater familiarity, even from ap-prentices.

"But this is me," he grinned, and blew past me like a fair-weather gust, drawing the heady flower scent and bird-chatter of the courtyard through the door in his wake.

Energy was Howie Marr's specialty: boundless, indefati-gable energy and the impression (his enemies would say illusion) of a fine intelligence properly leavened by keen commercial sensibilities. He and Micah had come along together in the business, colleagues since a youthful Howie had wrested the leadership of the Arkadie from the failing hands of its original founder, by means of an almost acci-dentally brilliant production-cum-pageant about the raising of Harmony's dome. Absolute surefire patriotic material: right-thinking artist-pioneers throw down their pens and brushes and take up their laser assault rifles to save a stretch of wasted Vermont farmland and found a sanctuary for Art and the Intellect. That play may also have begun Micah's

reputation, though for that honor there are many more
claimants and much dispute.

Since then, Howie had achieved other more minor suc-
cesses as a director, but his real triumph was the Arkadie
itself, now thriving under his producerial hand.

He swept down the narrow aisle between the desks,
grasping Crispin's quickly proffered hand, dispensing airy
waves to Jane and Songh like some Eastern potentate. He
breezed to a halt at Micah's shoulder to peer at the work
in progress as if already shopping for ideas. "How nice!
Crusader castles for the terminally rich."

Micah never walked around the studio. His bagged-out
slippers fell off if he took full-sized steps. But now his shuffle assumed a more stubborn weight. "Ah, Howard. You
lost your watch?"

"Couldn't wait, Mi. This one's too special. Always ask
you first, you know."

"Send me the script."

Howie spread his arms without apology. "No script yet."

"Howard, you know the rules." Micah bent over his
sketch.

"I'll *talk* you through it." Howie eased under the slanted
overhang of stucco and beam that made Micah's corner so
reminiscent of a cave. No machinery lived there, no artists'
prosthetics. The computers and effects simulators were
exiled to Crispin's end of the room. Micah did all his roughs
and sketches with brush, pen, or pencil. Prehistoric wall
paintings would have been as much at home as the tracings
and drawings that layered the rough plaster like molting
feathers.

Howie peered at a tattered watercolor, peeled back an
edge to squint at a pencil sketch below. "The piece is written, Mi. Just haven't got my hands on a clean copy yet. It's
not . . . well, it's not exactly *local*."

Micah ended a delicate stroke that left his brush suspended like a baton. He frowned faintly at the sketch. "Not
local?"

Howie grinned like a happy shark.

Crispin rolled his eyes disapprovingly and reactivated the
Marin holo. Jane sighed, though of course not loudly
enough to offer the appropriate public protest. Being an
apprentice is often like seeing an accident about to happen
while reluctant to cry out a warning, just in case it doesn't.

You see, Micah was extremely busy at the time, booked nearly seven years in advance. His projects were big, spectacular and complicated, and he liked to take his time with them. He liked to take ours as well, worrying every one of the details he was so justly famous for. We were already way behind schedule with the Marin project currently on his desk, even though it didn't go into actual production for another year and a half. There were models and spec sheets and drafting and programs backed up far enough to occupy another three people if we'd had room enough and terminals for them. But between his home, the studio, and the adjacent conference room shared with the studio on the other side, Micah had used every micrometer of his officially allotted space, and he wouldn't hear of an assistant working at home, out from under the Master's dogged supervision. I didn't really blame him. Three years had been enough to teach me how little I knew. But the point is, Micah was better at his art than he was at saying no, and right then, the absolute last thing we needed was another project.

"Has an outside producer attached to it," Howie added.

"Is that outside, or Outside?"

Howie laughed indulgently, and I pictured some sooty, raw-eyed Outsider shedding mud all over Howie's expensive leather chairs.

"It's Reede Scott Chamberlaine, from London."

"You're getting into bed with him?"

"He owns the script."

"Howard, think again."

"Yeah, yeah, he's a skinflint and he'll cheat me blind. Don't worry, I can handle him. We watch him close enough, we might learn something about making money. It's worth it. You'll see."

Howie ducked out of the cave, squared his shoulders, and let his eyes drift soulfully toward the skylight. The Big Sell was coming, but watching Howie sell was always entertaining, so we all stopped work to listen.

"The Ark's been in a real rut lately—one nice, uplifting spectacle after the other, no messiness, no waves. Sure, it's been great for the box office, but it ain't why I got into the business. Nor you either." He flicked a mocking glance at the crude profile of turrets and ruined battlements rising from the holo pad, then offered Micah his most earnest smile. "This piece is different."

"And?" Micah rinsed his brush noisily. He had a talent for making total skepticism sound polite. Most people never noticed when he was being rude, and if Howie noticed it now, he knew Micah too well to let it show.

"It's time to take a risk, Mi. A big one." The catch in Howie's voice was subtle enough to convince me he'd finally fallen victim to his own hype. "Time to knock that pseudo-liberal audience of mine on their asses! Send 'em out remembering more than their ticket price and the outfit the star was wearing!"

Songh and Jane glanced at me in mute alarm—as if there were anything I could do. I thought Songh must watch Jane very carefully to be always able to do exactly as she did. Micah's only reaction was a faint pursing of his lips under the dark brush of his mustache.

The Arkadie did not particularly cater to the daytime tourist trade that supported many of Harmony's newer theatres. Its audience of mostly local residents and their guests *was* liberal, certainly by Chicago standards. But as a result, it was more than usually self-satisfied, and Micah despised smugness.

Howie knew that. "Whadda ya say, Mi? Ready to stretch that underused brain of yours a little? Ready to do something you've never done before?"

He hovered before the display model of Micah's design for *A Dream of Red Mansions*, a multi-award-winner waiting to be shipped to a museum in the Beijing Dome. The glass housing was dark, and Howie's hand that could never leave well enough alone strayed to the keypad set into the base, selecting act and scene. The box came to life at the top of Two, four, with the portentous music of the entr'acte and holographic mists sifting down from midnight hills to coil around curly pines and painted pagodas lit by the glow of dragon-headed lanterns. I sighed. I loved that design, envied its darkness and mystery and the completeness of its conception. The downside was it made me despair of ever being able to come close to it in my own work.

"I flew to Glyndebourne for the evening just to see this," Howie murmured. He watched until the entrance of the tenor, saw he was losing us to the model's evolving magic, and switched it off in the middle of a crescendo. "Sublime, but exactly what my piece isn't gonna want. None of your usual spectacle."

Usual? Well, I thought Howie must be pretty desperate if he was willing to needle his old friend into saying yes.

But Micah always said anger took years off his life. In three years I'd only once seen him lose control, at a producer, and then it took two burly stagehands to hold him back. Now he rinsed his brush again and set it deliberately aside. "Songh, make coffee, would you please?"

I waited for Howie to be treated to one of Micah's intimidatingly articulate defenses of The Work, coupled with a lecture on the value of his time. But that was when clever Howie chose to tell us about the Eye.

He followed Micah to the narrow trestle table beneath the courtyard windows. Every other surface in the studio was crammed with tools and supplies, stray model pieces and research. These dark planks were kept clean and oiled, to show off a single vase of flowers from the courtyard. Order within Chaos. This week, Order was red gladiolus.

Howie waited, hulking in the filtered sunlight like some smartly dressed grizzly, until Micah settled fussily into his wooden armchair. He perched opposite. "There's this troupe, actor-dancers—"

"From?" Micah's chin folded into his chest.

"They're a touring company. They don't have a permanent space."

"I didn't mean what theatre, I meant what dome?"

"No dome, actually."

Micah glanced up, I thought, hopefully.

"No, they're not Outsiders."

Micah's mouth quirked. "Not ready to be that radical."

"The next best thing. They're from Tuatua."

Jane gasped. Crispin cheered and slapped the off switch on his holo. Songh's painstaking coffee making halted, his round moon face lit in joyous disbelief. Even Micah nodded with faintly raised brows. Howie leaned back to enjoy his carefully orchestrated sensation, and then I ruined everything.

"From where?"

Crispin made a face I wished I could hate him for.

"Tuatua!" Songh was innocent of malice. "You know, the Magic Island! Everyone's heard of it!"

Not me, from benighted Chicago, not even three busy, informative years later.

"It's a tiny island in the Pacific," Micah supplied gently. "Hasn't been much in the news once the initial furor died down."

"The Island That Time Passed By!" Songh waved empty coffee mugs in circles above his head. He was small but lithe and graceful as a dancer. My mental image of Songh was always smoothness.

"It really exists?" Jane murmured, as if she wished it didn't.

Micah nodded. "The only known community in the world to survive the Dissolution without doming. Quite the mystery, actually."

"Tuatua!" Howie beamed. "The very stuff of legend."

"Without doming? And they're all right?" I asked.

"Yup. Drives those science types crazy."

"Unique geographical isolation," Micah explained, "and that it stayed undiscovered for so long after the collapse."

"No, it was their magic powers," Songh insisted, arranging the mugs in a precise oblong on the tray.

The word *power* keyed a memory. I had heard of Tuatua before, or something like it.

Crispin ambled over, tightening the red bandanna that wrapped his glorious shoulder-length hair. "Stayed undiscovered until fifteen years ago, when some enterprising Tuatuan saw the profit to be made in fresh foodstuffs, packed up a war canoe with papaya and bananas, and sailed two weeks to the nearest neighbor to set up a fruit stand."

"Instant fame," nodded Howie. "Relative prosperity."

"And tourism," Micah added. "For those with dangerous tastes."

"And touring companies!" Howie gloated. "Or one at least."

Micah was wary. "Not another ethnic traditionalist dance company?"

"Hey! Would I do that to you?"

Micah shrugged delicately.

"Naw, they've done a lot of dance and folk drama, but they have this play they want to add to their repertory, expand their horizons a little. Reede Chamberlaine saw them in Kyoto and came to me with the idea of starting the new piece here. They call themselves the Eye."

"The Eye?" repeated Crispin. "What's that supposed to mean?"

Howie smiled. "Guess we'll find out."

Songh brought the coffee, balancing the laden tray as if his job depended on it, which in Micah's studio it did not. I tried to picture this undomed yet living island. I was glad it was unique. That it could exist at all raised too many disturbing questions.

Howie leaned into the table to wrap his big hands around a steaming mug as tenderly as a lover. His nails were clean and professionally buffed but bitten to the quick. "The very name Tuatua will be a big draw, but I got to tell you, this is no booking agent's idea of an easy sell—these guys are on the very brink of civilization, schizoid mystics deep into the magic and legend and taboos of yesterday, yet struggling to embrace the cold logic of today."

"Ah," remarked Micah, always at his driest when weighing a decision. "A preview of an upcoming press release?"

"Press, schmess! Micah, I'm talking a revolution in style here!" Howie rose, the famous Marr energy brimming like water at a spillway. "Away with your holograms and lasers! The power of the Eye will be the power of the live actor alone. Voice, movement, the transcendence of the word!" He threw out his arms like Moses receiving the inspiration of God. His sleeve toppled Jane's lamp, and her lunge after it scattered scale rule, pencils, and eraser to four points of the compass.

Micah hugged his coffee mug protectively. "Down, Howard, down."

"The time is right for it, Mi! A return to elegant simplicity! A new look! The history books will credit you." Howie bent to join Jane in pursuit of the lost implements.

Jane crabbed sideways and stood, beet-red, clutching her tools to her thin chest. She hated being involved in clumsiness, in case it might be held against her. "It's all right, Mr. Marr. I have them."

Howie clambered to his feet. "Gad, so early in the morning and already I'm exhausted." He dusted his expensive slacks, pulled their creases into the best order possible on his pudgy thighs. "Tell me, you guys believe in omens?"

"Oh yes," chirped Songh. Crispin snorted.

"Not so fast, now." Howie fished a yellowed tatter out of a silver card case and held it up between two fingers.

"Newspaper, the real thing. A genuine scrap of history. I found it stuck inside a pre-Dissolution atlas I picked up years ago. Added it to my idea file. Thought it might make a play someday."

Micah took the clipping and scanned it while Howie fidgeted.

"You see it? The remote island? The native tribesmen with their strange religion? Micah, it could be *them*! I've had that clipping for ten years. It's like I knew!" When Micah's only response was to regard him dubiously, Howie made a sound like a balloon deflating. Hype might be his stock in trade, but it required effort nonetheless. "Christ, Mi, how long you gonna make me go on like this? Does it make any difference I'm gonna direct this one myself? Please. I'd like you there to see me through it. Like old times."

I was amazed that Micah didn't say, forget it, I'm too busy. Instead, he offered up the clipping on his palm. "Have you seen this troupe perform?"

Howie folded the shred away reverently. "I've read a few reviews. Reede's booking them worldwide after they leave here. Damn, does it matter? It's the idea of the thing, isn't it? It's artistic freedom! It's . . . Tuatua!"

Micah studied his mug intently. "What are your dates?"

"Goes into rehearsal in July.".

"July what?"

"Fifteenth, by the current schedule. It might be tricky getting them visas and the like, them being unEnclosed and all."

"Howard, please. July of what *year*?"

Here, to his credit, Howie did show a fleeting embarrassment. "This July, Micah. Two months from now."

I couldn't believe the audacity.

Crispin was brave enough to be vocal about it. "You want an update, boss?" He jabbed at his keypad as if urging it to audible protest. "Bids for Marin are due end of this month, engineering specs for *Deo Gratias* by June tenth, drawings and model for *Cymbeline* before the first of July."

To save Crispin from being the only murdered messenger, I added, "And you did agree to have roughs for Willow Street's new piece by the end of June. Plus there's *Don Pasquale* for Sydney Opera to begin thinking about."

Micah nodded and nodded, staring at Howie, who somehow found the temerity to stare back.

"Remember, it doesn't want much," Howie prodded gently. "An image, an idea. We'll do it in our smaller theatre. Nothing much to build. It'll mostly be think-time for you, the part you really enjoy. Give me twenty minutes to lay it out for you. You don't buy, then God's honor, you won't hear another word about it."

Micah nodded a bit more, muttered, "Tuatua . . ." then plunked down his mug, and rose like a sudden flight of birds, winging for the conference room. He paused at the door, caught in his own momentary disbelief, then glanced at the old analogue wall clock that was our only timepiece. "All right, Howard, you've got your twenty minutes. See if you can convince me."

HOWIE'S RESEARCH: THE CLIPPING IN THE ATLAS

The Christian Observer, December 16, 1951

". . . stayed in the car, but my husband and I did not regret the steep and sweaty climb to the top of the promontory. There were flowers everywhere, as lush as if tended by human hand. The view of the island was unsurpassed: a bright green ring set in a mirror of blue. On a flat stone table near the summit, a native woman dressed all in blue feathers intoned a singsong ritual before a gathering of her tribe.

When pressed, our native guide translated a bit that the woman had repeated several times, and it went like this:

"Of the world's twelve stations, the first is Rock, the Father, companion to Wind, the Mother, and his name is Pirimaturamiram, who we celebrate in the first moon of the Turning and call on him for his approval."

I said to our guide that this must refer to God, being the Father, but he replied, no, this was not God, or even a god, but an ancestor.

"The rock is her ancestor?" I asked.

"And yours," he answered impudently. "She knows not to waste her time praying to gods who can't answer."

I did wonder then what the Mission had been doing in this lost land with our donations, if not bringing God to the tribesmen.

"If there is no God," I asked, "then who created us?"

"We have always been here, changing and growing. Is that not the business of life?"

So I answered him as I must: "The business of life is carrying out the work of God."

I thought it very quaint to be standing on a jungle promontory, discussing religion with a heathen savage as if we were two Church elders, but should anything I said urge him closer to godliness, I would not begrudge the time spent, for truly these are godless folk . . ."

MICAH:

You might want to know a bit more about Micah, even if you've heard most of it already. There's always some little bit of relevant detail that doesn't make it into the history files.

Micah had just turned forty-six when I arrived in Harmony. He was strong-faced and chunky, not the romantic Spaniard his surname had suggested, but with a touch of Quixote nonetheless in his droopy, dark mustache and in his willingness to go up against anyone and anything he considered Philistine.

Three years later, I was twenty-two and Micah's mustache had remained preternaturally black while the rest of his bristly mane was increasingly shot with silver. The Old Badger, Crispin called him in the privacy of our bed, insisting he meant it fondly. For once, I believed him. Not only was it the perfect physical image, but nothing better expressed the deep-rooted, earthy quality of Micah's determination.

Sometimes, as the years progressed, the wine was uncorked a little earlier in his workday, or the music turned up a little louder, as if to drown out the noise of the constant demand on his time and concentration, or the perennial offenses against his sense of what was just and logical. But he persevered, while others of his colleagues threw up their hands in disgust and retired on their laurels and healthy investment incomes. Even on a day off, if I went into the studio for a forgotten book or sweater, there'd be music filling the tiny room and Micah hard at work, pausing perhaps to conduct a passage with the shaft of his brush, reveling in his rare solitude and the beauty of Mozart.

A relevant fact: Micah wasn't born in Harmony, either, though he came a lot closer to it than I did. He comes from Buenos Aires, a rich man's son like Crispin, but from a long and illustrious line of them. He could have inherited servants and an estate large enough to warrant its own dome. He could have worked a short day and taken vacations. But he came to Harmony to escape a life of business and to study music, the violin. It's said he showed real promise as a composer.

I'd like to have been at the performance of *Die Zauberflöte* that changed his mind. He says it was not so much the actual production as what it suggested to him in the way of possibilities for a totality of expression that he had been struggling toward within his music. He left the Conservatory the next day (he says), and apprenticed himself to Andres Bohr, a master scenographer well into making a revolution in theatrical production styles.

Micah treasured the contradiction inherent to live performance, that his art existed for only as long as the event itself. For instance, though the intricate working models and drafting we produced while developing each new work sold quickly to museums and collectors, Micah did not consider them Art.

The same went for his sketches, which were very popular with the tourists. If you are skilled with the light pen and the airbrush (or in Micah's case, with old-fashioned pencil and watercolor), you can attempt to represent the ephemeral: the vivid spear thrust of the laser lancing through a storm-dark stage house, or the glimmer of a hologrammed warrior rising through the mists of an ancient moor. The result might be beautiful—Micah's always were. It might even be Art, but it will not be magic, the magic of illusion made real, of time halted, of history and fantasy brought to life as if in substance, living breathing three-dimensions, before your very eyes. This was the mystery that bound Micah Cervantes to the theatre forever. He called it his "lovely anarchy."

Micah had no children. We were his children, and those who came before and after us. He lived with Rosa Fein, the poet, who spent much of her time closeted in her workroom, or out on tour, doing readings and guest professorships. She would occasionally drop in for lunch at the studio, but with the long hours that Micah put in, we wondered when they ever saw each other. Still, the relationship had held through the years, perhaps as the only appropriate accommodation for two people who were neither hermits nor aesthetes, but who loved their work above all else.

Shall I tell you more? That Micah loved animals, but would never allow one in the studio? That he would have worn nothing but white if we didn't get after him? That he loved good food and good drink, and even better, a good argument? Or that there were things, beside Rosa and the music, that meant nearly as much to him as his work, such as integrity (his own as well as others'), the rich experience of collaboration, and above all, friendship.

HOWIE'S RESEARCH: A LONDON DANCE CRITIC'S REVIEW

Review/Dance

EXOTIC MYSTERIES, SURPASSING SKILLS
by Glynna Farquharson

. . . Though their meaning and purpose remained obscure, there was no question about the passion and skill exhibited last night at the Aix Festival by an unusual dance theatre troupe called the Eye.

This is a new (to us) company of remarkable perform-

ers whose combined skills offer a rich and original blend
of music, movement, voice, and song. While their chosen
idiom remains that of the small Pacific atoll where they
are based, the three pieces on the evening programme
(selections from a twelve-part work entitled Stations)
were no slavish reproduction of traditional island dances.
Here is potential for an exciting fusion of the old and
the new, tantalizing but as yet unrealized, lacking only
the textual coherence needed to guide an urban audience
along the intended metaphorical journey.

The opening piece, *Mother Wind*, was a series of interlocking duets and quartets for four performers who
played their own haunting accompaniment on flutes and
pipes as they danced. The choreography was both athletic
and sinuous, full of spectacular leaps and catches but at
its most expressive when borrowing from the movements
of Nature. The graceful, trailing masks and cloaks of sky
blue and white feathers here, as throughout much of the
evening, disguised each dancer fully, so that it was often
impossible to distinguish sex, age, or race. This reviewer
considered scolding the management for neglecting to
anywhere list the performers by name, but perhaps the
Eye intends this further air of mystery, even to the point
of concealing the size or makeup of their company.

The middle work, *Fish Sister*, was stylistically ritualistic
and though it employed the troupe's dramatic gifts, was
less successful. A mythlike story of impenetrable plot was
danced to a chanted text including oddly juxtaposed quo-
tations from nineteenth-century mystic H. D. Thoreau
and the Bible, as well as less famous . . ."

THE ASSISTANTS:

Jane was quiet the rest of that day, even for Jane. I knew
she was working up one of her major worries when, after
an afternoon of Marin meetings plagued by unusually vocal
tourist visitations, she dogged Crispin and me all the way
back to the dorm.

Cris showed his malicious streak. Knowing Jane avoided
the perimeter, he led us the long way round, over the little

stone bridge across East Avon Brook and up through the quaint warehouse maze that hugged the generator wall (not even in Harmony would anyone in his right mind build a residence within sight of the Outside). It was nearly six. The little street-cleaner robots were nosing up and down the paths like dogs on a scent. We'd soon be late for dinner at the dorm. But Jane stuck like glue. At the perimeter, while Crispin idly bounced pebbles off the force field, she turned her back and faced inward toward Town.

"He's going to take that show of Mr. Marr's, I know he is."

"The Marin thing might push him into it." I wanted to ask about Tuatua, but I thought I'd exposed enough ignorance for one day.

"I like Marin," Cris announced.

"Sure, it's a programmer's dream. But Micah's so bored with sleeping princesses and rune swords, he's open to the mere whiff of something unusual."

"Hope springs eternal," Crispin sniffed.

"Micah's as vulnerable to hope as any of us." I considered how much hope I'd expended on Crispin early on, then stood with Jane to take in the view. After three years, this verdant beauty still stunned me with gratitude and joy.

The Vermont hamlet that Enclosed as Harmony was nestled in a giant natural bowl in the Green Mountains. Her Founders built their field-generator wall around the rim, enclosing rich farmland and a deep, spring-fed lake. They dammed up the outflow, built their Gate in the drained riverbed, their service domes in the fluvial valley beyond, and hid all of the residence dome's working systems—climate, power, water, and waste—beneath terraced and planted hillsides. From the heights along the rim, the entire five-kilometer spread of the dome opened before us like one of Crispin's holo models. Tree-softened hills, quartered by artificial mountain streams falling from the four points of the compass, embraced eight villages, then rolled down to a flattened center where the glassy twin spires of Town Hall, Harmony's only high rise, rose out of the dark green of Founders' Park. At their feet, an oval lake shot back ripples of artificial amber dusk.

Older citizens, especially the surviving Founders, complained that by swelling over the years to fifty thousand inhabitants, Harmony had lost its rural atmosphere. But I

was sure it was the most beautiful place on Earth, even
though I'd seen only one other. Chicago had sacrificed all
its parks to housing construction. Harmony seemed like one
big park. Even the bright domesticity of its low-slung architecture soothed and pleased. In Chicago the air recondition-
ers often malfunctioned. Here the air was always fresh and
sweet, my grandpa's "green air."

"Wonderful, isn't it?" I murmured. A mild jasmine-
scented breeze ruffled my hair, and in the upmost arc of
the dome a puffy gathering of cloud promised an evening
shower. Harmony's wild-programmed climate offered the
treat of unscheduled "weather."

"Actors' Collective in Underhill's interviewing for designers," Crispin called from the wall. "Saw it in Micah's e-mail
this morning."

I left Jane to her worries. "You think we're really
ready?"

"Hey, get the job, then worry." Cris draped an arm
across my shoulders. "They're real loose over in Underhill,
all those weavers and potters, what do they know? I say
you're ready as you want to be. You're a First now, Gwinn.
You should be getting your stuff out there." He squeezed
me briefly. "But you don't want, I won't send your file over
with mine."

"Let me think about it."

"Yeah, sure." His arm slipped away, to resume tossing
stones with slow, sinuous arcs of his arms, like a dancer
checking position at the mirrors. Crispin's mirrors were in
his head.

Each time I came to the perimeter, I promised myself
not to stare, and found my eye caught anyway. Because
Harmony's art-export business thrived and because she was
a tourist mecca full of successful artists able to shoulder a
huge tax load, her field technology was state-of-the-art. The
quality of light Inside was said to be more "natural" but
more to the point, the Outside was clearly visible through
Harmony's dome.

From the generator wall, the land fell away into a dry-
bottomed moat. It rose again a half kilometer beyond in
abrupt slopes of gray rock and scrub. Further off, mountains
loomed. Their scrubby spring growth was spiked with
burned-out evergreen and the tall, fortified towers that
enclosed the dome's exhaust vents. The Gate and shuttle

port were on the opposite side of the dome, but the dozen hemispheres of the farm domes were visible off to the left, and beyond them, Power and Recycling, glinting through the haze.

Huddled against the exterior of the Wall, the Outsider bidonvilles shared the meager shelter of the moat: clusters of junk-built huts wreathed with the constant smoke of trash fires, teeming with Outsider families bent on the drear business of survival. I'd have found the same had I ventured outside Chicago (unthinkable) or any dome, anywhere in the world.

They rarely looked up, the Outsiders. Even seeing them in detail—a man's twisted leg, the missing buttons on a woman's jacket replaced by filthy twine, or a child with matchstick limbs picking invisible grains of food out of the dust—even then I distanced myself out of long habit. Unknowingly, the Outsiders encouraged the distance by refusing to acknowledge the apprentice princes and princesses gaping at them from the battlements of the fairy castle.

It never occurred to me there might be injustice in the fact that they were Out and I was In. I was dome-born, they were not. Outsiders *deserved* to be Outside, because of criminal acts or mutant inferiority. The way I'd deserve it, if I couldn't measure up in Harmony.

Now, Cris in his rich-boy confidence might mock Jane's avoidance of the Wall, but I understood it. Of the few thousand apprentices admitted each year, only a few hundred could expect to be in Harmony ten years later. Each visit to the perimeter, each glance Outside was a reminder you shouldn't get cocky. Until you're proven talented enough to win your citizenship, you're living on borrowed time.

"You change your mind about Underhill, let me know." Cris shook his black hair free of the red bandanna, worn piratelike when working his precious machinery. I knew I had disappointed him. He thought I lacked ambition. Sometimes I thought he was right.

Cris had arrived in Micah's studio the year before, knowing exactly where he was going and what he wanted to do. I made him an object of study, thinking a mere hint of insecurity might render him less intimidating. I envied that damnable confidence. Perhaps I hoped a little of it would rub off on me.

But confident is not the same as mature. Cris pivoted away, waving his bandanna like a flag, shedding his studio persona, the one where he posed as a responsible adult. "Tuatua! UnEnclosed! Magic and taboos! Damn, I can't wait to meet these guys!"

I said carefully, "I met a Tuatuan once. I think."

"Sure you did."

"Really, I think I did. At the Gate, the day I got here."

Cris knotted his scarf around his neck. "You think they just run around the world at large?"

"Why not?"

"Jeez, they're practically Outsiders! What dome's gonna let the likes of them in, except as a special event?" He danced away gleefully. "Damn! It's dynamic!"

I followed more decorously. After all, my stranger hadn't claimed *she* was Tuatuan, only the necklace. And maybe I didn't even have that part right.

"Why does Micah always do this to us?" Jane tore at the flowers in the hedgerow, then gazed in guilty horror at her handful of shreds.

"First he does it to himself, and *then* he does it to us."

Jane tossed the broken petals under the treads of an oncoming cleanerbot and sidestepped it quickly. Destroying plant life was a serious crime in Harmony. Even the unfrequented warehouse district was planted within an inch of its life. All that lush greenery was the real secret of the sweet air under Harmony's dome.

"We'll manage," I continued. "We always do." Micah had assured me that studio morale was part of the First Assistant's job. "He'll only take the show if it really excites him, and that's when it's the best, not like Marin."

"But what if it's too weird?"

Cris hooted. "That could make Howie a hero. Champagne and celebrations! Vine leaves in his hair! His trustees will give him a plaque." He vaulted onto the low stone wall bordering the lane. "Mothers and fathers of Harmony! Art took a great leap forward tonight, as our box office records will reflect . . . !"

Ahead, a brace of camera-laden ladies in the bright new clothes of day-pass tourists had strayed from the beaten path. Racing to clear the Gates before Closing, they halted to consult their faxmap, the flimsy kind from the public newsboxes, just about the only thing you could get for free in Harmony. One of them snapped a few quick ones of the raven-haired scarecrow declaiming from a public wall. Our blue apprentice coveralls marked us with mysterious privilege.

"But if he really offends them . . ." Jane pursued.

"He meant excite, not offend," I said.

". . . the Town Council might . . ."

"Make him mayor?" Cris waved his arms, tottering on the wall. "Jeez, Jane, we're talking *Tuatua* here! Major fame! Major life adventure! I've wanted to go there ever since I heard about it!"

"Then go! We don't need them coming here!"

I'm slow sometimes when it comes to people, but finally the real source of Jane's worry came clear to me. Her apprenticeship renewal came up for review in September, just after Howie's "revolution in style" was due to open. I glared at Cris to back off.

There was a nasty little mind game we apprentices played among ourselves, where each would speculate on their chance of survival if put Outside. Crispin had an endless appetite for this game. He was sure he'd survive. "Intelligence is survival," he'd proclaim. "I'd go off into the Badlands with my gang. I'd found my own colony! Wouldn't catch me taking charity in some domeside slum!"

I was less certain of success and, lacking Crispin's rich and powerful father, less assured that I'd never have to play the game for real.

Jane was from Providence, one of the strict Calvinist communities in what used to be Switzerland. I'd heard it mocked in Harmony as a god-dome. Like me, she had sacrificed her citizenship to come to Harmony. Often I wondered why. Only her obsessive dedication to the hands-on craft of design gave any inkling. Jane refused to play the Survival Game at all. Concerned about causing offense if she actually voiced her loathing, she'd go cold silent if the subject even came up. Cris said she was more of a drag on our fun than if she simply left the room.

"Audiences like a little adventure," I assured her. "Besides, even if Howie went too far, no one would blame you."

What "too far" might be, I wasn't sure. I'd seen some pretty outrageous performances during my time in Harmony, though admittedly not at the Arkadie. "Nobody blamed the designer's apprentice for the twelve nudes painting each other last season at Interaction. They didn't even blame the designer."

"Should have blamed somebody," Cris put in.

"Jane, if Howie flops, it's not going to affect your review."

She flinched at my comforting touch, then accepted it with schooled tolerance. She was so tense and thin, as if there was no skin softening the bones beneath the blouse of her coverall. "If the Council censored Micah, it could."

"Oh, Jane," Crispin scoffed, "this is Art. That's Politics!"

"The Town Council's authority is civil, not artistic," I reminded her. "No one legislates aesthetics in Harmony."

"Except the gallery owners," murmured Cris.

But Jane was in her terrier mode. "If Howie got them mad enough, they might decide Micah doesn't deserve four apprentices." Her arms rose and fell in suppressed panic. "Oh, I wish I were Songh!"

Crispin's laugh got an edge to it. "You want to be SecondGen? So you could run home to Mommy and Daddy every night?"

"Like you could if they threw you Out?"

"That's not true!"

Jane's eyes raked him unbelievingly, then slid away. "At least if I were SecondGen, I wouldn't have to worry all the time!"

Around the curve, the sprawling three-story brick and timber bulk of our dormitory appeared from among its surrounding oaks. The BardClyffe dorm was one of the smaller ones, housing only three hundred apprentices. The exterior was modeled on ancient university residence halls like the few surviving in the Oxford dome. Inside, it was a rabbit warren. I didn't want Jane storming in there in one of her hysterias. I had to stop and grab her for a little shake. "No one's going to throw you Out! You know Micah couldn't do without you. You're carrying your weight just fine!"

But even as I said it, I wondered.

We left Jane at the dining room door, while Crispin deciphered the menu. Most domers'd be content with nice, legible computer readout. In Harmony, it had to be handlettered, in calligraphic pen and ink. I wouldn't be surprised if they'd used a goose quill.

"Too healthy," Cris announced, groping me there in the

hall like some dirty old man. Fool that I was, I loved it. I thought that's what sex was all about. "Your palace or mine, princess?"

"Mine." It hardly mattered. All our rooms were the same. But I had sudden interest in searching up that piece of jewelry I'd stashed away three years ago and forgotten about, until now.

Bedtime with Crispin was athletic and speedy, as if pleasure was just another thing to be accomplished. For me, it rarely was. We never talked feelings afterward, we talked careers. His career, mostly, though occasionally we'd spend time trashing other people's, those Crispin saw as his particular rivals.

"You think Jane's got reason to worry?" I mused between rounds. I'd found the braided necklace and fastened it around my neck. "That could have come from anywhere," he'd said.

Now he stretched as luxuriantly as he could in my narrow bed. I thought he looked very beautiful, all smooth and golden in the dusk light that squeezed through the single window, heating the beige walls to salmon. He ran his fingers negligently through his hair, letting the ends coil along his collarbone. "If Jane didn't have stuff to worry about, she'd invent it. If she gets thrown Out, it's not going to be because of Howie Marr's politics. I mean, c'mon—this isn't some proto-marxist enclave like Chicago."

I let that pass. "Micah does need her. That's got to be some kind of insurance. She's the ideal studio assistant. She's earnest and diligent, she's a skilled and experienced draftsman, and a total obsessive crazy when it comes to details. She has patience with stuff that drives me up the walls. She's passed four reviews so far just fine. No reason why she shouldn't make the next one."

Cris yawned. "Except that after nine years, she's still not so hot when the shit hits the fan in the theatre or if Micah's not around to make decisions, and the only show she's ever done on her own was that little workshop Gitanne got her at Images." He raised his eyes to the ceiling. " 'The applicant's potential as an independent artist remains undeveloped' . . ."

"They do say ten years is the cutoff point. If you're not made journeyman by then . . ."

Cris grinned and drew his forefinger across my throat. "Jane's afraid Howie's show might tip the balance against her."

"Do we have to talk about Jane?" Crispin did not feel responsible for Jane as I did, or had come to, upon my elevation to the position of her superior.

"But it's not fair! There should be a place for skilled technicians."

"Who do you think builds our scenery? You just got to make citizen first."

"Or be born here."

Cris shook his head impatiently. "If Jane can't accept the risk, she shouldn't have come to Harmony. Not everyone can make it here." He sat up, dragging the sheet away. "What've you got to eat?"

"You should have thought of that before you turned your nose up at dinner."

Jane's worry had dampened my mood. Even in the flush of victory from my recent promotion, my own sense of vulnerability was easily awakened. Not all the rumors I'd heard in Chicago had been true. Harmony was indeed proud of its unique Outside Adoption Policy, but even Micah had once remarked that the intent of the OAP had never been to add to the day labor pool. As I learned soon after arrival, there were plenty of ungifted sons and daughters of Harmonic citizens to fill those posts. SecondGen, we called them. Like Songh. A sweet kid, but not exactly on the ball. As an experiment in eugenics, Harmony had not totally succeeded. As a result, an odd double standard prevailed. Songh, a native son, did not have to earn his citizenship as we did. He'd have to commit a very serious crime to be put Outside.

And there were more and more of him every year. Citizens in Harmony were law-abiding and there were few unlicensed births. But in the newly healthy environment of the dome, there were far fewer deaths than the Founders had counted on. And many applicants for residence who were already too famous and successful to pass up.

So Jane did have cause for worry. Many did, whose birth-domes would not take them back. If we didn't measure up as artists who could add appropriately to the GNP, Harmony didn't need us hanging around. I pictured Jane, bone thin in rags, stirring a stew pot in the perimeter slums. In the dorms, Jane made sure never to miss a meal and still she was as thin as a fever victim. Outside, starvation and disease would fell her within a month.

Cris slid down beside me, ready for another round of fun and games. "Now me, I'm going to be famous *before* I'm a journeyman. You too, if you let me send your file out." He tugged at the braid and bead around my neck. "This thing's really in my way."

I nudged him warningly. "Pride goeth before . . ."

"Pride is exactly what Jane is lacking," he replied seriously. And I could not disagree.

VTH/TOWN HALL REPORT

TOWN MEETING: 05/15/46

ATTENDANCE: 43%

TOWN COUNCIL MEMBERS PRESENT: Addison [Amadeus], Topa [BardClyffe], Lazarevna, Kata [Eden], Aftuk [Fetching], Lee [Lorien], Morales [Silvertree].

SPEAKERS: Healey, T. Boeck, Yoshimura, Valkenberg, C. Brigham, Ho, Chiovaro, Roskelly, S. Reilly, Stulir, V. Gogolen, Beadle, Rand.

MOTIONS PASSED: 3
MOTIONS TABLED: 2
MOTIONS DEFEATED: 2

MAYOR'S AGENDA: Proposal to increase appropriation for OutCare due to falloff in private and corporate donations. Her Honor singled out recent reports of unrest Outside other domes as reason enough to keep OutCare afloat.

TOWN COUNCIL AGENDA: Counterproposal re: last week's motion to extend Friday visiting hours.

Mr. Addison suggests: "Open the Gate at ten in the morning instead. Save energy not having to light the damn place up all night."

DISCUSSION:

19:35 Mr. Rand spoke in favor of the extension of Friday visitor hours until 21:00. Projected figures estimated increased box office revenues and gallery sales.

19:52. Ms. Roskelly expressed the concern of the Crafts Merchants Association about the apparent increase in unlicensed peddling in the village markets by foreigners gaining entry via day-visitor visas. A more thorough screening of visa applications was suggested.

20:18. Arguments were heard for the proposed construction of a Francotel-financed luxury hotel in Bard-Clyffe Village. Arguments against were scheduled for next week. A complaint was filed citing the BardClyffe Chamber of Commerce for opening negotiations with Francotel without making their intentions known at Town Meeting.

21:50. The issue of population pressure was raised again. Because so many citizens spoke over their allotted three minutes, this topic will be taken up early in next week's meeting.

SEAN:

The morning after Howie's paean to "elegant simplicity," Micah hated everything he'd done for the Marin project. Even the ideas the writers and director had creamed themselves over the afternoon before.

Disquiet reigned in the Badger's den. Mutters of "over-complication" and "the essential purity of the line" accompanied the sound of X's being hand-drawn through vast portions of my neatly drafted and freshly printed-out ground plans. I finally saved the third-floor plan I'd been revising, closed the Marin file, and called up the full-scale details for *Deo Gratias*. No point bothering with Marin until the Master's malaise had run its course.

This went on for three days. Somewhere around mid-morning Friday, Micah emerged from his storm cloud. "Sean's coming to lunch."

"Thank god," I whispered to Jane. "Sean'll calm him down if anyone can."

"Mr. Marr's sending him over to convince Micah to do the play."

"Oh, come on," I said, though Micah had been unavailable to several of Howie's phone calls, and she was probably right.

The Master punched Wagner into the sound system, rolled his sleeves higher, and returned hell-bent to his destruction. Crispin by manly effort concentrated on the Tuatua research Micah had requested while two weeks of preliminary Marin programming went down the drain in megabyte-sized pieces.

Micah's agent had convinced him to take the Marin job to make up for the financial losses on his higher-minded projects. Such a client could not normally hope to lure Micah Cervantes. The concept was a multilevel, walk-in environmental entertainment for the Marin sea dome, grand and gaudy on a medieval fantasy theme, without even pretensions to being art. Its greatest challenges were technical, such as involving the audience in the action without seeming to control their movement or their responses. The producers were young and greedy, the writers were laughing up their sleeves: the design process should have been fun and breezy. But the director was still trying to convince herself that there were reasons other than money to do the piece, encouraging Micah to indulge himself likewise.

And now with Howie's bee in the Master's bonnet, the Marin job lay on his desk in a shambles.

I longed for lunchtime as if it were the Second Coming.

Sean could tell something was up the minute he walked in, with the Wagner blaring before noon and Micah not favoring him with an immediate greeting. He browsed quietly among the tables, leaned over Jane's shoulder to peer at the *Deo Gratias* model. She was building the triple-arched facade of a Romanesque cathedral, with carved portal figures of stern and saintly glance, and a detailed Last Judgment frieze on the tympanum. It was beautiful. You could practically hear the grim monks chanting in the background.

"Ah, Janie, me gerl. You do one hell of a model." Sean eyed it with an exaggerated squint. "Too bad I'm not building the show."

"We wish you were." Jane gave him a shy smile. She was quite taken with Sean, but hoped that no one noticed. She wouldn't want anyone to think she'd look twice at a married man.

Sean Reilly was Master Carpenter at the Arkadie. He was a native son of Harmony, but one of that first generation born beneath the dome, when Harmony's survival was still a question. "Fourth kid born after they raised the lid," he'd remind you proudly. Sean was no wimpy SecondGen. His very special kind of genius lay in being midwife to the genius of others.

His father was a sculptor who had favored Art over Religion, and left Dublin in disgust when it Enclosed as a Catholic theocracy. Sean had been born with a cutting torch in his hand, and had all the other usual shop qualifications as well: an organizational mind, an attention to detail, an encyclopedic knowledge of materials, the stamina to work long hours, and the incipient beer gut of a onetime athlete spending too much time at a desk. Micah had brought him to the Arkadie and thought him a treasure, a standard to which all others in his profession should aspire, and a well of sanity in an increasingly irrational business. We all agreed, mainly because he had such a good effect on Micah.

Sean winked at Jane, tossed a jaunty nod to Crispin and Songh, and wandered over to lean into the faint glow of my desktop. His forefinger traced the bowed outline of a flying buttress with absentminded sensuality. "Hell of a crowd out there today."

"Every day," said I, like the old hand I was beginning to feel.

He leaned in closer, as if murmuring little seductions. "What the hell's got Micah so worked up?"

He smelled of fresh sawdust and after-shave. I sympathized with Jane. Sean at forty was going soft around the edges, but he had what the Irish call laughing eyes and his body still remembered how to move with confidence and grace.

"It's Howie," I whispered.

"Ah. I know *that* problem." He moved on to the Master's corner. "Say, buddy, didn't you invite a guy to lunch?"

"Invited yourself, as I recall," Micah grumped. "And you're early. The lunch hasn't arrived yet." But he offered up a weary grin and turned down the Wagner.

Sean nodded at the chaos on the drawing board. "So, Mi. Whatcha up to?"

Micah raked both hands through his bristly hair. "I'm trying to . . ." His shoulders sagged. "You don't want to know."

"Hey. Try me." Through some kind of companionable magic, Sean inserted himself between Micah and the drafting board. "Hmm," he said over the drawings. "Hah! Dragons! We could use a few o' them at the Ark right now. Things have been pretty dull lately."

Micah regarded him skeptically, then shrugged. "Well, since you're here, there is one thing you might take a look at . . ."

But then the lunch arrived, and Micah never did have the chance to pick his favorite technician's brain for free on the subject of the Marin project.

Lunch at Micah's was a major event. Because the studio lacked a kitchen and the village restaurants were priced for tourists, too dear for the likes of us poor apprentices on any regular basis, and because Micah loved to eat but hated to eat badly, he had lunch catered every day and encouraged friends and colleagues to drop by. It was his homage to the social contract, his attempt to further communications within the field, his substitute for family dinners, his (and our) one moment of relaxation.

The mess hall was our little conference room. Often, Marie Bennett-Lloyd, the costume designer who had the other studio in the suite, joined us with her apprentices Mark and Bela, whom we called the Blond Twins. With guests and tall Josie who brought the food and the food itself and the bookcases and filing drawers lining three walls, it was quite a crowd and altogether the break one needed after a morning of intense concentration. The one thing it rarely was, was quiet.

Marie and the Twins were on location that day, so there was more room than usual. Sean canvassed the food avidly, grinning at Josie as she passed around tumblers of iced tea.

"You weren't at Town Meeting last night," he scolded. He wagged a stubby finger at Micah. "You either. Bet you didn't even watch it on the vid. Christ, democracy in action."

"I was working," said Micah. Josie shrugged and smiled.

"It's an election year, Mi! Don't you care what's happening? The population issue's heating up again. Did you know it's a fact we've been letting in some fifty people every year for the last forty just 'cause we like their looks?"

"Their talent," Micah amended sternly. "Artists of world stature."

"Yeah, and Cam Brigham says proven salability, but pal o' mine, we got no more place to put 'em! And here's the kind of solutions being offered: some asshole running for T.C. from Amadeus says, hey, start a program to encourage expatriation to other domes." Sean eyed me slyly. "So, whadda ya say, let's all move to Chicago!"

I laughed. "They could use you in Chicago, Sean."

"Are all the women as sexy as you? I'll go." He threw himself into a folding chair and stretched his legs. "So. I hear Howie's been exercising his particular neuroses around the premises."

Jane's look to me said I-told-you-so. I shrugged and watched Sean stir three heaping spoons of sugar into his tea. He did it with coffee, too. Every time, I wondered what he had left for teeth.

"Howard has a lot of damn nerve sometimes," Micah grumbled.

Sean chuckled. "Told me he's gonna direct this one himself."

"Ummm."

"Been awhile for Howie. Do him good to get back to it."

"Umm-huh."

"Tuatua, huh? You gonna do it?"

"Haven't read it yet. He hasn't seen fit to grace me with a script."

"Me neither. They choose 'em without running 'em by me first, then they bitch when the damn shows go over budget!" Sean leaned in to grab a plate. "They're talking the July slot in Theatre Two."

"I know."

"Max Eider's *Crossroads* for the mainstage'll be in the shop then. It'll be tight. You know Max, always gotta be on the cutting edge of technology."

Micah nodded without noticeable sympathy.

"Hey, c'mon!" Sean spread his arms, plate in one hand, fork in the other. "You know I'm the first one to jump on a problem that wants a new solution. That's where the fun comes in. But sometimes a thing's best done tried and true, instead of wasting your time tryin' to reinvent the friggin' wheel!"

"I thought Howard sent you over to be encouraging."

"Hell, no. I'm just here for the free lunch." Sean took a bear-sized bite of chicken in basil cream. "Bringing in real Tuatuans, eh? That oughta be something. Some pretty weird stuff got aired when that place was rediscovered. Hoodoo, and magic . . ."

Micah laid squares of cheese on dark brown bread. "Crispin might be able to offer us more than rumor and conjecture, after three days in the library files."

Cris swallowed eagerly. "Yeah! Don't have much on the Eye yet, but there's great stuff on the island. Its real name is Tuamatutetuamatu."

Yes, I thought. That's what she called it. *Tuamatutetuamatu.*

"That a name or a mouthful?" snorted Sean, with his mouth full.

"It's east of the Fiji Domes, just about where it starts to look like open ocean on the maps. It's a caldera, what's left of a big volcano that blew up a hundred thousand years ago, so the island's actually a ring eighteen miles in diameter with a nice lagoon in the middle." He looked to Micah. "I could show you if . . ."

Micah nodded. "Anyone mind eating in the dark?"

Cris rescued the conference table's remote keypad from between the avocado salads and the cheese plates. The walls of the room disappeared, replaced with a vista of turquoise water, black sand beaches lined in palm, and toothy green mountains behind. Rolling surf sighed beneath the sharp cries of seabirds. Salt tang mixed with smells of heat and vegetation. A breeze ruffled the soft fall of hair across Sean's forehead.

A soft "But . . ." escaped me. No smoke? No gray? No ruins? This couldn't be Outside.

"Welcome to Tuatua," Cris announced smugly.

"Why would they ever leave home?" remarked Micah, though he knew better. No eighteen-mile atoll could provide a big enough audience to support a theatre company. The Eye, whoever they were, had to tour in order to make a living.

"There's more," said Crispin. A roar of water shuddered the room, silver strands falling out of darkness into leaf-ringed pools. Rain forest trees clung to green cliffs wreathed in fog. I shivered in the sudden damp. The violent death of its volcano had bequeathed Tuamatutetuamatu a rugged siren beauty that quite belied the island's diminutive size. I'd seen pictures like this, in books about Before, but it was hard to believe this existed undomed, *now*.

A flight of rainbowed birds shot past to dazzle our ears and eyes.

"Kinda empty, isn't it?" murmured Sean.

"Before Dissolution," Cris continued, "nobody much bothered with the place but missionaries. Development wasn't cost-effective. The world just sort of lost track of it for forty years or so, during the worst of things. But now . . ."

The mists cleared and we sat in neatly tended fields on a terraced hillside, acres of shiny-leafed shrubs bright with clusters of red and green berries.

"Coffee plantations. Also tea and banana, some rubber, pineapple and avocado, papaya and cardamom. The climate is ideal for agriculture, and the ground remarkably fertile."

In the brighter light of the open fields, Sean reached for and opened a beer. "But no good eating it, growing out there like that."

Micah sectioned an apple into eighths. "We might be eating it now, if they're exporting what they grow."

Sean frowned at his plate. "We wouldn't import Outside fruit."

"It's not Outside, officially."

"I don't care what those scientists say, the sea ain't gonna keep out the airborne crap. It was the whole system broke down. You believe the Pacific could get clean out there all of a sudden?"

"I live in hope," said Micah mildly. "They do appear to be managing marvelously well without a dome."

"Voodoo," I suggested. "Isn't that what the legends say?"

"Yeah, right," Sean snorted.

Songh giggled, and I grinned at him. "You probably believe there is such a thing."

"The local tribes don't call it voodoo," said Crispin. "They say it's the power of the Ancestors." He fingered the keypad, and around us the neat plantations flared into the glaring, bustling streets of a city, tall and white. Squinting into the Pacific sun, Cris resumed his lecture voice: "But maybe their power's not working so well anymore, because the big news about Tuamatutetuamatu, besides gourmet coffee and pineapples, is that there's practically a civil war over whether or not to Enclose." He glanced at Jane and flapped his eyebrows wickedly. "Oh-oh. Politics . . ."

Sean nodded. "Yah, well, there's always someone thinks they're against a doming, but they get used to the idea soon enough."

"This debate's gone on for twelve years," said Cris.

"Why dome now," I asked, "if they've been okay without one?"

"The pro-domers claim being undomed isolates them from the world community. They say—"

"I don't think we need to go into the sociology right now," said Micah. "You can print it out for me later."

"There's just this last," Cris insisted, and we were perched on a parapet, looking across at steep hillsides encrusted with lavish single-family estates. Gardens, pools, the heart-stopping works.

Sean let out an admiring whistle. "Somebody's done all right by themselves on this little rock."

"Somebody sure has. Descendants of settlers from Before. Tuatua's new entrepreneurs. But I'm not supposed to bore you with that." Cris shoved his keypad aside. The white room re-formed around us.

Micah ignored Crispin's sulk. "Thank you. Excellent work on such short notice."

It was. Cris had exploited a minor research project into an affecting design exercise. I was only mildly jealous.

"You didn't show us any Tuatuans," I complained.

"Oh, right." An array of flat pix flashed up on our one blank wall. Dark faces, naked bodies, flowers and feathers, and a child with a braided necklace strung with a large carved bead. I shot Cris a look and sat back satisfied. He killed the pix and tucked into his lunch without comment. Cris hated being proved wrong.

Sean drained his beer. "So what's this play about?"

"Misunderstanding and betrayal, Howie says. Among other things."

"Sounds right, for Howie." Sean rocked back in his chair with a deep, and deliberate belch. "You gonna do it, Mi?

Be good to have you back in my shop. Take the show. I'll put the beer on ice."

"I told Howard I'd read it and let him know."

Sean laughed, shaking his head. "C'mon, you're gonna do it. Tuatua! How can you resist? Now, if we stay together on it, we might just keep the Howie beast under control. You got all my best, you know that. When d'you think you can get me drawings?"

"I haven't said I'd do it."

"Sure, Mi, I know." Sean grinned at him. "So when can you get me drawings?"

That afternoon, Howie faxed over the script. We all clamored so loudly that Micah had Songh make up four copies and sent us home to read it. Jane was still working on the castle revolve for *Deo Gratias* at the Paris Opera. It wasn't due for another month, but she was convinced that Songh should stay to help her finish it. Songh pressed his bundle of still-warm pages to his chest and jittered like a six-year-old until Micah shooed all four of us into the courtyard. We ran off whooping and laughing, just as a clutch of black-veiled Arab women arrived at the gate for open studio hours.

I slowed, listening for the music of metal and glass beneath the dark flowing robes. But these women were short and wide and moved like toadstools. I felt only vaguely guilty that we'd left Micah to deal with them alone.

CRISPIN'S RESEARCH: A LETTER AT RANDOM

April 2, 1957

Dear Father Wilhelm,

Please forgive the several-months gap since our last report. The materials for the school finally arrived, and we have been beside ourselves gathering manageable work crews and organizing the building in weather that does not always suit our habits of work.

And time, I fear, has somewhat dampened the euphoria that possessed us upon our arrival. You must not think that we are disheartened, but so often the things that one expects should be easy turn out to be the hardest to accomplish.

For instance, the issue of agriculture. Though the ground is prodigiously fertile, the native diet is sadly limited and starchy. Though they do not complain, they cannot be expected to know any better. I felt from the first that we must put serious effort into improving nutrition if we want the human ground to be equally fertile to our Mission here.

Well, Father, I promise you we did our best to introduce some of the excellent European varieties we brought with us, such as the improved legumes and grains, and resistant vegetable strains, ones that we were sure would thrive in this happy climate and provide for a wealth of nourishment and a more various diet.

We grew test plots right in the Mission yard, using the new intensive methods, and at harvesttime, invited the chiefs in with their advisers to view the results, which were fruitful beyond even our own expectations.

Ivar and I loaded giant baskets with squash and sweet melons, tomatoes and beans, together with packets of seed for each. The chiefs smiled and thanked us, then each lugged a basket home to his village and set it up in front of the Men's House like a battle prize, where of course the produce soon rotted in the sun.

And no curious farmer came to consult about the planting of the seed or our new growing methods. All continued to grow what they'd always grown in the way they had always grown it.

When we remarked on this, several of the Mission workers hastened to compliment us on our wondrous crop, as if concerned by our distress but lacking the thought that this success might be repeated in their own fields season after season, with the benefit of improved nutrition. My Beryl, always the voice of wisdom, suggests this is because this land already supports its people well enough and their need to change is not urgent.

As for the school, the pages that follow are Ivar's summary of our progress on that front. He and Beryl . . .

HARMONET/CHAT

05/16/46

Just keeping you up-to-date, friends and neighbors, and we know you want to be kept up-to-date when you just happen to meet Mr. World Famous Cellist TUI-PIKIN at the corner table in the café down the street. Or even if it's only your old friend SALLY. You'll want to be chatting with the best

***You're gonna want to slip it to him (or her) that you heard **somewhere** how L'EVANA WILLARD's unhappy with her recording contract with Ho'town Studios over in Amadeus, how she's sure she can go world-wide with her utterly *rip* holo, *DIE FOR ME*.

***Or how 'bout our man-about-town CAMPBELL BRIGHAM? Never the Prince of Fashion, our Cam, but he sure knows who to have dinner with. Our question: who regged the tab? Cam or FRANCOTEL? You guess the dinnerchat. Perhaps an elegant BardClyffe branch for Cam's Lorien gallery in that gorgeous hotel the boys from Marseille want to build?

***While we're on Cam, we'll send along our compliments to him and the rest of the Arkadie Rep trustees for a totally *rip* evening at Monday's benefit for Out-Care. Were YOU there? Everyone ELSE was. Our favorite little fireball CORA LEE could charm the credits out of a cleanerbot, but where does she get that Fu Manchu wardrobe??

***And speaking of the ARK, what's HOWIE MARR got up his sleeve this time? TUATUA and REEDE SCOTT CHAMBERLAINE? Can we put those two together in our wildest imaginations, friends and neighbors? Beauty and the Beast? Question is, which one's which?

Remember, you DIDN'T hear it here!

THE SCRIPT:

Cris and I didn't go home with the script. We went down to the Brim.

"She's following us," he hissed as we snaked among the tourists mobbing the hedge-lined lane to the village square. He pulled me under a handy tree, kissing and fondling me until I squirmed and Jane had slunk off on her own.

"Cruel, Cris, cruel." I pushed him away so I could breathe.

"I'm tired of her long face around everywhere."

Our village must have been called BardClyffe out of some Founder's nostalgia, since there were no cliffs. But there were hills, some quite steep, with low white houses cut into the slopes and narrow streets stone-paved and white-washed, like the Greek villages it was modeled on. Maybe it had been "Birdcliff," until some theatre maven got hold of it. There were a lot of birds. Birds thrived in our wild-programmed climate, perhaps because the programmers had limited themselves to mild breezes and gentle rains. No hurricanes. No snow. No thunderstorms or tornadoes. Still, you could get drenched without warning. Did this keep the creative juices flowing? The Founders apparently thought so.

The BardClyffe market was jammed, as always. Weekday tourists meant heavy business at the brightly canopied glass and ceramics stalls out in the open plaza. Weekends brought the big money to the painting and sculpture galleries in the surrounding two-story arcade. The art in BardClyffe was low-tech and conservative, for the most part. You wanted high-tech or avant-garde, you went across town to Franklin Wells. The Chat always implied that BardClyffe did the better business.

At the head of the square, we passed under a raw metal scaffold thrown up around a lovely old stucco town house. Cris slowed to peer through the chain link fence.

"Big flap over this at Town Meeting last night, until they got sidetracked onto overpopulation."

Apprentices were not invited to Town Meeting, but Cris was an avid spectator of power games. He kept up with

Video Town Hall, as well as WorldNet/News and the Chat. I didn't pay the news services much heed. The Chat amused me occasionally, but I'd had my fill of small-town politics in Chicago.

"The BardClyffe C. of C. was going to tear this down without clearing it through the Town. The issue of village autonomy is suddenly a hot one."

"Tear a whole building down without asking?" I shook my head in wonder. In Chicago, you couldn't paint your bathroom without permission."

"You wait. The Town Council finds a way to okay anything that encourages tourism."

High on the chain link, a fancy signboard announced the construction of the multinational Francotel's twenty-story luxury hotel. With the exception of Town Hall, three stories had been the legislated limit since Harmony's founding. Travel brochures touted our "Old World charm," but tourists complained about the scarcity of available bedrooms.

Two overalled architects' apprentices on ladders scrubbed at the sign furiously. Scrawled red lettering vanished under their foaming brushes. A small crowd had gathered. Beat Street, a roving street theatre from, you guessed it, Franklin Wells, had arrived on the scene to improvise a little mime satirizing the scrubbers *and* the crowd. Quite the event. Public graffiti were unheard of in Harmony.

"Se . . . the . . . oor?" Cris squinted at the lettering. "Boor? Poor?"

"See the boor?"

"House the poor?"

"There are no poor in Harmony, just us apprentices, and they certainly aren't building us more housing."

I felt the first drops of an unscheduled shower and grabbed his sleeve, heading for the rain canopy at the Brim. The Brimhaven was the one café on the market square that apprentices could afford: since it was on the third floor, you had know to about the Brim to find it—plus they gave theatre folks a discount.

We waved to the owner on the way in. Gitanne had been with Images, the local dance group, until her retirement. She still did her barre each morning in the restaurant's main salon, gazing bravely into the long wall of mirrors, seeing perhaps not today's rather robust grandmother, but the pale, black-haired sprite of fifty years ago.

Gitanne had been lucky. Her licensed two children had both turned up talent. Her daughter now ran Images, so the dancers were in and out of the Brim like their own living room, or in the case of the apprentices, the living room they didn't have back in the dorms.

Out on the canopied terrace, the Blond Twins had already commandeered our favorite table. The rain had stopped as suddenly as it had begun, and Mark and Bela sat with heads close together, hands clasped beside thin, frosted glasses and little plates of cake. I smiled just looking at them. Seeing them together, you were struck by their sunny beauty. Apart, they seemed unremarkable, two pleasant-faced youths whose main distinctions were Bela's gift as a raconteur of human foibles and Mark's uncanny ability to look stylish in apprentice coveralls. They were the sweetest couple I knew.

Cris and I joined them and the four of us sat there grinning at each other. On days like this, Harmony felt like a gift from that gentle and loving deity in whom I generally did not believe. The sun on the rain-washed terrazzo, the gay sounds of commerce from the market, rich espresso in a porcelain cup and the company of friends. What more could I want, besides success and my citizenship, or that Cris and I might be as devoted as Bela and Mark? But that would've been asking too much.

Mark Benedict was from the Leningrad dome. Bela Mellior was from Prague. Mark said Leningrad was a "crazy" place. Cris told me there'd been a conservative coup there just before Mark arrived in Harmony. Mark didn't talk about it but you hardly noticed, since Bela was always going on about Prague and the preservation of the architectural wonders of her Old City. The shadow on his hymn of praise was that Prague, like Chicago, wanted its children trained in so-called useful trades and would not take a "deserter" artist back again.

"Got the script," Cris announced. He hauled out his copy and plopped it on the table. The smooth paper shone brighter than the surrounding gleam of white tile and stucco. He balanced it in one hand. "Needs cutting."

Bela nodded sagely. "Fails the weight test."

"The Gift," Cris read. "Hmmm. Not very auspicious."

"The critics complained, 'The title gives everything away . . .' "

Crispin gratified me with a smirk and peeled back the top page. "Jeez, they're gonna have to do something about these names. They're unpronounceable."

"You don't have to pronounce them," Mark noted. "The actors do, and that's what actors are good at."

Bela raised a delicate brow. "Some of them."

"Is Marie going to do the show?" I asked.

Mark said, "She's considering it. We have two ballets and an opera to turn out this summer."

Cris let the script flop closed. "So do we read it or not?"

"Read on," Mark ordered.

We took turns, through a second cup of espresso and later, through the market, empty after Closing, past the sign scoured of its mysterious graffito and along the twilit lanes toward home. The BardClyffe dorm, unprestigious residence that it was, was out along the rim and nowhere near a Tube stop. A trip to the village meant a long uphill journey home.

"Keeps us in shape," I said, as I always did.

"I'm living downtown when I'm a journeyman," said Cris, as he always did.

"We're moving to Underhill," said Mark. "Into the country."

"Sure," said Bela. "Four rooms, a little yard for my herbs."

"Studio attached," Mark added. And we all sighed in unison. We knew it was wishful thinking. Tourists were not the only ones worrying about bedrooms. The housing turnover in Harmony was miniscule. Respected talent went on living in the dorms well into their journeyships. If the Town Council was allowing high-rise buildings, I decided it should be for resident housing, not tourist hotels.

"We'll be lucky to find anything at all," I concluded, as I always did.

We took our scripts to dinner. Cris read in a stage whisper, passing the pages around under the table in a secretive manner calculated to arouse the curiosity of even the dullest of diners. Bela egged him on while Mark and I exchanged tolerant glances. It was not always apparent to those around us that Cris and I were, within a month, the same age. I valued my dignity. Crispin valued visibility.

When it got late, I gave Mark my script. Cris and I read the last act in the privacy of his room which was identical to mine except that he'd laid his mattress on the floor and set the metal bed frame upright against the wall where, with a few minor modifications, it was managing rather well as a bookcase. Upon his accession to journeyman, he said, it would convert nicely into housing for the computer his father would then be allowed to buy him. It was no use pointing out that the bed would be needed by the room's next occupant, or that his rich father could eventually send along an entire com center. Once Crispin got hold of an idea, he ran with it like a thief.

"So. What do you think?" He tossed the script aside and lay back, studying the ceiling.

"I like it." Truth was, I didn't know what to make of it.

The plot was simple, like a fairy tale: a plantation owner wishes to expand his coffee plantings into an area containing a secret native shrine. An idealistic tribesman decides that the only way to make the planter understand why he should not desecrate the shrine is to take him there to experience its magic, even though this violates a major tribal taboo. The gods show themselves in the planter's presence, but he's too busy computing the site's commercial potential to notice. Angered, the gods send a tremendous storm that wrecks the harvest, but the planter's house is stone, and in it he survives. For his heresy, the tribesman is ceremonially murdered by his elders. End of play.

I was moved by the murder of the tribesman, an innocent caught in the cross-cultural vise, but the dramaturgy was awkward here and there. It had the patchwork quality of a communally written work, and somehow, the ending didn't quite happen.

"But with all this talk of new and daring . . ."

"Yeah. You expected something more . . . exotic." Cris dropped a hand to the discarded script, thoughtfully riffling the pages. "But you know, there's more to it than it seems right off. I wonder if even Howie knows. Tuatua's Enclosure crisis is barely covered by WorldNet. I really had to dig for it." He rose to his elbows. "What Micah didn't let me explain today is that the real issues in the dispute are magic and religion. There's a group of tribes still keeping the ancient practices who claim that doming will interfere with their rituals. They say Tuatua's survival has nothing to do with geography, that it's their magic keeps it pure and alive." He lay back, pensive again. "Got to check up on actual climate conditions there."

"Must be some reason the others want to Enclose."

"Money, what else? With their limited landmass, agriculture can get them only so far. They want to expand their tourist trade beyond the few who think it's macho to spend a week Outside."

With Jane's worries in mind, I was not eager to discover a political motive to this play. "You blame everything on tourism lately."

"I know," he agreed, as if that proved his point.

The play did not leave my mind as quickly as I'd expected. "Odd how this script reads like a straightforward play, realistic dialogue and everything, despite all the weird shit going on: visions at the shrine and all the totems and talismans, the magic and the ancestor gods and the singing of the curse."

"That stuff *is* realistic to the Eye. All the research says these tribal guys really believe their magic. I mean, really."

Magic. I pulled the thin sheet up around me, my eyes tracing the rational geometry of the cubicle's four walls. No one talked about magic in Chicago. Even in church, miracles were seen as feats of the human spirit. Without training in the irrational, I found it scary but fascinating. Micah often used magic as a metaphor in his work, but *The Gift*'s nonchalant mixing of magic with the everyday was an entirely new concept. Magic offered as reality either turned your world upside down or forced a retreat into skepticism, where the whole idea could be dismissed as primitive ignorance.

Was the Eye going to arrive expecting us to believe? I recalled at last my jewelry peddler's words: *Wear it honestly, child. There is power in it.* What power did she mean? As gullible as he was, the tribesman in the play seemed to have some wonderful secret. You wanted to share it with him.

Cris flopped over restlessly. "It's very sad, this play."

I laughed. "I thought you were a progress-at-all-costs man."

He gave me a withering look. "One more coffee orchard is hardly my idea of progress. Progress can also be expressed in the evolution of ideas. What's sad is that the planter can't *see*."

"In Harmony, the shrine would have been preserved."

"Yeah. Like the town house in the square."

"Well, it may be yet."

Cris laughed at what he called my "pop-optimism." I wasn't really optimistic—I just needed to believe in things that showed some sign of being good and true. Harmony was one of those things. But I was used to his laugh, and to allowing (if not forgiving) it. *The artist mustn't temper his opinions*, he'd declare. *They are his daily bread!* I rolled over and snuggled in next to him. "What will they be like, the Eye?"

"Like nothing we've ever seen."

His tone made me shiver deliciously. "I can't wait to meet them!"

And we lay there quite happily, wondering what Micah would make of *The Gift*.

CRISPIN'S RESEARCH: EXCERPT FROM A SOCIAL HISTORY

(A Far Island, Pacific Books, 1963)

. . . now, I been workin' coffee for a lotta years out here an' I've hadda come to an understandin'. It ain't that these bozos isn't smart, ya see—they just got different ideas about what workin' means. I mean, they'll come in right on time, say, even early one mornin', the next they're three hours late and not understandin' why I'm yellin' at 'em for it. Or one day, they'll work steady fer the full eight, better'n any white man, even in the heat o' the day, then next they'll take off mid-afternoon without so much as a by-yer-leave. Just walk off with a wave and a smile, even as yer standin' there.

An' drink? Oh, ya gotta keep 'em away from the sauce. Most right places won't sell ta 'em anymore when they come 'round. Even their own folks is gettin' after fer it now. Seems they ain't gettin' the work done at home neither.

But they do got some good stories in 'em. Yah, we'll take lunch in the shade o' some big ole tree 'longside the field, and one a them'll get goin' with what happened to his cousin the very last night, an' before ya know, he's got ya on the edge a yer seat and the hair standin' up with some wildass tale o' spells an' spirits walkin' an' people turnin' inta dogs, all kinda craziness, and you believin' him every minute!

Like all them taboos they keep. Serious, ya know? I'm always gettin' the long eye from one a them 'cause I ask about somethin' I oughtn't. An just let some woman come roun'! Man, there's not hardly anythin' they's allowed to know about, don' matter what color she is! An' that's one place me an' them bozos see eye to eye . . .

SONGH:

Jane and Songh lay in wait for us the next morning, slouched like co-conspirators on the long neo-Gothic bench outside the dining hall. Songh's smooth, round face, rarely clouded, showed signs of trouble.

"What? Here on a Saturday? They stop feeding you at home?" Crispin patted the boy's dark head as if he were a dog. "C'mon in, we'll see what we can do."

Songh scuffed his feet on the polished slates, his hands tucked under his knees. He was nearly twenty but looked fifteen, with the body of an adolescent, not gangly but slight and flat-muscled, the sort that wouldn't thicken until well past middle age. He had a bad case of hero worship where Crispin was concerned. Cris enjoyed and encouraged it, then made rank fun of him behind his back.

"I'm not allowed in your dining room," Songh reminded him without complaint. "What did you think of the play, Crispin?"

"That it's a play like any other play. What, is it a morning emergency what I think? Ask me after I've had some breakfast!" Cris turned on his heel and shouldered through the oak-planked double doors into the dining hall. Laughter and the rattle of plates escaped in a rush as the doors swung home behind him.

Songh turned his puppy eagerness on me. I was second

best but would have to do. "Jane says Micah's gonna get in trouble if he does this play."

When I frowned at Jane, she looked away. I noted how tightly her curls hugged the back of her head, and wondered idly if fear could actually curl your hair. "Oh, Jane's probably worried about Tuamatutetuamatu's Enclosure dispute. But *The Gift* has nothing to do with Enclosure."

"Jane says when the farmer wants to plant on the native's land, it's a metaphor for Enclosure."

Typical. While I had struggled with magic and religion, Jane had read purely for the politics. "Why should that bother anybody? There's no Enclosure dispute in Harmony. Never has been."

"I know. But there's this . . . what about . . ." Songh ground to a halt, then shrugged. "Never mind."

"Come on, Songh." Jane turned from her intense scrutiny of the notice board. "What about the Closed Door League? That's what he was going to say."

"The what?"

"When you live at home," said Jane, "you hear things we don't in the dorms. Or at work."

Crispin stuck his head between the doors as a crowd descended on the dining hall. The morning rush was on. "You coming or not?"

"In a minute. Go stand in line." I turned back to Songh, who was pressed against the tiled wall by inbound traffic, looking like he wished he'd kept his mouth shut. "The Closed Door what?"

"League," Jane prompted. "He overheard his parents talking about it."

Songh nodded miserably. "Awhile ago, after a party when they came home late. They didn't know I heard. It wasn't about the theatre or anything, but they were real secretive, like they were worried or a little shocked, and then when I read this play . . ."

"And you were talking to Jane . . ." It was hard not to lay all of this in her lap: in the eight months Songh had been with Micah, there'd been little indication that he ever cross-referenced his life at home with the work he did in the studio.

"Even before," Songh insisted with some pride. "I mean, doesn't this play say everyone should have the right to decide the use of the land, not just the owner?"

"You could see it that way."

"But that's it! The Closed Door people think . . ." He glanced at Jane, then blurted, ". . . only people born in the dome should have that right."

"Second-generation types," supplied Jane. "Not even people like Howie or Micah. People like . . ."

"Me," murmured Songh.

"And people in the League," I said.

He offered his hangdog nod.

This was not an original notion. In many domes it was policy. But not in Harmony, where one in every three citizens had been born elsewhere. "Who *are* these people?"

He shrugged. "It's secret. Even my parents didn't know."

"Why keep it secret? Anyone can say what they like in Town Meeting. That's what it's for."

"I'm only telling what I heard."

"Oh, great. An underground movement in Harmony." Perfect fuel for Jane's paranoid fantasies. I wondered if Micah had any notion of it. "But, Songh, if this mysterious organization identifies with anyone in the play, it'll have to be the tribesman, the real native. The planter wasn't born on his land. He's the newcomer and the bad guy. *The Gift* should be very popular with these Closed Door folks."

Songh frowned and looked to Jane. I'd guessed right. With skewed logic, Jane had equated her own sense of disenfranchisement with the native's martyrdom, without exploring the question of usurpers and property rights.

"Besides, our audience will focus on the universal human tragedy, not on the obscure domestic politics of some island in the Pacific." I glared at Jane before she could object. "Even a famous one. There's nothing to worry about."

Songh's face smoothed. "I want them to come anyway. They're magic!" Perhaps his real worry had been that somebody might prevent them. "What do you think they'll be like?"

I echoed Crispin. "Like nothing we've ever seen."

Mark and Bela clattered by, late for breakfast.

"Be nothing left!" warned Mark, careening through the doors.

"Pan scrapings!" Bela seconded gleefully. "Burnt toast!"

The dining room doors at breakfast were not the best spot for serious debate. "Have we put this to rest?" I asked. "I'm hungry."

Songh shrugged. "Sure. I'll see you guys Monday."

"Oh, come in and sit with us," I urged. If he were with us, he wouldn't be brooding about the script. "Nobody'll toss you out. You can have my second cup of coffee."

He smiled, beatific in his gratitude.

"You see," said Jane, but sadly, not in malice, "Songh can get in anywhere he wants."

WORLDNET/NEWS

05/17/46

JOHANNESBURG, 05/16/46

Rescue operations were called off today after a twenty-four-hour air and ground search failed to provide any sign of two OutCare workers who vanished after leaving their dome on a charity mission Wednesday. Extensive questioning of Outside residents turned up no clues to the disappearance.

STOCKHOLM, 05/16/46   *Special to WorldNet/News*

Avowed Open Sky spokeswoman Ingrid Hibberd was taken into custody today and remanded to the Civic Hospital for psychiatric testing. Ms. Hibberd's organization has been increasingly vocal in its criticism of Stockholm's policy for dealing with the local Outsider population. The name "Open Sky" refers to the members' conviction that doming is unnatural and should be considered a temporary measure to be done away with as soon as Outside conditions permit.

MARSEILLE, 05/17/46

Representatives from thirty domes worldwide are meeting with business leaders to discuss the proposed turnover of inter-dome vacuum transport to private management. The ten-dome consortium that has administered the Tubes since their completion in 2019 has been operating at a deficit for the last two years under the cloud of charges of corruption and incompetence, due to the increasingly frequent loss of materials sent through the Tubes.

Megacorps Taido, CONPLEX, Francotel, and Bunicorp have tendered bids to assume operation of the service. A spokesman for CONPLEX, the mining supergiant, was heard to remark, "We built the damn tunnels. We ought to know how to run them."

TUAMATUTETUAMATU, 05/15/46

Planters' Association President Imre Deeland, while attending a wedding reception Tuesday, was overheard by an alert press when he admitted to his host's five-year-old daughter that he had indeed heard stories about the Conch, the mythical hero adopted by local tribes as a symbol of their resistance to the proposed doming of the island. Mr. Deeland has previously denied all knowledge of the colorful folk hero, despite tribal claims that the Conch actually exists and that his magical powers are being employed in the service of their cause.

POLITICS:

Monday, we played the Survival Game at breakfast, while Bela convinced us that not only did he know all there was to know about jungle survival, but it could be uproariously funny as well. When Cris and I slunk into the studio ten minutes late, we found Micah leaning wearily against his drawing board with his arms folded.

"Quarantine!" Howie's voice blared from the speakerphone. "Can you believe it? Immigration's gonna make me shut 'em up for three weeks soon as they get here! For chrissakes, this troupe's been in Paris, London, Stockholm, all over the damn world without infecting anybody!"

Micah nodded to us absently as we settled onto our stools. "Odd for the mayor's office to take an interest in such matters."

"It's that new immigration chief the T.C. jammed down her throat. He's keeping a tight rein on work visas all of a sudden. They'll let in every tourist asshole in the goddamn world, but when it comes to genuine artists . . ." A sound like a shrug rattled through the speaker. "Well, I'll play it their way. Maybe I can turn it to some advantage on the publicity front."

"No doubt," agreed Micah dryly.

"See you at one, then?" Howie boomed, his cheer restored.

"One o'clock." Micah switched off, then looked up to four pairs of inquiring eyes. He smiled back guilelessly.

"So I guess we're doing it?" ventured Crispin.

Micah pushed briskly away from his desk. "Irresponsible not to."

Jane stood rigid at the cutting table. I wished she'd admit her worries to Micah, but she'd never risk his disapproval. He could at least ease her fears about the security of her position in the studio. On the other hand, in the first flush of his enthusiasm for the new piece, Micah might steam right over her without even noticing. He often said that committing to a play is like falling in love, and we all know how blind love is. So for Jane's sake, I said nothing, and regretted it later.

"Irresponsible?" Crispin always wanted the why as well as the what of Micah's decisions. He claimed the artist's take on the material mattered more than the material itself. Crispin's precociously clear image of himself as Artist was another thing I envied and admired.

"Irresponsible," Micah confirmed, his fists balled up tight for emphasis, those clever badger paws that worked such wonders. Micah wore his nails rather long, in the way of Latin men, and sometimes, in pursuit of an idea, when the sketch paper flew around his desk like leaves in a wind, I pictured him digging into the fertile earth of his imagination with sharp, sure strokes. "This play's about what we do for a living! It's about communication. And cultural context. Howie says betrayal, but the communication gap caused by massive cultural misunderstanding makes that betrayal inevitable."

He turned back to his corner and began methodically stripping the sketches from the walls around his desk. "We have an odd view of culture here in Harmony. We don't live it so much as use it. New apprentices arrive every year from domes all over the world, and the first thing we teach them is to assimilate, to defuse their personal history by converting it into a tool."

The pile of Micah's personal history built on his worktable. Some of the drawings had been on the wall so long that the tape was gummy and the paper gray and brittle.

"Sure, we do plays about the importance of culture, but most of them were written two hundred years ago, and the actors, however well intentioned, dredge up their character and motivation from the research files. The Eye was born knowing what their play's about! Do we ever do plays about Harmony? Not since *Domers*. We should be doing them all the time! It's the only thing we know about, I mean, *really* know, like the Eye knows *The Gift*."

He took down the last sketch, and the wall that faced him was as blank as I had ever seen it. Smudge marks and tape gum formed faint square outlines, the ghosts of all that work lying on the table. A silence settled into the studio, all of us transfixed by that blank wall. *Fill me, fill me*, it demanded.

"Howard's right about his audience." Micah's hands swung empty at his sides. "They are smug and complacent. We all are. We think we've got it right, here in Harmony. We are so busy preserving the Enlightenment against the anarchy Outside. But the Planter in the play's no different— a liberal thinker, not a bad guy. His problem isn't his intentions, it's his lack of vision. He just cannot see that there are other values as valid as his own."

He raised open palms to the wall as if communing with its emptiness. And then, his invocation complete, he shifted gears with a grinding sigh and faced the mound of drawings on his worktable. "I suppose that Marin bunch wouldn't take well to finding their project off the wall so soon . . ."

Micah did not want to fill that waiting space. Not yet.

I understood his reluctance, but in my gut rather than my head. "You might want to find a spot somewhere for *Cymbeline*."

He nodded, then dutifully sorted out the Marin and *Cymbeline* sketches and retaped them to the right of his drawing board, allowing the wall in front of him to remain bare. Micah regarded it with satisfaction and sat down to work.

The studio had just got peaceful again when Cris exclaimed from his console, "I don't believe it."

I enlarged the Marin elevation on my desk to do details. "What?"

"Totally amazing."

"What? What?"

"I stumbled across a mention of some big Tuatuan folk hero the other day and added him to my search list. Not a scrap showed up for two days and now, all of a sudden, here it is, an entire file, all neatly put together like someone collected it for me. Like . . . magic." He shook his head, almost a shudder. "I got to have twigged some library call code somewhere."

"For a file on a folk hero?"

"Well, why not?" But Cris was gazing at his screen as if it really were magic. Having never seen actual awe in his eyes before, I barely recognized it. "He's called Latooea, the Conch, after those big shells that islanders used to call tribal meetings with back when. Supposedly this Conch is invisible, he can be several places at once. He walks through walls and spirits anti-domer prisoners out of jail. He eavesdrops on Planters' Association meetings and reveals their secret pro-domer strategies." He looked back at me. "Dynamic, huh?"

Was he baiting me? I couldn't tell.

"Of course, the planters claim the Conch is anti-domer propaganda. But according to the tribes, he always appears in times of crisis, using his magic to protect the ancient ways. Neat, huh?" Cris blinked at me, shook his head, and sank back into communion with his keyboard.

I leaned toward Jane, hoping to jolly her at least a little. "See? Told you this play has nothing to do with politics."

She did not appreciate my irony. And I found my mind straying all morning. Magic Tuatuan revolutionaries, Micah talking politics—I'd never heard him express such vehement dissatisfaction with Harmony before, and undeniably, *The Gift* had inspired it. I didn't know what a rich kid's life in Buenos Aires was like, but if Micah'd grown up in Chicago, he'd be as grateful as I was for the advantages of life under Harmony's dome. You could say what you liked in Harmony, and do what you liked, and if someone didn't approve, they could get up in Town Meeting and tell you about it without fear of reprisal. Even then, you were required only to listen, not to come to an agreement. It was what Micah called "the encounter-therapy heart of Harmony."

Surely a little smugness was deserved?

But this Closed Door thing sounded like a lot more than

smugness. And why so secret? Constitutional issues had been submitted to open debate in the past. Micah'd once said the best way to defuse a hot issue was to talk it to death. Was that what the Closed Door League was afraid of?

So here was another thing I neglected to ask Micah about and regretted later. But I did decide to lend a more careful ear to Jane and her dogged paranoia.

CRISPIN'S RESEARCH: A CONCH STORY

Sydney Morning Herald, April 23, 1932

. . . and finally they allowed me into the hut. The child's father glowered suspiciously, but as I was under the Headman's protection, he jerked his head toward the corner where the older siblings sat. I didn't mind this insult, as the children soon lost their earlier awe of me, co-exile in this inferior space. Other relatives filed in. Soon we were two dozen, packed into a 15 by 20-foot hut, hunkered in the dirt, breathing thick wood smoke and the smell of each other's fear, for the child, for his awful disease, for what was about to happen.

We waited fully an hour, in silence but for the fire snapping and the night sounds outside and the boy thrashing and moaning in his fever. The mother sat by his bed of palm fronds and sang to him voicelessly, her lips moving in tireless prayer. One of the younger sisters sagged in sleep against my shoulder. I worried that the boy might die before the ritual began.

The palm log fire burned yellow and bright against the darkness past the doorway. The flames mesmerized me, all of us, I think, waiting in that closed-packed silence. I made sure not to doze or lose my concentration and with it this extraordinary opportunity to observe the tribal magics. Even so, the creature entered the hut without my notice. I was first aware of her easing around the fire toward the delirious child. I say "she" because the creature moved with such feminine grace and quiet. Otherwise, it bore the stature of a man, tall with lean, muscular limbs stained a peculiar blue with mud and ash mixed so smoothly to seem the skin's own natural color. It wore a mask of blue bird feathers with white cowrie shells for eyes, sewn in tight concentric rings.

This strange apparition seated itself and took the boy's feet into its hands. The silence continued, as if nothing more unusual than another relative had joined the circle. But soon the mother's chanting became audible, and those around me, even the children, took it up. *Latooea, Latooea,* they sang softly, over and over in ceaseless incantation. My legs ached horribly, bent under me on the hard-packed floor, but I did not stir. But I must have dozed again. Next I recall, the Headman rose and kicked at the dying ashes of the fire. Birds were singing dawn songs outside the hut, and the little boy slept peacefully in his smiling mother's arms.

The blue-skinned apparition was nowhere to be seen, but the relatives, filing out of the hut, one by one paused to touch the sleeping boy's head in awe and gratitude, each murmuring as he did the name of Latooea.

THE ARKADIE:

Micah settled down to work pretty well after the ritual purging of his corner. Once he'd allowed as how he'd gone about his revisions a little too freely and that it wasn't worth setting the Marin project back another six months, we spent the rest of the morning restoring his weekend spree of damage and disorder.

"Okay," Cris called from his console. "I'm clear on the sequencing up to Captain Seraglio breaking into the Sorcerer's secret library and burning the rune book. But then . . ."

"Don't forget the magic sword," Songh put in.

I was glad someone was interested enough in Marin to keep track of the more baroque details.

"The sword, the sword . . ." Cris fiddled at the keyboard, peering at the holo miniature on the model stand. "Got the sword. After then I'm lost, when the fire spreads to the

royal nursery." His glance at Micah dared a faint reproach.
"We never set the point where you want to switch from live
flame to the projection, or which walls you want to be
real—"

"Or for that matter," replied Micah, "how to prevent
some overly involved viewer from reaching into the cradle
and rescuing the damn princess."

I laughed out loud. It was okay to laugh at Marin. Even
Jane was snorting quietly to herself, while Songh pouted in
confusion.

Micah made a grand effort to pay attention, but by noon
he was terminally restless. He sharpened his pencil again
and again, insisting the machine was jammed and he
couldn't get a point. He complained about his brush and
the quality of the paper he was forced to use "nowadays."
It was soon clear that the rest of the Marin restoration
would be up to us.

But that was okay. You always learn more when you have
to make a few design decisions on your own, and Marin
was the perfect project to school apprentices with, where
maturity and subtlety were clearly not required or even
desirable. If Songh's grasp of the CADD system had been
better than hopeless, I'd have assigned him to draft Marin.
Enchanted princes, love potions. It was just his speed. I
decided I'd trust him to take charge of the model, and in
that little burst of optimism, I began to think we might
actually get Marin done in time for bids.

But Micah wanted me to go to the Arkadie with him. By
twelve-thirty he was waiting in the doorway.

He'd been inviting me to design meetings lately, ostensi-
bly to take notes on schedule and budget figures, those
crucial data directors so often hope to gloss over. But
mostly I was along to learn "the process," that mysterious
and touchy method whereby a design is developed and
agreed upon.

I turned off my desk and told Jane to do anything she
could to hurry *Deo Gratias* along.

We squeaked out just as the first tourists came nosing
around the courtyard gate, searching through the beech
branches for the nonexistent sign.

"This is the place," I assured them, though the real place
to visit, if you wanted to understand where the work came
from, would be the inside of Micah's head.

We edged away through the crowds streaming up from the village and took the Tube four stops to Fetching Green, home of the Arkadie Repertory Theatre. Fetching was larger than BardClyffe, being one of the "cardinal villages," the four original settlements ranged crosswise around Founders' Park. The green spaces between had filled in more rapidly than anyone had dreamed, but BardClyffe was one of the last villages to be incorporated and remained, along with Underhill, the least developed.

The Tube was packed with tourists. Residents no longer used the Tube during Open Hours unless they absolutely could not walk or bike to their destination. But it was a two-mile hike to Fetching, and Micah had never been seen on a bike in his life. Mind you, everyone rode bikes in Harmony. Apprentices passed them down like antique furniture, from generation to generation. But bikes were one Harmonic eccentricity that my boss steadfastly refused to adopt. Probably he wasn't much good on a bike, and his refusal indicated how highly he valued his personal dignity.

So highly that we stood pressed like sardines in the narrow, bright-lit car, suffering the one-way conversation of a skin-headed young man visiting from BosDome, where he attended a school which from his account was teaching him everything there was to be known in the universe and beyond. He had seen Micah's design for *Grasses* last season at the New Avon on the other side of Town. He had a great deal to say about how marvelous the production was, but you know, he *could* offer a few ideas for how it could have been done better, no offense of course.

I looked for the chance, during a convenient lurch, to crush his foot as flat as his nasal twang. But Harmony's Tube is magnetic. It doesn't lurch like the Chicago monoel, or clatter madly enough to drown out conversation. And Micah, however much he avoided converse with tourists and strangers, once accosted was unfailingly polite. He even contrived to look placidly entertained, which I thought was carrying civilization just a little too far.

"What an asshole," I breathed, when we had been released from our torment at Fetching Station.

"Just another theatre critic in the making," replied Micah, stepping heavily onto the escalator.

At street level, we crossed the broad circular plaza ringed with booksellers' stalls and picture galleries. Only through

great exercise of the will did Micah pass the rare-book dealers by. I would have happily lingered in the galleries. Two-
dimensional black-and-white photography was undergoing
a major renaissance. Reproductions of old work and new
originals were both selling well. During one of our weekend
wanders, I spotted an ancient picture postcard of the Wrig-
ley Building in one of these shops. Crispin bargained per-
suasively enough to be able to buy it for my birthday, even
promising to remember the dealer after he became famous.
He complained about it afterward, but I knew he'd enjoyed
the contest and its victory. He hadn't gone to all that trouble just for me. Anyway, it was good for him. No matter
how much his father leaves him or how famous he becomes,
there'll always be this bit of Crispin's life when he knew
what it meant to have no money.

The sun always felt hotter to me in Fetching Green, perhaps having something to do with Fetching not being all
that green anymore—another vote for BardClyffe's runaway
plant life. The market plaza was paved in alternating circles
of bright red and white marble. I couldn't look at it without
thinking of the expense. Heat shimmered above the polished stone, which never seemed to age or crack. Had we
been anywhere but Harmony, I'd have wondered if the
stone was genuine.

The august edifice on the far side of this marble ocean
was the Arkadie, tall, cylindrical, and white, very much the
image of a cultural citadel. The facade was windowless and
faced with smooth curved stone. The only detail was in the
fluted columns flanking the pedimented entrance, con-
sciously classical in both style and scale, scrupulously weathered as if flown in from the Parthenon itself. The name
"Arkadie" was chiseled in block Roman above the door.
No gaudy posters, no informational marquee. Nothing. I
never could quite decide whether this plainness was the ultimate in taste or presumption.

In the center of the plaza, a clutch of street cleaners were
hard at work scrubbing the already gleaming marble. As we
passed, I caught, with a jolt of déjà vu, a glimpse of big
red lettering disappearing under their push brooms.

I slowed. ". . . lose the . . . oor?" Not enough to make
sense of, but clearly it had read the same as the graffito on
the sign in BardClyffe. "Micah, you ever seen graffiti in
Harmony before?"

"Tourists sometimes carve their names on the trees, but that's about it. Nothing on this scale." Micah waved to his colleague Max Eider, who waited in the Arkadie's shadowed entry. Eider carried a fat roll of drawings beneath one arm and a pencil behind one ear. He was frowning darkly over the plaza.

"Well met, Max!" Micah trudged up the broad steps to join him.

Eider gestured with his drawings. "Ach, Micah! Look what goes on these days!"

Micah glanced around inquiringly.

"Slogans on the stone!" complained Eider heatedly.

I hung back. Eider scared me, though I hardly knew him. He was a diminutive elderly man of ferocious mien, with an accent, not like Micah's faint Latin rolling of the vowels, but a real accent, as if he had not been born speaking English as well as his local tongue. He kept his white hair long and combed straight back without a part. His dark suits were worn but always well pressed, and his black eyes could pin you to the wall. It was a surprise to me each time he opened his mouth that fire did not issue forth. In fact, he was usually very soft-spoken, which conspired with the accent to make him often hard to understand.

"Slogans?" Micah turned back with renewed interest. "What did it say?"

Eider shrugged, as if text were irrelevant compared to the outrage of defacing the perfect marble. "Howie, he says a piece of street art."

Micah laughed expansively. "Very likely. The empty space . . . the broad and glistening stone . . . I was often tempted myself in my Young Turk days. We've settled in too much, don't you think? A little street art would do us good. But, Max, how are you? Have you been in there giving Sean the business?"

I thought Micah let go of his curiosity very easily, but he was so amused and satisfied that I was left wondering what the devil was "street art" and why didn't I know about something Micah obviously regarded with such fondness.

The mention of Sean deepened Eider's frown. He shook his roll of drawings like a fist. "He is very hard to convince, this boy."

"But he's the best, Max. They don't come better. Did he tell you we'll be sharing the shop, you and I?"

"*Ja*, Micah, but don't worry—I am already onstage before he must start with you." The old man wagged his head disapprovingly. "This Howie, he does not think always his schedule so well."

"Sean'll work it out," Micah assured him. "He bitches and complains, but he always works it out. Is *Crossroads* a big show?"

Eider spread his arms until he looked like a frail and angry bird readying for flight. "What is big, Micah, these days? You know we must be always doing more and more each time, or they say, " '*Hein*, this was fine but too much like last time.' "

"Oh, I don't know, Max. Maybe it's our fault for allowing the bigger-and-bigger syndrome to persist for so long."

Eider's black eyes narrowed as if he suspected a joke. When he saw Micah was serious, he grasped his sleeve and drew him close to murmur so low that I had to sidle up behind to hear. "Watch out with Howie talking these big ideas of no scenery. No one asks the director ever to make do with less. He will go on and do the play as he wants, and only you will be left with egg on your face."

Max Eider had survived a long and bumpy career before arriving as a guest artist at the RoundHall some seasons back. His work was so instantly popular that his special application for residency was voted through Town Meeting on its first round. To listen to him, you'd think everything bad that could happen in life and the theatre had happened to him. Who knew? Maybe it had.

Micah briefly borrowed Eider's frown. "Howard's already out telling the world what the show's going to look like, is he?" He smoothed the folds of his loose white shirt as if brushing away doubt, then smiled. "To tell the truth, Max, I'm looking forward to being less distracted with the technical details of a big production. Howard and I want to create a truly integrated work."

Eider nodded, patting Micah's arm rather gloomily. "Well, you are still young. As for me, I cannot afford these risks."

"Nonsense, Max."

"No, I am known for what I am known for."

Micah's smile tightened. "Every once in a while, there comes a time—I'm sure you've been there, Max—when you can't afford not to take a certain chance, so that you'll be able to move on to the rest of your career." He paused. "So there will *be* a rest of your career."

Eider's look must have pretty much mirrored my own. Micah had already endowed this little play with a crusading significance. At twenty-two, I found this astonishing but somehow reassuring, that Micah at forty-nine was still willing to tilt at windmills.

Max Eider was not reassured. He summoned a sickly grin and gave his birdy little shrug. "Ach, Micah. You will make good of this, and then you will see them coming to the rest of us saying, 'Look what Cervantes has done! Why didn't you think of that?' "

Micah chuckled. "But, Max, it could be so satisfying, to be artists again instead of mere showmen."

"But we *are* showmen!" Eider hugged his drawings tight under his arm. "If not, why make our work in a theatre and not alone on the canvas?"

"I'll bet that's what you say to Sean when he's telling you to cut down on the expensive detail." Micah's amiable smile said he'd gone as far as he cared to with this debate.

Eider accepted the truce. "This is only how I get what I want from him."

"An example to us all." Micah was already moving up the steps, out of the glaring sun. "Good luck. See you around when the time comes."

Eider waved, heading out across the heat-shimmered plaza, past the street cleaners finishing up. "*Ja*, Micah, same to you. But only, watch out for this Howie!"

"Phew!" I said when we'd got inside, into the Arkadie's prizewinning lobby, suffused by sunlight filtered through panels of stone cut thin enough to be translucent. The walls glowed warmly, showing only a faint and carefully planned pattern of seams and fasteners.

Micah nodded ruefully. "Sean wasn't kidding when he said Max was a handful. He'll stand at a painter's elbow for hours, telling her how to lay in each stroke. One old carpenter at Willow Street nearly put a clip of nails through his head.

"But he does something very special that the audiences love, and he does it very well. What Sean won't admit in all his railing against the old man is that producers hire Max precisely because he can exact such good work from the shops."

"But you get good work out of them . . ."

Micah's laugh was deprecatory. "Oh, I grump and coerce. Max browbeats. And there are plenty who feel on principle that a designer's not getting the best for the producer's money unless he or she browbeats the shop. Those people don't tend to hire me."

What he really meant was he didn't accept those people's offers. Micah would rather be rude to a rich backer than insult a stagehand. The discussion with Eider seemed to have fired him up. He strode through the carpeted acres of lobby as if ready to take on the entire design establishment, which at that moment in Harmony, perhaps in the world, included himself and Max Eider and at most a dozen others.

At the door to the administrative offices, he punched the entry code and we stepped into pandemonium. People in motion, the clatter of simultaneous conversation, the skreel of the fax machines. The offices, where the public never set foot, were nowhere as luxurious as the lobby. Here, the space shortage endemic to life under a dome reasserted itself with a vengeance. The staff worked practically in each other's pockets. The aisle between the desks would not have allowed for a fat man.

The walls were painted a careful pale lavender but every inch that wasn't behind a desk or file cabinet was covered with clippings and notices and printout and schedules and subscription lists, and all the rest of the paper detritus of running a theatre. What old fool said computers would free us from drowning in paper?

"Micah! Welcome back!" The subscriptions director gripped Micah's shoulder as he squeezed past with a stack of printout under one arm. "I've only read the first act, but I love it!"

"This is going to be a tough one to sell, you think, Micah?" worried the head of Marketing, glancing up from her terminal.

A secretary I knew gave me the thumbs-up sign from across the room. The heavyset bookkeeper wriggled his shoulders in proud anticipation. "Isn't it wonderful? What other theatre would take this kind of chance?"

"Micah! About time you showed!" Kim Levin, Howie's assistant and right arm, hung over the railing of the executive offices balcony with a harried grin. "Get the hell on up here!"

We scaled the slim spiral stair as the child receptionist gawked after us. Kim met us at the top with brisk kisses on both cheeks. She was a thin, pretty brunette, always dressed to kill, with a street-wise manner that belied her native Harmonic upbringing. I wondered if both parents having been apprentices explained why they'd done right what so often went wrong with second-generation kiddies. Howie would have been lost without Kim and everyone knew it. And she knew we knew it. She never felt the need to throw her weight around. Plus, she always remembered all the apprentices' names. I expected she'd be running the Arkadie someday, when Howie got tired of it.

Micah slumped against the railing as if celebrating a narrow escape. "Time to petition the Board for more office space."

"Foolish man," Kim snorted. "Try something we might be able to afford, like more staff. We are ready for some new blood around here! We're so bored looking at each other all the time!"

"You're about to get your wish, I do believe."

Kim laughed. "Indeed. And I'm a big fan of surprises, but a touch more advance information would be heartening. So far all I know about the Eye is that they're great and there are ten of them."

Ten. Even Crispin hadn't uncovered that little kernel. I pocketed it to carry home in triumph.

"I suppose it's company policy that their reviews never mention individuals?" Micah asked. "Presenting only the communal identity?"

Kim groaned. "Oh god, I hope not. We've been through the group-decision number before. Everything stops dead in rehearsal while the entire cast votes on whether so-and-so should walk upstage on this syllable or that one."

She linked one arm in mine and the other in Micah's and drew us down the narrow, carpeted hallway. "*He* is a madman today. When I left, he was yelling at Reede Chamberlaine and had reached decision crisis over the lunch menu."

"How are things going with Reede?"

Kim hissed eloquently. "Slime, he is slime."

Rachel Lamb, the general manager, called a hurried welcome as we passed her open door. Several meetings were going on at once in her little cubicle, and a sidebar was starting up out in the hall. We squeezed by and found

Howie as promised, in his own cramped but well-appointed office, hunched over his vid with a caterer's menu clenched in his fist as if he were ready to ram it into the screen. His curly mane of red-gold and gray was more than usually disarranged.

"Then you damn well talk 'em into it, Reede!" he roared. "No, we can't push the schedule back! I have a season here! I have trustees and subscribers to answer to! Bring that famous velvet pressure to bear." Howie waved us into chairs without looking up from the screen. "We can't let these actors start here thinking our time means nothing just because they don't live that way. If they have to go home first, they have to, but the quarantine means I need 'em here three weeks early!"

Reede Chamberlaine's answering voice was an Oxbridge-accented purr, so casual in contrast to Howie's ranting as to sound faintly sinister. I tried to sneak a look over Howie's shoulder but moved too slowly.

"Right. Keep me posted." Howie slapped the cutoff with a growl, then spread the crushed menu flat with both palms. "Now, Micah. What don't you eat every day at the studio?"

Micah eased into a chair beside the translucent outside wall. The glow warmed his olive skin to burnished gold. He looked very youthful and relaxed, slouched deep in cream-colored leather as if on holiday. I loved to watch Micah's Great Master persona slip whenever he left the studio. He put his feet up on the chair opposite and waved me into a third.

"I solve this problem thusly: I let them send me whatever they feel like, with enough variety to allow plenty of alternatives."

"What if you don't like any of it?"

"It's never happened."

Howie pulled at his nose reflectively. "Maybe I should change caterers. D'you suppose yours'd charge me extra for long-distance delivery?" He turned to me. "So whadda ya say, Gwinn? Know what you want to eat?"

They might be willing to take up most of our precious lunch hour discussing the lunch itself, but I wasn't going to be a party to it.

"Lean corned beef on sisal rye with french mustard, cornichons, a side of red cabbage slaw, and iced tea with lemon."

Kim whistled. "I like a decisive woman. Make that two!"

I'd only learned to order like that since I'd come to Harmony. In Chicago, menus were a fable. You ate what was available.

"Three," rumbled Micah.

Howie grasped his temples. "But I hate corned beef!"

Kim levered the menu out of his hands and headed for the door. "I'll order you chicken salad."

Howie nodded. "Dull, dull. But no heartburn."

Micah folded his hands like a pasha over his solid stomach. "I ran into Max Eider on the way in."

"Max, Max. He's already driving Sean around the bend. I'm adding a rider to the standard contract: no designers allowed in the shop more than twice a week until technical rehearsals."

"He didn't much like all this talk of pared-down production."

"Good!" Howie cheered. "He's costing me an arm and a leg on *Crossroads*. Maybe you can teach him a thing or two."

"Maybe *we* can."

Howie blinked at him. "Whew. That sounded a bit pointed. Getting cold feet, are you, Mi?"

"No, no." Micah crossed and uncrossed his legs on the padded chair. "Just feeling a little . . . exposed. You do know not everyone will understand what we're trying to do."

"If they understood it, we wouldn't have to do it for them."

Micah nodded. "Fine. So how's Reede treating you?"

"*Now* I'm getting heartburn," Howie groaned. "Nah, ole Reede'll be here for first rehearsal and opening night, and if we're lucky, we won't see much of him in between."

"Is he putting in any money?"

"As little as he can get away with."

"What a surprise."

"Hey, we need him. He's booking the Eye's tour after the run here. The new Immigration guy won't let them in without a ticket home."

Micah frowned. "Unusually letter-of-the-law, isn't it?"

"And I'd like to know who's at the bottom of it. Cora Lee from my Board tells me he's got the backing of a majority of the Town Council." Howie's eyes slid wearily across his

poster-covered walls. "Great reviews aren't enough anymore. And I quote: 'This troupe's aesthetic value has not
been sufficiently proven . . .'"

"What happened to artistic autonomy?"

"Exactly. Never had this problem with imports before.
Cora says it because Tuatua's undomed. The T.C. is sure
the Eye will want to stay once they get here. They don't
know how wrong they are!" Howie grabbed a bulging
folder, then dumped Micah's feet off the extra chair, and
dropped into it with a smug, boyish grin. "I went there this
weekend."

"There?"

"Tuamatutetuamatu!" He upended the folder. Glossy
brochures, picture postcards, and pamphlets spilled across
the table onto the floor. "Goddamn Immigration gave me
every shot in the book."

"No quarantine?" asked Micah.

"Hey, I'm a citizen." Howie laughed. "But they were
worried."

"Did you meet the Eye?" I asked eagerly.

"No such luck. They're playing some dance festival in
Stockholm. They'll swing home before they come here,
we'll get a glimpse, then quarantine for three goddamn
weeks." Howie threw up his hands. "Elusive little buggers,
aren't they? But Christ, those planters want to open that
little place up, they got to make it easier to get to! A cool
hour to Sydney, then two puddle-jumpers and a seaplane,
five more goddamn hours in the air, never mind the ground
wait. A seaplane, for chrissakes! The whole place is like
watching some revival at the Film Archive!"

Micah rescued a handful of candy-hued cards from the
rug and pored over them hungrily. "Should I go?"

"Yeah, if you want to absorb the cost yourself. Bloody
expensive. And my general manager doesn't believe in
research trips for second stage productions. She even cut
the effects engineer from the budget. But we don't need all
that shit this time!" Howie laughed delightedly. "God, Mi,
how many shows have we done together?"

"Too many. What did you do on Tuatua?"

Howie leaned back. "Went around staring through the
locked gates of infuckingcredible plantations and asking
about native shrines. The whole island was on edge with
this Enclosure dispute. Rallies and protests breaking out,

leaflets blowing all over the streets. Get this: the day before, the police raided this dive where somebody claimed they'd spotted this native legend called the Conch. Seven feet high, covered in blue feathers, debating domer policies with some plantation foreman who'd just dropped in for a quick one." Howie grinned. "Wonder what *he* was drinking."

"And when the police arrived?" asked Micah.

"Not a sign of the Conch, since, as we know, he's invisible . . . Cops beat up on a few people, went home. Even with that going on, folks were friendly enough when they heard I was from Harmony—they're building a tourist industry and they wanted to pick my brain about how we do it. However, they had nothing to offer about native shrines, and things cooled off pretty fast if I pushed it."

Kim bustled into the office. "Lunch is on its way."

Howie ignored her. "So I searched around for someone who looked like they might know that sort of thing firsthand. I finally fastened on this old waiter at the hotel, obviously a local."

"How did you know?" asked Micah. Kim settled like a cat in Howie's chair to listen.

"Well, he was, you know, not white."

"Are all the planters white?"

"White or mixed, at least all the ones I met. I mean, this guy was really *not white*."

Micah laughed. "Howard, your own general manager is not white."

"Take my word for it."

Kim looked at me deadpan. "The bone in his nose was the real giveaway."

"Anyway, the guy was kinda grumpy and closemouthed, until I mentioned the Eye. All of a sudden he was interested. I told him who I was and about the play, and finally he says if I really understood this play, I would understand why he couldn't tell me where the shrines were—story places, he called them."

Micah chuckled. "Had you there, didn't he."

"But he said there were places he could take me that weren't so secret, to help me understand the play, and I realize he's talking about things in the play I hadn't even mentioned. Well, turns out he's seen it. The Eye already performed it there a few years back. He says it caused a big noise and everyone on the island saw it at least once, even all those rich planters who'd told me they'd never heard of the Eye."

"Interesting," Micah remarked, "how entire groups of people can become simultaneously forgetful."

Howie developed a sly grin. "The official line is the play didn't exist. The media were told not to review it, but everyone went anyway. Even the Conch, my guy tells me. Seems he quotes the play sometimes in his underground messages to the people."

"Invite him to the opening," said Micah, uncharacteristically glib. I've always wanted to say I felt a premonition stirring. Mostly I felt a little creepy.

Howie nodded. "Somebody in that Opposition sure knows how to exploit a legend. But wait." He leaned forward, dropping his voice. "Next morning, I meet my friend at this little café that the hotel desk has never heard of but a native cabdriver has no trouble taking me to. My man has a new guy with him, his cousin-with-the-Land Rover, and in we pile and off we go."

The intercom on Howie's desk beeped discreetly.

Kim hopped up. "Lunch. I'll get it."

"It takes the rest of the day, and I'd had other visits planned for the afternoon. But once he got going, there was no way I was going to stop him, 'cause what he's doing is driving us the full circuit of the island, which is a ring with water in the middle.

"Mostly we're driving past planted fields and terraces, and the plantations with their fancy gates and big shiny billboards pushing the advantages of doming. But every so often, we take a turn down some dirt track and the driver pulls over and we get out into some totally breathtaking piece of nature, and my guy says, 'This is Station Two,' or three or five or eight, whichever, up to twelve by the end of the day, for the twelve months of the year."

"Stations?" I pictured concrete arches and magnetic rails. But Latin-born Micah got it immediately. "Like the Stations of the Cross."

Howie was crestfallen. "How'd you know? That's exactly what he said to me. One of the native clans—he didn't call them tribes—has the duty of walking these 'Stations' all year long. The next year, another clan takes over. Twelve Stations, twelve clans, an endless cycle. Between moves to the next station, they live at the one they're at and maintain it—you know, clean it up and repair any damage caused by storms . . . or other visitors."

"Vandalism?" asked Micah.

Howie nodded. "Increasingly."

"Who?"

"My guy was reluctant to say. I figure the same casual tourist damage we have—taking home a piece of the rock—or it could be—"

"More organized," Micah supplied. "Burning churches has always been a favorite strategy of oppression."

"Why do the clans go to all this trouble?" Kim asked.

Howie wound up for a big finish. "Because they believe that if they don't keep 'walking the Stations,' the Ancestors will decide that humanity can't be trusted to care for the world anymore. Then they'll do us all in and find somebody else to do the job."

"Oh. Is that all?" Micah's smile was grave. "I'm sure all this fits into the doming controversy somehow?"

"On the mark, as usual. Doming any part of the island will cut off access for the clans' ritual circuit."

"And the Eye is . . . ?" asked Micah.

"From those clans."

"But not on duty at the moment."

"Apparently not."

My creepy little chill was not going away, but I was beginning to like it. Suddenly, this minor fairy tale that had seemed as remote as an old morality play took on the weight of reality in Howie's glowing, windowless office. Just what Micah had asked for: actors doing a play about politics they were actively involved with.

Howie stood, stretching legs. At his desk, he reached into a drawer. "When I thanked the old man, saying I thought I understood the play much better now, he gave me these. Said they'd help me with the Eye when they got here."

He held a folded paper in one hand and a small dark sphere in the other. He waved the paper. "Kim, we'll need copies. This was supposedly snatched from a heavily guarded planters' meeting by the Conch. Now that someone's actually circulating their secret minutes around town with the morning mail, the planters aren't laughing so hard when the Conch's name comes up." He twisted the dark ball lightly in his fingers and tossed it to Micah. "Take this with you, too. For inspiration."

I leaned in to look. A bit of wood, carved all around. Twelve facets carved with tiny birds and animals. My hand jerked reflexively to my throat. This was the exact match to the bead Cris had made me stop wearing.

Micah turned it round and round as if searching for operating instructions. Howie let out a cathartic breath and strode restlessly to the door. "Hey, what happened to that lunch?"

And as if enough had been said on the subject of Tuatua, the two of them spent the rest of our lunchtime discussing the latest standings in the men's amateur soccer league. But Micah hurried home brimming with ideas, and I was left mystified.

"That was a useful meeting—I mean, beyond the research?"

Micah nodded, scribbling madly at his desk, the boredom of Marin behind him. The little wooden bead offered its multiple faces from the worktable. Micah had unearthed a dusty pad of rough paper he called newsprint. Its edges were cracking with age, but there he was, filling sheet after sheet with broad, dark strokes of charcoal, tossing each aside, on his worktable or on the floor. He often worked as one possessed by the beginnings of an idea, but this newsprint routine was unusual.

I'd missed something. Some essential aesthetic communion going on between Micah and Howie. My panic made me querulous. "But we didn't even talk about design!"

"The best ideas," the Master murmured, "always come indirectly."

Indirectly? I'll say. I decided right then that no magic that the Eye could come up with, real or imagined, could be more mysterious than the birth processes of Art.

HOWIE'S RESEARCH: FROM THE MINUTES OF THE APRIL MEETINGS OF THE TUATUAN PLANTERS' ASSOCIATION

[Ms. Corso:]
The Chair recognizes Mr. Raul-Ortega.
[Mr. Raul-Ortega:]
Madame Chair, fellow members, apologies for speaking out of turn, but you know, we are just not facing facts here. This Conch business ain't going to simply go away.
[Mr. Deeland:]
Now, Rafael—
[Mr. Raul-Ortega:]
No, I got to say this. Nobody believes us anymore when we say a guy who goes around spreading seditious paper broadsides like some French revolutionary and pulling off taped broadcasts on our own channels . . .
[Mr. Deeland:]
We're working on that—
[Mr. Raul-Ortega:]
. . . we look like damn fools if we keep saying he doesn't exist! Even the city police have a unit out looking for him.
[Mr. Deeland:]
Well, Rafael, what would you suggest? Perhaps you'd like to invite him to one of your Sunday lawn parties for a little chat?
[Mr. Raul-Ortega:]
There's no call to talk like that, Imre.
[Ms. Corso:]
Gentlemen . . .
[Mr. Raul-Ortega:]
Yeah, yeah. Look, all I'm saying is, say whatever you want in public, but we got to do something real in private. *Somebody's* responsible for all this stuff going on, probably some guy pretending to be a mythical hero. Don't matter, it's hurting us. It's gone way beyond the Station Clans now. All my workers are in love with this

guy, even the ones who never had a political thought in their lives. We got to find out what we can: who's seen this Conch, what he looks like, you know, facts. You can't do anything without facts!

[Ms. Corso:]

Perfectly reasonable, Mr. Raul-Ortega. Do I have volunteers for a fact-finding committee to research the true-life identity of the Conch? Goodness now, don't all speak at once, Mr. Deeland.

AT THE BRIM:

I thought a lot about Art after that, as we settled into the early stages of designing *The Gift*. I pondered the relationship of Art and Politics. I hadn't really thought there was one. I mean, wasn't Art about history and romance and philosophy, the Big Topics? Everyday politics didn't seem . . . well, elevated enough.

I thought a lot about the Eye as well. I wore my Tuatuan necklace despite Crispin's satirical glances. I devoured his research and picked his brain mercilessly, even borrowed the few books on Tuatua still extant in the Town Square library. Me, a child of Chicago, reading actual books on paper. And it wasn't just me: we were all Tuatua-crazy. Even Jane couldn't resist.

There was more available about the Eye's beginnings than about their recent history. The troupe had formed about the time of Tuamatutetuamatu's rediscovery. They performed traditional dances and dramas based on local legends, and were very popular on the island until they lost their founding director to a plantation accident. After this setback, the data files dried up. Crispin pursued the Conch into obscure anthropological monographs that seemed to confirm a savior figure out of ancient clan legend, whose last appearances had been in the 1950s when the European colonists were dividing the island into plantations with total disregard for tribal claims and boundaries.

"Just came in with their guns and moved the people off the land," Chris complained, as if this was something new in the history of the world.

Weekly, Howie would call to say the show was all off, he couldn't get the work visas or the Eye had refused to submit to the long quarantine. An hour later, it was full speed ahead again. In the studio, there was a burst of productivity while Micah struggled with his muse. We delivered the Marin drawings to twenty bidders eager for the profit to be made on such a mammoth project. We sent *Deo Gratias* off to the Paris Opera shop and *Cymbeline* over to the New Avon in Eden Village. I even got Micah thinking about the next two projects on his calendar, when I could pry him loose from Howie and *The Gift*.

On our off-time, the Eye beat out the Survival Game as our favorite topic. "So what do *you* think they'll be like?" we'd ask in the fraternal privacy of the Brim. Howie had called them primitive, but it turned out we each had our own idea of what that might mean. The conflicting and colorful mythos stirred something deep and different within each of us.

Songh admitted he was afraid of them, but he ate up stories of the real power of their tribal magic. Jane identified them with the martyred tribesman in the play and therefore with herself, arguing any political point in their favor with the iron-jawed insistence of the self-consciously disenfranchised. Cris went on a lot about the parallel freedoms of the "natural" man and the artist.

I don't know what I did. I tried for objectivity, but it's tricky recognizing your own delusions, and each newly uncovered fact or legend was like dry wind to the wild sparks of imagining that Howie had lit in all of us.

My image of the Eye and their culture was a confusing one. I'd find picturesque photos of cylindrical huts roofed in palm fronds, of toothless old men squatting in the dirt among dark, naked children, of ceremonial dancers submerged in feathers, raffia, and cowrie shells. But in the next shot: neat rows of students in the Mission classrooms or business-suited tribal elders at Planters' Association barbecues. Or T-shirted women with their wrist calculators, selling beads and baskets in the tourist bazaars, looking nowhere as exotic as my mysterious jewelry peddler. Then always, there were the fantastical deeds of the Conch, weaving the brightest threads through the tapestry. The mix of ancient and modern, real and magical, was impossible to correlate. Where in all of this should I place the Eye?

We sat one afternoon under the Brim's rain canopy. A random downpour had cleared the market square as quickly as a bomb scare. Giant drops fell like pebbles, bouncing off the cobbled pavement in sheets of spray. While Crispin lectured Songh about respecting the Eye's taboos, I mused about magic and the Eye and Marin.

Visitors to the Marin Sea Dome would have a sophisticatedly complex relationship to magic. They would demand to be mystified and astonished, but their suspension of disbelief would be an almost conscious mechanism. They'd never really question the basic assumption that a clever technical explanation existed for each and every wonder.

Suddenly this seemed pitifully cynical. What about real wonder? What about willing submission to genuine awe?

The religious connotations of this embarrassed me, which kept my musings private, but imagine sitting in a theatre believing that what you see is real. Or if that's too much to swallow, then imagine asking yourself just for a moment if it might be. To be given in the theatre the gift of that doubting, of the possibility of miracle! Once a possibility is admitted, the reality hardly matters. To be able to *give* such a gift . . .

Mark stopped by the table, balancing carry-out plates of Gitanne's infamous sacher torte and Black Forest cake. He didn't sit. "Bela's ill," he announced.

Jane hovered between solicitude and caution. "What's he got?"

Mark smiled. "Vapors. I'm taking him treats."

"Take him the latest from WorldNet/News," offered Cris. "The Port City police on Tuatua have offered a nice fat reward for information leading to the capture of the Conch."

"They're admitting he's real?" Mark set the plates down and squeezed onto the edge of my chair. "I'll let him sleep awhile longer. What else have you heard?"

Later I mourned, "What will we ever have in common with the Eye? What will we talk about when they get here?"

Crispin replied, "What actors always talk about. Themselves."

But I thought, we all thought, even Cris for all his outward cynicism thought: no, these actors will be different.

Anticipation flared in me. I tingled with the promise of their strangeness. I could not wait for them to come.

And then one Monday morning late in June, the mail board was flashing "URGENT" when we trouped into the still-empty studio.

Crispin cued up the message, then let out a victory yell.

"What?" I demanded.

"What?" echoed Micah, entering behind us, frowning in concern.

"They're coming!" Cris did a mini war dance of exultation, pointing at the screen. "Howie says be at the Gate at five forty-five, 'no later, no fail.' It's gotta be them!"

Micah allowed a small private smile. "Well, well. Good for Howard. He got them in after all."

THE ARRIVAL:

The crowds at the Gate were naturally the worst just before six o'clock closing. At noon, the traffic flowed steadily inward toward the Tube and the villages, intent on restaurant guides and lengthy shopping lists, but by five-thirty folks were lingering in the broad, café-lined Gateway Plaza, nibbling at sweets from the vendors' carts, gulping a last espresso or Campari, refusing to end their precious day in Harmony until Security descended en masse to politely but firmly throw them out.

Harmony's Gates really look like old-fashioned gates, if you ignore the air-lock mechanisms. The towering arched facade was designed with frank reference to the Roman Coliseum. The bottom tier of arches is fitted with wrought-iron grilles, the work of a local metal sculptor. The grilles are for show, of course. They're impressive, but they wouldn't hold back a determined Outsider mob for long—the air locks do that, plus a secondary force field, invisible but impenetrable, activated outside the Gate when Harmony closes for the night. Even a prominent citizen couldn't get in (or out) after six o'clock closing.

It was hot in the plaza that afternoon, with all those homebound tourists sucking up the air. The public address, dubbed the Voice of Harmony, was announcing the final departure of the airport-bound hover fleet. Howie, Kim, and the general manager Rachel Lamb had secured a table in the café nearest the west end of the Gate. Howie's grin was an unsettling mix of exhilaration and worry. Rachel gave us her quick, cool smile, her attention fixed on the arrivals and departures board flashing above the second tier of arches.

"Should be in any minute now," said Howie brightly. He had twisted the napkin under his espresso into damp shreds.

Micah pulled up a chair and glanced around for a waiter before surveying the tight-packed plaza. "Whose idea was it to bring them in at Closing Time? I'd want a better idea of what's arriving if I'd arranged a triumphal entry."

"Word of mouth is the best publicity," returned Howie smugly.

Micah nodded. "The circus is coming to town."

"And," Rachel murmured, "Reede Chamberlaine is coming with it."

Micah noticed us waiting faithfully beside his chair. "The view might be better from above . . ."

"Awrright!" Crispin dodged away through the throng, yanking me with him. Songh sprang after us, eager as a pup. Jane looked like she'd prefer the safety of the café to a press of tourists chattering like patrons at a gallery opening. The Voice was now urging visitors through the Gate, and I wasn't sure Jane had followed until we reached the steep stone stairs that led to the observation deck along the second tier. But there she was, bumping cross-stream through the crowd, apologizing left and right and looking pained. Poor Jane, I thought. Life is so difficult for you.

The observation deck was empty.

"Mark's going to be sorry he missed this," I said. Bela was still mysteriously ill and Mark was still nursing him.

From the rail, we could see the bustle at the Gates below and stretching out along the wide boulevard to the paved landing field. The leaden sky was abuzz with aircraft. A thick haze hung over the Outsider slum that pushed against both sides of the boulevard. Every stick, every scrap of brush out there had been burned for fuel, every blade of grass trampled into the flat gray earth. The stream of departing tourists was a thick slash of color across a dull, dusty landscape.

On the outskirts of the camp, I spotted the retrofitted hulk of an ancient ground car, its boiler coughing steam alongside the cracked and weed-choked road that led off into the hills. Strong-arm Outsider gangs were said to rule those hills. I nudged Crispin to point out the ragged men in conversation beside the vehicle. One of them, tall and dark-skinned, moved with supple grace and was wearing a respirator. It was unusual for Outsiders to bother. When one did, it was supposedly an emblem of power. I glanced below. The Outside Security guards, their own noses safely buried in state-of-the-art breathers, had their heads together and their eyes on the steaming, shuddering car.

Cris pounded the marble rail and then my arm. "There! It's gotta be that one!"

The hover fleet was boarding its final round of passengers. A bit apart from the rest, a single hover settled on the tarmac, rotors slowing, its fans kicking up whirlwinds of dust and debris.

A blue-clad, air-masked loading crew trotted forward to unfold the fore and aft gangways. Any morning, the opening doors would have disgorged an immediate, eager torrent of humanity. Now they opened into darkness, the shadowed empty interior of the cabin. The loaders hesitated at the foot of the gangway, holding back the long, restless line waiting to board. A delay in boarding was sure to catch the interest of departing visitors, and just as every eye had fastened impatiently on the gangway, a tall, silver-haired man appeared in the forward door. Impeccably tailored in pearl gray, he stood straight and unsmiling. He gazed majestically over the muttering crowd, then nodded into the shadows behind him, and started down the gangway.

"Reede Chamberlaine," I guessed.

Crispin's nod was unsure. "I expected bald and fat."

"And greasy."

The crowd stilled. They knew an Entrance when they saw one.

The empty doorway filled suddenly with a swirl of black. One, two, five, ten veiled and hooded figures detached themselves from the inner dark and swept down the stairs onto the tarmac.

Without a glance behind him, the silver-haired man set off across the landing area toward the Gates. The faceless ten whirled after him like a flock of giant blackbirds swooping to the attack, wings of fabric and glittering feathers twisting, rising around them in the gusts from the hover fans.

"Weee-ooh!" breathed Crispin.

They could have been male, they could have been female. They were mystery incarnate. Nothing about them was definitive except their blackness and their constant, almost floating movement. I was conscious of my mouth hanging open. I shut it before Songh could notice that I looked exactly like he did.

Chamberlaine reached the head of the crowded boulevard and chose a path straight down the middle. The throng parted like the Red Sea before Moses.

"They think he's royalty or something," Crispin hissed. "After all that's gone on, the damn fools are still in love with royalty."

"No, it's what's following him." But privately I admitted that if there had to be such a thing as royalty, Reede Scott Chamberlaine was what it should look like. But no chance, from what we were told, of him *acting* like royalty, except for the high-handed part.

"But they're *not* following him," Cris exclaimed.

The Eye had collectively strayed from the center of the boulevard, deserting the "safe" aisle Chamberlaine had so ostentatiously opened for them.

Suddenly they broke rank and danced in among the confused but delighted tourists. Flowers and colored feathers and shimmering silver balls materialized in twirling gloved hands, brilliant flashes against the black, tossed and juggled, then presented into eager tourist paws. The throng cheered and applauded, soundlessly to us behind the dome, giving their flapping hands and mouths a surreal quality, like watching the vid with the sound off. Meanwhile, the Eye moved around and through them, but ever toward the edge.

Cris was beside himself with admiration. "Now, that's what I call working a crowd!"

"Upstaged Chamberlaine, all right . . ." Jane murmured.

"I knew they'd be great!" Songh leaned so far over the observation rail that I feared he'd brush the force field, and I wondered how I'd explain it to his father if that smooth, young face were scarred for life. I hauled on his arm to pull him back.

"Look!" cried Cris.

Songh broke free. "What are they *doing*?"

The Eye danced now along the edges of the boulevard, five on either side. Their flowers and feathers had become bread and fruit, which they were tossing to stunned Outsiders as fast as they could produce them, seemingly out of the air. The Outsiders stirred from their apathy and pressed forward in response. Sooty, grasping hands walled both sides of the boulevard. The tourists drew together like herd beasts, gaping. Even from our elevated perch inside the dome, I sensed the heartbeat of the crowd quickening in fear.

"Well, this is a fine way to start!" Jane reconsidered her approval.

"They don't come from a dome," I reasoned. "They don't really know about Outsiders."

"They've been on tour around the world."

"Then it's a gesture of greeting. They don't know how dangerous it is here." Surely this feeding of Outsiders was too grossly obvious to be meant as a political statement, especially in a place like Harmony, where charity laws were written into the constitution along with taxes.

"Or maybe they do . . ." Crispin put on a wolfish grin.

I could see Reede Chamberlaine clearly now as he strode toward us, almost at the Gates. His pale face was aquiline and arrogant, still impassive, but his head was cocked back ever so slightly to monitor the goings-on behind him and his eyes seemed to be searching ahead of him, imperiously, showing no fear.

Sure enough, a fresh brace of green-uniformed Security appeared beneath us, easing themselves quickly but unobtrusively through the press of onlookers. Their obvious skill made me suddenly wonder who made up Harmony's Security force, and how or where they were trained, and also why hadn't I asked myself that before.

Songh and Crispin whooped again in delight. I turned back to see four of the Eye leap into the center of the boulevard, their robes billowing around them like pirate sails. In precise and grandly gestured unison, they unfurled a silken banner painted with a giant eye.

Distracted, the crowd relaxed, applauding like happy children. Two more dancers joined the four. Six, then eight black-clad bodies leaped and twisted with the rainbowed silk held high, and the banner grew with each pair who joined it, ten, twenty, thirty feet long, increasing again as the final pair took hold. Behind the giant eye unfolded blocks of smaller painted symbols, dark and mystical against the shimmering silk.

"Even the Outsiders are applauding," Jane noted with awe.

Which they were, if only sporadically. I saw that day my first Outsider smile, on the face of a young boy with a ripe mango in one hand and a mirrored ball in the other. Rapt, he gazed from one to the other as if unable to decide which was the greater prize.

A flash of light caught my eye, like a sudden reflection off polished chrome. One of the smaller dancers seemed to stumble. The flash came again.

Cris leaned abruptly into the rail. "Omigod."

The tourist throng still laughed and clapped, but the Eye dropped their banner and the Outside Security bolted straight at them. A fresh block of guards spilled out of the air locks, stunners at ready. Scattered panic broke among the crowd, and a surging backward toward the Gate. I saw Reede Chamberlaine hustled inside by a pair of guards. Another half dozen pushed in behind, herding the shifting cloud of black that was the Eye. The rest moved out to quell the rising pandemonium and train their stunners on aroused Outsiders already reaching for clubs and rocks. The last outgoing tourists were hurriedly cycled through the locks, and the iron grilles swung shut. Seconds later, the secondary field snapped on.

The boulevard was cleared with astonishing speed. The loader crews sprinted over to bundle the frightened tourists into orderly lines and urge them across the tarmac into the waiting hovers. No wounded were revealed lying on the pavement, only scattered flowers. There was no discarded laser rifle. Even the silken banner had disappeared. The only signs of disturbance were the burly squads of Security guards ranking either side of the boulevard and the dying stir among the Outsiders.

"What happened?" I gasped, when I could breathe again.

Cris whirled away from the rail. "Come on!"

We tumbled down the stairs, ducking clear of a red police hover, the only motored craft beside the ambulances allowed inside the dome. It settled among the vendors' carts and the cleanerbots already working the emptied plaza.

Across the square, a knot of Security stood alert around the café where we'd left Howie and Micah. Reede Chamberlaine's silver head nodded among the green uniforms and the black robes of the Eye. We started for the café, but the Security knot reformed around the Eye and hurried them toward the hover. I'd never seen so many bared stunners in my life. Between the stout backs of the guards, I saw that one black-robed figure was lagging a bit, supported by two others.

"Somebody was hurt," said Crispin avidly.

Then they were inside the hover and gone.

We rushed the café with a babble of questions. Howie leaned against a wall, looking shattered. Kim and Reede Chamberlaine conferred with a Security guard. Still seated, Micah silenced us with a calm, dark look of reproof.

"But are they all right?" I whispered.

"Nothing serious. A flesh wound."

"Was it a gun?" asked Crispin.

"They shouldn't have done that stuff!" Jane burst out. "With the Outsiders!"

Crispin rounded on her. "You're saying it's their fault?"

"Perhaps they should not have," agreed Micah pensively.

"Where are they taking them?"

"The hospital, then quarantine."

"Was it a gun?" Cris repeated.

"A gun, yes. It would appear so."

"But where would an Outsider get a gun?" I asked. I naturally assumed an Outsider was responsible.

"Indeed. Especially a laser weapon small enough to conceal in a crowd."

No one asked why an Outsider would try to kill a total stranger.

Inside the café, Howie had recovered enough to be drawn into animated debate with his silver-haired co-producer. Rachel Lamb stood a bit apart, studying Chamberlaine with clear misgivings.

Micah rose, moving out into the open. "The first thing Reede wanted to know was why we didn't have more Press around." He shook his head and walked away toward the Tube.

Crispin laughed excitedly when Micah was out of hearing. "Press? Who needs the Press? We just got all the publicity we need!"

HARMONET/CHAT

06/24/46

Just keeping you up-to-date, friends and neighbors, and we know you're desperate to be up-to-date when Ms. NeoRealist CARMICHAEL, who just sold for fifty million, is trapped there right beside you in the Tube.

***So do we care, we mean *really* care that GEORGE PEERZADA won't sing Don Giovanni at matinee performances, and that SILVERTREE OPERA is suing for breach of contract?

***No! Because the *only* thing we want to know is: just what went on at Gateway Plaza last eve at Closing? *SOME ENTRANCE, HOWIE BABY!*

***"A freak *OUT*break of *OUT*sider resentment," says our suave friend from LonDome, REEDE SCOTT CHAMBERLAINE. We wanted to buy his suit, but he swore he has only the one. Then he invited us to get in line at the Ark box office.

***Well, that didn't set our heart at rest about armed bandits Outside our Gate maybe thinking of taking a bead on any ole unsuspecting visitor . . . or returning citizen! Ms. ROLLY DINOPOLIS of Security Task Force Four agrees. She was doing Outside duty at the time and confirms reports of strange Outsider activities just moments before the *Incident.*

***And of course the usual channels were unable to uncover an *official* medical report, but the Chat is, a doctor was called in.

***So remember a little place called *Tuatua*? What about these exotic dancer folk? We hear we have to be *really* careful we don't offend or they might turn us into FROGS or something. Madame Mayor, do we *really* have to wait THREE WEEKS to find out? Chat is, WorldNet's being besieged with demands for better coverage of rumored troubles back on our mystery guests' bizarre little island home. Come on, WorldNet! We have a right to know!

***And first thing we're going to ask when they come out is, what's this elusive fun fellow the CONCH *really* like?

Remember, you DIDN'T hear it here!

WAITING:

If their three-week quarantine was painful for the Eye, it was excruciating for us, awaiting their reappearance before the full story could be told.

Advance sales soared at the Ark's box office. Both WorldNet/News and WN/Commentary developed a belated interest in Tuamatutetuamatu, where the Enclosure dispute appeared to be boiling toward open civil war. As strikes and demonstrations rocked the island, WorldNet actually reported them. Maybe it was the abrupt availability of news that made the crisis seem so sudden.

So politics intruded into Art, the world rediscovered Tuatua, and Howie had his hands full with the Town Council, who were ready to send the Eye packing.

"What the hell's wrong with airing the plight of the dispossessed," he demanded at a midweek design session. "Especially in a politically stable environment like ours? But I said, hey, look at the figures: tourism increased after the Eye arrived, and then again when WorldNet decided to cover Tuatua."

"WorldNet's coverage is totally one-sided," insisted Cris, who was showing a minor genius for coaxing data out of hidden files. "They only report anti-domer riots and sabotage, never mentioning the police brutality and unlawful detentions, or the firing and evictions of Station Clan workers without cause."

Howie nodded sickly. "There're always two sides. Thank god most of my Board's behind me on this."

With his Board's help, Howie flattered the Town Council into submission with reminders of their superior enlightenment, convincing the required number that visiting artists should not be made to answer for the political troubles of their homelands. He retained the Eye's work visas and gained entry permits for their props and costumes as "artworks." In the halls of the Arkadie, he was congratulated on a major political triumph.

The Chat got a few days' worth of good material out of the Incident, but the Eye's arrival grabbed first place on the apprentice gossip roster and stayed there. Not only the question of what had actually happened, but a debate about what had been intended by it.

"Street theatre!" Cris held forth at top volume as we sailed our bikes along the empty lanes, a morning exercise detour on the way to work. A grove of tall, old trees marked the border between BardClyffe and neighboring Lorien. Our raucous passage violated the reverent silence of their ancient shade, but Crispin was in oblivious high gear. "They were making a piece of Art!"

"They were making an entrance!" Jane replied. "A dangerous, exhibitionistic, *stupid* entrance!"

"True art must be truly dangerous," Crispin sneered.

"Jane, they're actors," I soothed. "They're supposed to make entrances!"

"Inside the theatre! Not Outside and scaring everybody to death!"

"And getting actually shot!" panted Songh from behind.

"Right on cue," Cris pointed out.

Songh's eyes ballooned over his handlebars. "You mean they maybe meant to . . . ?"

"Genius is the willingness to risk!" yelled Cris airily as he bent to his pedals and pulled ahead.

We sped out of the grove and swooped down among the stucco and glass mansions of Lorien's high-rent district, home of agents and gallery owners. I tossed Jane a look of complicity. "Great with the epigrams, isn't he?"

But she was staring straight ahead, jaw tight and her knuckles white on her handgrips.

I figured now was not the time to ask if Songh had heard anything further about the Closed Door League.

THE SHOP:

Despite the controversy, or perhaps spurred on by it, the design progressed. Micah's charcoal fantasies for *The Gift* became strong-lined pencil sketches, and a rough paper model was developed. A rough model is a working tool, not always an articulate expression of the design—a declaration of intent, Micah called it. We spent several days tearing this one apart and sticking it back together again. Finally the Master said, "Meet me at the shop tomorrow morning. Time to check in with Sean."

"With this?" I said in dismay.

He cocked his head fondly at the ragged little construction of paper and tape. "Sean knows how to read my shorthand."

The maintenance workers were busy again when I rode into Fetching Plaza the next morning, a crowd of them down on hands and knees scrubbing at the pavement. Howie and Rachel Lamb looked on from the steps of the Arkadie.

"How's it going, Ike?" he called to one of the scrubbers as I parked my bike.

A balding man shook his brush sourly. "The creep used some nasty high-tech paint this time! Goddamn bonded with the marble!"

"They painted on the street again?" I asked.

Micah arrived with the model wrapped in plastic. "It's been awhile. I was sure our street artist had moved on to other projects."

Howie grinned. "This time they'll have to bleach it out. Or repave! Ha!" The desecration of Fetching Plaza actually amused him. "Sort of an ongoing conceptual work, I'd say. Remember when we thought this kind of stuff was Art?"

"It's more about Art than it is Art," said Micah.

"And that's okay, too. Heading for the shop?"

Micah nodded. "Want to come along?"

"Not just yet."

We climbed the steps to Rachel's side. This neat, coffee-colored woman was not as sanguine about the graffito as her boss. The scrawly red letters were at least two meters tall and only a few shades paler where the cleaners had worked on them.

"That's weird," I muttered.

Howie squinted into the bright sunlight. "Can you make it out?"

"Yeah." I could read it just fine.

"And we have an audience tonight," Rachel mourned. Does she know? I wondered.

Clearly Howie did not. "They'll love it," he boomed. "A little something new in the old plaza! Course, it'd help to have the artist around to interpret the work!"

Meanwhile, I'm thinking, *These guys are getting serious.* The lettering read: CLOSE THE DOOR.

The long, three-story shop was sandwiched between the unequal half-moons of the Arkadie's two theatres. Railed galleries ran around three sides. The fourth was occupied by a movable paint frame wide enough to hold three eighty-foot drops, hardly big enough for a theatre producing as much and as often as the Arkadie, but better than most theatres could offer. Carpentry, sculpture, and metal-working were spread across the main floor. Plastics was one flight down in a series of rooms that vented the noxious by-products of that work into holding tanks to be shipped out of the dome.

The props, sound, and electrics shops were next door, squeezed into three rooms that would have done better as one. A plan to find new space was offered at the beginning of each season, always without results. Below Plastics lurked several filled-to-bursting levels of warehouse sunk into the Green Mountain granite. The costume shop sweltered in the attic space above the ceiling of Theatre Two.

The horn had just blown for afternoon coffee break. The saws were quiet. A tall stack of shrink-wrapped lumber waited to be moved out of the open bay of the vacuum tube terminal. Sean was very proud of that terminal. Not all theatres had their raw materials delivered directly to the shop.

The crew hailed Micah like a long-lost brother and shoved hot cups and giant sugared pastries into our hands.

"Gonna bust our balls this time? Gonna keep us up nights?"

"Naw, we won't have to sink a screw! Those tribal guys'll voodoo the friggin' scenery onto the stage!"

"You think they do love potions? I could really use one."

The men laughed. "Can ya help him, Mi? The boy's in *need!*"

"Old Howie, stirrin' up trouble," an older hand remarked.

"The hell, let 'im!" roared a tall redhead. "Christ, we're fuckin' sick and tired of Easy Street down here!"

I loved watching Micah go into action in the shop. This man who had no patience for the usual social trivia knew every crew member by name, knew their spouses, knew the names and ages of their kids. He admired their craftsmanship, he asked about their current projects. He worked the floor of that shop, any shop, like Howie worked an opening-night crowd. He loved it, and so did they.

While I stuffed my face with unneeded sugar, Micah strolled among the worktables with the shop foreman, Ruth Bondi, to inspect a new material she was eager to show off. The carpenters joked with me, but their eyes followed Micah possessively. The crew felt they could bitch with him about the administration and tell funny stories in Max Eider's accent, and know that Micah would return their fraternity by never repeating what he heard or naming names to the front office. Crispin slipped once and called him the Badger in public, and the nickname raced like wildfire through every shop in Harmony, though like us, none of them would think to call him anything but Micah to his face.

This was always the best time to visit with a crew, with the problems of your last show there forgotten and the problems of the next show not yet confronted. But the rough model remained in its opaque wrapping. Revealing it to Sean was one thing, but it was not smart to show something so nascent, so inchoate to the crew. They'd only be disillusioned.

Ruth returned, chortling with Micah, as the horn declared the end of the break. "Well, folks, seems like we're in for some real exotica. And I don't mean just the cast!"

Micah smiled innocently. "Keeping you on your toes."

The crew went back to work laughing, and we climbed toward Sean's office. Soft goods lived off the second-level gallery, along with mechanics and animation, holography, projection, and miniatures. The computer clean-rooms were up on the third level with the special-effects labs. Micah stuck his head into Animation to say hello and waved at the stitchers tending their huge machines in Soft Goods. A printout production schedule clipped to the door listed twenty-two separate drops of various sizes and materials for *Crossroads*.

Micah took a deep breath. "I'd like to get away with just one."

Well, I thought *that* was pretty radical.

Sean's office was the sort that began each day as neat as a pin and devolved into chaos by quitting time. Though it was only mid-morning, entropy had already taken its toll. The wide interior window that overlooked the shop floor was plastered solid with the *Crossroads* elevations also papering every bit of wall. Sean was on the phone, arguing with his lumber supplier in Singapore. I always kidded him about using the old black handsets like my parents had in Chicago, but telescreens broke down and cost you money, Sean said, and he had little need (and no desire) to see his dealers face-to-face. He tossed a wave as we came in and went on arguing.

The property master, Hickey Kirke, slouched over Sean's huge drawing board. More *Crossroads* plans were spread out like the pawed-over goods in a market stall. Tall and dark and dour, Hickey was Sean's antithesis. They didn't socialize much, but balanced each other well in the workplace. I was always careful with Hickey, who struck me as painfully vulnerable.

" 'Lo, Hickey. What's new?" I asked while Micah leafed absently through Eider's drawings, waiting for Sean to dicker the dealer down to a price they could both live with.

Hickey shrugged, his long face solemn, then flicked me a guarded smile. "Not much. The Eye's show props arrived via the Tubes, but I'm not allowed even to crack open the crates. Taboo, you know. Guess they'll cut off my left ball or something."

"Maybe just sacrifice your firstborn." I deposited the model on a pile of printout and peered over Micah's shoulder. Eider's apprentices' drafting didn't look any better than mine, though the title-block labeling each plate was bordered with a complex egg-and-dart motif—much flashier than Micah ever wanted.

"Done," Sean concluded. "I'll need it Monday . . . Yeah, it's friggin' sudden! I get *sudden* drawings thrown at me every day now! Hey, up yours, Carlos, have I ever traded you bad credits? You just get it here. My order came in short last week . . . Yeah, sure, the Tubes swallow things, right . . . Hey, I'm on time more than most of your customers! . . . Fine. I look forward to it."

Sean dropped the archaic phone into its cradle. " 'Will the money be there' . . . ! Friggin' jerk! After all the business I give him! That's the trouble when your supplier's not next door. You can't just go over and threaten to beat the crap out of him."

"When was the last time you beat the crap out of someone?" Hickey inquired, as if he really needed to know.

"Well, it always sounds like a good idea." Sean shoved back his chair and stalked to his cooler. "Just about beer time, isn't it?"

Micah continued his study of Eider's excruciatingly elaborate ground plan. "What have you got?"

"What I've always got. Damn, Micah! You know I only stock one beer in here!"

"We can't afford that imported swill you drink, Mi." Hickey's strangled little cough was his idea of a laugh. Sean was famously loyal to the local brand brewed in Harmony's farm domes.

"You want one or not?" Sean demanded.

"Is it cold?"

"Jeez, Howie must be givin' you some hard time, huh?" Sean put aside his irritation with the lumber dealer and opened four frosty beers. He passed two along to Hickey and me, then stood in front of Micah, holding the others and nodding expectantly at the shrouded model. "So how's it going, fella? How's the dragon thing?"

"Out for bids." Micah ran his finger along the track of a magnetic winch drawn on the plan and clucked his tongue.

"Gwinn, get those friggin' drawings away from him, will ya?"

I played the magician pulling the tablecloth from beneath the twelve-course dinner.

Micah took his beer. "Well, it's not going to be what you'd expect from me." At his signal, I slid the model out of its wrappings. It was a simple-looking construction in brown paper and cardboard, a little bent from the trip. I tweaked it back into shape. Micah came and stood over it. "I think it'll end up as one set with a few minor changes and some special effects."

"And a shitload of props," predicted Hickey darkly.

"Most of which the Eye has brought with them."

Sean stared at the little model. "C'mon, really? This is it?"

"The basic idea of it," Micah drawled. Sean's genuine astonishment delighted him.

"No kidding." Sean circled the table as if searching for hidden complications. "One-setter, eh? Jeez, like the old days."

Micah wagged his head from side to side, at his most badgerlike. He could go from banter to dead serious so fast, most people got lost catching up. "Not quite like the old days, I hope. When I say special effects, I mean something quite out of the ordinary. Something that, in this innocent, untechnical environment that we create, will come as a complete surprise and blow their socks off."

"I thought these guys came with their own magic," said Hickey.

Sean said, "Hell, we can manage a little magic."

"Have you read the play yet?" Micah asked.

"Sure. Well, most of it. Not my sort of thing, y'know?"

"Fine, but give it some real thought for a moment."

"Yeah," said Hickey. "Don't just mouth off like some asshole."

Sean tossed his empty bottle at Hickey's head, then banked his grin to listen.

"The characters in this play believe that magic is real, remember that. Now, just before the climax, an Ancestor god dances with something called a 'Matta,' then delivers it to the clan elders to use in their ritual murder of the heretical clansman. They 'wind it about him until he is no more.' " Micah seemed to be studying the inside of his beer bottle. "What I need you to do is make an actor, a live actor, disappear downstage center instantaneously and without using flashpots, smoke, or any of the recognizable decoy techniques."

"Sure, I, well . . . it has to be a live actor?"

"Oh yes."

Sean glanced at the wide-open downstage sweep of the model. "If you can move him upstage a little, I could—"

"No. It has to be right down there in the middle, so that the audience thinks it's magic. Real magic. The whole piece is going to turn on it."

I should explain something of Sean's predicament: the smaller of the Ark's two theatres was a modified arena: blunted wedges of seating framed three quarters of a circular stage that extended forward from the remaining 90 degrees. Broad ramps pushed the playing area in between the seating wedges so that the action could, in effect, surround the audience.

Downstage center meant out in the middle of God's country, with skeptical viewers on three sides. Working with holos and lasers and smoke projections and the like as we usually did, we could make all sorts of stuff happen in this no-man's-land. But to cause a living actor to vanish into thin air with no visible effects was a very tall order down there. We hadn't yet perfected matter transport.

Hickey handed Sean another beer. "Better give it some thought, eh?"

Sean said, "I better give it some thought."

Micah nodded. "Let me know."

"I will. You bet I will." Sean took a great swig of beer. "Hey, you sure they couldn't just do it with voodoo?"

RENEWAL:

It was very quiet in the studio when we got back.

"Someone painted in front of the theatre again," I announced.

Crispin's head snapped up from his screen. "Could you read it this time?"

"Yeah. It said, 'Close the door.' "

There was a rustle at Jane's desk as she slid from her stool and fled toward the conference room.

Micah and I blinked after her.

"She hasn't been feeling too well," I lied, and sped off in pursuit. I found her sitting pale and dry-eyed, her hands spread wide on the broad tabletop as if it might tip over and crush her.

"Jane, it's only words . . ." The instant I put my arm around her, she collapsed sobbing to the table.

"Bela wasn't at breakfast this morning, did you see?"

"No?" I'd slept in with Crispin before heading off to the Arkadie.

"He wasn't renewed!" she blurted.

"What?" I dropped into the chair next to her. "But . . . I didn't know he was up."

Jane shook her head savagely. "Nobody did."

"Not even Mark?"

"I don't know. He's . . . I just couldn't talk to him."

"Bela. Oh no." That was how it went. If you said nothing to your friends, and you didn't pass your review, one morning you just weren't there anymore. They said Security spirited you out in the middle of the night and dropped you Outside your birth-dome. Perhaps if we'd had to watch our friends dragged away kicking and screaming, we wouldn't have accepted the situation so readily, with mourning but without question. Domer children have been taught to accept in the name of survival what earlier eras would have called atrocity. I'd dream about failing review once in a while, and wake up in a cold sweat, boundlessly grateful to find myself in my narrow dorm bed instead of Outside Chicago. Yet it never occurred to me to ask, *Is this necessary?*

"Jesus. Poor Mark."

"Poor *Bela!*"

"Jane, I know you're up for review yourself soon, but . . ."

She collapsed again. "September," she wailed, as if it were tomorrow. "I don't understand it! Bela's work was good. Marie needed him! Why didn't they renew him? Why?"

I agreed it was odd that Bela hadn't made the cut. People less talented than he made it all the time. This was going to make a lot of apprentices very nervous.

"Don't worry," I murmured uselessly. Jane was unlikely to be soothed by the usual reassurances, especially if delivered from my position of relative security. So I held her, deciding it would serve her best if I just let her weep.

ADVICE FROM THE MASTER:

No more was said in the studio about the graffito.

But when Jane had recovered sufficiently to go back to work, I invited Micah into the conference room to explain that because Jane was so worried about her own upcoming review, Bela's failure had set off an attack of panic.

Micah looked at me oddly. "I didn't know he was up."

"Me neither. I don't think Mark even knew."

Micah smoothed wrinkles from his smock. He was pensive for long enough to make me glad Jane wasn't there listening, then said, very delicately, "It might be of some help with Jane's situation if she had encouragement from her peers to work more on her own outside the studio."

The way he said "situation" chilled me, as if the word were a fragile eggshell placed on the table between us. "But she's only got until September . . ."

"Wouldn't hurt," he continued, "for you and Cris to be thinking about it yourselves."

"We are!" My surge of fright must have been visible in my eyes.

Micah waved it away. "Just think about it. Willow Street's looking for young designers to work in their second space, and Gitanne tells me Images is putting in a new holo system that will make working with them much more challenging."

He stood, a bulky white shape against the blank white wall, punctuated by a dark mustache. He had much more to say to me. I think he was considering whether this was the right time to say it.

Finally he leaned against the wall as if grateful for its support. "When you take your oath of citizenship, you swear to promote and preserve not the quality of life in Harmony, but the quality of its output, its artistic product.

"There are many in the world to whom this implies elitism or decadence, Art raised above the more 'humane' priorities. But it's not just Art we're preserving here in Harmony. It's civilization itself. Art may not be necessary to life, but it *is* integral to civilization." He pushed away from the wall, moving slowly along its cool white expanse. "Without Harmony and the other enclaves like it, nothing except life, mere existence, unadorned, would have survived those twenty years of death and destruction. We'd all be living like Outsiders, reduced to the pursuit of animal comforts, living without history, without mirrors, without images of our great human potential to urge us upward."

I murmured, "Without the science that gave us domes and the industry to build them, nothing would have survived at all." But that was my mother talking, my painter-mother, once painter, who had not been fortunate enough to find a haven like Harmony. I answered my own protest at once: without messy old Art, Science and Industry gave you neat, clean, soul-parching Chicago. Chicago was not Micah's idea of survival, and if it had been mine, I guess I'd have never left it in the first place.

Micah's slow progress brought him to the end of the wall, and the connecting door to Marie Bennett-Lloyd's studio. He studied it thoughtfully, then turned back the way he'd come. "The Apprentice Administration is under pressure lately. There've been complaints about renewals being granted too leniently."

"But Bela's work was fine!"

"Yes, I would have said so." Micah shook his head. "But Mark has also been protecting him, making his work look even better than it was. Mark, you see, has unusual talent. Mark is what the Outside Adoption Policy was created for. But he's hardly likely to develop his full potential if he's spending half his energy making up for someone else."

He gazed straight at me. I tried not to look away but failed. The cold white surface of the table was easier to look at than the compassion in Micah's eyes.

"We're not making up for Jane in any way," I mumbled.

"No, you're not." He gave a brief, dry laugh. "I am. And I'll continue to do so for as long as I can get away with it. But in doing so, I am betraying my oath, my solemn oath, out of pure selfishness, because she is useful to me."

I felt the first stirrings of revolt. "Some of the designers who made citizen in the past aren't as good as either Bela or Jane."

Micah nodded. "Perfectly true. But the past is not now." He returned to the table. "I'd been meaning to say something to you all. Even if Jane hadn't, well . . ." He squeezed my shoulder briefly. It was rare for Micah to be demonstrative with us, so I was grateful, but I realized if he saw the need to break his pattern, we all had reason to be frightened.

"Thank you. Yes. I understand."

"Do you? I'm not sure I do. I fear this pressure on the Admin is motivated less by aesthetic concerns than by a few powerful people's concern that overpopulation will lower Harmony's standard of living. Look to the future, Gwinn. You're going to have to fight for it much harder than I did."

He sighed, a growly release of regret and relief that did not quite satisfy him. "But still, it is odd. Marie didn't say anything to me, and the Admin is supposed to inform the craftmaster a few days ahead of time if they're going to lose someone. In fact, I'd swear she said Bela wasn't due for review for another six months."

Later, I found the courage to stick my head into Marie's studio. It was empty but for a lone tourist, looking querulous and lost.

"Are you Ms. Bennett-Lloyd?" He frowned.

"Not me," I replied.

"Well, where is she?" he demanded as I withdrew.

Mark wasn't seen anywhere for two days.

I was worried. "He's got to eat."

"Leave the guy alone," Crispin muttered.

Finally I loaded up a tray at dinner and knocked on Mark's door. He answered it unshaven and haggard.

"Oh, Mark," I whispered. I offered him the tray. To my surprise, he took it.

"Thanks, G. I . . . really couldn't face the mob downstairs."

"You ready to talk?"

His bruised brown eyes wandered, then refocused on me with effort. "Um, no, not yet. I . . ." He set the tray down inside and hovered miserably in the doorway. Impulsively I put my arms around him. He clung to me, shuddering. "He wasn't up, you know. It wasn't his time."

"Are you sure?"

He jerked away. "You think I wouldn't know about a thing like that?" He whirled into his room. "Gwinn, they took him!"

"They can't just take people at random."

Mark reached the far wall and rebounded toward me. "So they tell us, but they did. They just took him when they had no right to!"

WORLDNET/COMMENT

07/02/46

SEATTLE

When the mayors of ten North American domes meet under Seattle's dome next week to discuss the proposed affiliation that some have styled the reUnification of the States, topics are sure to include how such an organization would be financed, where its headquarters would reside, and what would be the legal responsibilities of each member.

We watch these overtures with mixed feelings. The smaller towns like Harmony have benefitted greatly from the total autonomy they have known for the past forty years. Would such an affiliation of city-domes presume to include the unEnclosed territory in between? What about other non-signatory domes which happen to lie within the affiliation's geographical boundaries? Will the loosely symbiotic exchanges of goods and services devolve once more into a weapon of economic diplomacy?

We fully understand the need for inter-dome discussion and cooperation at a time when the tide of anti-dome sentiment is on the rise, but we hope the mayors in Seattle will also find time to debate the wisdom of establishing anew a bureaucracy that could grow again unchecked into the overweening burden that made the Dissolution inevitable in the first place.

The Open Sky anarchists and the Outside are not the only threats to our prosperity and peace of mind.

THE DESIGN:

But life and work went on. Mark came dutifully to Marie's studio every morning and went back into hiding as soon as the day was done. Jane pulled her work over her head like the proverbial ostrich. Even a mention of Bela was forbidden.

The simple eloquence that Micah was striving for in his design for *The Gift* did not come easily. His first impulse toward bold abstraction required thoughtful articulation, and Howie needed weaning from the literal-minded habit of his normal directorial style. Between the first rough model and the final design, the two of them ransacked and devoured six working models. Progress on any other front—the Willow Street piece or *Don Pasquale*—slowed to a crawl as we raced to have construction drawings and a presentation model of *The Gift* finished by first rehearsal.

Every so often Micah would call Sean to ask if he'd discovered how to accomplish the downstage center magical disappearance we were counting on. Micah was convinced that the success of the design as well as the play relied on that single piece of business.

"Got some ideas," Sean would say. "Just working out the details." Meanwhile, the rumor mill reported that the Arkadie's shop was in way over its ears with *Crossroads*.

But we were too busy to worry about that right then.

The design that at last evolved was so spare and elegant that it took me awhile to see how truly brilliant it was.

It took its textural inspiration from Tuatua's volcanic bedrock, but the overall lines were as sinuous and lyrical as jungle mists and sunrise. Micah played a lot of French Impressionists as he worked. He said there was more of himself in this design than in anything he'd done in a long time, and that he understood how the clansman felt in the play, offering up his most precious private magic to public view. His eloquence convinced me, and Howie too.

"Well. No bullshit here," said Howie finally. "It's . . . it's truly humble."

And he looked at Micah and smiled.

I put all of us to work on the final model, even Crispin.

We reproduced Micah's sweeping collage of texture and color in the finest degree of finish. Jane spent a whole week on the backdrop alone, incising fine strata lines and pebbly grit into its undulating surface with the precision and tireless patience that was her most remarkable asset. The model cost a fortune in time and materials, but Micah said it must represent the finished set exactly.

"Translating models is a learned skill," he worried. "We don't want the Eye thinking they're getting anything less than our best."

We set the completed model in a fully detailed scale replica of the theatre, to show its dynamically eccentric placement within the space. Micah always said, if you want to grab their attention from the start, focus the space so that the seating is an element in the total composition. This draws the audience "into" the set, without doing something pretentious like putting them onstage with the actors.

It was completed the day of first rehearsal, with minutes to spare. Jane remained at my elbow all morning as scrub nurse, handing me tools. We crated it up like the precious object that it was and just before noon, hurried off to Fetching to meet the Eye.

PHASE II
Rehearsal

THE EYE:

Gift rehearsals were not to be at the Arkadie itself. Both theatres had shows playing in them, and all the in-house rehearsal space was taken up by the complications of *Crossroads*. The secondary space was a small and ageing warehouse on the edge of Fetching's commercial district. Howie rented it for a nominal sum from Campbell Brigham, the chairman of his Board of Trustees. Cam owned a prestigious print gallery in Lorien and apparently needed a tax break.

The Ark staff called it "the Barn." Micah explained this was a nostalgic gesture to the mythic days of summer stock, which even he couldn't remember. It didn't remind me much of the gleaming white metal tunnels in Harmony's farm domes. It was rectangular, with a peaked and girdered roof and lots of columns breaking up the space, which made it hard for the stage managers to tape out the ground plan on the floor. Also, it needed a good coat of paint. But it had great, tall windows along two sides, and stood on an open corner that got lots of light.

At noon, the Barn was empty, except for the stage managers. Micah strolled in and immediately began rearranging the furniture.

"We'll use this table for the model. Pull the big one over here longways so they can look at the set while they read."

The production stage manager, Liz Godwin, a freckled, smiling woman with an outrageous mop of curly red hair, watched calmly while her assistants raced to replace disordered chairs and water pitchers and rescue their careful arrangement of clean scripts, pads, and pencils that Micah had shoved aside in his search for the right table to show off the model.

"It's only because you're cute that I'm allowing you to get away with this," Liz called after him from the production table.

Micah pulled his chosen model stand a fraction closer to the long central table where the cast would sit to read through the play for the first time. He stood back, contemplating.

127

"Fine," approved Liz. "It's fine, it's perfect! Gwinn, get that thing over here before the mad decorator changes his mind!"

Micah smiled, but distractedly. He hovered like a mother hen as we set our precious package down on the table.

"How'd it do?"

"Good," said Cris. "We only dropped it twice."

Jane flashed Micah a look saying *she* understood there were some things that just should not be joked about.

Most actors see scenery as simply a backdrop for their own work, so a model of the set only has to be pretty to keep them happy. But with *The Gift* Micah was presuming to create within a foreign, exotic culture. He wanted the Eye to take one look at his model and know he understood exactly what their play was about.

Cris lifted the model out of the crate, and we freed it from its packing one layer at a time like archaeologists unwrapping a mummy. The stage managers clustered around to watch. Our peace and quiet ended when Howie bustled into the hall with Marie Bennett-Lloyd. Marie had finally agreed to coordinate the clothes and design whatever the Eye had not brought with them. She and Howie were nodding and gesticulating like a pair of tandem robots. Rachel and Kim followed more sedately, with Mark behind them, alone and solemn.

"Just find me an hour sometime, okay?" Marie was insisting. "I'm not telepathic."

"Funny. I always thought you were." Howie wheeled away to confer with Liz. Marie descended on us as the last fold of plastic wrap slid off the model.

"Have you seen them yet?" she demanded cheerfully. Marie was tall and a bit of a whirlwind, always in motion within her many layers of clothing. I felt dowdy and reserved standing next to her. Today she wore a flowing, skirted wrap in tie-dyed blues reminiscent of water. I thought Marie and the Eye should get along very well in matters of dress.

"I haven't a clue what they've brought!" she exclaimed. "We weren't allowed to unpack the trunks. Then no resumé photos, no one could get measurements! Honestly, sometimes I wonder about Howie!" She glanced expectantly at the door, as we all were doing. "I just hope they're cooperative!"

Mark eased up beside me. "Did you wear it?"

"No, but . . ." I pulled my bead and leather necklace partway from my pocket. "For good luck."

A wan smile was still the best he could manage. "I wouldn't have been able to, either, not right out in front of them."

"Now we'll finally hear what happened," I murmured.

Marie drew Micah aside to talk about color. Sean sauntered in, a roll of blueprints under his arm. He saluted us from across the hall but chose a route that would take him past the greatest number of pretty women. Kim snagged him briefly when he paused at the coffee table to load up with goodies. I watched them both turn on the flirty charm. Sean's stubby, sensuous hands always caught my eye. He handled a piece of machinery or a woman's body with the same sure respect and appreciation. When Sean moved on to his next stop, Kim came our way, noting my amusement.

"He's got to get in his quota of suggestive remarks to the stage managers," she offered wryly. "Otherwise his ass will be grass when he needs stage time come tech week." She greeted the model with enthused circlings of her arms. "Micah, it's a beauty! At last, scenery that won't cost us the entire season's budget!"

"It is beautiful," agreed Marie hastily, having forgotten in her preoccupation with the lack of measurements even to look. "It's so clean, so simple, so . . . exposed. You're very brave, Mi. Wait 'til Lou sees it! Looks like you designed it just for her!"

Louisa Pietro was the lighting designer, and this particular set *was* a lighting designer's wet dream.

Micah searched the crowd vaguely. "I don't suppose she'll be here?"

Kim snorted. "You gotta be kidding."

Louisa was a constant globe-trotter and characteristically unavailable until the final week of rehearsals. But she caught on fast once she arrived and she was well worth the wait.

More Arkadie staffers drifted in, the publicity and subscriptions departments and the head of the costume shop. They cruised the model table, nodding and smiling, then moved on. I noted a few raised eyebrows.

"They don't know what to say."

"They've never seen so little scenery in their lives," whispered Crispin. "They're wondering if he's forgotten something."

The Barn filled up with people and shop talk. A noisy clot formed around the coffee urn for the usual exchange of gossip. Howie's voice boomed at the stage managers' table. The hubbub seemed louder than usual, the laughter shrilled by more than the normal first-rehearsal excitement. I was about to get coffee for Micah and myself when Hickey Kirke slouched up, wearing his habitual sober face and a striped pullover that looked like he'd slept in it.

He surveyed the model. "So where's the props?"

Micah was fussing, arranging and rearranging some little half-inch-scale rocks, unable to settle on a way that suited him. He waved one in front of Hickey's long nose. "Here."

"Unh-unh," said Hickey. "Carpentry does rocks."

"These rocks get moved about like furniture."

"Props does rocks at the RoundHall," teased Crispin.

"No way."

Micah bent his head to hide his grin. "I really think these'd be a good project for you."

"Sean and I will have a discussion about this." Hickey moved around to peer into the rear of the model, putting his back to a nearby conversation. "Any more word on who caused the Incident?"

Micah shrugged, noncommittal.

"Reede," murmured Hickey. "He benefits the most."

I had to lean in close to hear. "You're saying they planned it? The gun and everything?"

"Reede," said Hickey. "It's not Howie's style."

Cris had suggested the Incident had been staged, but I couldn't believe that. "But someone was actually hurt!"

"Did you see any blood?" Hickey inquired loftily.

Micah turned his head to gaze at him. "In fact, I did."

Hickey blinked. "You did? Really? Jeez, he's worse than I thought."

Sean finished his rounds and joined us, coffee and donut in hand. He pointed a sugared finger as Micah again bent over the model. "Uh-unh, Mi. Too late. The drawings are in. You can't change it now!" He eyed Hickey drolly. "Friggin' designers! Never leave well enough alone! This guy's worse than Eider!"

Micah straightened with a wounded look.

"Only a joke, Mi. I remember, this here's the one where

we all get to go home at four o'clock." Sean held out his cup. "Coffee?"

His laugh seemed strident, but only because the loud shop talk and gossip had fallen suddenly away. Reede Chamberlaine stood murmuring into Howie's ear. People were staring while pretending not to. The staffers were as curious about our imported producer as they were about the Eye. I certainly gave him a closer look, after what I'd just heard.

He was a handsome man, tall and impressive, but it was his polish you noticed, his clear, expensively ageless skin, the tight grays of his palette. His precise business tailoring made Howie's brightly casual director suedes look self-conscious, almost frivolous. I was so intent on trying to overhear his conversation that I didn't notice the small crowd that slipped in behind him.

Then the undercurrent of chatter died into real silence, and there they were. Ten of them, sticking close together.

I didn't want it to be them, no fanfare, no grand entrance. Just, you know, walking in like that.

"Well." Crispin's murmur was flat with disappointment.

They were tall and short, dark and light, four women, six men, in blue jeans and mirrored sunglasses, with classy dance bags slung over their shoulders. They wandered into the room not like magical strangers at all but like any other actors walking into any other rehearsal hall. One already sported a T-shirt that read, HARMONY SINGS in rainbowed letters, the one where a *W* was careted in above the *S* and the *I*. The women wore chic, luxuriant hairdos. The men sported the latest and most expensive athletic shoes. They all looked healthy, rested, well-fed, and extremely up-to-date.

"Not quite what I expected . . ." I heard Marie hiss to Micah.

I wondered what Micah had expected. Feathers and nakedness? Like I'd assumed that they'd all be black? I felt premature envy of the troupe's white members, that they should be included in the mystery and not me. But what mystery? No matter how much I'd said about them being actors and such, I hadn't expected them to look so . . . normal.

By now no one was pretending not to stare. The pause in the room lengthened uncomfortably, we hoping they'd do something weird to satisfy our heightened expectations, they no doubt awaiting some reassuring gesture of welcome. It was the urbane Reede Chamberlaine who broke the impasse. He gestured grandly toward the ten. "Ladies and gentlemen, may I present to you, the Eye."

With equal ceremony he led Howie over for the introductions that had never taken place in the confusion of their arrival. When fluent, crisply accented English accompanied the actors' smiles and handshakes, the long breath held in the hall relaxed.

Then I noticed one of the young women had her arm in a sling.

"I'll let the troupe introduce themselves." Chamberlaine had taken complete charge, but Howie didn't seem to mind. "Don't worry about remembering names—you'll get to that later, and Tuatuan names are a little complicated at first." He nodded to the woman standing nearest him. "Omea?"

She dropped him a playful curtsy, then smiled around the room with perfect poise, to Howie, to the office staff hovering at the coffee urn, to the production staff clustered around the model. She was a buxom, pleasant-looking woman of about forty-five, with crackling black eyes, a cloud of dark wavy hair, and a resonant performer's voice. "I am Pirea-Omealeanoo, but as Reede says, don't worry about names. Call me Omea." Her smile invited our complicity. "I'll know who you're talking about."

She flattened her palms together in a way that might have been personal mannerism or ritual gesture. "I will be your translator and encyclopedia. I will speak of and for the Eye . . . that is, when it isn't speaking for itself."

Polite laughter rose and fell.

Omea continued, "And my first job is to say how grateful we are for the chance to work in an atmosphere that supports creativity and experiment. Your welcome for these few months will allow us to grow into the richer, more dramatic material we have been longing to try our hand at." She saluted the gathering with her joined palms. "Our deepest thanks. And now to our introductions."

She turned to her right, where a sober and beautiful young man stood beside a shorter, somewhat crabbed older fellow with a dark, mobile face.

"This fine one here is Te-Cucularit, who we call Cu. I will tell you our titles with our names, though you will find we all do a little of everything. Cu is named our archivist and company historian."

Proof of strong links with the past, I noted. Domers were not often into preserving the past. It was a bad memory to them. Even a theatre as large as the Arkadie didn't have a company historian.

The young man nodded silently and looked down.

"And this gentleman: our choreographer, No-Mulelatu."

"No gentleman," grinned the older man. "I'm Ule the Mule." He did a little leap and kick. "You'll know me."

Next was a sultry girl-woman who already had the eye of every straight man in the room and some of the women.

"And this, Telea-Muatamuatua," Omea supplied.

"Just Tua," smiled the girl with lowered lids and a willowy toss of thick black hair. She was the sort of girl men always say reminds them of a deer or perhaps a flower, but I suspected steel and ambition beneath her silky brown skin.

"Guess they don't list 'sexpot' as a job title," muttered Sean aside to Hickey.

"Bet she's high on the Muchee Taboo list," Hickey returned.

Omea moved on. "Pili-Peneamanea, or Pen." She grinned maternally. "Our movie star. Pen has given up a big holo contract to be with us on this tour. For the play, you see, because he feels it's so important to do."

I was working hard to store away names and faces. The company was younger than I'd expected. Half of them would have still been children when the Eye was founded. This Pen, I guessed, was about my age. His mirrored lenses flashed as he nodded with preening grace. He was smoothly handsome and defensive, a bantam cock.

"Trouble," murmured Sean.

"You just don't like the competition," Hickey returned.

"You wait. You'll see."

The two women next to Pen, girls really, were identical in the perfection of their height, weight, and proportions, except that one was pink and blond, and the other creamy dark and wearing the sling.

"Lucienne LaGrange," nodded Omea, "and Dua-Tuli-nooribil, called Tuli." Tuli gave no indication of being upset or in pain, and the sling was not mentioned.

Marie whispered, "Isn't it wonderful how dancers are the same the world over?"

Micah eyed her glumly. "Is it?"

"And that's Sam next along, just Sam," Omea continued with a smile, "our other paleface. Sam is our consulting Magic Man. When the Ancestors cannot do it, Sam usually can."

Sam took a half step forward and bowed with casual flourish. He was close-cropped and solid, with a watchful eyes-on-the-horizon manner. He could have played an old-time sailor without changing a thing except his spanking new sport shoes. Though Omea called him paleface, his skin was closer to Rachel Lamb's color. When he rose from his bow, he held a shimmering red bird which he sent winging with a presentational flick of his wrists. It flew three perfect circles above the heads of the troupe, singing what Micah later swore was *Pagliacci*, and landed on Sam's sturdy shoulder.

Howie was the first to applaud, and it was a few minutes before Omea could continue her introductions. I looked, and the bird had vanished.

"There's hope for these guys yet," Crispin declared.

Of the last two, the first was a huge and spectacular black man of obvious African descent, but it was the second who caught my interest. He was tall and thin, with long arms and spindly legs and a lifetime's experience packed behind his eyes. He lifted his chin faintly to acknowledge his audience and my heart contracted.

How had that simple move communicated all the sufferings of the world?

"That's him," I murmured. "He's the tribesman."

Cris looked at me sideways. "As opposed to the rest of them?"

"I mean, he'll play the guy who gets killed."

"Our musical director, Moussa N'Diaye," Omea was saying of the smiling African, "and Sa-Panteadeamali. Moussa and Mali." She pressed her palms together a final time. "And there you have us."

More applause, then after a brief hesitation, the Eye relaxed out of formation and the Arkadie staff surged around them. The groups mingled for the usual coffee and small talk before sitting down to read the play, but in less than a minute, a problem developed. I watched Liz Godwin take Howie aside.

"They don't drink coffee?" Howie could not imagine this.

"I'll send Ted out for fruit juice," said Liz. "And by the way, Reede grilled me about lunch and made me cancel the beer."

"What the hell for?"

Liz looked embarrassed. "He says, um, they're not good with alcohol."

"They? Oh, *they*. Christ, that paternalistic son of a bitch!"

"I didn't think it was worth an argument."

"No, not at the moment. Later, yes." Howie already looked tired. He shook his head as if he did not consider this an auspicious beginning, then waved to Micah, and came in our direction. "How 'bout we show them the model?"

Something very like terror fleeted across Micah's face, then disguised itself as gruff readiness. All my allegiance was his at that moment. He cares so much, I thought.

"All right, everyone! Over here!" Howie gathered the room into a semicircle in front of the model, except Reede Chamberlaine, who had drawn Rachel Lamb aside to talk. "For the sake of our honored guests," he boomed, "and for anyone here who's spent the last twenty years in a cave somewhere, I'll introduce our master scenic designer, the great Micah Cervantes."

He laid a proud hand on Micah's shoulder. "We are more fortunate than I can possibly express to have him with us on this production. And there, to his right, another of Harmony's national treasures, Marie Bennett-Lloyd, who will be helping with the costumes."

The applause from the Arkadie staff was prolonged and genuine. Howie raised his hands for silence, turning back to the model. We awaited the traditional director's overview of the play, using the scenery as specific illustration, often including a short recap of the design process, and certainly an explication of how the choices supported and expressed the director's intentions. This was the moment that introduced the whole concept of the production.

Instead, Howie gazed at the model briefly, then offered Micah a big, encouraging smile. "Well, Mi, you want to tell us something about your work?"

Your? I nearly screamed at him. *What happened to our?* I must have moved threateningly, because Crispin grabbed my arm and shook his head.

Micah returned Howie a level gaze, looked thoughtfully

at the model for a few seconds, and began to talk. And because he was Micah, he did a creditable job out there on the limb by himself, though he was no public speaker and there were few things he loathed more than having to explain to people what he'd just spent weeks, often months trying to make self-evident.

But he could do it, because his intellect was as sharp as his instincts, and he'd come prepared. "Mostly they don't want to work it out for themselves," he'd said to me once. "The audience is often less lazy than your own colleagues."

When he finished talking about encouraging a new focus on the actor, and how the simplicity of the line should complement the universal truths of the story, he smiled graciously and asked for questions.

There weren't any. The shadings between convinced and dubious were impossible to read on all those faces trying so hard to remain safely noncommittal.

("What's the matter with them?" I raved at Crispin later, after I'd gone on about Howie's cowardice for at least an hour. "Does everything have to be proven before they'll get behind it?"

"Of course," he replied, as if my outrage was just too innocent to be believed.)

So Howie said, "Well, take a good look, everybody, then we'll sit down and read it through." Then he came back with that big bullshit smile. "You've done it again, Mi."

"I'm glad you like it, Howard."

"It's beautiful. Really."

"Thank you," Micah replied. I could see him taking into consideration everything that Howie had to deal with, and finding patience with him. But when Howie turned that bullshit grin on the four of us, he got back two stony faces, Jane's neutral mask and one wide-eyed glare of accusation that Songh didn't have the wit to hide before dropping his eyes to the floor in confusion.

Howie didn't even notice.

Meanwhile, Reede Chamberlaine hadn't given the model so much as a glance, being fully occupied off in the corner with the business end.

And there was still the Eye's reaction to get past.

Omea was first, bringing her spokeswoman's graciousness and the magician Sam at her elbow. They showered Micah with compliments on work of his that they'd seen, omitting comment on the present one but casually, as if comment wasn't required. The stunning African musician Moussa stared into the model, engaging Ule the little choreographer in a low-voiced discussion about the placement of instruments and whether it would be comfortable where he was going to sit. Ule played with the little rocks and tweaked Micah with a humorous comment about the unevenness of the floor surface and dancers' clumsy feet. The rest offered public smiles and nods and wandered off to find seats around the reading table.

When they'd all moved on, the tall, thin one, Mali, lingered, studying the model with hands clasped behind his back, his shoulders at a slipping, pensive angle.

This man charges the very air around him, I thought. Not with anger or pain, exactly. Something like both.

Micah waited in silence. When Mali looked up, there was challenge in his eyes as well as understanding. But then he smiled, and the smile was profound and genuine, a total transformation of his face from darkness to light. I stared at him covertly, trying to understand why anything about him should seem so familiar.

"This is good work," he rumbled.

Micah nodded gravely, but I could see he was thrilled. We apprentices glanced our relief to one another. At least we'd gotten through to one of them.

PROPS:

Of course, we never did get the "true" story.

"But was she shot or wasn't she?"

This mattered more to Songh than to the rest of us. I'd have thought Jane, but she'd already decided the answer was yes, and that Outsiders were responsible. Cris and I were more interested in the mechanics: if it was Reede Chamberlaine, how did he manage it? How did you make deals with Outsider assassins to stage a shooting?

At breakfast, the long dining room was full. The wooden barracks-style tables, stained and scarred by forty years of apprentice abuse, rang with the usual catcalls and chatter.

At the serving counter, Mark loaded up his tray to eat upstairs alone.

"Why don't you just walk up and ask her?" Crispin lunged into his boardinghouse reach for the sugar bowl. Like most of our dishes it was a hand-thrown reject from a local potter's studio. "Oh, miss, you're very lovely and I'd like to see your scar . . ."

Songh blushed. "Oh, I'd never dare *speak* to one of them!"

Songh's new habit was showing up outside the apprentice dining room at breakfast so we'd invite him in for coffee with the rest of us. When teased about it, he'd stammer a bit and say it made him feel more a part of "the process." I wasn't sure if he meant the studio process or the apprenticeship process. Whatever his reasons, his work in the studio was improving. He was concentrating much better, as if he'd suddenly decided to take life seriously.

"Then write her a note," drawled Cris.

"You're making fun of me." Songh's eyes were round and reproachful.

"You finally noticed," said Jane with grudging sympathy. However she envied the security of his inherited citizenship, she was never as hard on Songh as the rest of us, who considered SecondGen hazing to be part of *our* process. "Now that you're onto him, maybe he'll lay off for a while."

"Oh, he's such a damn wimp all the time," Cris grinned. "How can I resist?"

"Unrepentant to the end," I remarked into my oatmeal.

Crispin's spoon became a battle flag. "It's good for him! You think you can afford to be a wimp in this business? In this world?"

"You can," replied Jane, "if you were born in Harmony."

"No, you can't!" With more heat than I thought him capable of, Songh shot hurt looks at both of them. "I mean, I'm not. You'll see!"

"With bated breath, I wait." Crispin always assured me there was benign intent behind his mockery when I scolded him about it in private. Occasionally I even believed him. But right then it didn't seem so benign to Songh, who stared into his coffee cup with beetled brows and tried not to pout.

Events took on a strangely heightened quality after the

Eye arrived. Maybe it's just my memory adding hindsight significance. Cris and I fought a lot, then made up equally spectacularly. In the studio, we seemed to pass from one extreme to the other, from high hilarity to deep despair, neither particularly warranted by the given moment.

For instance: a routine morning prop meeting with Liz Godwin occasioned vast excitement. Even Micah put down his brush when she walked in.

"Is it my perfume?" she laughed. "I don't usually rate this warm a welcome!"

Hickey leaned against the wide front door, looking patient and disregarded.

"How's it going?" asked Micah lazily.

Liz was not fooled. "How's it going with them, you mean."

Micah shrugged, smiled. "We are naturally curious."

"Yeah! Songh especially!" Cris called from his terminal.

Songh squirmed. "I am not!"

"He's dying to know, was she really shot?"

Liz's sigh said she'd heard this one before. "Don't know. They're not talking about it. It's as if it never happened."

"They made it un-happen," said Hickey blandly. "They can do that."

I could stand it no longer. "Liz, Liz, what are they like?"

Liz considered. "Have you got about a week?"

"Abbreviate," I pleaded.

"Give them every tenth word," Hickey suggested.

"Well, they do keep you guessing." Liz laughed at our avid faces. "Okay, it gets pretty weird in there from time to time, like when we stop for the occasional song or chant, but at least Mali and Omea have stopped telling Howie what was done in the original production, and Howie's stopped asking Sam how he does his magic tricks. So far, the biggest problem is they're not real happy with their housing."

"Where are they staying?"

"The Fetching dorms. They say they feel like they're in jail."

"I've often felt that," muttered Cris across the room.

"I don't see what's wrong with the dorms," said Jane primly. "It's not like they're used to luxury . . ."

"Who says?" I objected. "We don't know what they're used to."

"What they're used to is more open space," Hickey volunteered. "The little dance man, Ule, told me the thing he hates most about touring is having to sleep indoors all the time."

"They want to sleep outdoors?" Songh gasped. "What if it rains, or someone steps on them?"

Crispin rose, retrieving a fresh print run from the slot further down the console. "And he means OUTdoors. No roof, no dome . . ." He stretched his long arms in an arc and the printout fluttered like feathers. "Only the great *open sky*."

"Ughh," said Jane.

Hickey grinned. "Them's fightin' words."

"He's just tormenting Jane," I told Liz. WorldNet was keeping domers well informed of the growing threat of Open Sky anarchists while supplying very little actual fact. As a result, they were Crispin's latest research project.

Liz avoided the issue. "Well, we're looking for someone with a big house who's out of town for three months. Reede's staying an extra day or so to try to pull some strings."

"A Londoner can pull better strings in Harmony than Howie?"

"Different strings. The retired successful that don't do Art anymore, just sell it." Liz touched Micah's arm as he turned back toward his corner. "Howie hopes you'll come down and watch now and then. The cast complains about being isolated over in the Barn. Omea says they're used to having people around while they work, friends, family, I don't know. Whoever walks in off the street, I guess. Except the Press—they won't let the Chat reporter inside the hall. But you should come. They're up on their feet now and it's getting interesting."

"I'll get there. Tell him I will." Micah gestured at the pile of sketches on his desk. "I'm trying to get a bunch of work out of the way so I can concentrate on him again."

She smiled at him winningly. "It means a lot to him, Mi."

"I know. I know. I'll get there as soon as I can."

I hauled Liz off to the conference room to talk props.

"It really has been crazy around here." I dragged scattered folding chairs up to the table. "We got way behind during the *Gift* push, then Micah had to take a few days in Paris with *Deo Gratias*." I shoved aside a stack of Marie's costume sketches and two piles of multicolored fabric swatches, bright florals, and exotic batik prints. "Now the bids are back on this giant project for the Marin Sea Dome and Micah's got to cut it, which always gets him nuts, plus he's got—"

"Whoa! It's not an emergency." Liz plopped down, finger-combing her red curls back from her face. "Howie's just extra-nervous. This piece has to be as special to everyone else as it is to him."

Then he should stand up for the design in public, I thought. "It's very special to Micah, believe me it is."

Hickey and Crispin came in, a matched set of tall and dark, except that Crispin rarely slouched and Hickey rarely didn't. I once heard Marie ask Hickey, as earnestly as a vid reporter, if he bought his clothes two sizes too big on purpose. He growled that no audience was staring at him while he worked and he saw no reason why he shouldn't be comfortable.

"You're keeping tabs on Tuatua?" Hickey was saying. "Whatever for?"

"C'mon, Hick—it's interesting!" Cris handed me the top sheet on his stack of papers. "The latest from the Crispin Fox Tuatuan Remote News Service, Inc. Wait 'til you see the last. Those planters'd be smarter not to record their meetings . . ."

Hickey peered over my shoulder. "Does he do sports?"

I scanned the WorldNet release on top. "Left the island?"

Cris raised a brow. "If you can believe their sources."

"The planters want the people to think he's left?"

"Cuts him down to size," he agreed.

"Who?" demanded Liz and Hickey simultaneously.

"Latooea," Cris supplied.

When they both looked blank, I realized that our favorite Tuatuan hero was a household word only among ourselves. "The Conch."

"Oh yeah, the Conch." Liz nodded. "The Eye talk about him sometimes."

"Like he was God," said Hickey.

"The symbol of the anti-doming revolution!" Cris enthused, like the twelve-year-old his passion for the Conch recalled in him.

"Actually," I pointed out, "the anti-domers are only trying to maintain the status quo. And no one's sure the Conch is a he."

Cris mistook my meaning. "Naw, he's real. He's some amazing charismatic guy, and they're trying to kill him off!"

"They?" Liz and Hickey spoke again as one.

"Jeez, don't you guys do any research? Look, never mind, hey?" Cris tossed the rest of his papers on the table. "Here's the info you wanted, Hick. Gwinn, read the bottom sheet. Check you later."

He stalked away and Hickey groaned into a chair. "Well, we finally got the Eye's prop crates opened, under that Cu fellow's gimlet-eyed supervision. Can you believe, he actually would not let the women on my crew touch anything? I mean, he stood over them until they backed off. Except with the Matta. He said that was okay because it's traditionally woven and painted by women."

"What is a Matta, anyway?" In the script, the Matta was used by the avenging ancestor-god to effect the miraculous disappearance of the tribesman.

Hickey pulled Crispin's research over and thumbed through it. "Let's see, ah . . . the first source says, 'The object called a Matta was too sacred to be revealed to the uninitiated.' "

"Typical," said Liz.

"Now, wait . . . okay. Here he quotes some obscure anthropological journal. The author was allowed to view a matta that had been 'desanctified' for repair." Hickey regarded me over the considerable length of his nose. "And I quote: 'A very long strip of coarsely woven cloth, painted with the history of the Ancestor it is dedicated to, and its own history as well. Many Mattas are reputed to be several hundred years old.' " He handed me the paper. "The guy wasn't much of a draftsman but here, take a look."

He was right. The writer was mostly interested in recording the Matta's storytelling pictographs, but he did think to include an estimate of its length.

"Eighty-five feet?" I exclaimed. I hoped we didn't have to vanish all eighty-five along with the actor playing the tribesman.

Liz glanced at the drawing and let her tongue loll. "Eighty-five feet of tiny little drawings."

"Time-consuming," said Hickey.

"Expensive," I agreed. "Thank god they've brought it with them."

"Well . . ." Hickey drawled, "there's a problem about that . . ."

There were tourists in the studio by the time we'd finished our meeting. A scholarly looking couple muttered appreciatively beside the model display shelves behind Songh's desk. I wished all the tourists were like them. Another pair, white-haired and wheezy, fanned themselves in the chairs beneath the window. At the cutting table, Jane patiently explained the uses of the scale rule to an earnestly pigtailed ten-year-old.

"Here's the thing," I reported to Micah. "The matta they brought is from one of their dance dramas, so it's dedicated to the wrong ancestor and we can't use it. They forgot the right one, they don't like the Burinda they had from the old production, and a few other things got lost between then and now, no explanations and no apologies."

Micah nodded slowly, intent on the prints mounded on his drawing board. Crispin stood by with the Marin spec file in one hand and a thick stack of bid sheets in the other. Hip-slung in a pose of self-conscious grace, he was pretending to ignore the pretty teenage girl who lurked at his elbow munching an apple.

The Marin bids had come back high and in a very wide range. The lowest bids were from shops Micah had advised against even inviting to bid, shops he considered unreliable or downright dishonest. He always warned producers that the difference between low- and medium-range bids would be made up in additional charges: any detail that wasn't precisely noted on the drawings or spec sheets would be termed an "extra," sometimes even the glue and fasteners.

So Micah was searching for cuts that would not sacrifice the look or function of the project. He'd suggest them to the shops he trusted, to help them bring their prices within range. I used to think this was sneaky, unworthy of him, until I realized the survival of quality work depended upon it.

Right now I wasn't even sure he was listening to me. "The Eye will supply exact specifications, so Hickey can build replacements, and they'll do all the painting."

Micah studied the drawings for the Sorcerer's secret

library, shook his head, and slid them aside to his worktable. "Nothing there I can see doing without."

Cris checked his papers. "I thought maybe that full wall
of old books might become windows."

"Windows in a hidden room?"

"Well, how 'bout cabinets that are always locked?"

The tourist girl smiled up at him. I could see she liked
his looks. Cris flicked her a conspiratorial grin. Had-I-but-
world-enough-and-time, and all that.

"The Eye will do all the painting," I persisted. I refused
to be made jealous by a tourist teeny. "It'd be taboo for us
to do it, even though they're going to fake the symbols
anyway, because it would be taboo for us to see the real
ones. Oh, and Hickey's a little worried about time."

"Already? Well, if there's a problem, I'll send one of you
over to help him finish up."

"I hope it won't come to that." We always fell way
behind when one of us had to spend time out of the studio.
We were already late on Willow Street's *Doubting*, now
retitled as *Fire!*, and *Don Pasquale* was developing very
slowly. Micah was never easily satisfied, but ever since *The
Gift* and our boss's obsessive policing of his own process,
even the paint he used was subject to special scrutiny.

"So, Liz'll send along their little sketches, and I'll draw
them up properly and—"

Micah laid another drawing aside. "Nothing here, either.
Why don't you go over and talk to the Eye yourself? The
less lost in translation, the better."

"I was hoping you'd say that."

The teenager finally got bored and sulked off. Micah
regarded me dryly across the pile of Marin. "You are welcome to make a suggestion when you think it's the right
one."

Don't forget about *The Gift*, I wanted to say. "Okay.
Thanks."

"It's the least I can offer after three years of excellent
service." Then his mind was instantly back on Marin.

"I want to know," said Cris over Micah's bent back,
"what they think will happen if we violate a taboo."

"They'll be pissed as hell, of course."

He made an impatient face. "I mean, what will *happen*?"

"You mean, actual events?"

"Yeah. Will the sky fall in? Will lightning strike us?"

I shrugged, too glibly. "Maybe they'd be supposed to sacrifice us, like the tribesman in the play."

"I'm going to ask them when I see them."

Micah raised a bristly amused brow. "Best way to find out, after all. But I wouldn't expect a direct answer if I were you."

CRISPIN'S RESEARCH: FROM THE MINUTES OF THE JUNE MEETING OF THE TUATUAN PLANTERS' ASSOCIATION

[The meeting continued after a ten-minute break.]
[Ms. Corso:]

The next item on our agenda is a discussion of the strategies we wish to apply against the growing influence on the voters of this figure called the Conch.

The Chair will first take a report from the fact-finding committee, then open the discussion to the floor. I'd like to note for the record that our campaign to identify the Conch with various criminal activities around the island has convinced only the police, and has if anything added to his potency as an image of resistance to authority. Now: Mr. Deeland?

[Mr. Deeland:]

Thank you, Madame Chair, fellow planters: the task this committee set itself was to gather up all possible information, then try to separate out truth from fiction and hearsay.

This unfortunately has left us with little fact.

You may be pleased, Madame Chair, to know we cannot even reliably establish a gender for the Conch.
[general laughter]

It is, of course, the Conch's very success in maintaining this cloak of mystery that has given credence to the claims of magical powers that are made on his (or her) behalf.

[Mr. Deeland here showed some "inconclusive" slides.]

That this is the best we have may help to illustrate the nature of the problem. Though many claim to have seen him (or some, her), some swear she's tall and black, others that he's white. All the broadcasts have been traced to a voice simulator.

But our dilemma is not hopeless. First, though the media balked at our gag order, we have succeeded in convincing them not to air the speeches sent in by tape. Our tribal-born members suggest that with the Conch effectively muzzled, it is unlikely that the literal-minded Station Clans will continue to rally around a ghost and a cipher.

Thus, our strategy should be to turn this advantage of anonymity into a disadvantage, by maintaining the position that the Conch does not exist, thereby forcing him into the open in order to preserve his credibility.

This should be pursued immediately, as the Conch myth can certainly be credited with the recent inroads made by Open Sky agitators among the numbers of unde-cideds. We have isolated certain informers among the tribes who have been made to understand the rightness of our cause, and who should be able to supply us with more factual information in the future.

Only when we have flushed him out can we proceed with our original aim of elimination.

REHEARSAL:

I didn't really believe the Eye would consider human sacrifice.

I'd said it mostly to show Cris I could be provocative, too. What I really expected from taboo violation was disdain and ostracism, sort of like you'd farted in public, but to tell the truth, this worried me just as much. I didn't want the Eye to think I was some jerk who'd run roughshod over their social customs. I wanted them to be bizarre and magnificent and mystical, but I also wanted them to like me.

Still, now that I'd seen them, I kept thinking, they're only actors. Isn't there something a little egomaniacal about claiming the world will end if you don't perform a certain religious ritual?

But I was excited as I gathered up my lists and hopped on my bike, already formulating questions for the Eye that wouldn't sound too ignorant. It was prime tourist rush hour, so I took the High Road, always less crowded because it looped up around the Perimeter. I stopped along the rim for a breather and a look at the view.

Though it was July and probably sweltering Outside, the weather computer had blessed us Inside with an afternoon chill. Harmony spread soft and green below me like a fairy kingdom. The whitewashed walls shone like witches' sugarice cottages. The village markets bustled with commerce and color. The twin towers of Town Hall rose tall and proud, the magic crystal castle.

With my heart full of my good fortune, I remembered Bela and turned my gaze to the Perimeter slums. The Outsiders had stripped down to their innermost rags. The fierce heat Out There lent a false air of repose. Sunburned women fanned themselves lazily in the shade of patched and stained tarpaulins. The children fought their dusty battles in slow motion. No overt signs of sickness or deformity. Not thirty yards from me, a group of sweating men played cards on a stack of crates drawn into the shadow of the moat. The crates were stamped "OutCare," identifying the huge inter-dome charity organization, and they were still sealed. Either these men were powerful enough to be hoarding, or there'd been a recent donation and this particular enclave was well fed enough to relax for a while. It seemed almost, well, normal. The men were enjoying their cards, laughing, gesticulating. I imagined I could hear them hurling amiable insults back and forth. We always said Outsiders had time only for survival, but now I found myself wondering what else they did for amusement.

What would they think about a play, for instance? Some may even have been born in domes and attended plays before committing the crime that had lost them their citizenship.

Of course, you could never let them *in*, to get to the theatres. Especially if they were going to go around taking potshots at visiting actors.

I considered the standard nightmare the bogeyman of my childhood: visions of disease-ridden Outsider mobs ravaging the city like a swarm of ravenous locusts. Rape, pillage, and worse. I heard again my mother's voice: that's why we must keep the laws and follow the rules. That's what could happen to us.

But Tuatua survived without a dome. Did magic protect it from Outsiders as well as the natural horrors? Or were there places Outside that were safer than others? OutCare workers went Outside all the time, and nobody shot at them, though they sometimes came back with scary stories which the Chat spread gleefully. And then there were those who didn't come back at all.

The cardplayers discovered me watching them. For once, they chose to stare back. They elbowed each other, leering, and showed their yellowed teeth. When one pulled out his pale penis and shook it at me, I shrugged and turned away. I had enjoyed them enjoying their cards. That might have been something positive we could share across the distance. At very least, I had hoped for more imagination than a cheap obscenity.

With a sigh I descended back into my magic kingdom, and arrived at the Barn in Fetching just before rehearsal was due to end.

I tried to slip in unnoticed. I still felt like an intruder when I walked into a rehearsal hall, like a guest arriving too early and surprising his hosts in a private act. Liz motioned me in, putting a finger to her lips as she drew out the chair beside her at the table. But the room was not quiet.

Howie straddled a folding chair in the middle of the hall, listening intently as Omea and the girl Lucienne ran through a scene at a volume inaudible even from the stage managers' table. I guessed it was the moment where the clansman's wife frightens the planter's overprotected daughter with tales about the magic of the ancestors.

The rest of the company lounged in a corner with their bare feet up on the prop tables, chatting and joking as if nothing else were going on in the room. The dancers rehearsed with Ule. The dark one, Tuli, wore long sleeves but no sling. Moussa, the musical director, worked out a noisy percussion riff on the arm of his chair. In front of a long mirror leaning against the wall, Sam the magician rehearsed a complicated sequence of hand movements over

and over with tireless patience. And up in the Barn's cathedral ceiling, chirpings and rustlings echoed through the
rafters.

I nudged Liz. "How can anyone concentrate in here?"

She made a don't-come-to-me face. "This is the way they
work."

"Howie doesn't mind?"

"He's adjusting."

"And how's the housing problem?"

Liz sighed. "Reede had an emergency in London, so it's
back in my lap. Is Micah coming?"

"Not today. He sent me over for the prop info."

She registered official disappointment, then softened it
with a smile. "Try to get him down here, okay? Howie
really wants to talk. There's a few things about the set he's
not sure about."

"Things the model can't tell him?"

"Well, you know. Things he's got a clearer idea about
now he's been moving the actors around a little."

I felt a familiar sinking feeling. "Things he might want
changed?"

Liz's smile got businesslike. "You'd really have to ask
Howie. Best thing'd be to get Micah here to see about it
himself."

The little two-scene in the middle of the hall ended. The
women broke their pose and converged on Howie with their
scripts. In her red leotard and flowing black rehearsal skirt,
Omea looked both regal and voluptuous. Lucienne looked
like a little girl.

Howie rose. There was no trouble hearing his voice.
"That's great, ladies. You're really beginning to pull out the
intimacy of the moment." He turned back toward Liz. "I
think that's it for today. Will you give everyone their calls
for tomorrow?"

He beamed at the actresses and thanked them again,
standing close to touch their arms and shoulders, continuing
the scene's intimacy. Omea wanted to discuss her dramatic
action and describe the sense memory she was using for
motivation. Lucienne giggled and murmured. Howie
laughed his big, booming laugh. But as he turned back to
the stage managers' table, he was pensive.

He looked hopeful when he saw me. " 'Lo, Gwinny.
Micah here?"

"Not today." I tried not to let any lingering resentment show, but I was going to be a little more careful with Howie from now on.

He glanced around the hall, biting his lip. The way he aligned his body to the walls told me he was picturing himself in the theatre.

"Liz tells me you have some questions about the model."

"About the set," he corrected. "Some stuff I think Micah should take a look at."

"If it's something simple, tell me, so I can catch Sean before he's built it already."

"I really think Mi needs to see it for himself." Howie's brow creased faintly, and I backed off. He wouldn't be the first director to take out his irritation with the designer on the designer's assistant. Why push it?

"I'm here to get prop info," I offered neutrally. "You want to be in on it?"

Howie shook his big head. "They'll tell you what they need. Speaking of Sean, how's he doing with our vanishing act?"

"I was going by the shop after to check on that."

"I'll walk you over when Cu's done with you."

"Cu?"

"Te-Cucularit." He nodded toward the dour young archivist. "He's their ceremonial expert. He determines the right and wrong of the rituals."

"Wasn't that determined ages ago? I thought their religion was very old."

"Ancient but forever in flux, they tell me. It seems to be all in the interpretation."

My image of a ritualist was rather more gray-bearded.

Howie took my arm. "Handle him real carefully, now. He's bothered enough already by the way we do things around here, and they don't like it when Cu's upset. Call me when you're done."

Howie gathered his script and retreated to the stage managers' table. The company was packing up their dance bags and making dinner plans in three languages. I looked for tall Mali. He was still slouched in the corner, his thin body draped crosswise over an ancient armchair, reading a book as if the day held no other purpose.

"They must look like this."

I jumped. I'd been sneaked up on. Te-Cucularit stood

behind me, holding out several ragged-edged sheets of paper. A grade-school spiral notebook, worn soft with use, was clamped under his arm next to his playscript. The script was neatly page-tabbed and folded open to his big scene in Act One. with all his lines highlighted in Day-Glo green. Elaborate doodling textured the front and back covers of the notebook. Repetitive linear motifs framed fantastical representations of birds, fish, and animals. I looked at the papers he'd pushed into my hands. There were drawings of a Burinda, a schematic of a Matta, and several other unidentified items. The same doodling decorated the surfaces of the drawn objects and formed borders around each sketch.

"These are fabulous!" Cu was abnormally handsome and it was easier to stare at the drawings than at him. My eyes strayed to his notebook. "You did them?"

He nodded, glancing away, less shy than remote, clearly uninterested in conversation. All my carefully considered questions fled from my head—how irritating that mere biology can be such a weakness. This guy would soon be the heartthrob of all those staff ladies who lusted after the unattainable types.

"I wrote the measurements down," he noted. "You must follow them exactly."

These Tuatuans spoke better English than old Max Eider. I studied the sketches again. Te-Cucularit's figures were precise and graceful. "Sure. Okay."

"We will need them quickly, to paint them."

I traced the complications of his patterning with a finger. His disapproval was intimidating. I hadn't even done anything yet. "That'll take awhile, I guess?"

He nodded again and turned to go.

"Umm . . . ?" I was afraid to call him by name. I might say it wrong and offend him further. "I know about the Matta and the Burinda, but could you tell me what these others are?"

He reclaimed the sketches brusquely. "This is a *Duli*. This is a *Puleale*. I give you their short names. This is a *Gorrehma*."

"It would be useful if, umm, Micah will want to know what they're for . . ."

"They are for ceremonial use," he replied, as if I'd asked him to sell his grandmother.

"The ceremonial use of the gorrehma," rumbled a voice behind us, "is for Moussa to sit his big black ass on when he plays his drums."

Mali loomed like a great, dark stork, book in hand, dance bag slung over his shoulder. He smiled down at me, his transforming brilliant smile, rich with what I dared to interpret as sympathy, though it was rather more complicated than that. "Cu likes to go by the book. Don't you, bro?"

Nothing in Cu's manner challenged the older man. He nodded faintly, his face as tightly closed as the notebook beneath his arm. I saw that Mali had intervened not to clear up any misunderstanding but merely to defuse it.

"Ask our Master Cervantes if he might not be more satisfied to discover a knowledge of these objects as they are actually being put to use."

Get him to come to rehearsal, you mean. Mali's gentle formality reminded me of the way one speaks to a child when trying to make it feel grown up.

"I'm sure Micah will understand," I said lamely.

"I'm sure he will." Mali hiked up his dance bag and nodded to Cu. "Pack up, bro. Dinnertime."

Brothers, I wondered? Though both were tall, Mali was much darker, as if he stood under a cloud, and thin to the point of awkwardness, all knobs and sticks, while Cu had that perfect dancer's body.

Mali slipped his book into an outer pocket of his satchel. Made bold by his civility, I asked, "What are you reading?"

He laughed, and I wondered if I would ever hear a sound from him that did not seem to have at least three meanings.

"Everything I can get my hands on!" He patted the book in its pocket. It was an old hardback stamped "HARMONY FREE LIBRARY" on the page ends. "There aren't a lot of books on Tuatua, never mind a whole library!"

He'd gone out the door with Cu in tow before I realized he'd satisfied my curiosity without actually answering my question.

BRIGHAM:

I stared after Mali, probably looking dumb, then stowed Cu's drawings between the pages of my pad, and joined Howie and Liz at the production table. "Do those guys ever give a direct answer to a question?"

Liz smirked. "Not if they can help it."

"But why?"

"They don't trust us." Howie wagged his head sagely. "They've been so isolated out there on that little island of theirs, they don't feel a real part of the Arts fraternity. Once they see we're all after the same thing, they'll come around."

The stage managers bustled about straightening chairs and feeding rubbish into the recycler. On our way out, I asked, "Are those birds up in the rafters?"

Howie nodded. "And they come when Moussa calls them. Uncanny."

As it was past Closing time, only the usual army of cleanerbots kept us company along the lanes as we trudged the long mile to the Arkadie, me wheeling my bike to keep Howie company.

"I guess Tuli's okay, huh?"

Howie's chortle was not as complacent as he probably intended it to be. "Ah, they'll play that mystery out until there's no one left who remembers it."

The Outside sun cut through haze and dome to mix its dirty orange with the programmed pinks and ambers of the dawn/dusk artificials, lending the landscape a Turneresque quality: turbulent, smoky, and faintly sinister. The warehouses loomed, laying long bands of shadow across the pavement.

Along the edges of the residential district, we passed several construction sites.

"Higher and higher," mourned Howie. "No more room to build out."

"Those foreign hotel people finally tore down that beautiful old town house in BardClyffe," I said.

"I was at that meeting. Christ, even Micah came. You

should have heard him, insisting that only five years ago such zoning variances were 'anathema.' " Howie chuckled. "Only Micah could pull off a word like that. The mayor nearly wept as she agreed that the Founders had not planned adequately for the needs of an expanding economy. But we did manage to knock Francotel down from twenty stories to ten. Fit to be tied, they were."

Build, build, build, I thought in gloomy panic. Someday even Harmony will look like Chicago.

Howie got pensive again, tromping along like Big Foot.

"How'd it go today?" I asked him finally.

"Fine, just fine."

"You sound a little tired."

"Well, they wear me out. Whoever said theatre was a universal language had his head up his ass." He waved with hastily summoned energy to an elderly woman standing in the rose-twined doorway of a mock-Tudor cottage. Fetching's style tended away from the Greek hill village ideal and more toward the Cotswold hamlet. "This issue of religion is a bitch. I'm not allowed to sound skeptical, yet if I try to talk in their terms, I'm either co-opting what doesn't belong to me, or I'm being condescending! I have to think twice about every word, theirs and mine, just to be sure we're understanding each other. I mean, hell! We're speaking the same language and I still need an interpreter!"

"Omea can't help?"

"Omea is also my leading lady. Who translates for Omea? Even she's been asking me if they could take a walk Outside now and then! I mean, come on! They've got to know better than that!"

A walk Outside? "Hickey says the dome makes them feel confined."

"They live on an island! What's the difference? Listen, I think I'll come along while you bother Sean about the vanishing act."

"I don't know, Howie . . . the artistic director in the shop? They'll think someone's died."

"Yadda yadda. At least I know the way. Better'n many I could mention." But first he steered me through the columned portal and across silent acres of salmon-colored plush, in the direction of the upper lobby. "Gotta make nice with Cam Brigham. Rachel says he's here checking out the display for *Crossroads*."

Like most of Howie's Board of Trustees, Campbell Brigham came from a Founder family that had prospered. His gallery in Lorien Market did most of its business in eight figures over the com lines.

"I didn't know he bothered with stuff like that."

"Never has before. But Bill Rand, who's directing *Crossroads*, is a longtime pal of his. Whenever Cam's pissed at me, he threatens to desert the Arkadie for Bill's theatre over in Silvertree."

"Willow Street? We're doing a piece with them next fall."

"Yeah? Good play?"

The stairs to the upper level seemed to float unsupported in the flush of sunlight through the translucent stone walls. The polished brass rail was a warm golden curve beneath my hand, as sensual as skin. Howie took the shallow carpeted steps two at a time. I raced after him, panting.

"Not bad. 'Cept they keep changing the title."

"Typical. I'd hate to be their publicity department."

"At least they don't keep changing the play, like some theatres I could name."

Howie tossed a defensive glance over his shoulder. "Hey, kiddo, plays are like fish. Sometimes they get away from you."

He slowed at the top of the stairs and rounded the corner strolling. He hailed Cam Brigham as if we'd just happened to be wandering the upper lobby at six in the afternoon.

The display area was the curving inner wall that separated the lobby and the bigger theatre's balcony level. Photos of the current production, and often rehearsal shots or research material relevant to the play, were mounted behind broad sheets of glass. They were there, Micah always said, to give the audience something to talk about besides each other while they nibbled their intermission snacks.

Now the cases were empty. Photos lay stacked against the marble wall or stretched out across the peach carpet. Several minions from Publicity scurried around, hanging and labeling.

Cam Brigham stood with hands clasped behind him, staring down his nose at an eye-catching blowup of an actress in eighteenth-century costume. Howie fell into an identical posture at his side.

"Everything to your liking, Cam?"

"Oh fine, just real fine, Howard."

Brigham was a fat man, no bones about it. He made bear-like Howie appear svelte. His pale blond hair was thinning and made his head look small compared to the pear-shaped rest of him, and as he seemed determined to play the jovial fat man, he carried himself like one, shoulders pulled way back, belly advancing, arms slightly akimbo to balance his weight.

"Glad to hear it," said Howie.

"Oh well, I had them move a few things around, that's all." Brigham smiled at me expectantly. We'd met at several Arkadie opening nights, but I wasn't important enough for him to remember longer than the five minutes required for an introduction.

"You know Gwinn Rhys, Micah's assistant," Howie supplied smoothly.

"Of course. I'm always telling Micah how lucky he is to have someone around who's both talented and lovely."

Yuck, I thought, but I smiled for both Howie's and Micah's sakes, and did everything but curtsy.

"So what'd you move around?" asked Howie casually.

Brigham laid an inflated hand on Howie's shoulder. "We were thinking we should leave more space for the color shots of the finished production, and actually, I thought you might want to put all the materials for your show downstairs nearer the entrance to Theatre Minor."

It was thought clever, among certain of the staff, to refer to the two stages as Theatre Major and Theatre Minor, but I knew Howie did not encourage this.

Howie considered a moment, or pretended to. "Yeah, might be. Only problem is there's not much room down there, and it's really too poorly lit for display."

Brigham gave this an equal split-second's consideration, then gestured at the impressive photo in front of them. "But you know, How, the contrast won't do either any good."

I moved away, out of the firing line, and perused the *Crossroads* pictures. The show was a richly costumed period epic, the sort that photographed well even in rehearsal clothes, with actors in long skirts and elegant poses. The historical material was stunning, and the final production shots, taken with the set finished and the actors in full costume, would be huge, lush, and gorgeous. Boards of trustees loved displays like that: they made the theatre appear lively and prosperous. I could sort of see Brigham's point, especially when I came upon the pile he'd discarded.

I recognized a lot of the stuff from our own research. Alongside the tall, bare-shouldered actresses of *Crossroads*, in their powdered wigs and acres of silk and jewels, the Tuatuans in their beads and T-shirts put on a poor showing indeed.

But Howie smiled, offering up intellectual conspiracy as a prize. "Cam, contrast is exactly the point."

Brigham laughed broadly. "Your point. But maybe not Bill Rand's point. No fair weighing down one show with the exotica of another, eh? Let our audience come to both and draw their own conclusions. Especially now we're considering those new tourist matinees."

"I didn't give the okay on those, Cam."

"Not yet."

Howie looked ready to do battle, but Brigham headed him off. "Howie, Howie, let's go easy here. I've had enough flak from the other trustees for letting you do this little play of yours in the first place."

"*Letting* me . . . !"

"And bringing these Outsiders right into our own theatre. Now I hear Liz wants to put them up in somebody's house!"

Howie flushed. "They're not Outsiders!"

"Excuse me. UnEnclosed. Same thing."

"No, Cam. These guys are *legal*. For chrissakes!"

Brigham patted his arm. "There's things going on in the world, Howie. All I'm telling you is the Board's not happy with it."

"First I've heard of it! I've consulted the Board every step on this. Prill and Jim and Cora have been behind me all the way."

"Well, Cora always was a little radical. As for the others . . ." Brigham shifted his weight from one thick leg to the other, smiling apologetically. "You know how people are."

"What, they've changed their minds?"

The fat man shrugged, still smiling. "People don't always know their minds right off, you know how it is."

"No, I don't!" Howie jammed his big hands on his hips and glared around at the *Crossroads* photographs as if all this was their fault. I wanted him to leap to the Eye's defense, but instead he let out an explosive breath and said, "I guess I'll just have to take your word for it."

Brigham looked hugely satisfied. "Atta boy. Don't pout, now. You'll see I'm right."

Howie fumed the whole way to the shop. "It's him, damn it! Fucking stick-his-fingers-into-everything Cam! He never liked the idea of bringing in the Eye, and now the sonofabitch is working on everyone else! He says, why go so far away and to so much trouble? Perfectly good plays being written here at home. I said, yeah? Show 'em to me! They're all fucking boring!" His usual bearish stride lengthened. The narrow concrete corridor echoed with his steady clomping and my clattering to keep up. "Have to get to the others right away. Go to work on damage control. Cora will help."

I was silent. I wanted to know why he'd let Brigham push him around the way the fat man was pushing around the rest of the Board members, but it wasn't the sort of thing you come right out and ask somebody. Howie probably deserved it, after leaving Micah high and dry at first rehearsal, but I was trying to learn from Micah's compassionate example.

So I grunted the appropriate agreements and pondered something else: that Brigham had referred to the Eye as Outsiders. It reminded me of the graffiti.

Our failure to turn up any solid information about the Closed Door League was somehow more threatening than if they'd been haranguing right under our noses. Exactly what were these policies they were keeping so secret? If they wanted the home-bred to be running Harmony, that wasn't so scary, but what did they think about the Outside Adoption Policy? Were they Exclusionists? Would they, given the chance, try to throw all non-natives out?

I wasn't too happy to find myself suddenly thinking like Jane.

Sean's irreverent boisterousness was a relief, and Howie was soothed by the respect automatically accorded by the shop personnel to the man who signed their paychecks. As we threaded a crooked path among the crowded worktables, I saw a lot of *Crossroads* being built and nothing at all that I could recognize as part of *The Gift*. I was surprised the show hadn't been started yet, but figured that Sean knew his own schedule better than I did.

"Cam's up there taking my pictures down!" Howie complained to the plans and elevations lining Sean's office walls.

Sean's T-shirt read: *Don't start with me. You know how I get.* He handed each of us a beer. "Cam's a jerk. He's a fat man. He'd put up his family album if you gave him the chance."

They laughed, and the creases in Howie's brow softened.

"Ah, I gave in to him, the asshole." Howie took a manly slug of his beer. "Keeps him outa my hair. He's only on the Board 'cause he's rich as Croesus. Let him run around taking his petty victories, so I can get on with the real work, like directing my play!"

"A world-class jerk," Sean agreed. But I was pretty sure Brigham's victory had not been so petty.

I was relieved to discover the prints of *The Gift* laid out on Sean's drawing board. I leafed through them absently while he and Howie did their fraternal number. Reassuring notes were jotted here and there, measurements and materials specifications, little sketches showing a crosscut detail or how to make up a certain joint. At least some work was getting done on the show.

"How's it going, Sean?" I asked eventually.

"Good, me gerl." He put on his father's thick brogue. "Sure 'n we've got our hands full, but we're allus on top of it. How's me auld boyo up there in Bardycliff?"

I sighed. "Still struggling to cut Marin."

Sean mimed scissors as long as his arm. "It's the only way, you know." He smiled my way, his soft blond and gray hair falling in front of come-on eyes. Sean's sexy clowning usually inspired teenish giggles, much as I wished to appear professional and mature. But at the moment I was thinking, *Sean's SecondGen. Ask* him *about the Closed Door League.* But not in front of Howie. Howie had enough problems.

"We're wondering how's the magic trick," announced Howie genially.

"Coming, it's coming." Sean shuffled some papers on his desk.

"Yeah? And how do you figure it?"

Sean moved over to the drawing board. He hauled the ground plan out from under the pile of prints and smoothed it flat with splayed hands. "Show me exactly where you need this guy to disappear."

Howie stabbed a forefinger at a spot downstage center.

"Right," said Sean. "Well, what I'm thinking is maybe a light curtain, a one-man elevator, and a small reflecting force field around it, set into the deck."

Howie whistled. "Small enough for one man?"

"Yup." Sean was still not meeting Howie's eyes.

"You ever seen one that small?"

"No, but me and my mechanic are working up some modifications to the smallest one we can order. It's expensive, but it'll be just the thing."

"Invisible?"

"I'd rather say *transparent*. Totally new look. Not effectsy, y'know?"

"And it's safe?"

"Hey, have I killed any of your actors so far?"

Howie chuckled. "Hell, go for it. The business is crucial, so don't worry about the expense. If we have to, we'll take it out of something else."

"What else?" I worried. But I was delighted to have at least one bit of good news to carry back to my boss.

"Just so long as we don't bankrupt the entire organization," laughed Howie.

"Oh no," said Sean, "*Crossroads* is going to do that."

This reminded Howie of Cam Brigham again, and he frowned into his empty beer. "Sean, my man, who do I talk to about getting some better lighting down in the lower lobby?" He turned to me with a wolfish grin. "I'll show that s.o.b. I'll turn that piss-poor lobby into the best damn gallery in Harmony!"

WORLDNET/NEWS

07/23/46

BANGKOK, 07/22/46

Mirek Labs revealed today that six tons of pharmaceuticals were lost in shipment between Bangkok and Lahore last week. Mirek investigator Rima Parseghian discounted rumors of Outside interference. "Vacuum-tube technology is far too sophisticated for any Outsider to understand, let alone manipulate," Ms. Parseghian stated. "Even if they could dig a hole deep enough to access a tube, the idea of them being able to do it in the Indian Wasteland is even more absurd." She advised that her company will begin secretly marking drug shipments to be able to trace the stolen goods when they reappear in the marketplace.

STOCKHOLM, 07/22/46   *Special to WorldNet/News*

Civil order has been reestablished in all quarters after Tuesday's outbreak of violence during a circum-dome march to protest the detention for psychiatric evaluation of Open Sky spokeswoman Ingrid Hibberd. The radical anti-dome faction had promised a peaceful demonstration, but Security Police were summoned when Open Sky marchers assaulted bystanders who pelted them with vegetables and rotten fruit.

TUAMATUTETUAMATU, 07/21/46

The Port City police declared a "state of urgency" today in response to the latest series of strikes by plantation and hotel workers protesting the planned Enclosure of the island. A "state of urgency" is described as having lesser status than martial law. It imposes a ban on public assembly and rescinds the civil rights of laborers remaining off the job after the declaration goes into force.

The Planters' Association made accusations of sabotage last week when fire destroyed two warehouses containing a recent harvest of coffee beans. Several suspects are being held for questioning, but the police have been unable to apprehend their chief suspect, the mysterious Conch, despite the substantial reward being offered for his capture. The Conch was recently indicted on charges of inciting to riot, sabotage, and treason. Tuatuan officials have said the trial will proceed in the Conch's absence if he refuses to appear as ordered.

MARK:

"It *sounds* feasible," allowed Micah the next morning when I told him about Sean's force-field idea. "Have Cris look into it."

Cris was running a test of some Marin reprogramming in the conference room. Through the open doorway, I saw little red and purple holographic dragons squaring off over the white tabletop.

"Sean said it would be expensive," I told Micah. "I got the feeling it was still very much in the planning stages." With non-computer-generated special effects, we usually knew what was possible in theory, but were at the mercy of the "outside experts" when it came to the mechanical details. This was one of the things that made a thinking, innovative builder like Sean so valuable.

"Well, he's got time, if he moves along with it." Micah went back to his sketch for Willow Street's *Fire!* Sean didn't have a lot of time, just under four weeks before the set was due in the theatre. Micah's confidence in him soothed any real anxiety, but I'd have felt easier if the build had at least been started.

It was after that, really, that the problems began.

With Bela gone, we had expected a new face in the studio next door. But Marie reported that the Apprentice Administration had finally suggested she make do with one assistant for a while.

"Sure, I'll manage," she allowed, "but really!"

Mark sat further down the cluttered lunch table, empty chairs to either side of him. After three weeks his sad, angry manner still asked for space to mourn. Songh sat opposite, shy but solicitous as a nursemaid, honoring Mark's vigil with his own soulful silence.

"Perhaps some form of formal protest . . ." Micah offered.

Marie fluttered her hands. "Not worth it. Plenty of Second-Gen kids working in the costume shops—I'll groom one of them."

Micah looked thoughtful. "Attrition," he murmured.

"Beg pardon?"

"Attrition. That's how they'll do it."

They exchanged sober glances over the lunch table, then Marie changed the subject abruptly. "The stitchers are saying the Eye's laid a curse on the costume shop."

The perfect intro for a shop tale, but shop tales had always been Bela's province. We'd suffered through some sober lunches lately without him.

"Well, not the whole shop," Marie explained. "One of the sewing machines, actually. The one that's been biting people a lot because the shop's too busy to retire it for repair. Now nobody'll use it."

"Why do they say it's Eye?" I asked.

"Because it's more fun than the real reason. Haven't you been hearing the voodoo rumors running around the theatre?"

"The Eye does not practice voodoo," said Crispin.

"Well, whatever you call it. Plus all these threats about what happens if you violate a taboo. One of Liz's assistants fell off his bike the other day, and now he's saying it was Te-Cucularit getting even because this kid scolded him for being late to rehearsal. That got the girls in a state." Marie smiled, leaning over her plate. "Or how about this? We had a fitting with two of the men the other day—they showed up an hour late, which for them is almost on time, but all the tailors had gone home. Jorgen said go ahead anyway, then was called to the phone. Ah, the look on little Sarah's face when those two hunks, Moussa like some oiled ebony god and our young holo-hero Pen, dropped trow right there in front of her!"

"She works in a costume shop," Cris said. "She should be used to seeing people undress."

"But, my dear, you do have to get extremely intimate to fit this particular garment. It's nothing but a long strip of cloth, and it requires some, uh, manual adjustment to get it into place."

"As it were," said Micah.

Out of respect for Mark, I was trying not to laugh out loud. Marie was so bright and animated and a wonderful mimic, especially of Jorgen, the sour, self-pitying head of the Ark's costume shop. He was good at his job, but nobody liked him much. Sarah was a SecondGen seamstress, and only seventeen.

"They could have left their jocks on," remarked Jane.

"Moussa thought he could make it easier if he helped, but because he's as naughty as my five-year-old, he couldn't resist teasing her a little . . ." Marie writhed like a belly dancer, pitching her voice as low as she could to groan in comic ecstasy. "Then Pen got impatient and uppity like he does, and by the time Jorgen returned, poor Sarah was in tears and a terror with the pins and Jorgen finally had to send her home."

The thought of Jorgen dampened Marie's hilarity. She stirred her coffee, tapped the rim with her spoon. "Jorgen said later they ought to be thankful they're in Harmony instead of back home in all that mess and why don't they behave themselves? Now he's pissed at me and Howie and the cast and starting to give me reasons why he can't do this or that, and the stitchers still refuse to use machine seven and Jorgen blames that on the Eye as well." Marie flopped back in her chair with a sigh. "What ever happened to professionalism?"

"They do seem to be a handful," Micah conceded.

"They're not so bad! They're just . . ." Marie's blousy sleeves and dark hair flew about her head. "Well, so we're getting a lot of attitude! Most of the time they're just trying to have fun! These people sit at the sewing tables all day and gossip and bitch about how bored they are, then when something new shows up, all they do is complain that it's not what they imagined it would be!"

Mark broke his silence suddenly. "It's just like clothing."

All of us waited for him to continue.

His eyes were tired, half-lidded, and his full mouth tight from holding in his grief. But his voice was steady with conviction. "It's a question of signals. Because we live in the same small world, us and the Eye and everyone, we share a set of surface signals—clothing, haircuts, expressions—but all these signals carry subtext, and subtext is very local. We didn't grow up in the Eye's subtext, so the signals get crossed. We misinterpret them. Because the surfaces are often familiar, we interpret some signals as if they were our own when they're not, and some as different when really they're just the same. People get uptight when they suspect they're misreading someone. They feel ignorant. It makes them want to blame the other person."

This was a big bite to chew on. Finally Micah shifted in his seat, nodding gravely. "Very well said, Mark."

"Yeah," Cris seconded softly. And since there was not much one could add after that, lunch ended then and there.

Songh's glance followed Mark back to Marie's studio. I decided he had found a new hero, one who might not give him as hard a time as Crispin always did.

Back at my drawing table, I said to myself, *Now, that's the way a costume designer should think.* But was any talent worth sacrificing the less talented? Would keeping Bela on really have meant the eventual loss of both? How could such choices be weighed? The only thing I was sure of was I was grateful the decision wasn't mine.

RUN-THROUGH:

What finally pushed Micah out of the studio was Sean calling up to complain. "Damn stage managers won't give me the friggin' model 'til you and Howie have a little chat about it!"

But Howie wasn't at rehearsal when we arrived, sweaty and irritable from the Friday matinee crowds. There was a basketball game going on. Not on the video feed. Right there in the room.

The hall shimmered with noise and pounding feet and a rainbow of racing, naked skin. Mali and Cu, stripped to their jeans, were teamed with Omea against Moussa the giant, young Pen, and Sam. Only the magician Sam wore shoes, I noticed. Omea's flowing rehearsal skirt was hiked up around her thighs. Lucienne laughingly guarded a trash can at one end of the hall, and Tuli a smaller metal wastebasket at the other. Matching goalies, dark and light. Even the sultry siren Tua cheered like a tomboy from the sidelines.

Liz Godwin's amiable calm was showing strain. She sat at the production table winding the ends of her red curls around her pencil and tapping her foot. The other stage managers pretended to be busy, even the assistant with the splinted ankle, fresh from his mysterious bicycle accident. Overhead, birds fluttered in the rafters.

Micah surveyed the chaos with bemused astonishment. "Did Howard give up and go home?" I was amazed myself. Serious, dignified Mali and maternal Omea scrambling around like adolescents?

"Howie," replied Liz heavily, "is down at Town Hall, bailing out our choreographer."

"Whatever for?"

Harmony's jail was a block of small holding cells where inebriated tourists could sleep it off. To discourage its use as an impromptu hotel, bail was exorbitant.

Liz shut her eyes and took a ragged breath. "Security found Ule asleep in Founders' Park this morning. Just lying there, right on the grass, happy as a clam."

"And?"

"They arrested him, of course."

I looked to Micah. "Is that a crime?"

He sucked his teeth uncomfortably. "There are vagrancy laws, I suppose."

"He's not a vagrant!" I recalled what Hickey had said. "He just hates sleeping indoors!"

"Indoors is where you're supposed to sleep!" Liz shook her head, realizing how that sounded. "I mean, he should have known better. How's this going to look for Howie and the Arkadie? They give you these big airs of spiritual superiority, then they go and do a thing like this."

"He probably never thought—" I protested.

"Well, he should have!" she snapped, and immediately regretted it. "Look, it's just, you know, the world is watching."

The ball slipped through Pen's damp fingers and careened toward us. Sam bounded after it, silent and agile as a cat. He snatched the ball away an inch from my head, then grinned at my defensive cringe, and spread his arms wide. "Ha!" For an instant, the ball vanished. Then he had it again and was whirling back to the game. His T-shirt, as he turned, lifted to reveal long, parallel scars across his lower back. Old scars, pale against his biscuit-colored skin, at least a dozen of them. I stared after him.

"And then," Liz was saying, "there's this charming little thing."

She grabbed a fold of paper and flipped it open in front of us. An e-mail printout, without identifying lettercode or signature.

" 'Citizens of Harmony,' " Micah read, " 'the door is open. Do you know who your neighbors are?' "

"What is that?" My vehemence surprised even me.

Micah eyed me curiously. "It was in the public-message board this morning."

Liz said, "It was also taped to the front door of the Arkadie, and to the door here, and not to any other door I know of."

"Howie's street artist?" I offered brightly, wishing I'd never heard of the Closed Door League. "Trying out a new medium."

"Yeah? So why is he picking on us?" She stuffed the paper away in her notebook. "Don't tell them."

"Them?"

She nodded toward the basketball players. "Howie doesn't want them upset by stuff that doesn't concern them. They're distracted enough by what's going on back home."

A rolling clatter rocked the hall as Pen darted beneath Cu's guarding arm and dunked the ball into the wastebasket. Cu was dancer-graceful but too controlled to match Pen's loose, aggressive style. Tuli clapped her hands to her eyes and squealed with laughter. The wastebasket toppled and rattled off into a corner. Pen hooted and strutted. Cu scowled. He sent Tuli a rude gesture, which only made her laugh harder. Noting her lean bare arms, I began to doubt my memory of that first rehearsal day. Was it Tuli who'd been wearing the sling? Certainly no sign of injury now.

Mali trotted after wastebasket and ball. "Ho, Cu, you gotta watch out for these little guys!"

Pen tossed a punch at his ear as he passed. Mali ducked and swerved, laughing. Pen swore and bolted after him to swing at him again.

"Yah, bro!" Mali danced out of the younger man's reach. The troupe's pensive elder statesman was transformed into a grinning maniac. He whirled and sprinted away to scoop up the ball, then dribbled it a few times in Pen's direction, tempting him to swing again. Tuli scrambled to restore her wastebasket. Cu moved in to cover. In the center of the hall, Omea leaped and yelled for the ball, while big Moussa and solid, compact Sam waited like a wall of dark and light behind her. A flock of small birds landed in a line on the overhead crossbeam, watching.

Mali sighted on Omea and stretched his long, flat-muscled

arm to throw, the ball balanced on his palm. He hesitated, then pivoted, and lobbed the ball in a high, gliding arc toward the front entrance.

All eyes followed this sudden change of trajectory. The ball hit the floor once and bounded straight into No-Mulela-tu's hands as he jogged through the doorway.

He was barefoot in ragged cutoffs. A knitted wool cap perched on his braided hair. His plain white shirt hung open to his chest, the long shirttails flapping. Small wonder Security took him for a vagrant. On a thong around his neck, he wore a dark, carved bead just like mine. The one I still wasn't wearing around the Eye.

The little choreographer caught Mali's throw without breaking stride. He bounced the ball twice, let out a high-pitched yodel, and charged into the game. The others cheered in welcome.

I scolded myself for easy credulity, but it was hard not to see prescience in the perfect timing of Mali's throw.

Howie halted in the doorway. "What is this, recess?" he growled at Liz. "Are we doing a run-through today or not?"

She look back at him helplessly. I thought she might cry, but she caught herself and produced a stony grin. "Just letting the children run off a little steam."

Across the hall, the game wound down into a muttering huddle as Ule spun the tale of his arrest. Howie turned on Micah instead. "Well. You picked a fine time to show up!"

"What's a better time?" inquired Micah mildly.

"Forget it. I should be glad you've spared us a small moment from all that other shit you've got going." Howie moved away. "Liz, try and establish a little order here, will you? Micah, let's get this over with."

The model waited in exile against the wall. Howie loomed over it like a thunderhead. "I'm having a real problem here with the scenes inside the Mission and the public bar." His big hands chopped at the interior space like knife blades. "I'm losing all the intimacy out here in the open, and there's all this business that has to get done and no goddamn place to put anything!"

Micah peered into the model speculatively. I stood back.

"I need something," Howie went on, "like a wall that comes in."

"A wall?"

"With a door in it, so I can get these entrances working right."

"A real wall with a real door?"

Howie shoved past the warning in Micah's voice. "And some shelves or cabinets to put all the props in. We'll fly it in. Shouldn't be too hard for Sean to work out."

"Not for Sean, no."

"Okay. And we're gonna need some kind of little hut . . ."

Only the shadow moving along the floor alerted me to Mali's arrival. He was damp from his exertions. He stood silently at my shoulder, observing, surrounding me with his clean, earthy smell.

". . . out here for the scenes in the village."

"Howard, whoa."

"What is it?"

Micah kept his tone admirably neutral. "I'm concerned about breaking style here, Howard, about jarring the viewers' expectations where we might not want to. If we drop a realistic wall into this imagistic environment, it'll look like it fell in from another play."

"So make it look like it belongs. What's the problem?"

"Howard, don't you think the whole idea of a realistic wall might be contrary to the style we've worked so hard to establish?"

"All the style in the world's not gonna help me if there's no place for my actors to play the damn scenes!"

Howie in extremis, Micah would say later, with simultaneous exasperation and compassion. But just because Howie'd had a rough morning at the jail didn't mean he was allowed to take it out on his scenographer, on his friend.

Micah placated. "Let me look at it. See what I can come up with."

I wanted to yell, *It's not the set's fault if you can't make the play work!* I may have even taken a breath or opened my mouth. A light touch on my arm restrained me. Mali. His fingers were there and then they weren't, and my angry impulse passed. Saved again. I'd slipped him a glance of gratitude before it occurred to me to be amazed that he'd read a virtual stranger so effortlessly and so well.

Howie stood rigid, as if boxed into a man-sized cubicle. "If you'd been around a bit more and had some sense of how the piece is shaping up, you might understand my problem."

Micah nodded. "You're having a run-through? I'll stick around."

Howie noticed Mali beside me. He cranked out a smile that would have shattered if you'd dropped it. "Just working out a few set details." He gave a stingy bit of the smile to Micah. " 'Course we don't have to worry 'cause this guy Mali can make anything work, anywhere, anytime. We should have whole companies of this guy!"

He moved past Micah and looped a bearpaw arm around Mali's stooping shoulders. "What do ya say, *bro*? Shall we get to work?"

And I hated him for the false ring of it on his tongue.

So we stayed for the run-through, and it was your typical halting second-week effort. It had been three years since the original production and the piece had been rewritten so much they might as well have been starting from scratch. But for Micah and me, the script that had been mere words on a page and the troupe that had been a faceless exotic import at last became individual performers in a living event.

The magician Sam was gruff and driven as the Planter and his brashest, flashiest sleight-of-hand symbolized the great wonders of technology he would bring to the benighted natives. Later, as an ancestor-god, a cooler, subtle illusion became his very essence. As the doomed clansman's wife, Omea sang and chanted a haunting narration, twinned by Ule's sensitive panpipes. Moussa's rolling percussion swelled in and out of the action like breaking waves. Lucienne and Tuli lent an air of abstraction as attending spirits who sometimes mirrored, sometimes mocked the human dilemma.

The sultry Tua blossomed irregularly as the village maiden, the clansman's daughter. She hadn't played the role originally, so was behind the others in her preparation. Pen was attractive but somewhat stiff as her youthful suitor. You could tell he'd been doing vids—he kept looking for the camera, then remembering where he was. As the clansman's friends, then executioners, Cu was a grim and stalwart straight man to Ule's more fluid comic pacing.

Mali, playing the clansman as I'd guessed, seemed to have

decided to use this rehearsal as a technical exercise. He marked his way through most of his scenes, running his lines, checking his moves and timing with mechanical efficiency. But every so often he'd forget. Then the energy in the room would ignite and the other actors would be drawn into his fire. For long moments he'd have us on the edge of our seats, until he recalled that he hadn't meant to be acting that afternoon.

And he made it seem effortless, as if he could slip in and out of his skin at a second's notice. He made no lengthy preparation, used no vocal tricks, no body mannerisms. He just suddenly *was* the betrayed and martyred clansman, and you couldn't tear your eyes away. His pain was your pain and his dying breath your own very last.

At the end, there were only six of us to applaud, but we made it sound like fifty. Howie was up on his feet and roaring, and in Micah's eyes I saw something very rare: undisguised, near boyish admiration. This was the Mali who had gazed into the model and seen the design for what it was.

"That was great, everyone! Just great!" Howie waded in among the company, scattering individual praise like rose petals. The actors were excited. Omea's contralto laughter spiraled like smoke toward the girders. Sam juggled the woodblocks while Moussa looked on with a benign grin. Ule already had the girls reworking some of their harder combinations, railing at them in falsetto so they'd break up laughing and misstep. Even sober Te-Cucularit allowed himself a small smile of satisfaction.

Mali received Howie's compliments gravely and drifted off to pack up his bag. I thought he looked tired suddenly, older and preoccupied, his stoop more pronounced.

"Don't think it's as easy on him as he makes it look," Micah advised quietly. "The soul of a great artist cannot die once a day and remain unaffected by it."

"Twice on matinee days," I murmured. I rolled my wooden bead in my pocket. I understood now that what I needed was their permission to wear it. Mali's permission.

Mali passed us on his way out with a nod and the quick flash of a smile. But his eyes were remote, defended as they had been that first day. There were matters other than us on his mind.

"Well, Mi, what'd ya think? If it works in the rehearsal

hall, it'll be pure gold onstage!" Howie's elation was blinding in light of his recent treatment of Micah. The need for an apology didn't even occur to him. "I knew I was right about this! Nothing touches the heart like a great performer working the waiting void!"

Oh please. I frowned and pretended absorption in my notes.

But Micah, amazing Micah, extended a hand and a wryly forgiving grin. How could he not require the rest of the world or at least his colleagues to behave as decently as he did? "Looking good, Howard. You could make an international star of that man."

Howie beamed brighter at Mali's retreating back. "Something, isn't he? We've got some pacing problems here and there, but the rest of 'em ain't bad, either. Moussa, eh? Sam and Omea?"

Micah nodded. "Remarkable."

"Even little Tua's gonna wring their hearts. We have really got something here! Look, Mi, about the set . . ."

Micah raised a palm. "Let me look at it first thing tomorrow." He grasped Howie's arm, shook it a little. "Don't worry. We'll work something out."

Howie looked grateful, but he'd have had to get down on his knees to mollify me. "First thing tomorrow" really meant all day tomorrow and maybe Sunday—the long extra hours it would take to find a solution to his demands.

"Good thing you were pushing so hard on Willow Street," I remarked on the Tube to BardClyffe. "While you still had the time."

Micah stroked his mustache with comic sagacity. He was relieved not to have left things with Howie on a sour note.

"You knew this was coming?"

"One must always be prepared for the possibility," he admitted. "At some point, things will get tough in rehearsal and the director, or somebody, even you yourself, will come down with a case of cold feet."

"And then?"

"Well, then you just have to roll with the punches."

I scowled. "I don't like it."

"Who does? Why do you think there's so much bad design around? In all the chaos attendant on making a production, the original impulse often gets lost in the shuffle.

Sometimes it's up to the designer to haul it into the light again."

I was still mad at Howie. "If nobody else has the guts to do it."

"If nobody else notices it got lost in the first place."

"Directors shouldn't be allowed to change their minds after a certain point."

"They are and they do, so get used to it." Micah chuckled. "Sometimes you'll even thank them because sometimes they're right."

But walking up through BardClyffe Village, as if fifteen minutes hadn't passed since he'd last spoken a word, he said, "But I didn't see too many signs of a revolution in style in there . . . did you?"

HICKEY:

The stunning run-through lit some kind of fire under me. I worked late that Friday and all day Saturday, formalizing Cu's prop sketches. Saturday evening I rushed them over to the Arkadie, where the shop had gone on weekend overtime to finish *Crossroads*.

Fetching Plaza was empty, puddled from a recent rain. The bookstalls were folded up and shuttered like deserted houses. I pedaled over the S in CLOSE, still ghosting through its many bleachings and scrubbings. I left my bike unlocked in the theatre's rack, noting with pleasure that I could never have done that in Chicago.

I padded through the silent lower lobby. A lone electrician was installing new lighting fixtures in the low-ceilinged, boxy space in front of Theatre Two. He took my lingering as an excuse for a break and stood back with me, wiping his hands on his thighs, to inspect the one completed wall.

"That's a bit cheerier, eh? Now they'll be able to see where they're at."

"And that these walls need a serious coat of paint," I smiled. No polished marble here. No brass and plush. Instead of Minor and Major, the wags should call them Theatre Plain and Theatre Fancy.

It was well past quitting time, even for an overtime Saturday. But Hickey Kirke's home life was the Arkadie. He was more in than out on weekends and usually stayed late. I was sure of finding him still squirreled away in what the crew called Hickey's Cage.

I pushed through the shop door into a vast darkness lit by the flash and dance of sparks. The welders were still hard at work in the metal shop. Pale light glowed in a far corner. Shop foreman Ruth Bondi was hunched at her terminal.

"How's it, Ruth?" I murmured, stopping by her elbow.

"It goes," she nodded. Ruth was a solid, red-cheeked woman with a surprising waist-length waterfall of brown hair which she usually wore piled up under her hard hat. Tonight the hat was on its peg and the hair gleamed softly around her shoulders as she leaned into the light of her desktop.

I squinted at her monitor. "So what's this?"

"What else?" She made a deep-throated dog noise. "My newest nightmare is I'll be building this show for the rest of my life!"

"Mr. Eider been around much?"

Ruth rolled her eyes. "When hasn't he been?" She flattened both palms on the backlit drawing as if to shove it away. "This is a rebuild of a cornice we rebuilt yesterday! No, we didn't build it wrong. Max just keeps having these little changes of heart!"

"Little?" I glanced around. By the flicker of the welders' torches, I picked out a giant curved staircase, several pilastered walls, an elaborate colonnade, at least a mile of carved "stone" railing, and a forest of unfinished topiary. Nothing that I recognized. "Uh, listen, Ruth, has *Gift* been started at all?"

Ruth bent low over her terminal. "Better ask Sean about that."

"He only cracks jokes when I ask him. C'mon, I won't hold you to anything. Is it even on the floor yet?"

She sighed. "Don't put me in the middle, hey?"

"Just yes or no, Ruth. No sources cited, I promise."

"Talk to Sean."

"Not even for Micah's sake?"

She rubbed her snub nose, sniffed, and rubbed it again, then sat back. "We've done all the working drawings, the materials are on hand . . . but no, nothing's been actually started so far."

"Nothing." I'd been hoping she'd reveal the hidden corner full of our half-built scenery. "But why?"

Ruth folded her arms into her chest. "We don't have the men or the space. It was total madness to schedule another show alongside *Crossroads*! It's got us out flat all by itself!"

"Would more overtime help?"

"Are you kidding? We're in from six light to nine dark as it is! The men have got to eat and sleep sometime!"

"But something's got . . . what are we going to do?"

"I don't know," she laughed wearily. "Die young."

"When do you think he'll start on it?"

"Probably when *Double-Take* closes. I think he's looking at building *The Gift* in the theatre."

Double-Take was the show currently occupying Theatre Two. "Next week? That's less than two weeks before *Gift* goes into technical rehearsals!"

"It's a small show," she reasoned.

My voice broke like an adolescent's. "Doesn't he care?"

Ruth hushed me quickly. "Of course he cares! He's doing the best he can! You know how it is. *Crossroads* was in the shop first, we got a momentum going with it, and he's afraid if he breaks men off to start another project, we'll bog down and never finish. It's been a long, hard season. All our usual extra hands are unavailable. And, hey, Sean gets tired same as the rest of us."

"Bring in some new help."

She shook her head. "You gotta start all over with new people."

"But what am I going to tell Micah?"

She trilled her fingers stubbornly on her keypad. "That *Crossroads* is one motherfucker of a show!"

I took a breath. No use beating up on Ruth. "I gotta get him down here."

"It'd be a good idea."

I watched for a bit while she figured moulding lengths for Eider's again-revised cornice, then nudged her arm. "Hey. Thanks."

"Don't mention it." Then she smiled wanly. "Really. You'd better not. For my sake."

I gave back my most earnest smile. "Not a word."

*　　*　　*

Hickey's Cage looked deserted when I peeked in, but the overhead lights were glaring as if it was midday, and a fresh cup of coffee steamed on the prop master's littered desk.

"Hickey?" I squinted up into the four-story jungle of metal storage scaffolding crammed with furniture, statuary, weapons, and household items from three thousand years of human history, in facsimile reproduction, of course. "Hey, Hick! You here?"

I heard a distant rattle down along the narrow aisle between two towers of shelving, then a clanking across the upper catwalks. The noise halted above my head. Then some more rattling, and Hickey spidered down the ladder beside his desk.

" 'Lo, Gwinn."

" 'Lo. You look all dusty, Hick."

Hickey brushed at his rumpled shirt, then wiped his face on his sleeve. He yanked at the homemade belt that cinched his oversized pants to his skinny, high waist. "Eider swears we've got this Empire fire screen in stock that he used his first show here," he grouched, "but the computer disagrees and I sure can't find the damn thing! Must be somebody else's stock he's remembering."

"So tell me. Are you as far behind as Sean is?"

"Is Sean behind? Hell, we're moving right along in here. Nothing I can't handle 'long as sleep isn't important." His expression was sour, but Hickey wasn't known for sweetening the truth when he could lay you flat with it, or at least darken your day.

"Good, good, 'cause here are a few items I *know* you don't have in stock." I untaped my slim roll and spread out the *Gift* prop drawings on the faux-marbre top of a Victorian washstand.

"Ah ha!" he exclaimed. "Geegaws!"

I giggled. "Don't let them hear you saying that. These are muchee taboo."

He waved a dismissive hand. "Oh, I'm cool with those guys. People around here think they're stuck up, but they're all right. Nothing a few centuries of cynicism and civilization wouldn't cure." He slumped at his desk, drew a big hunting knife from a cubbyhole, and dug delicately at a splinter in his thumb. "I like 'em. They've got good drugs. The kind you grow in the ground and smoke."

"How archaic." Not to mention illegal. Not the drug part, of course, just the smoke.

"Don't knock it until you try it."

Drugs from the ground? I wondered if that was safe. "I'll pass the word to Cris."

"You do that."

"If I can get him to listen long enough."

Hickey smiled tentatively. "Problems?"

"Nothing that couldn't be solved if I were someone else."

"Or he was, hunh?"

"Yeah." I smiled back, grateful. "So you're getting pretty friendly with these guys?"

"We've hung out a coupla nights. Ule and Moussa, mostly. Guess they decided I was okay after I unpacked their props with due ceremony and respect." He tossed the knife down and went after the offending splinter with his teeth.

"What do you talk about?"

Hickey's shoulders flopped up and down like a loose-stringed marionette. "Stuff. Drugs. Their tours. Politics."

"Politics?"

His head sank into his chest, but his eyes looked up. "Yeah. So?"

"Nothing. Just, well, their politics have been sort of an interest around the studio."

"Ah. Right. I remember. The Crispin Fox Tuatuan Remote News Service. Maybe I should subscribe."

"So . . . what kind of politics?"

"Oh, how they feel about ten thousand years of religious tradition and their rights to their homeland being threatened by the greed of recent immigrants, little stuff like that. It's the old story, you know. Their way of life is simple, non-aggressive. Colonizers moved in without a fight. Tuatua's such a backwater, nobody realized the colonizers had taken over until the doming thing."

"Do they say anything about the end of the world?"

Hickey hesitated between a cough and a laugh. "It comes up now and then."

"And what do you say when it does?" An idea had come to me.

"As little as possible. Why wreck a blooming friendship?"

I gave the idea some rein. "Hick, can I ask a personal question?"

His eyes grew wary. "Sure. I guess."

"You're SecondGen, right?"

His head eased up, the puppeteer tightening its string. "No, actually. I'm not."

"Oh." This left me planless. "Gee. I assumed—"

"Most people do." His laugh was a short bark. "Only the stars could be FirstGen, right?" He glanced away.

"I didn't mean that."

"No. Of course not." He hesitated. "Shit, what the hell. You want the whole number?"

I felt obscurely privileged. "Yeah, I'd like that."

He blew air silently through his lips. "Hokay. The Story of Hickey Kirke. I came here twelve years ago to study furniture making and design. Worked hard, struggled through my apprenticeship, survived to journeyman, got my citizenship, a hole-in-the-wall workshop, a gallery . . . then just couldn't get enough commissions to make it go. Not chic enough. Well, not commercial. The tourist trade was just catching on in a big way then and . . ." He shrugged, but it was nothing casual. "Furniture's tough to carry home as a souvenir. So I lost the gallery. Lost the shop. But I'd been doing some free-lance work around the theatres, so when this job opened up . . ."

"I see." And I did. And was glad I'd had always the sense to treat him gingerly. "But you survived, Hick. You're still here."

His eyes flicked around the Cage. "Here?"

"Harmony."

"Oh. Yeah." He picked up the big knife again, idly testing its balance across his forefinger, then just as idly set it aside. "Why d'you ask?"

"Just curious."

"Unh-uhn. You worked up to it much too carefully for 'just curious.' "

"Did I?"

Hickey leaned forward, shoulders gathered up, hands shoved deep into baggy pockets. "So what's up?"

I wondered why Hickey Kirke was going to be the first full citizen I told about this. "Have you ever heard of something called the Closed Door League?"

His eyes narrowed to study me a moment. Then he fished among the piles on his desk and pulled out a sheet of e-mail printout. "Anything to do with this?"

This one was a little more direct: CITIZENS OF HARMONY!
DANGEROUS RADICALS ARE AMONG US. CLOSE THE DOOR!

"This came this morning?"

"Like the first one. What's it all about?"

"That's what I'm trying to find out." And then I let it
out all in a rush, Jane's worries, what Songh had said. I
was so relieved to tell it to someone more experienced with
the politics of the citizenry. I finished suddenly, like running
out of fuel, and gazed at him breathless. "Hickey, I don't
think you're surprised."

"No. Not very. Except that it's taken this long."

I cocked my head in question.

"For the territorial imperative to reassert itself."

"But who are these people? What do they mean by 'dangerous radicals'?"

"People who don't think the way they do."

"Like us, for instance." I swore him to secrecy even as
he was mulling through a list of SecondGen friends he might
safely worm some information out of.

"Why not Sean? Surely we could ask Sean."

Hickey didn't even consider. "Nah, I don't think so.
Sean's got enough on his plate right now."

Funny. Same reason I'd used for not telling Howie or
Micah.

HARMONET/CHAT

07/26/46

***Just keeping you up-to-date, friends and neighbors,
and just imagine if you weren't up-to-date when you find
yourself seated next to Reigning Queen of Shakespeare
KIRI REDSTONE at the Eden Philharmonic?***

***But if you can't get a ticket, go east to BardClyffe.
We're racing right over to partake for ourselves at
GITANNE ENTREMONT's newly refurbished *Brimhaven Bistro,* formerly known to all you pub-crawlers as
just the BRIM. You'll all remember Gi from her stellar

performances with Images in the early days. Her third-story hole-in-the-wall has climbed out of apprentice-dominated obscurity to become the latest *rip* joint to jump for the visitor set. We picture Gi on her terrace early, gazing across the square at the FRANCOTEL site, just counting the credits. All those extra visitors gotta eat, right?

***Meanwhile, doesn't little ole HOWIE MARR have his hands full? A sleep-over in Founders' Park?? Is this a stunt or what? And the way they *look*! Casual dress doesn't mean NO dress, friends and neighbors, for those of you who've just joined the civilized world. We liked 'em better in their robes and feathers. But, hey, don't worry, Howie. We'll tell you when you go too far.

***Besides, the word on BILL RAND's production of CROSSROADS is mouthwatering enough to forgive anything. And so's all the money he's spending!

Remember, you DIDN'T hear it here!

OVERTIME:

Overtime was technically forbidden in the apprentice program. Weekends were legislated: apprentices were expected to pursue their independent futures on Saturdays and Sundays, in the dormitory studios or out among the galleries and performance spaces, observing the work of others, making contacts.

But it's hard for anyone except writers or maybe miniaturists to manage anything but sleep in a five-by-eight dorm room. And the communal studios were always crowded and noisy, more conducive to arty clowning and debate than to serious accomplishment.

So we worked in Micah's studio. This tradition had been instituted by a clever former apprentice, one of Micah's first. The Master allowed us the studio on Sundays in return for a few illegal hours here and there when a crunch was on.

Only problem with Sunday was it really meant Sunday morning, working as efficiently as possible, because once the Gates were open, Sunday was a total loss.

We were in early that Sunday, even before Micah. At breakfast, I'd browbeaten Jane about resurrecting a neglected project she'd done some very nice work on.

"There's no point," she replied. "I mean, it's too late for me, isn't it?" But she came anyway, perhaps for the company on a lonely Sunday morning.

The door of Marie's studio, brazen with red and yellow stripes, stood wide to the morning breezes. Mark's battered racing bike stood in the courtyard rack next to Bela's, its twin. I called out cheerily as we passed the door. Bent over his drawing board, Mark raised a hand but not his eyes.

"He was never in Sundays when Bela was around," I murmured.

"Then Bela will not have failed in vain," Cris replied.

Jane looked like she would happily murder him if he showed even the hint of a smirk. I went around noisily propping open the skylight panes and swung the front door flat against the wall. Letting the air breathe freely through the space could make you question the need for walls, and hopefully it could lighten our fractious mood.

Crispin cleared the rough white-paper model of *Fire!* from Songh's table and sat down. We called up our projects from the files and settled in to work.

"I'm sure Mark's lonely in there all by himself," said Jane after a while.

I grunted. I was finally making progress with my modern-dress version of *Lysistrata*. I'd decided that Greek city-states and autonomous city-domes had something in common. My scheme mixed huge, animated marionettes with high-tech robots. The sound and atmospheric effects were going to be so complicated, I'd need Crispin's help with the programming. (Never confine yourself to what you know how to do, he always said. Hire an expert.) Now that I had a look that I liked, I wanted to get on with the details. But I'd been thinking it was time to include Mark in on the Closed Door mystery. "Let's invite him in to work with us."

"Leave the guy alone," said Cris. "Work is the only true solace."

Lately, Jane delivered her attacks on Crispin to me. "How can you waste your time with someone with so little human feeling?"

"I'm not really sure," I replied seriously.

"She needs me around," he laughed. "She'll never be a player unless I push her into it. Right, Gwinn?"

"That must be why she's the First and you're not," Jane countered bravely.

Cris snorted. "Micah's no fool. He knows who'll always put his interests before her own."

"Your way is not the only way," I said.

"Better way than sitting waiting for it to happen to you. I make things happen, and I make 'em happen for you, too. Don't I?"

My file had come back from Actors' Collective with an invitation for an interview. "Yes," I admitted.

Jane eyed me pityingly.

"And there are a few other human feelings beside pity and fear." Cris threw in his final salvo and let the matter drop. We worked in the enforced concentration of discord until Micah arrived an hour later.

Most Sundays, if he came in and found us working, Micah would make the rounds from desk to desk, favoring us with nuggets of advice and criticism, which we stored away like chipmunks against that wintry season when we'd have to do without his guidance. He had the natural teacher's gift for unraveling, with a well-aimed observation or two, the tangled knots both in your head and on the paper. He taught us that ideas were cheap, that we must never hesitate to throw them out in order to make room for the solutions, which were the real gold.

That morning he came in hunched and solemn. He greeted us abstractedly and retreated immediately to his corner, where he rolled up his sleeves and sat down to work without putting on his smock. He had on one of his good shirts, a fine drapey white cotton trimmed with embroidery at collar and cuffs—flashy, for Micah. He'd dressed up for his Sunday breakfast with Rosa, then forgotten to change before he came in. If I didn't do something, the shirt would be gray by noontime and he'd be upset, despite his insistence that the real and only purpose of clothing was to intercept dirt.

I got his smock off its hook and padded over. "Anything we can do to help things along this morning?"

Micah stared blankly at the smock, then shrugged, and put it on. "Until I solve this, we're pretty much at a standstill."

He meant the changes to *The Gift*. The original sketches were laid out on his board, buried under smeary overlays of tracing paper—embryonic ideas touched in in pencil, then worked over and over. The increasing coarseness of the line cried out his dissatisfaction with each successive solution. All day Saturday, while I'd churned out prop drawings, Micah had struggled to answer Howie's demands without sacrificing the clean simplicity that was the heart and soul of the design. Carving into it was like dismembering his child.

"Reconceiving after the fact is a contradiction in terms," he muttered.

"Would it help to talk it out a bit?"

"I doubt it."

I didn't take it personally. Micah was mostly angry with himself for being unable to shake free of his original mind-set. I retreated to my own dilemmas. By the time I'd got up to speed, it was noon. Time for the weekend tourist invasion.

The problem with the weekends wasn't only the greater number of tourists. It was the weekenders' odd presumption that they were on holiday not only from work but from other aspects of civilization as well, such as manners and social restraint. They ate more. They drank more. To the gallery owners' delight, they bought more and bigger. They talked louder and moved faster, and while the weekday tourists tended to accept that what went on in a studio might actually be work they should allow to proceed undisturbed, the weekenders expected the world to come to a halt the moment they arrived.

The first shadows over the sill that day were three plush couples whose accents placed them in one of the Texas domes. They were rich and high-profile. One of the men carried a substantial hip flask that Security should have confiscated at the Gates. As he flashed it about, I wondered where he'd hidden it coming through the detectors. Cris enlightened me later about the thriving mail-order trade in objects made of non-detectable materials: flasks, syringes, cameras, recorders—the sort of things rich boys know about. What was illegal in one dome was a profit industry in another. He'd even heard of weapons made of the stuff, not just blades but guns and explosives. I felt a lot less safe after that.

The flask, however, was the only thing these folks were trying to hide. They gleamed and jingled. All six of them were sheathed in leather from head to toe. The women wore their wealth like African tribeswomen, bracelets to the elbow and rings on every digit.

"So this is the place."

"Small." The woman's heart-shaped face was so perfectly manicured, I wondered how she dared smile.

"A true artist can work anywhere." Her friend was a buxom brunette with a cowhide beret angled over a full mop of curls. A clear jewel the size of a cherry sparkled on her hatband. A diamond? I contrived for a closer look. Even in Harmony, diamonds were none too common.

Crispin, Jane, and I smiled the welcome that apprentice regulations required. Micah hunched his shoulders and kept working.

"We'll just look around a bit." The thick, pale-faced blond strode possessively around the studio, stopping at Crispin's console. He lifted the dust cover. "Jeez, look at this old antique!"

Crispin drew his blade along his straight edge with a vicious squeal. I joined him at the cutting table. "Don't slice off your thumb." The women stared at my faded coveralls.

The flask man, tall and broad-shouldered, already flushed with drink, leaned in at Micah's side. When the work on the drawing board disappointed him, he turned to the nearby walls, with their collage of roughs and plans. He pointed at a *Cymbeline* sketch tacked in the upper corner.

"How much for that one?"

"That is a work in progress, I'm afraid," said Micah politely.

"That's okay. Looks good to me."

"I mean, it can't be sold until the production has opened."

The man grinned slyly. "But you could just make 'em another one, right? They'd never know."

The three women were already bored. They took turns with the two chairs beneath the front windows. Two

younger couples appeared at the door, boisterous and gig-
gly. Newlyweds, I guessed. Behind them, five elderly Asian
men, dressed in identical business suits set off by eye-catching ties with little sayings on them. Our little studio now
resembled the Tube at rush hour. The pudgy blond drifted
into a technical reminiscence over the computer. The tall
drinker pestered Micah to make a deal. One of the new
couples introduced themselves heartily to the women in the
chairs.

"When do we break out the cocktails and canapés?" Cris
grumbled.

I nudged him. "Look."

Mali stood in the doorway, barefoot, eyeing the crowd
as if reconsidering his visit. In his worn jeans and plain
black T-shirt, he seemed surreally tall and dark against
the pale plaster and the roomful of pasty faces. His eyes
picked out Micah, besieged by the would-be buyer. The
five Asians had drawn up in an avid semicircle to observe
the bargaining.

"Why isn't he in rehearsal?" hissed Cris. The actors'
workweek at the Ark was the traditional Tuesday through
Sunday.

"Maybe he's not called today."

"How could he not be? He's in almost every scene."

Mali frowned our way. The faintest motion of his head
demanded explanation. When I shrugged, he rolled his eyes
impatiently. Next thing I knew, he was leaning like a willow
in the wind to murmur to the Texas ladies in the chairs.
His body seemed to lengthen as he bent over his clasped
hands in a continuous curl from head to toe. The ladies
pulled away instinctively, but for all they knew he was just
another denizen of Harmony, one of those eccentric artists
they'd come two thousand miles to stare at like animals in
a zoo. A flash of Mali's brilliant smile won like three surprised
but willing nods. In a moment they were up on their booted
feet, teetering off to urge their husbands toward the door
with hushed, excited explications. Mali moved in on the
newlyweds.

He had the studio cleared in six minutes. The chatter in
the courtyard burbled like water over rocks, the satisfied
sound of tourists who feel they've gotten their money's
worth. The last of the Asians took his departure under
Mali's companionable arm. The tall Tuatuan waved the lit-

tle man off with incomprehensible salutations that made him
and his four cronies smile and bow in delight.

Mali shut the door and leaned against it. "Phew."

Crispin raised a clenched fist. "Man! You are hired!"

Micah was as chagrined as I'd ever seen him. "How the
hell did you manage that?"

Mali blinked. "Is it like this every day?"

"Sundays are the worst," I said.

"This is not right. Such distractions to your work."

"Been much worse since the T.C. raised the price of a
tourist visa," Cris explained. "Now they figure they own us
already."

"What did you say to them?" Micah asked.

Mali relaxed with a modest grin. "Only what they wanted
to hear."

"Please. Enlighten us."

Mali's voice softened to an unctuous purr. "Oh, kindest
madam, I do so deeply regret this disturbance to your recre-
ation, but I have the inestimable high honor to be First Aide
to the Chief Protocol Officer for His Extremely Exalted
Magnificence, the Prince of Cairo. I must ask you all to
leave, so that His Magnificence might grace Master Cervantes with a royal visit."

Cris and I broke up. Jane looked bewildered.

"And how was His Magnificence to get in, with that mob
in the courtyard?" asked Micah dryly.

"Arab princes always use the back door," Mali replied.

"Ah, but there isn't one."

"Ah, but do they know that?"

Micah chuckled at last. "Shameless."

"Effective." Mali smiled with him, then eased away from
the door. "And so. How are you coming with the changes?"

Micah's smile cooled. "Coming along."

"I thought it might be that, when there was no word in
rehearsal."

I hadn't noticed before how tired Micah looked. Not just
tired, wrung out.

Mali stooped under the slanting eave of Micah's corner,
hands shoved into his pockets. He studied Micah's face
rather than the drawings on the board. "I might offer some
assistance."

The only thing Micah hated more than tourists telling him
how to design his shows was hearing it from the actors. But

true admiration can overcome such prejudices. He settled back on his stool. "Please. Tell me your idea."

Mali laughed softly. He picked up the carved bead from Micah's worktable, dusted it off on his pants, and held it between both palms as if warming it. "No idea, Master Cervantes. I am not so bold. An observation merely. It's all in the seeing, isn't it? How you are *seeing* these new things he requires?"

Micah rubbed the bridge of his nose. "Go on."

Mali put the bead back where he'd found it, then pulled up a stray stool, and straddled it, bringing his eyes to level with Micah's. "Seeing. If you are seeing Howie's new demands as objects, you naturally feel they'll be out of place in an environment of ideas. But if you could see them as ideas, well, then their natures could be moulded to your needs."

Micah sighed. "Would that reality were so ephemeral."

"Mine is." The Tuatuan grinned with sudden mischief. "It is . . . Mali-able."

This was either truly profound or total bullshit. I was unsure for which to cast my vote. I looked to Cris. His straight back imitated Mali's, his mask of sophistication was set aside. He was transfixed.

"If you'll permit me," said Micah, somewhat stiffly. "Beyond its philosophical nature, an object's reality is not so, ah, *maliable* when it must exist in three dimensions in an actor's hands."

"Then its nature must be determined before it is real. While it still exists in the realm of ideas."

"Sophistry!" Micah growled. "The problem is having to change the idea in order to accommodate the new object." He turned for proof to the confusion on his drawing board. There, something caught his eye. He fingered the frayed corner of a tissue overlay, then snatched it aside, and balled it up violently. He pressed it between both hands, staring down at the board.

"Aha," said Mali quietly.

"Maybe." Micah was as stubborn and irritable as ever a badger could be. He tore two more layers free of their tape, balled them up with the first, and tossed the crumpled wad onto his worktable. He laid a fresh sheet of tracing paper over his sketch, lowered himself heavily onto his stool, and braced his head in his hands. "Just maybe . . ."

Mali sat back. He nodded two or three times, a motion faintly more than breathing, then glanced across at our astonished faces. He shrugged negligently and ambled over. "The rest of you take the day off."

His audacity made me laugh. "Actually, we already had it off."

"Take it again. Leave the man to his muse."

Delivered ever so lightly, it carried the weight of an order. And we were too in awe to refuse him anything.

"You are a magician," breathed Cris.

"No, that's Sam. I'm Mali."

"He knows that," I said.

"Then he knows more of me than I of him."

I ticked off our names and we shook hands all around.

"So, Jane and Cris and Gwinn: where do you get lunch in this Birdy Cliff?"

Cris and I cheered simultaneously, "The Brim!"

MALI:

He might have been the Pied Piper, the way we trouped after him so willingly. I feared we'd find the courtyard jammed with tourists awaiting a glimpse of His Magnificence of Cairo, but their chatter had long ago faded down the lane.

"Better lock it," Mali advised outside the gate.

"Micah doesn't like that," said Jane before she could stop herself.

Mali studied a red lizard clinging to the stucco. When he touched an inquiring fingertip to its triangular head, it did not bolt. "You want to help him over the hump or not?"

I locked the gate and pocketed my key with ceremony. "Don't know why we don't do it more often."

Cris placed himself at Mali's side. "Boy, you sure got Micah going again!"

Mali trailed a long arm through the foliage overhead, blue-green and glossy as silk. "Easy. He only needed reminding that the solution was already within him. While you all sat about with glum faces as if there wasn't one."

"Glum, huh? I guess we were." Cris attempted to match the Tuatuan's gangling stride.

"Yah. I saw you."

I prevaricated. "Changes are usually real easy for Micah—"

"In a familiar landscape, sure. Harder in foreign territory."

"It's not just the culture, *your* culture," added Cris. "This kind of design is . . . foreign for him, too."

"I know that." Mali halted at the top of a long flight of shallow whitewashed steps overhung with hibiscus, vermilion, and fuchsia against the earth brown of his ringleted hair. With an actor's sixth sense, he consistently placed himself in contrast with his surroundings. "But you—you just stand at the border of the known and wring your hands?" He frowned at us paternally. "Venture out there with him! Support his courage with your minds as well as with your skills!"

"Yessir," mumbled Cris.

"Micah'd never ask us for help with an idea," I said.

"He's too proud to ask us," Jane seconded.

Mali started down the steps. "Are you sure you've been listening?"

We slouched after him, sunk in self-pity, while Mali admired the blooming hedges and nodded cheerfully to passing tourists who looked askance at his worn clothing and his bare feet. Finally Cris asked disconsolately, "You still want that lunch?"

Mali returned a surprised glance, then laughed, and clapped him hard on the back. "No one ever scold you before, bro? Well, I don't live here under this dome, so I don't have to spoil you like you're used to. You give me those anything-you-say dog-eyes, you got to be ready to hear it when it comes, hah?"

Crispin's mouth tightened. "I suppose."

"Of course I want lunch. Who the hell wouldn't want lunch? Maybe some overfed boss man wouldn't want lunch, maybe some fat-cat producer."

Cris could not hold on to his sulk. "Reede Chamberlaine—"

". . . wouldn't want lunch. But me—"

"We—"

"We want lunch," I chimed in, unable to resist the sudden lilt in Mali's step and the jaunty rise of his chin.

"We want lunch!" we chanted as we clattered down the stairs. The tourists stared. Mali tipped an invisible hat. Jane lagged behind, disclaiming us. I averted my eyes, both embarrassed and delighted by our raucous, childlike behavior. If challenged, I'd have pointed to Mali. It's him, I'd say. He's magic. He made me act this way.

By the time we got Mali up the narrow stairs at the Brim, Crispin's spirits had buoyed and Mali had sobered. A young man in evening clothes stopped us at the door to the main salon.

"Excuse us," I said, "we're just heading for the terrace."

"The terrace is full."

Our favorite table was often occupied since Gitanne had redecorated. Her landlord, one of the local galleries, had raised her rent. She'd been obliged to put in a fancy sign at street level to encourage tourists to discover the backwater pleasures of the Brim. Mali hummed a little song to himself as we struggled with the realization that the Brim now had a maître d'.

"We don't mind sitting in the rain," said Cris suddenly.

The young man turned. A surprise shower was emptying the outer terrace. The kid was new to his job. He couldn't think what else to do but let us by.

Mali eased among the crowded tables with quiet dignity. I followed, thinking how right he'd been about Cris. Cris hadn't been scolded much in his life. Not by his parents. Certainly not by Micah, whose idea of scolding was to let slip a dry remark or two and expect the offender to make the adjustment on his own. But this required understanding what you'd done wrong in the first place. Reading Micah was not always as easy as Mali had made it seem.

The rain stopped as we squeezed into a small table along the wrought-iron railing. "That's better," said Mali.

Jane squinted up at the high golden arch of dome. I found myself trying to imagine the heat and the summer stink of the slums Outside. Mali leaned over the rail to study the teeming crafts stalls in the market square. Windows and doors were open along the surrounding gallery arcade. Paintings sat outside on easels or propped against the walls, big lush landscape oils framed in gilt and picturesque rural scenes painted last month of a world that hadn't existed for a century. Below, a street musician doled out Gershwin on the violin. No synth players on the paths of BardClyffe. You had to go over to Amadeus for that.

At the far end of the square, a plastic bubble swelled like a giant blue growth over Francotel's construction site. Fine white dust dried in droplets on the table and dulled the broad leaves in the terrace flowerboxes.

Mali sighed. "Just one big marketplace."

"Oh no," Jane countered softly. "We have all sorts of beautiful homes and museums and parks—"

"Parks you can't use," he retorted.

"Parks you can't sleep in," Cris amended recklessly.

"Yah." Mali turned away from the rail as if something smelled bad. We glanced at each other, uneasy and self-conscious.

Gitanne, with the unerring herd instinct of performers, wheeled over to welcome him with iced cappuccino on the house. Mali covered his sourness with a winning grin, and the two of them went to work charming one another, dropping the names of touring houses and sympathetic restaurants around the world. "Bring the others in soon!" she bade him when she was called away to the kitchen.

Mali slouched back in his chair. He nodded at the bright trellised vines, the white tile, and bleached wooden furniture. "Sure, I will. Not bad here, as the Inside goes."

We grinned foolishly, delighted that our place, our Brim, had won his seal of approval.

"In Fetching," I pointed out, "Gitanne couldn't afford to be so generous to the likes of us."

"Us?" he asked.

"Apprentices."

"Ah." He nodded. "Apprentices and other second-class citizens."

"Fetching," said Cris, "is real high-rent."

"Unlike the rest of Harmony?" Mali laughed his bitter, open laugh. "Under this lid, bro, the very air smells like money."

One of Gitanne's ThirdGen granddaughters popped up to take our orders. Mali disappointed us by choosing a prosaic cheese sandwich and a beer. I'd half hoped he'd exhibit his alienness by demanding something not on the menu.

"So," Cris ventured at last, "tell us about Tuatua."

"What's to tell about a little place so far away?"

I flew eagerly in the face of his gentle mockery. "Everything!"

"We've been studying it." Cris got more boyish by the minute. "Ever since we knew you were coming."

"Then you know all there is to know, young bro."

Cris frowned. This was not going according to his plans and fantasies. Since I couldn't imagine what interest the Eye would have in me, I'd kept my own fantasies safely limited. An opportunity to socialize was an unexpected bonus.

"Please tell us," begged Jane suddenly.

Mali turned his complex stare on her. Even then, he was gentler with Jane than with the rest of us. "What is it you really want to know?"

She went tongue-tied, twisting her hands.

"How do you live without a dome?" I asked, for her sake.

"Is the air really that clean?" asked Cris.

"Wouldn't life be easier with a dome?"

Jane found her voice, barely. "How do you keep Outsiders away?"

When our onslaught had subsided and we hung on his word like eager students, Mali said, "Children, listen to me. The only dome Tuamatutetuamatu needs is the one great dome of the sky."

We gazed at him nervously.

"Yes, I know. Such talk caused riots in Stockholm. But if you've studied up on Tuatua, surely it's no surprise. Can you not imagine that some in this world do not want to be Enclosed?"

Jane shook her head. "You must keep safe from the Outside!"

Mali smiled. "But we are Outside."

"No!" Jane rasped.

"What do you know of the Outside? Firsthand, I mean."

"I was Outside when I came here. The air was poison."

"Plenty people out there breathing it."

"Outsiders."

Mali didn't answer immediately. Then he sighed, as if starting something he must but hadn't wanted to. "The air Outside is neglected. The water is sick, the land diseased. The earth needs our care. Instead we put all our best science magic into carving it up and shutting the best of it away in little boxes."

"Conservation of resources," said Cris.

"Quarantine," said Jane.

Mali frowned. "I just got out of quarantine. Nearly went mad in there. Tuamatutetuamatu lives while we care for her. I would not for my life put her in a box just to make my task easier."

"How do you care for her?" I asked.

"We walk the Stations."

Not one of us was ready to touch that yet.

"The Open Sky people say the domes should come down everywhere," challenged Cris. "Is that what you think?"

"I think we should not use walls to avoid our larger responsibilities."

"We do it to survive," I said.

"Outsiders survive," Mali reiterated.

"I mean, long enough to fulfill that larger responsibility. Outside, you can't do anything but survive."

"And do you also believe that it rains sulfuric acid out there, and every child is born with two heads?"

Jane's stare was glassy. She stopped asking questions.

Mali eased off his accusatory tone and hooked his arms over the back of his chair. "Look, it has to be someone's job to remind us that walls and boxes and lids are not the natural order of things."

"Your job?" Cris ventured.

"My job is the telling of the tale."

"What tale?"

"The tale of the life of Tuamatutetuamatu and how to save it."

"How do the planters fit into your tale?" Cris pursued.

"The ignorant shall learn, the misled shall be redirected."

"But what if they win? The money and guns are on their side."

Mali's lids flicked like bird wings. "Were I gifted with the spirit vision, I would answer you. But my gift is another."

"What is your gift?"

"As I said, the telling of the tale. Proclaiming the true story of the present to those who will create the future."

Cris had a vise grip on the edge of the table. "Like the Conch?"

I noticed Mali's fractional hesitation only because I was listening so hard.

"How do you mean?" he asked softly.

"That it's the revolutionaries who create the future. Your domeless future for Tuatua."

Mali relaxed. "I see your studies taught you something, after all."

Cris flushed. He copied Mali's lean into the table. "Have you ever seen him?"

Mali wagged his head slowly, not quite a negative. "I have been where Latooea has been, I have heard Latooea's voice." His words rolled out hushed and sober, like a litany, like prayer.

Cris wanted more. "But if you've never seen him, how do you know he exists? Maybe he really is only a myth."

"Only a myth?" Mali sat up very straight. "Do you think a myth cannot walk? Or that magic lives bodily like you or me?"

The waitress arrived, her tray piled high with sandwiches of thick brown bread. We drew back from the table, suspended in silence while she doled out the plates. Mali snatched his beer out of her hand and downed a long, cold swallow before setting it down with a grunt of satisfaction.

To Cris he said, "You want what I cannot give you, young Crispin. You want proof. But that's because your only stake in Latooea is a boy's romantic notions."

"No, I—"

"Yah, you are drawn by the legend, not the cause. Were you Tuatuan, your need would create faith enough."

I'd have hung my head. Not Crispin. "Then you don't believe the Conch fled Tuatua? A walking myth wouldn't need to run away."

"Left, they said. Not run away." I fingered the carved bead hidden in my pocket.

Mali read the label on his beer bottle with interest. "If Latooea has retired from the battle, I must believe it was for good reason, to return when it's time to take up the fight again."

"No point in being a martyr," I offered. "If he is a real person, that is."

"Martyrs are useful only when a cause is already lost," he agreed. "But see, here we are, neglecting this fine lunch."

I pulled the necklace out of hiding and offered it to him on my palm. "Please, I wanted to ask—"

The look he gave me was quick and as penetrating as a laser, but he took the bead and leather from me casually enough. "Where did you get this?" He smiled as my story unfolded. "But why keep it hidden away? Will you not wear it?"

"I didn't—I wasn't sure—I thought it might be—"

"Sacred?" Mali held the bead up between two fingers. "This carving honors the twelve Station Clans: each of the twelve figures is a clan totem. Here is my clan: the Rock. You will offend no one by wearing it."

"What did she mean, saying there was power in it?"

He handed the necklace back with a sly and mysterious grin. "Twelve totems is a lot of power." He took another long gulp of beer and a huge bite of his sandwich, then sat back. "Now. Here's my question for you."

He pulled crumpled papers out of his back pocket, spread them flat on the table, and slid them toward us with thumb and forefinger of both hands. I recognized the recent anonymous e-mailings:

CITIZENS OF HARMONY! DANGEROUS RADICALS ARE AMONG US!

Mali cocked his head. "What can you tell me about that?"

While we explained about the Closed Door League, I fastened the bead around my neck, and have never willingly had it off.

CRISPIN'S RESEARCH: FROM THE SONGS OF THE STATION CLANS

The Twelve Stations

Of the World's Twelve Stations, the First is Rock, the Father, companion to Wind, the Mother, and his name is Pirimaturamiram, whom we celebrate in the first moon of the Turning and call on him for his approval.

The Second is Water, Laukulelemelea, the Birth. In the second moon, we give thanks for the gift of life and sing Water's songs to the full circle of her hearing.

The Third is Wind, the Mother, who carries the Birth in her womb and is mother to all creatures. Her moon is the fat third and her name breathes in all of us slow and fast, Moorililil, Moorililil.

The Fourth is Earth, and he is the Death, whose moon is dark but soon shines in a sliver. He is called Nawki, brother to Water, and his songs are both sad and glad, for he is the end and the begining.

The Fifth is Fire, our Uncle the Sun. He stands with Wind his sister to guard the Giving. In the fifth moon we sing of his goodness to woo him from anger, calling him Wurimutonutonu.

The Sixth is Tree, our blessed cousin of a thousand shapes. In the shelter of her leaves we praise her strong magic. She is Mishimishi-Medangin our protector, healer of Moorililil and companion to our kinsman Earth.

The Seventh is Fish, sister to Water, brave provider to our needs, whose color is moon and we name Atiapelu. Her song we sing each time we meet in Water's embrace.

The Eighth is Bird, brother to Wind, who carries our dreams where we cannot. Him we call Timbulele for his music is laughter. . . .

CHANGES:

Cris didn't invite me along that Sunday when he biked back to the studio after dinner to power up the research files. I went to bed early and alone, and told myself I didn't mind.

In the morning, he tossed brightly colored weather maps onto my desk. "It's true, you know. Tuatuan air is better."

Jane looked up from the paper model of *Fire!* "It can't be!"

"Better than some domes. Better than Chicago, I'll bet." I refused the serve. "That wouldn't be hard."

Cris turned back to Jane. "It's a famous mystery phenomenon among climatologists. Seems like everybody's taken a crack at it. They claim a unique dynamic of wind current and temperature creates an anomalous eddy that keeps airborne pollution away from the island."

"Voodoo," Songh intoned.

I touched my bead. "Totem power."

Micah was looking profoundly satisfied that morning as well. The revisions rolled off his table as fast as I could snatch them up. By judicious manipulation of shape and volume, he'd met Howie's need for windows and doors by creating a "zone of reality" pocketed within the larger abstraction.

He let this "reality" enter the world of the play on a long track curving from upstage right to downstage left. The transition into and out of its smaller, more mundane world would be smoothly gradual, a cinematic zoom to close-up detail. Jane and I threw together a paper mock-up for him to look at.

"It'll force those scenes to comment on themselves in a way I'm not happy with," he mused. "But one can only go so far with telling a director what's good for him."

Brave Micah. Still fighting for that revolution in style.

We tracked down Howie Tuesday before rehearsal in the lobby of Theatre Two, where he was supervising the rehang of his *Gift* display material. The new paint did wonders, even with only half the lighting installed. The finished *Gift* model, once I'd brushed the shop dust away, looked spectacular against the creamy satin-white walls. But it was not the best time to be trying to win Howie over.

"Why the hell didn't you send him back?" he ranted.

He meant Mali, of course.

Micah bent over the model to nudge the mocked-up additions into a happier configuration. "Howard, I am not aware of where your actors are meant to be at every moment."

"He was meant to be in rehearsal, where did you think?! There we are working, things are going great, we take a break and poof! he's gone. No one even saw him leave!" Howie halted his arm waving to glare at me. "Hanging out at the Brim? And he's the most responsible of all of them! Jesus H, they show up late, they disappear in the middle! How am I going to get this play ready if my cast thinks rehearsal is something they can take or leave?"

"You needn't question their commitment," returned Micah calmly. "The problem is their somewhat altered sense of priorities."

"Somewhat . . . ! The other day Omea was insisting we all take the afternoon off to visit the farm domes. Christ!"

"Mali came to talk to me about the set. He evidently thought it important."

As important as rehearsal, he meant. But Howie wasn't listening for subtleties. He leaned both palms against a gleaming wall, suddenly weary. "You hear I got hauled into Town Council last night?"

"No. Why?"

"The mayor wanted to know was there any truth to the rumor I'd brought 'dangerous radicals' into Harmony. I said she'd better hope they were something at least that interesting!"

Micah straightened up from the model. "The Eye?"

Howie nodded darkly. "Seems someone's decided our e-mail artist is referring to them. Someone like Cam Brigham, my own goddamn fat-ass chairman, who just happened to mention to Her Honor recently—just a point of information, of course—that our actors belong to the same clans that are the focus of the anti-Enclosure movement on Tuatua. He's got her worrying about the Eye spreading Open Sky propaganda around Harmony. I scoffed, but she comes back with the riot in Stockholm last month. Then Cora Lee from my board demands to know if we'd all forgotten the difference between radicalism and creative thinking. She got so mad she offered that castle of hers for the Eye to stay in."

"At least that solves your housing problem," Micah observed. "The Eye can't help but be happy living at Cora's."

Howie regarded him balefully. "And won't Cam be pleased. His place is right nearby."

It did me good to see them both laughing together, so much that I didn't even resent it when Howie okayed the changes without asking if they'd compromised the design.

"And what does the Eye make of all this?" Micah asked.

"Didn't tell them. Hard enough getting them to concentrate on their work as it is."

Well, guess what? I thought. They're way ahead of you.

But what we'd told Mali about the Closed Door League already needed updating.

We took the model and headed for the shop. The front doors of the theatre stood open, spilling bright sun from the plaza onto the unusually long line at the box office's advance-sales window. Cam Brigham's completed display for *Crossroads* was already arousing tourist interest.

Shop noise assailed us from halfway across the lobby.

"I forgot *Three Sisters* was loading out today!" Micah groaned.

The connecting corridor was an obstacle course of Victorian furniture and storage crates piled high with flowery chinaware and gilt picture frames. The fire door was propped open with an upholstered rocking chair, upon which rested a large silver samovar.

The shop was a madhouse. The south wall loading door lay open to the cavernous stage of Theatre One. A logjam had formed between stage and shop, dead scenery waiting to be stripped and recycled. A load of pipe and canvas had just arrived in the vacuum tube bay. Amid the screech of saws and the snap of the cutting torch, Ruth did one-armed semaphore while bawling instructions through a bullhorn.

"Bring that on through! Stack 'em over there for now!" She lowered the horn when she saw us coming. "No room to breathe in here! Gotta get some of *Crossroads* out on-stage!"

"Sean around?" I yelled, hiking the model box over my head to squeeze between two loaded dollies.

Ruth jabbed a thumb upward, then spun aside to waylay a shop apprentice who was about to toss his load of scrap onto a carefully cut stack of spacing rods.

The dark-suited figure of Max Eider hovered at the paint frame like a guilty conscience. There were four drops hung on the frame, two full-stage eighty-footers and two smaller, at various levels of completion. All were richly detailed and pictorial, lots of foliage in seventeen different greens, amber sunlight, and late rococo architecture. Very painstaking, very time-consuming, but the stuff that painters love to show off with. Twelve painters were lined up along the frame, happily absorbed in their work.

Micah gazed briefly at this bravura display, then shook his head resolutely and led me upstairs.

Sean was a blur of edgy movement around his office. He had on hard hat and work clothes. His jeans sagged low on his hips, bagged out in the rear. Judging from the condition of his hands, he'd been onstage helping with the strike.

"I know, I know! We're a little behind. But don't worry. *Double-Take* loads out of Theatre Two on Thursday. With *Three Sisters* gone, we'll get some of *Crossroads* off the floor, and that'll free up men to start on your show. You gotta trust me on this, Mi. We'll save time building it in the theatre."

One of the younger carpenters strode into the office and handed Sean a sheet of bright blue paper, so blue it drew your eye and made you smile. "Thought you'd like to see what came in with the luan."

"What, through the Tubes?"

"Again."

Sean was not smiling. "What is this shit? Was there more?"

"Four bundles. Already in the recycler."

"Good. That's where this crap belongs." I thought he would show it around and mock it, but he crushed the paper in his fist and a bit of light went out of the room. "Friggin' advertisers won't leave you alone these days!"

But I'd caught the headline over his shoulder, bold-faced across the top of the page: THERE IS A WORLD OUTSIDE. I waited for him to toss it aside and forget about it, so I could retrieve it on the sly. Instead he shoved the wad in his pocket.

Micah was busy projecting helpful concern. "I could ask Rachel for more men."

"Nah," said Sean. "She'll just say we can't afford it."

"Never hurts to try."

Sean snatched up a drawing, tossed it down again, dropped his hard hat on top of it. So early in the day, the clutter was already winning. "They think we're machines down here! They don't understand what they do to me when they schedule things this way! One of these days, real soon . . ." He paced away from his drawing table to glower at the revisions in the model. "You sure Howie's gonna stick with this? We can't waste time building shit, then rebuilding it over again."

"No," said Micah evenly, "only Max Eider rates that."

Sean stared at him, then down at the model. He exhaled

deeply and grinned. "Okay, you smart bastard. Go talk to Rachel. You've always had a way with her."

We trudged back upstairs.

"This is the boring part," remarked Micah with what remained of his good humor.

Rachel was fielding a rush of phone calls, nodding and smiling what sounded like excuses into the screen. Kim met us at the door, looking like the latest summer fashion plate except for the baggy cardigan she'd borrowed to ward off the chill of the air conditioner.

"*He* thinks it's just peachy that Cora Lee's taken the Eye into her house," she grumbled cheerfully. "Some of her neighbors aren't so overjoyed."

"Why's that?" asked Micah.

"Well, you know . . . Cora does live in the high-rent district."

Micah's bemusement was a trifle disingenuous. "Actors have been housed in Lorien before."

"Stars, Micah. They have no objection to stars."

"What are their objections to the Eye?"

Kim laughed. "Hell, they don't know. They've 'heard things.' "

"Dangerous radicals," I reminded him.

"You needn't stand in the doorway," Rachel called, offering us the same smile she had given the vid screen. Rachel gave the same friendly face to everyone, which because it was so restrained, never seemed totally sincere. Micah said it was the most she could allow to seep through the armor a manager must wear, dealing day in and out with people's problems, demands, and complaints and never vocalizing her own. When Rachel and Micah spoke together, it was in the shorthand of two people with no relish for small talk. Retreating to a corner to be inconspicuous, I studied the pale blue walls, empty but for three smartly framed eighteenth-century architectural renderings, maybe even the real thing on loan from Cam Brigham's gallery. I wondered how Rachel managed to fight off the clutter that invaded everyone else's office.

"We've a problem brewing in the shop," said Micah.

Rachel folded her brown hands on the empty deskpad in front of her. "*Crossroads* is much bigger than anyone expected. We're hoping it won't be so late we have to cancel a preview."

"It's not *Crossroads* I'm worried about. What's the chance of putting more men on *The Gift*?"

"Micah, it's a little premature—"

"The show loads in in two weeks and he hasn't even started it."

"Sean assures me that as soon as *Crossroads* is finished—"

"*Crossroads* is a long way from finished. I was just down there."

"Micah, we really don't have—"

"The money. What about Reede Chamberlaine?"

"Our deal does not require him to put any money up front."

"It wouldn't hurt to give him a call."

Rachel resurrected the careful smile. "Well, I think Howie would have to do that."

"Howard has his hands full directing this play. He needs help producing it."

Rachel's lips compressed without moving.

"Rachel, if we schedule shows this tightly"—Micah gently stressed the *we*—"then we've got to be ready to back Sean up when he's in a bind."

"All right. I'll see what I can do. But I'm not promising anything."

I left the Arkadie with a bad taste in my mouth.

Part of a designer's responsibility is supervision. This is bound to involve making sure others are fulfilling their responsibilities, and designers often get accused of throwing their weight around. Micah had total faith in Sean, but he knew a problem when he saw one, one that everyone else was apparently too distracted by the pressure of *Crossroads* to do something about.

It wasn't until we got back to the studio that I recalled we'd forgotten to ask how the magic trick was progressing. My mind was full of that sky-blue paper and its provocative headline: THERE IS A WORLD OUTSIDE.

ULE:

I was back at the shop by the end of the week. Te-Cucularit was due to inspect the props Hickey's crew had built from my prop drawings.

I stopped to check in with Sean. Ruth said he was in conference with Eider and *Crossroads* director Bill Rand. I saw them over in a corner together: Rand, short and balding, more like a rich art dealer than a director, and talking as always; Sean for once quiet, listening as if this natty little man was enlightenment itself.

Being in a shop without Micah *was* enlightening. Some folks had more time for me, some had less. Some saw me as the ear of the prince, others as his spy. In any case, the truth was a little easier to get at. Talking to the right people, I began to realize how far behind *Crossroads* really was.

The crew hadn't had a day off for three weeks. Now they were working evenings as well. Amazingly, they were still willing. They'd passed through the initial stages of exhaustion and were into adrenaline high. Though burnout lurked just around the corner, their bravado made it hard to tell how far.

"Beats me why he hasn't gone and thrown your show at us along with everything else," one of my informants commented as she turned out an elaborate baluster mold in the plastics shop. Her grin was weary but her pace unflagging. Eight dozen newly made balusters lay stacked on the floor by her bench. "That way they'd both be late, but they'd both be done."

"Or neither of 'em would," added the guy working behind her. "The flashy one's gotta come first."

"F'sure. Upstairs'll have his balls if they gotta cancel any of those sold-out previews—"

"Sean won't let it get that far," I said.

My friend shrugged. "Who'da thought he'd let it get this far?"

"It's really unlike him," I said to Hickey as we waited in his multitiered Cage for Te-Cucularit to arrive.

"Sean's protecting his crew. He's tired of burning them out by mid-season." Hickey wore a baseball cap with "HARD HAT" stenciled on it in gold. His black hair stuck out in wings to either side. He tossed a bunch of little cloth bags at me, pointing to the silver coffee service resting atilt on a nearby crate. "Wrap that up for me before somebody steals it."

"Nobody'll steal it here," I protested.

"One of them Tuatuans'll magic it away."

"Hickey . . . !"

"It's happened. 'Course, they always bring it back . . ."

The load-out from *Three Sisters* still clogged his minimal floor space. Lyre-backed ladies' chairs and turned mahogany plant stands awaited a lift to storage in the upper stratosphere of the Cage. Near the door were gathered what seemed to be every artificial bush, tree, and plant Hickey had in stock.

"What's all that for?"

"Greenery for the Barn. Emergency request. The Eye can't stand it in there anymore without."

I eyed the pile dubiously. "But it's all fake."

"What'dya want me to do, cut down Founders' Park?" He dropped into his old wooden office chair, setting off a chorus of creaks. I perched on an upholstered straight chair.

"Don't sit on the props."

I got up and wandered. "So, Hick. Any word on the CDL?"

"Not a peep."

"You saw yesterday's e-mail?"

Hickey brandished a rumpled sheet of printout. " 'CITIZENS OF HARMONY! BEWARE SUBVERSION MASQUERADING AS ART! CLOSE THE DOOR!' "

"I don't think you're taking this very seriously."

"Yeah, I am, but you gotta admit, their rhetoric leaves something to be desired."

"Howie says they're after the Eye."

"Mali and Omea agree."

"Cris says if they're this hard to smoke out, it means they're very well organized."

"Un-hunh. Only pretending to be the lunatic fringe. My friend at Town Square News says it costs a bundle to buy an e-mail widecast if you don't have nonprofit status."

"Who does have it?"

Hickey resettled on a stool-sized crate. "Oh, the charities, educational organizations, most of the theatre and dance companies."

"Like the Arkadie?"

"Sure, we're nonprofit." He gestured at his unkempt desk and his baggy, paint-stained clothes. "Can't you tell?"

"Could your friend at Town Square find out who the CDL 'cast was charged to?"

Hickey smiled at his fingernails. "She's already on it."

"Really? Hickey, that's great!"

"Don't expect the right name'll turn up that easy, though. How 'bout the latest entry?"

"What latest?"

"Probably still sleeping at eight A.M."

I made a threatening face. "In the shower. What was it?"

"Ten unbroken minutes of bright blue screen on the public-access channel, at the end of which was superimposed in pearly white: 'The Color of Open Sky.' "

Bright blue. "No shit."

"Another county heard from. Damn well about time."

"You think there's Open Sky sympathizers in Harmony?" I had a sudden image of the dark earth below us seething with underground movement. They say worms are supposed to be good for the soil.

Hickey stirred in his chair, cropped his feet from the desk, and stretched them thoughtfully in front of him. "You know, Sean thinks it's high time management listened to him about scheduling. Could be he's chosen *The Gift* to teach them a lesson."

I settled down on a box labeled LACE CURTAINS, ANTI-MACASSARS. I'd have preferred to pursue that ten minutes of blue screen, but Hickey's rhythm was more indirect. "Why *The Gift*? *Crossroads* is the real backbreaker."

Hickey's shrug was more like a shudder. "The main stage gets priority? Sean wants to pressure the office but not the subscribers? Maybe he just figures Micah will understand."

"I can't believe Sean would take advantage of a friendship like that."

"Between you and me, Sean doesn't think our audience will take too well to *The Gift*. It's not about them, he says."

"Neither is *Crossroads*."

"Ah, but they'd like it to be."

I packed the silver into its bags and the bags into a crate, then wandered over to check out the newly built *Gift* props, laid out for inspection on Hickey's workbench, the only remaining clear space. I found them properly and satisfyingly exotic: the round Gorrehma, squat as a wooden toadstool, the hollow, resonant box of the Duli, and the strange Burinda, like a paddle made of tree bark.

"Nice work, Hick."

The curves were fluid and smooth, the joints tight. The broad-grained, colorful woods shone richly even in an unfinished state. The Matta was a towering pile of shimmering greens. I fingered its silky, dense weave. Lightweight, but would drape like a dream. "Mmmm. Great fabric. A shame to put paint all over it." I picked up one of the sticklike Puleales. The others were longer, shorter, fatter. The purpose of none of them was evident.

"They get feathers and a leather cross-wrap, but Cu'll want to do his taboo number on them first."

"So *this* is the Heeckee's lair!"

A dark troll face peered around the doorframe. Gray hair spiked out in all directions from a white-fanged maw. Hickey shrank into himself, then gave up an embarrassed snort. Te-Cucularit brushed past the leering apparition, glancing his disapproval, and stalked to the workbench.

"No feel for cheap humor," the troll sighed. He tossed his string mop and ivory chopsticks into a handy packing box, then favored his somber companion with a tolerant sneer and capered up to slam Hickey familiarly on the shoulder. The little dance man wore his usual ragged cutoffs and multicolored braided cap. His body was knotted and veined like an old prune, but it improvised motion as if it were a jazz riff, not always melodious or even in tune but in rhythm with the moment, part commentary, part counterpoint to the more regimented music of speech.

"Oh, Heeckee, I heard her today, singing those woman's chants." He squeezed his butt onto Hickey's crate, shoving the bigger man sideways until Hickey stuck out a foot to keep from toppling off.

"The Mule has arrived," Hickey laughed.

"The very same! No kidding, Hick, I heard her. Watch out, boy. Women's magic is strong stuff."

Hickey glanced at me sidelong. "Come on, Ule—"

"Don't blame me if she takes you by surprise!" No-Mulelatu planted his hands on his knobby dark knees and grinned at me. "Now who's this?"

Hickey mumbled an introduction.

Ule bounded off the crate and straight at me. When I recoiled from this whirlwind of public nakedness and energy, he guffawed hugely and snatched up my hand to bend over it with a courtier's smooth flourish. "My lady," he murmured.

Speechless, I giggled.

At the workbench, Te-Cucularit set down his well-worn notebook and cleared his throat. The sharp crease of his tan slacks and the tight roll of his sleeves were softened only by feet as shoeless as Ule's. Hickey levered himself off his crate and slouched over to join him, head cocked at an angle of listening and respect.

Ule settled more comfortably onto the crate and threw me a long, slow wink. "Ver-ree serious biz-ness here, y'know?" His legs did not quite reach the floor.

I made getting-up motions. "I should really—"

He slapped at my knees, urging me down. "Take a break! Keep me company. I'm so easily bored."

I sat. Ule kicked his legs idly against the crate, then reached out, and flicked the bead at my throat. "Good you decided to wear it."

Word gets around with these guys, I noted, stroking the leather braid. "Isn't it an interesting coincidence?"

Ule laughed. "Is that what you think?"

"Well, it was three whole years ago . . ."

"The blink of an eye. Time is not yesterday and tomorrow to everyone, you know."

"No, I guess not." That really left me casting about for conversation. "So how's your new housing?"

I'd seen Cora Lee's famous mansion during a spectacular opening-night party to which even the apprentices had been invited, that being Cora's style. Cora Lee was Howie's wealthiest board member, as well as one of Lorien's two Town Council members. She was close with certain information about her past, plus it was rumored she owned her own private hover. She lived in a true fairy castle, dressed stone and pointed turrets, leaded windows and tapestried great hall, at least twelve bedrooms and a spectacular skylit studio in the top of a tower for Cora's large and very popular paintings. All this in half scale, which brought the great-hall doors down to normal size and miniaturized the castellated architecture's more militaristic details into the sweet and quaint. And no automated home services. No hookup to the Town network. No vid. Cora was a first-class eccentric.

"Not bad for Insider digs." The gnome's mouth twisted faintly and his nostrils flared as if testing the wind. "A real lawn, nice grove of trees at the back." He made a bored, regretful face. "We'll manage."

I detected mockery but couldn't tell if I was its target or merely its audience. "Sounds like you'd prefer to be Outside."

He cackled merrily. "You domers."

"What do you mean?"

"You make it sound crazy, like some kind of aberration. You ever been underwater, ladykins? For a time, I mean. Breathing through a tube, the only natural sounds you hear your own?"

What on earth was he talking about?

"That's what it's like Inside, when you're used to the open. You ever seen the sun rise? For real, not on some damn vid box. Ever seen the thunderclouds, Moorililil's messengers, glower along the horizon or crowd up against the mountains, waiting to dump their piss and rage all over you?"

"We have weather here. We have—"

"Pah! An obedient, programmed air current. You call that wind? That's man's magic, not the world's."

"Man's magic saved the world."

Ule sat back and tilted his head. "My, my, ladykins, perhaps you are stupider than you look. Let me try it out in domer words: like the human body, the world is a coherent system. If your body falls sick, you don't go separating the parts of it and walling them off from each other. Now, man's medicine is certainly more evolved than man's politics. There the practice is to treat the whole body, taking all its complexity and interrelatedness into account."

His tone riled me. "The domes are the only coherent system now. The Outside is . . ."

"So much leftover trash?"

"No, chaos."

"Living creatures are a system, too. All of us. Think about it, ladykins." He pursed his lips, nodding sagely. "Think about how much of your human 'body' has been left outside the walls. How long do you think you can manage to go on without it?"

I was outmatched. No-Mulelatu had passion and eloquence on his side. I had only my childhood assumptions, never deeply questioned. I glanced again at Hickey and Te-Cucularit. "I really must . . ."

Ule chuckled and let me go.

At the workbench, the tall Tuatuan cradled the unfinished Gorrehma in the crook of his arm. His long-fingered hands stroked its satiny curves with an appreciation nearing reverence. He was nodding gently, his already perfect face suffused with the surprising grace of an inward smile, rarely seen in life but often painted on the faces of Renaissance madonnas.

The soft smile vanished as I moved into view. Cu's questing fingers found a flaw in the working of the wood.

"This will need further attention before you paint it," he said. He set the Gorrehma aside and moved on to examine the Burinda.

Hickey and I exchanged glances.

"*You* ask him," I whispered.

Hickey's posture shifted from respect to submission. "I thought you were going to do all the painting yourselves?"

Cu nodded. "We had intended to."

"I mean," pressed Hickey, "I thought we weren't allowed."

"This we can allow. I will show you how to do it in the way that will properly honor the Ancestors."

"I hadn't really planned—" Hickey began.

Behind us, Ule said, "What Cu means is, we just can't find the time to do it now, so you'll have to do it for us."

Te-Cucularit glowered, Hickey frowned.

"And of course," Ule added, "it must be done."

Cu flipped open his notebook. "The drawings on the wood tell the secret history of the world." He painstakingly separated several leaves from their binding, each filled with the same elaborate designs that decorated the cover.

"This is the surface." He pointed to the background cross-hatching. Small patches of fine parallel lines jostled together into a crazy quilt of opposing directions, like herringbone gone awry. "It means the world. Into the world enter the things that live in the world. Here are some that you can use without . . . prejudice." He spread the loose pages across the bench, indicating symbolic representations of animals and plants worked into pauses in the background. "Allow no snakes to enter your tale, or lizards. Birds and fish are very neutral. If you tell an incorrect tale about them in your ignorance, it will not be grave."

Hickey traced a graceful almond-shaped eye set inside a border of leaves. "This one's nice."

"You may not use it. That is ours. I'll add it later if I think it right." Cu sent a chill flicker of smile to Ule on his crate. "What if you write us into your tale where we don't belong?"

"Right," said Hickey. "Don't want to do that."

"Damn right you don't."

Hickey glanced up. "Hey, Sam."

The company's official magic man strolled in, hands shoved into the pockets of a dark brown coverall. With that and his solid, unremarkable looks, he might have been a visiting repairman.

"When Howie asks," he remarked amiably, "I'll just say it was you kept the boys so late."

"Sure, sure." Hickey nodded. "Just one more thing for him to blame me for."

Sam surveyed the Cage with a methodical sweep. "Holding a rummage sale?" When his intent gaze reached my heading on his inner compass, he nodded and offered a bland if pleasant smile. His eyes took in my necklace. It seemed to amuse him. "Gwinn Rhys, isn't it?"

We shook hands. His voice had a light, non-actorish timbre and the remnants of an Aussie accent. As our hands parted, his wrist flicked and the same palm that had pressed empty against mine mere seconds before came up holding a single white rose, which he presented to me with a diffident bow.

"Always the gentleman," snickered Hickey.

At my elbow, Ule advised, "You want to watch out for Sam, now. A real lady-killer, he is."

"I'm sure." I stared at the rose in my hand, fresh, fragrant, and real even to the thorns. Only a moment ago, I had wondered how this very ordinary man made his way in company with the Eye's beauty and eccentricity.

Hickey laughed. "Just don't ask him how he did it."

"Wouldn't dream of it."

Sam let the banter flow around him. "They're waiting on us, Preacher."

Te-Cucularit grunted. He snapped his book shut and stuck it briskly under his arm as if hurrying off to rehearsal had been his idea all along. "I will come now and then to see the tales you are telling." He sent Ule an imperious jerk of his head. The little choreographer bounced off the crate with a bow to Hickey, a mad grin and a "my lady" to me, then capered out after the young archivist like the court jester trailing the prince.

"Bye-bye." Sam winked at me and followed at a more leisurely pace.

I turned to Hickey. "Preacher?"

"That's what Sam calls him. No wonder. That Cu has a real rod up his ass." Then he gave me his most woebegone face. "So how busy is Micah really? Looks like I could use some major help down here."

THE SURVIVAL GAME:

The Survival Game took on a new edge, not only because of Bela. After his disappearance, we began to hear of others who'd been expected to make the cut and didn't. The custom had been not to talk about the failures, but now the rumor mill was keeping track.

In the late Friday dusk, our usual group hunkered down at the Brimhaven, still Rumor Central for the BardClyffe apprentices. The air was motionless and heavy, the weather computer's idea of deep summer in Vermont. Our cheer had been already dampened when we were asked to move to a small table to make room for a party of tourists. Asked to move, in *our* Brim. I was scandalized.

It was Yolanda's turn at the Game. She was a strong, serious girl apprenticed to a ceramicist a few streets away from Micah's. Her big hands could do remarkably delicate work. Cris had been chatting her up a lot lately, but I noticed she wasn't chatting back. For some reason she considered me a role model. She looked to me when she said, "I keep a pack under my bed now, with everything I'll need, so I can grab it quick if Security comes for me."

"Do we know they'd let you take it?" I glanced to Cris for a rules check.

"We don't know they wouldn't."

Yolanda continued. "A complete change of warm clothing, basic medicines I've cadged from the dispensary, matches, knives, you know."

"What about food?" I asked.

"You better bring fishhooks," spoke up little Ivan, a first-year apprentice in the same studio as Yolanda. We knew he must be extraordinary to have qualified so young, but that didn't keep him from being a pain in the ass. He tagged after Yolanda mercilessly.

"What's fishhooks?" asked Jane, who had lately begun to see the practical applications of this Game she hated so much.

"To get a fish, you know, a wild one," the boy explained.

"I suppose there might be fish Out There somewhere," I mused.

"Probably nothing you'd recognize as one," said Cris.

"I saw in an old vid once how travelers used some pills to purify drinking water," Yolanda went on.

"No, you just boil it!" insisted the boy, who didn't understand yet that keeping to the proper sequence of turns was part of the seriousness of the Game. "And you gotta take seeds!"

"Cram it, Ivan," said Yolanda.

"Seeds wouldn't be a bad idea," noted Cris. "Out There, healthy germ stock could be bartered for more immediate needs. That's the key, of course—to bring stuff you can trade."

Yolanda slouched into her chair. "You guys aren't letting me finish."

"Yerevan Dome lets people back anyway," little Ivan admitted guilelessly. "They need people with training."

"That's what they tell you when you leave." Yolanda dug around in her coverall, hoping to scare up enough change for another beer.

Jane shot Ivan a rankly envious look. "Do they ever take people who aren't born there?"

"Ssssh!" Yolanda nudged me hard and pointed.

In the mirrored main salon, where the light seemed harsher than it used to, Mark eased toward us through the crowd. Gitanne had added several tables and cut-glass crystals on all the old brass chandeliers. Mark eyed them dubiously as he passed.

"Now I'll tell what I'd do!"

"Not now, Ivan," Yolanda advised.

Under the stuccoed terrace arches, Mark tried to greet Gitanne as she raced past him to usher in new arrivals. Evenings had been quiet at the Brim until Late Closing, a recently instituted policy that kept the Gates open until nine o'clock Fridays. I was amazed how noisy the place could get, even out here on the open terrace.

"First time I've seen him out and about after work," I said, "You know, since—"

"Look who's with him," said Cris. Songh trailed Mark by half a pace, wearing the same intent face.

"What's he doing here?" Yolanda demanded.

"Free country," I returned lightly.

"I know, you've gotta work with him. But this is the Brim!"

Cris looked around at the sea of bright, fashionable clothing, at the tables laden with unfinished food, at the aisles choked with bulging shopping bags. "What's a SecondGen or two compared to all these interlopers?"

Mark gave us a self-possessed smile and pulled up a chair next to me. "How's the Game going?"

Nobody said anything.

"Don't stop on my account. I can take it. We're all going to need the practice."

"We were just finishing," I said.

He looked brushed and rested, with a briskness I'd never seen in him before. "In that case, I've put together a little research that might interest everybody."

Yolanda eyed Songh darkly.

"Songh's okay," I said, looking at him hard. "You won't blab, will you, Songh?"

His back straightened in reply.

"Songh's our mole," said Cris.

Mark spread a length of printout flat among the empties and condensation rings. "Figures from the Admin's files. Just to confirm what we already know, I looked at the twenty years preceding. The yearly average of new apprentice admissions was fifteen hundred. Of each class, twelve hundred made the first cut, five hundred the second, an average of thirty-three percent. Approximately three hundred and fifty of those could expect to gain citizenship. Generally, forty to fifty citizenships were granted per year." He bracketed the final set of numbers with his hands. "Now here's the bad news: in the last ten months, no citizenships have been granted and renewals at all levels are down to twenty percent." He leaned back, arms folded across his chest. His thick blond hair draped a diagonal veil across his eyes. "So?"

I gazed at the printout as if it were a death warrant, which in effect it was. Even Jane sat quietly, having passed her hysterical-in-public stage. How many weepy and sleepless nights she endured I could only guess from the depth of the hollows under her eyes.

"No wonder Micah's been pushing us so hard to find work outside the studio," I murmured.

"The sooner we make ourselves indispensable to some organization, the better," Cris agreed.

Mark flicked his hair back impatiently. "This job, that job, forget it. Look at the numbers! No citizenships. It's not going to matter how good any of us are!"

"You said there were still renewals," Cris objected. "They're just raising the review standards, in response to population pressures. We'll have to work extra hard, but the best of us will make it through. Survival of the fittest— and we are the fittest."

Mark did not leap to Bela's defense. "Look at the numbers."

"Okay, so they're playing with the numbers!" Cris stood up, leaning excitably over the table. Like all of us, he was off the usual Brim rhythm. What was once healthy debate sounded shrill with all these tourists about. "They can't cancel the program completely—it's written into the constitution. It's the law!"

"Harmony needs us," I insisted more quietly.

"Why should it need us," Mark replied silkily, inclining his head toward Songh, "when it's got so many of him?"

Crispin's fists clenched. "Yeah? Well, look at him! Christ, I've been trying to pump some guts into him for half a year! Harmony survives by selling its art, the art we will produce! If we go, you think he's prepared to fill the gap?"

Songh bunched up his face to riposte.

"Such sound, such fury!" Dark hands descended on Crispin's shoulders. "What could excite such youthful fire, O my brothers?"

Cris dropped like a stone into his chair.

"I did promise I would bring my friends," Mali smiled. Pen and Tua were behind him and Sam following, as Gitanne shooed them all in the direction of our far corner. She did not look pleased with their bare feet or Pen's tank top in her establishment. Mark and I shoved over to make room.

Mali took the chair between me and Mark. Tua smiled at Cris and slipped in next to him. Pen squeezed in between Jane and Yolanda, turned his mirrorshades on Yolanda's dark braids and voluptuous shape, and his back on Jane. Yolanda glanced my way and I smiled back reassuringly. Sam eyed the remaining space skeptically and wandered off looking for a waitress.

Mali offered a shrug and an expectant grin. "So what's up? We felt this energy surge all the way over in Fetching!"

Mark pinched a corner of his printout and drew it away casually. Mali reached, pinned the paper under his palm. "Is this the bone of contention?"

"It's, ah . . ." Mark tugged at it faintly.

"Oh, let me pry!" Mali was suddenly so much the gossipy old woman that I laughed out loud.

"Let him," said Cris.

Mali took up the paper for study. Sam returned to the table with a giggling waitress. He'd lured her away from a table full of strapping young Germans by making daisies appear in her cleavage. I decided my white rose was the more dignified tribute.

"Two double vodkas," said Pen immediately.

"One single," Sam advised. Pen's eyes glittered unnaturally. I was sure he'd already put a healthy dose of something down his throat or into his lungs before arriving at the Brim. He glowered at Sam, then smoothed back his glossy black hair and turned away to lecture Yolanda about the last adventure holo he'd starred in.

Sam saw me watching them. "A rough day in rehearsal," he said.

In the late amber light, his eyes were very blue. There was a toughness about him I hadn't noticed earlier, a weathering you don't see in domers, except among the really dedicated OutCare workers. Sam's skin was not that biscuit color naturally, it was tanned by the sun. The Outsider sun of Tuatua. He was probably younger than I'd thought, thirty-five at most. Before I could ask why rehearsal had been so bad, he gave an odd little salute and wandered off again to nose around the terrace by himself.

"You ever see *Mission to the Wasteland*?" Pen asked Yolanda.

"No . . ."

"I was in that. How about *Down the Tubes*?"

Tua had cornered Cris with a detailed complaint about the rehearsal. She declaimed with the same passion and gravity as one might about the end of the world. Her perfect teeth flashed, her brown hands flew about like birds to the music of her voice. Cris was mesmerized. Even I had to admit she was distractingly lovely.

When the drinks arrived, Mali laid the printout down, tapping it pensively with his forefinger. "*No* citizenships?"

"Not for ten months. It's unprecedented."

"Who determines these things?"

"The Apprentice Administration and their citizen advisers."

"But who are they?"

We looked at each other. I hadn't wondered about actual names.

Mali sipped his beer, blotted his lip delicately on the back of his hand. "So what's the plan?"

"Plan?" Jane echoed.

"Not much we can do," shrugged Mark. "Just be ready."

Mali shook his head. "My bros, there is always something you can do."

"We can work like hell," I offered. I frowned at Cris across the table. He should be listening to this, not to the sultry siren.

Pen bolted his vodka, glanced around for Sam, then snagged a passing waiter to order a double. His arm eased around the back of Yolanda's chair. "So I told the director I always do my own stunts . . ."

"I mean in addition to working," said Mali.

Mark folded his arms, an uncharacteristic show-me gesture.

"But you've begun already." Mali fluttered the printout. "Fact-finding is the first step. Gathering for purposes of discussion is the next. What turns talk into action is organization."

When we returned him dumb stares, he chewed his lip thoughtfully. "I see. The concept is an alien one."

"I don't think you understand, sir," said Mark. "Our contract pledges us to abide by the rules of Harmony."

"Are there rules against apprentices organizing?"

"I don't know."

"Be thorough, bro, be thorough."

"I'm sure there are rules," said Jane. "There are always rules."

"You have no social clubs, no sporting teams?"

"Oh, that kind of organizing . . ." I stopped, as what he was suggesting finally sunk in. No small talk for Mali. He just plunged right in. "Lots of SecondGen teams. None for apprentices."

"Organizing is anytime people get together in greater numbers than you can fit around a table, to talk about problems they share." Mali nodded patiently. "This paper implies the rules are being changed. After the fact. Seems to me that voids the contract and gives you the right to action."

"Action . . ." Jane murmured fearfully.

"Apprentices don't really have rights in Harmony," I said.

"Basic human rights," said Mali.

"What's it to you?" Mark asked suddenly.

"Ah." Mali studied him. "Ungrateful as well as unimaginative."

"Mark . . ." I chided.

"No, I mean, why should you care about apprentice problems?"

The Tuatuan turned on Mark his most intense and dignified regard. "Bro, I must always care, or lose myself in passive reflection. My father is the Rock."

In our puzzled and uneasy silence, Pen's background patter rose toward oration. "And then the fuckin' idiot couldn't even shoot the scene 'til I showed him how to do it!"

Yolanda flicked a pleading glance at me as Pen drew her close. A couple at the next table stared in disapproval. Sam, who had seemed to be acting as Pen's keeper, had disappeared. Even Tua was distracted enough from her tale of woe to reach across Cris and pat Pen warningly on the arm.

"I'm talking," Pen growled.

"I know you are," Tua replied. "So does everyone in the restaurant."

"Fuck off." Pen threw Tua's hand aside. Yolanda gave a soft shriek and pulled away from his encircling arm. Her chair overbalanced and tumbled her backward.

Mali sprang to his feet. Sam appeared out of nowhere. Pen got off one drunken backhand swipe at Tua before Sam pinned him in a bear hug. Glasses shattered. Silverware clattered to the floor. Tua ducked, then fell gracefully into Crispin's arms. He caught his breath as she pressed herself against him, weeping prettily.

Pen writhed in Sam's grip and spat incomprehensible invective at Tua, at Sam, at the table in general. Diners nearby set down their forks and readied themselves for escape. Several waitresses headed for the kitchen. Mali came around the table and murmured to Pen in the strung-out, rolling syllables of their native tongue, words like the movement of oceans, more suitable to reason than to rage.

Pen snarled and lashed out with his feet. "I don't have to take this from a fuckin' second son!"

Mali's hand moved so fast I never saw it, only heard the single resounding crack that shocked the room and Pen into silence. The calls of the vendors in the square below were suddenly very loud. Somewhere on the terrace, a woman moaned. A man hushed her impatiently. Gitanne halted under the arches, watching.

Mali's anger was forbidding, first blowing up like a windstorm, now so obviously held under tight restraint. As Pen sagged slack-jawed against his chest, Sam eyed Mali with wary concern.

Mali took up what was left of the double vodka and poured it out at Pen's feet. "The Second is Only, now, in case you'd forgotten." He turned away and dropped into his seat, slouching low, letting the tension run out of his long, bony body with a ragged sigh.

Sam righted a toppled chair with a deft hook of his ankle. He lowered Pen into it, then stayed behind him, massaging his shoulders companionably. The cowed bantam cock sat still and stared at the table.

"Like I said," Sam remarked blandly, "a bad day at rehearsal." He glanced at Mali, gave Pen a final pat, then produced a clownish grin and a handful of colored glass balls, delicate and glittery as soap bubbles. Humming a very silly tune, he juggled them among the nearby tables, passing out self-deprecatory jokes and apologies.

Mali laughed softly. The rest of us took this as a sign that the worst was over. Except Yolanda, who chugged the rest of the beer I'd bought her and jogged Ivan's elbow.

"Gotta go," she excused, "before they close the mess hall on me."

Ivan trailed after her with sorry backward glances.

"Mark," I murmured, "where's Songh?"

"Here . . ." Songh was actually under the table. "You're all going to laugh at me."

Mali grinned. "That's right, little bro. Come on up here and face it."

"Yes, sir." Songh crawled out and into his chair.

"That's better." Mali stopped laughing and none of us dared do otherwise.

Sam pocketed his trinkets, then rescued Yolanda's chair, and joined us at the table. He caught the eye of his friendly waitress and signaled another round. Chatter on the terrace and in the main salon returned slowly to normal, but our own conversation lagged.

Finally I asked, "What was the problem at rehearsal today?"

Tua straightened out of her protector's arms as Cris tried very hard to make his sudden interest look professional. "This director is so rigid!"

Cris and I gave the same astonished laugh. "Howie??"

"He's always worrying about the logic of the literal moment. Life isn't literal! Dreams happen, irrelevant thoughts, visions!"

"Excuse," Gitanne interrupted. "May I sit for a moment?"

Sam eased out of his chair and held it for her. "*Permettez-moi . . .*"

"Ah!" Gi returned a coquettish smile. "*Merci!*"

Mali slipped on graciousness like a glove. Tua and Sam made agreeing noises while the bad rehearsal story was trotted out and aired once again. Pen sulked in silence like a forgotten child.

"I know, the pressures," nodded Gitanne. "My daughters are putting in their own café at Images, so the dancers will have a place to unwind. The public restaurants have been so busy lately!"

I was not liking the sound of this.

"You must come again when we aren't so crowded. But right now I need from you a very great favor." She paused in confusion as Mali unfurled the full brilliance of his smile. "One of my customers has threatened to report me if I serve this table another round."

"Right," agreed Sam. "Fruit juice all around."

Gitanne took a breath. "Actually, under the circumstances . . ."

Cris was confident he understood the situation. "One more beer for the regulars and off we go."

She smiled at Crispin sadly. "No, I'm afraid not."

"Are you asking us to leave, Gi?" My voice sounded very small to me.

"I'm afraid I must. But don't worry, I won't say anything."

"Anything to who?" Sam asked quietly.

Gitanne's hands strayed to her bun, which was immaculate and needed no tending. "Please, you must understand . . ."

"I'm sure we will," said Mali.

She focused on him entirely, murmuring secretively as if no one else was at the table. "Forgive if I speak too boldly, but we are colleagues, no? It is best for these children if they are not seen socializing with your company. You will go on, tour the world, go home, but their future is still being determined."

"Ah, yes," said Mali, "I do understand."

"Oh, *cheri*, I knew you would!" Impulsively she leaned over and kissed his cheek, then smiled broadly for the benefit of her surrounding customers. "Please, you will all be my guests."

When she'd fled as gracefully as she could, Sam remarked, "Well, the cold box at Cora's is well stocked . . ."

Mali was watching us.

Cris was the first to get angry. "I don't believe this!"

"Anyone here ashamed of the company they keep?" demanded Sam.

Mali silenced him with a glance. "You are all welcome to join us."

"I think we will," replied Mark slowly.

Songh nudged him. "I . . ."

"I know." Mark appealed to Mali. "He'd better go, or his parents'll never let him out of the house again."

Jane got up with him. "I have so much work to do . . ."

Mali waited until they'd left, then rose, drawing Mark and me up on either side of him. "This party will repair to Cora Lee's. The smell of fear in here's too strong to breathe."

"Domer sonsabitches!" Pen muttered.

And there we were again, with Mark our latest recruit, marching after our own Pied Piper through the darkening streets of BardClyffe Market, along the restaurant lanes ringing with the chime of laughter and glassware, past the busy galleries lit with neon and laser fire, beneath the Chinese lanterns of the crafts stalls open late. The Tube was still crowded, but the oddness of our party and the collective grimness of our faces encouraged tourist and citizen alike to give us a wide berth.

Cora Lee's fairy castle was set in a wooded glade cleverly shared with several other mansions in a way that made it appear to be all her own. It was dark under the trees, though the path was studded with ground lights. Cora's entrance was a trefoil Gothic arch set in a pale stone wall, grilled with frothy metalwork from the same workshop as Harmony's own Gates. Beyond, a miniature drawbridge spanned a moat of black water dotted with water lilies.

Mali stopped within the soft light from a round filigree lantern hung in the arch. He dug in his jeans pockets for the key, then noticed the gate was ajar. "Didn't Moussa close this when we left this morning? Cora must be home early."

Sam did an odd thing. He lunged forward and caught Mali's wrist as he reached for the iron grille. He stepped between Mali and the gate and herded us back to the path among the trees. His easy jocularity had vanished. "Sit tight and don't move."

"Sam, it can't be," Mali said. "Not here."

"You think trouble doesn't travel? You want to take the chance?" Sam hunkered down and studied the gate. "Wish I had my damn bag of tricks."

"Thought you never got caught without it," muttered Pen, looking sober for the first time since he'd walked into the Brim.

"That's only what it says on my resumé."

"What is it?" demanded Cris. "What's the matter?"

"He thinks the gate's been wired," Mark whispered.

"Wired?" I asked.

"Wow," Cris murmured.

Mark joined Sam in his crouch. "This is, um, a smart-gate. There's a telltale on it, you know."

"No, I didn't. Where?"

"You usually hide them behind a bush somewhere." Mark moved forward and searched carefully among the thick vines climbing the wall. "Here it is—looks brand-new. It says the gate's clean."

Sam went to see for himself. A tiny box the color of the surrounding stone housed a panel of LEDs. "I'll be damned." He brushed the ivy back in place. "A little easy to find, though."

"Only if you know what to look for," said Mark. "Don't want the consumer losing his own marker. It's a popular brand, 'cause you can have the gate material shaped to your own design, so it doesn't look smart. You can get remotes if you don't want to get too close."

Sam studied him. "Where'd you get to be such an expert?"

Mark shrugged diffidently. "A man I knew at home had one."

"Just some guy?" Mali urged. When he turned those grave, trust-me eyes on you, it was hard to resist.

"My, um, my father."

Mali laughed mirthlessly. "A rich man's son!"

I was amazed that after three years I still hadn't known this. With Crispin you could tell right away, and if you missed it, he'd let you know.

"Get to know this kid," Sam advised. "He could prove useful."

"He already has."

"Let's find out." Sam was at the gate and through it before anyone could stop him. Several steps onto the draw-bridge, he halted in a stage magician's presentation twirl. I pictured the long black satin cape swirling behind him. "So far, so good," he called.

Mark paced Mali step for step. "Did you guys get to be this careful on Tuatua?"

"There's a war on," snapped Pen. "Maybe you heard."

Mali draped an arm across Mark's shoulder. "The planters never mind there being one or two less Station Clansmen around."

"Our news services still call it a 'domestic conflict,' " said Cris. "They don't say anything about killing."

"Would you let them if you controlled the media?" said Pen.

"Then forget the media. I'm the best source of real news about Tuatua around here."

"That so?" Pen had dismissed him already.

"If I can't coax it out of the files, nobody can."

Tua caught up with him. "Programmer?"

"Among other things."

She slipped her arm through his. "Me, too. What hardware?"

Cris reeled off numbers and letters.

"Can I come play on it sometime?"

"I'm glad there are no wars in Harmony," I murmured, mostly to myself, figuring no one was listening.

But Mali was listening. "There are always wars. Some just lie quiet longer than others."

At the far end of the drawbridge, a long, barrel-vaulted passage hung with tapestries mounted a shallow flight of stone stairs. Sam moved ahead, signaling us to stay back. On the top step, he stopped abruptly. "Damn!"

We rushed the steps two at a time. Sam held us at the doorway, then eased into the room.

Cora Lee's beautiful great hall had been trashed. Her fine leather furniture was overturned, cushions tossed aside. The precious tapestries woven from her own designs had been torn off the walls. The giant vases of flowers, Cora's pride and joy, were tipped and scattered across the priceless Oriental rugs. A huge oil mural, her own work, hung askew over the great stone fireplace.

"Cora?" Sam opened the door to the music room, shut it, and continued his circuit of the room. "Everything's all right in there. Cora? You here? I hope she didn't surprise them at it."

"They wouldn't . . ." worried Tua.

Mali called louder. *"Cora?"*

Pen said, "I think she had an OutCare meeting tonight."

Cris waded though the confusion to the fireplace. A sheet

of paper was pinned to the wooden slab of mantel with a nondescript pocketknife.

"Don't . . ." called Sam from across the room.

". . . touch it. I know." Cris leaned in to read the scrawled writing. "Just more stuff about subversives and dangerous radicals. 'Anarchy stalks the streets of Harmony.' Wait, listen to this . . . 'How long will we allow it? We have *eyes* enough of our own!' "

The Tuatuans converged on him as a group.

"There's more . . . wow!"

I shoved a chair out of the way to get to him.

Cris read: " 'The fugitive felon hides among his sympathizers! Close the Door on the Conch!' "

Mark's gasp beside me was as quick and silent as my own.

Cris straightened. He gazed at the actors breathlessly. "Are you guys hiding the Conch?"

Mali reached languidly for the paper and jerked it free of the knife blade. He scanned it, passed it aside to Sam. "Do you believe everything you read, young brother?"

"No, I—"

"If he does," said Sam, "imagine how readily the rest of Harmony will believe it."

Tua took the paper from Sam. "The next e-mail widecast."

"The truth won't matter one way or the other," said Mark.

"It rarely does," Mali replied. "Well, my bros, let's think. Is the purpose of all this to scare us into leaving or Cora Lee into evicting us? Should we clean it up or make it public?"

"Clean it up, of course," said Cora Lee from the entry stairs.

"Cora, thank the good powers!" Mali spread his arms in welcome.

"Were you worried, my Mali? I'm flattered." Cora bustled in, a plump, immaculate Asian woman in close-cut green silk. A diamond-studded comb sparkled in her tightly bound black hair. "Of course we should clean it up. What earthly good would it do to show the world we're vulnerable?"

"The sympathy vote," suggested Tua.

"Phooie," said Cora. She tossed her jeweled purse down on the back of an overturned armchair and looked around. "What a mess! I may have to start using that fancy alarm system Cam sold me to go with the gate."

"I'd say you'd better." Sam surveyed the wreckage with what seemed to me a very practiced eye. "I don't think they've actually damaged anything. Somebody's been rather careful."

"Of course. They want *you* out, not me. I pay taxes." Cora stalked a little circle in her green silk pumps. "Damn, I hate being muscled! I came here to get away from that!"

"And therefore you wish to clean it up and ignore it?" chided Mali softly.

Cora planted her feet. "If you can ignore people shooting at you, I can ignore this! Besides, who said I'm going to ignore it?"

Mali captured her tiny, well-ringed hands and smiled at her. Her nose came barely to his breastbone.

"I've stayed away from the struggle long enough." She tore her hands away to gesture impassionedly. "Tried to pretend I was free from it when it's been here brewing all along. Now, before we put this room back to rights, is anyone hungry besides me? A three-hour meeting about how to feed the starving and they can't even provide us with a little snack!"

Cora sailed off to the kitchen with the Eye in tow. Mark and Cris and I stood in the middle of the ravaged hall, staring at each other. Mark was pensive, I was struggling to put it all together, but Cris had one thing only on his mind.

"Is it possible?" he whispered, "Could they actually be hiding the *Conch*?"

CRISPIN'S RESEARCH: ANOTHER CONCH STORY

Indy/NetEntertainment 5

It's . . . the big world of Julian Cover, between the Domes. 06/14/46: Today, TUAMATUTETUAMATU!

Hullo, Julian here . . . moving on from death-defying anniversary leaps in Bangkok to bravery and magic on the little isle of Tuatua . . . this week's story will really make you wonder.

We got word of a sighting, but worried that our source had alerted us too late. The fire was well out of control when we arrived with our crew. The field bosses shouted futile orders while the pickers and sorters raced back and forth with buckets. None would venture into the blazing warehouse to answer the screams of those still trapped behind doors mysteriously jammed or locked from the inside.

Suddenly the big metal doors at the front broke open. A tall man appeared through the wall of black smoke and flame, carrying another on his shoulder. He beckoned to the field hands, then dropped his burden outside, and charged back into the fire.

The workers yelled at him to come back, save himself. Almost before they'd hauled the rescued man to safety, the tall man was back at the burning doorway with two more lucky ones and a girl staggering behind, dragging a young boy by his waistband.

I ducked in close with the cameras, but the choking smoke and intense heat threatened to melt our lenses. Even our telephoto couldn't make out the man's face, almost as if he hadn't any. One moment, a tall shadow against the blaze, the next, swallowed up in it again. I was amazed he could move in and out so fast, and that his clothing was not in flames, like those he'd rescued. *This is the real thing*, I told my crew, *or that guy's a fucking hero*.

Next, a cry went up at a side door, and workers rushed to grab the limp body of an old man from, no, not our fireproof man but a strong young woman who grinned and saluted our cameras as she whirled back into the roaring blaze. *"Where'd she come from?"* demanded my astonished audio. We'd seen no one else go into the building. Then other locked doors were bursting open and other flaming bodies staggering free. The workers rushed up with water and buckets to put them out while the older men and women who had gathered chanted encouragement in eerie, wailing tones. Incredibly, not one of the rescued was badly burnt, though four died when the roof finally collapsed. None of the bodies found in the wreckage fit the tall man or the laughing girl.

Twenty-nine were rescued before the roof collapsed. Each gave the same name to his rescuer: Latooea, THE CONCH.

Until our next meeting with the Incredible and the Inexplicable, this is Julian Cover, between the Domes.

SPECULATION:

Crispin didn't press the issue that night. After the rest of the Eye came home and we'd restored Cora Lee's great hall to its former magnificence, he celebrated with the rest of us. But later he could talk of nothing else, convincing himself gradually that the Eye was indeed sheltering his hero, the Conch.

In the morning, he visited my new paint shop, actually Theatre Two's chorus dressing room, commandeered by Hickey the minute *Double-Take* closed.

"Gotta go send out Marin for the rebid." But he prowled about as we worked and picked up a brush anyway. Props and paint paraphernalia sprawled across the plastic drop cloths protecting the white counters lining both sides of the narrow room. Since there were no actors in residence, the air was off. We'd suffocate if we didn't leave the door open. The whine and buzz of the *Double-Take* strike wafted in from down the hall and we kept our voices low.

"I bet he came in as a tourist and never left."

"And they're hiding him at Cora Lee's house?" whispered Jane.

I had a private image of the Conch now, tall and darkskinned and laughing. He wore bright colors and an aura of power. But I couldn't make out his face, or rather, it was changeable. Brash, wise, male, female, human and more than, shifting with each new tale I heard.

"If sneaking into Harmony was that easy, everybody'd be doing it." But I recalled my jewelry peddler's entry on an innocent apprentice's arm. Cora's castle would make a perfect hideout. "You think·Cora knows?"

"Oh yes." Cris laughed excitedly. "Can you see it on HarmoNet? 'Town Council Rep Hides Fugitive Revolutionary!' I love it!"

I mused over the section of cross-hatching I'd just completed, cool white against a rich sienna background. I'd chosen to paint the Gorrehma because I liked its sensuous shape, but the application of millions of tiny parallel lines on its curved surfaces was painstaking in the extreme. It required a steady, patient hand and what we liked to call a two-hair brush. The muscles between my shoulder blades were knotting up in protest.

"He doesn't have to be hiding. He could be one of them." Jane was painting perfect concentric circles of yellow and red on the smooth side of the Burinda. Her voice was flat and scared. I was glad she hadn't been at Cora's the night before.

Cris snapped his fingers. "Damn! Wish I'd thought of that!"

"The Eye spends half their life on tour," I countered. "You can't manage a revolution long-distance!"

"So he wasn't always with them. New to the company, like Tua. Their publicity's never mentioned individuals since that guy who died—you wouldn't notice a switch. Things got too hot for him at home, the Eye passed through Tuatua on their way here, dropped somebody off and picked up"— he beat a drum roll on the counter with his fists—"the Conch!"

"Shhh!" said Jane, glancing at the open door.

"Cris, you can't just stick an untrained somebody into a company of professional actors and expect him to blend right in."

"Any old somebody, yeah, but we're talking about the Conch! The elusive Latooea, master of illusion and disguise!" He tossed away the brush he'd been dawdling with. "You guys just don't want him to be here! She's too scared and you can't imagine it!" He began to pace up and down the narrow room. "Now, which one? Mali talks politics, so that's too obvious. The Mule's too wacko. Moussa?"

"I notice you don't even consider the women."

"Sam!" Cris did his little victory dance. "It's gotta be. He's so, you know, cool. Staying in the background, playing the supporting roles, but you saw how he took right over in a crisis?" He crowed delightedly. "A magician! The perfect cover!"

Jane began to look interested. "Well, it certainly isn't that Pen person."

"Or Te-Cucularit," I added disgustedly, leafing through the archivist's many pages in search of something new and different among the officially sanctioned motifs. "Too anal."

"I wouldn't rule him out," mused Crispin. "That could be an act."

"So could Pen's drunken bully be an act."

"Draws too much attention."

"What about the women?" I insisted. "Maybe the Conch isn't some great romantic hero. Maybe he is magic. Maybe he's your friend Tua."

Cris scoffed. "Sam's the best bet so far."

I wasn't sure. If it had to be one of them, I'd have said only Mali had the required charisma. But I couldn't imagine Mali ever being inconspicuous enough to suit the Conch's elusive habit. I preferred the notion of an eleventh, perhaps truly magical Tuatuan living invisibly in the towers of Cora Lee's fairy castle.

"It's not right." Jane's head bent low over her work. "Bringing someone like that into Harmony. I mean, if they did."

"Someone like what?" Cris challenged.

Jane turned on him. "You and your stupid kiddie games! Revolutionaries kill people! You think your precious Conch wouldn't walk right over you if you got in his way?"

Cris smiled smugly. "But I wouldn't."

"How would you know ahead of time?"

"No one's accused the Conch of killing anyone," I reminded her.

"He's a convicted criminal!"

"Political crimes!" Cris shouted. "Crimes of expression! He was tried and convicted in absentia!"

"Time for a coffee break." I lanced my long-handled brush into the water bucket and looked at Cris. "Shouldn't you be getting back to the studio?"

I crossed through Theatre Two on my way to the crew room. The stage was nearly cleared. A few stacks of plat-

forming waiting on dollies, a few piles of scrap left about,
a few crewmen pulling stray fasteners out of the floor,
and a new load of pipe and lumber sitting in the open
loading door. Was Sean finally going to start building *The
Gift*?

Raised voices drifted in from the shop, Howie's voice,
very loud, and somebody whose responses I couldn't distinguish. Cris joined me as I sidled up to the doorway.

Howie had cornered Sean by the water cooler,
explaining with great animation something Sean apparently didn't want to hear. Howie's big hands scythed the
air in parallel blades. Sean shook his head and slapped
his hard hat against the side of his thigh. The shop crew
was giving them room.

Howie spotted us trying to slip past.

"They were there!" He waved us over. "The whole place
upside down, isn't that right, kids?"

We both got real still.

"It's okay," Howie urged. "Omea called me first thing."

Cris stared back at him. "Cora told us to keep it quiet."

Howie's cheeks puffed up. "Yeah, well, come on. We're
all in this together. It won't go outside the theatre."

Sure it won't, I thought.

"It's a security problem! I've got actors at risk!" Howie
had finally realized the e-mails were not some young media
artist's journeyman project. I wondered how his blood pressure was doing.

Sean turned tired eyes to me. "He wants to move his
rehearsal into the theatre."

Our expressions were identical and eloquent. Sean turned
back to Howie. "See? They don't like it much, either."

"Nobody likes it!" Howie's hands chopped away again.
"But I can't have my actors' concentration disturbed by
some asshole's harassment campaign! They need a secure
place to work!"

Sean jammed his hat on his head and regarded Howie
from under its neon yellow brim. "So where am I supposed
to build your goddamn set?"

"We only rehearse eight hours—the rest of the time, it's
yours."

"Graveyard shift? Jesus, Howie, my men are exhausted!"

"Then hire some more!"

I nudged Cris. "Er, we're on coffee break . . . ?"

Cris led the retreat.

"This coffee's weird." I stared into the mug I'd borrowed.

"Pedro puts salt in it," said Flick, my friend the mold maker.

"Salt, huh? That's novel."

Flick's short dark hair was like a glossy bowl upended on her head. She had a ready smile and an equally ready tongue. She'd staggered comically into the crew room when the official break horn sounded to gulp her coffee as if it were water in the desert.

The low concrete room was furnished with props Hickey couldn't be bothered to store anymore. A dozen or so crew-folk lounged around in the broken-down assortment of chairs, benches, and stools, castoffs from past shows. In the rickety sofas at the far end of the room, several spent bodies sprawled in sleep. The rest of the crew was working through their break.

Flick stirred a cube of soup into hot water without rinsing her mug. "I hear Hickey's getting it on with one of your dancers."

"Hickey?" This was interesting news.

"Yeah, of all people!" Flick guffawed. "Never seen some-one look so soppy in all my life!"

"Lucienne," said Cris. "She's been singing him all week."

So. He'd been keeping things from me. "Yeah. You want to know about the Eye, ask Cris. He's real close with their sexy ingenue."

As soon as I'd said it, it sounded mean-spirited. Flick's glance was shifting back and forth between us when the door slammed open and Sean stormed in.

"There better be coffee in here or you're all fired."

Flick tossed her head. "Big Chief. On the warpath."

"Asshole," declared Sean to nobody in particular. He steamed over to the coffee table and snatched up a mug. "Stupid fucker."

"Howie," I guessed.

"Yes, Howie. Bad enough he has Hickey turning the joint into a goddamn greenhouse! The Barn's been good enough for every other cast that's worked in it. Who do these peo-ple think they are?"

"It's not them, it's this security issue . . ."

Sean dumped sugar into his coffee. "I just got started building. How'd Micah feel if I stopped?"

I nodded. He looked too tired to argue with.

"Well, fuck 'im. I told him he couldn't have it."

"The theatre."

"Yes, the theatre! I told him he could bring his goddamn actors where he goddamn liked, but I'd be in there with my hammers and saws and there'd be fuck-all he could do about it."

"I guess that told him," said Flick.

Stirring angrily, Sean spilled hot coffee on his hand and swore.

"Asshole," Flick observed.

Sean chuckled, caught her eye, and started to laugh.

HARMONET/CHAT

08/02/46

So! Are we up-to-date, friends and neighbors? Have we heard the *ultimate* latest? We would be so-o-o-o embarrassed if we didn't know what went on at the BRIM yesterday!

It's not that we wish to fill *all* our airspace with the folks from Tuatua, just because they can't manage to behave themselves in public . . . though we WOULD like to know what the tall one was muttering sotto voce as he stalked out. But their little family squabble was only the start of the evening's events. After they left, the *real* fun began!

First there was the hailstorm on the terrace. *HAIL* in Harmony? When did they add THAT to the weather program? But believe it, f&n. Chat is, Gitanne still has some squirreled away in her freezer . . . as evidence against charges of serving hallucinogenic beverages without due notice.

Then there were the flies in the soup. In EVERY-ONE'S soup. Or so we hear. Not a one of those *alleged* critters survived to tell the tale. We prefer Gitanne's story about floating peppercorns.

As if that wasn't enough to ruin the Brim's business for at least a week, then came the fainting spells! And not just the old ladies, f&n. Three strapping young men, five women of indeterminate age, and two grandfathers *out cold* on the floor! Had to be revived with generous doses of food and spiritous liquors, on the house! Try fainting next time the check comes at the Brim!

So now that you know, you STILL don't really know. But you don't believe in the Evil Eye . . . do you, f&n?

Remember, you DIDN'T hear it here!

MICAH'S VERSION:

The e-mail bulletin naming the Eye waited until Sunday morning.

"More people bother to read their public mail on Sunday," Micah pointed out when we raced in with newsfax in hand. We stayed to work on our projects, but concentration came hard.

We told Micah about Gitanne at the Brim. He said the face of Harmony was changing and he had to admit he wasn't happy about it.

We told him about Sean and Howie. Micah insisted that Sean was imperturbable, and that he himself would talk Howie out of needing the theatre.

Finally we unburdened ourselves of our theories about the e-mails. Cris reeled off his process of deduction concerning the identity of the Conch.

"A hero in hiding. What a charming conceit. I wonder what the Eye wants us to believe."

"They said no."

Micah nodded. "But they act yes."

"You mean they might want us to think they're hiding the Conch even if they're not?"

"What, for the publicity value?" Crispin looked as if he needed to spit. "They wrecked Cora Lee's for the publicity value?

"No, no. Just took good advantage of what happened." Micah stood back to squint at his *Don Pasquale* sketch. "I like this troupe more and more. They're as brilliant offstage as they are on."

"Micah, that's cynical."

He shook his badger head. "It's the greatest compliment I could pay them. Mali said it right here in the studio: reality can be manipulated. It's . . . 'Maliable.' Did we ever get a clear answer on the shooting incident? No. The challenge is to play as many versions of reality as you can at once, not only to prove that no single version holds precedence but to get as close as you can to portraying reality's true complexity." He set the sketch aside and laid down a fresh sheet. His hands worked at the paper long after the last wrinkle was pressed away, enjoying the sensual pleasure of the smooth whiteness against his palm. "A performance is not always an act. At its best, it's a direct expression of an ideology. Remember, these Tuatuans are genuinely mystical. Their T-shirts and tantrums can lead you to forget that."

I recalled the total conviction with which Mali had announced that his father was a Rock. "Yes. They can."

Crispin eyed Micah suspiciously. "I supposed you'd say they intend that confusion as well."

Micah tilted his head at the blank stretch of paper. "Encourage it, rather. As a diversion, as an expression of their worldview."

"They take real-world politics more seriously than you think."

"I never doubt their seriousness. But there are other ways to serve a cause than the obvious one. And the cause itself may not always be the obvious one. What if the cause is Art, and politics merely the means to express it?"

Cris sulked the rest of the morning, without even the grace to pretend that he wasn't. I managed some good work on my *Lysistrata* until I hit a serious conceptual snag around noon and was shaken by an irresistible upwelling of futility. My new confidence foundered. Even if Mark's figures were alarmist, I couldn't believe I was brilliant enough to survive the more rigid culling that seemed inevitable.

Suddenly I could see no reason, if the Admin was going to throw me Out anyway, why I should bust my ass on a Sunday for a paper project that would never be realized.

Besides, where I really wanted to be was at rehearsal.

THE RAID:

Micah and Crispin were so engrossed in their work, they didn't see me leave the studio.

I thought about that, alone in the sunshine of the empty courtyard. Not only was I losing faith in my work, but my supposed lover didn't notice when I left the room. I watched a feathery argument among a quartet of finches that hung around the yard because Micah fed them. Maybe I didn't mind. Crispin's approval, though often withheld, had bolstered my self-esteem. But I'd gotten too used to letting him take the lead in things, deciding where we'd go and what we'd do. Maybe it wasn't going to be that way anymore.

A door shut softly behind me. Not, as I feared, Cris come to steal my re-evaluated solitude, but Mark, closing up Marie's studio.

"Hey, G."

"Hey, Mark. Thought you weren't bothering with home projects anymore."

"I'm not." He hauled out his bike. It was candy-striped, orange and magenta. Bela's, its twin, still waited in the rack. Mark didn't allow it a moment's glance. "Coming or going?"

"Rehearsal . . . I think."

He raised a brow at my air of confusion, but left it at that. "I'm meeting Songh. Walk you to the fork?"

A batch of tourists clattered by outside. I waited until they had passed, then locked the gate surreptitiously behind us.

"Chamber of Commerce'll have us arrested," Mark murmured.

"We only do it on Sundays . . ."

It was good to hear him laugh—it had been awhile. I studied him as he wheeled his bike along. Mark was what you'd call a fine-looking young man—straight-cut blond hair, earnest blue eyes, precise features, sort of like Christopher Robin grown up. People didn't stare at him in the street like they did Cris. Their glance swept across him and beyond, but often their faces changed, softening, relaxing just a bit, as if some subtle reassurance had been gained in the passage. I decided he looked good. This new determination suited him. "So what were you up to in there?"

"A little further research."

"More numbers, Mark? Don't we have enough?"

"No, I was reading the constitution."

I laughed.

Mark dipped his head stubbornly. "Mali said, be thorough. I thought I'd find out exactly what rights we apprentices do have."

"Do we have any?"

"I'm just getting started. All this legalese is slow going, even for a lawyer's son."

The foot traffic thickened as we neared the market square. Avid faces all around, chattering like finches, about what they'd bought and how much it had cost them.

"Want to hear something weird?" Mark asked.

"Always."

"I was at Willow Street last night."

"To see that musical? I hear it's a big hit."

"Packed to the rafters. And the show's no good." He shook his head wonderingly. "Typical Bill Rand stuff—real old hat. At any rate, the first weird thing was the box office refused my apprentice pass and made me *buy* standing room."

"Buy? Like, with credits?"

"Had to borrow from an usher I know."

Our tiny apprentice stipends couldn't hope to cover the costs of Harmony's increasingly tourist-oriented ticket prices. "Are the apprentice freebees voluntary?"

He shrugged. "First I've heard of it. But wait—at intermission the lobby's so tight you can barely move. All around I hear talk about 'those radicals at the Arkadie.' There are a few other apprentices there, but mostly it's locals and a lot of overnight tourists. I hear this couple behind me complaining about the crowd. The woman asks why there are so many apprenctices in the audience. Her much older friend reminds her that our training program requires us to see as much of other people's work as we can. 'Well, I don't like it,' she says, 'they shouldn't be allowed to take up seats meant for tax-paying citizens!' "

We reached the fork in the path. "Micah says the face of Harmony *is* changing," I sighed.

"I think it's the heart that's changing, G." Mark swung a leg over his candy-striped bicycle. "That's what really frightens me."

I sneaked into the Barn and sat at the back by the door.

Pen and Tua faced each other in the middle of the hall, working through the quiet first-meeting scene between the clansman's young daughter and her suitor-to-be. The rest of the Eye sat cross-legged along the side, watching with unusual attentiveness. Or so I assumed, until Omea passed along to Sam a stack of papers she'd been reading. The bright blue caught my eye.

The Barn smelled stale and smoky. I wished it was real, all that fake greenery arrayed about the room in optimistic clumps. The Barn needed a little of my grandpa's green air.

The scene wasn't going well. Tua had made great strides since the week before. It was no longer obvious she was new to the role and to the company. She had her lines down, and disencumbered of her script, she settled more easily and consistently into character. But Pen was withholding, his concentration poor. He gripped his rolled-up script like the proverbial blunt instrument. His line readings were not character readings, they were Pen readings. Tua pushed too hard to keep the energy up. The wooing of the shy village Juliet by her eager Romeo slid toward something else entirely.

"Hold, please." Howie padded onto the floor to huddle with the actors.

I pulled my chair up to the production table. "How's it going?"

Liz growled softly in her throat. "Pen came in half lit again."

"Ah. Did Howie say anything about moving into the theatre early?"

"Tuesday, after the day off."

"Damn."

"I know. Sean'll never speak to me again."

I sniffed elaborately. "It smells funny in here."

"I've been instructed not to notice." She nodded toward Ule as he passed something to Moussa and eased back on his elbows to exhale luxuriously. A thin trail of smoke followed Moussa's hand to his lips.

"They don't know it's illegal to smoke in a dome?"

"They know."

I watched, fascinated.

Out on the floor, Howie's voice rose in spite of itself. "But why can't you?"

Pen snapped, "Because she can't get it fucking straight!"

"You're the one needs to get straight!" Tua snapped back.

"Guys," Howie reasoned, "this isn't useful."

Liz leaned closer. "Pen claims he can't do this scene 'cause Tua's from the city and doesn't understand the proper role of women in village life."

"Jeez."

"I know. But Mali says it's a clan problem: he's Fire, she's Water. Some old dispute from their grandfathers."

Fire and Water? "Older than that," I noted.

"And get this: Cu raised a big stink this morning when he found out there's no men on our running crew. He says it's taboo for women to handle the puleales or the gorrehma."

I felt a shiver of guilt, a genuine frisson, at the memory of my woman's hands on the smooth, forbidden curves of the Gorrehma. *Goodness, what was that?* I wondered. Not belief, surely not. "Who does he think's been painting the damn things?"

"Has he been around to see you doing it?"

"No, but . . ."

Liz shrugged the weight of the world and let it settle back on her shoulders. "Out of sight, out of mind with these folks. They use these taboos as a convenience."

"Oh, I don't think so, Liz." I smiled carefully. "We were warned about their taboos."

"Does that mean we have to buy into them? Damn! You and I wouldn't be here working if we did! Hey, you know me, I put up with a lot of shit from actors. But sometimes"—she glared at Te-Cucularit, who was doodling in his notebook, intent as a five-year-old—"I'm convinced they're taking advantage of us. They know we've been told to give their differences a lot of room, so they flaunt them, just to goad us into proving we're every bit as philistine and bigoted as they expected us to be."

"I like it when they flaunt their differences."

"You wouldn't if you were here in the tank with them every day!"

"Maybe it has nothing to do with being different," I suggested. Color was in motion again—Sam passing the sheaf of blue papers on to Moussa, Moussa passing a tiny red pipe back to Ule. "Maybe Cu's just an asshole. A Tuatuan should be able to be an asshole same as anyone else, I guess."

Liz stared at me as if I were simple. "Then we should be able to treat him same as any asshole!"

Behind us, the door swung open. Liz glanced around. "Good Lord."

A Security patrol spread quick-step across the rear of the hall, twelve green uniforms crisp and tight against the peeling white paint.

"Uh-oh. Smoke detectors must have alerted them." I looked at the line of actors, apparently engrossed in the rehearsal. The little pipe had disappeared. The squad captain headed our way. Only in Harmony would the police interrupt a rehearsal and know exactly where the stage manager was. Except in Harmony you didn't call them the police.

The Green leader was younger than me. She leaned in to murmur to Liz, something about a security search.

"Now?" Liz demanded. "In the middle of a rehearsal?"

The woman shrugged, then signaled her squad to proceed. Four of them poked unconvincingly among the artificial flora. The other eight headed straight for the Eye.

"Hold it," Liz objected. "You said 'search the *hall*.' "

I felt it, a subtle shift of the energy in the room. Out on the floor, the volume escalated abruptly.

"No way!" Pen yelled. "She does that, she takes the scene entirely!"

"Whoa, easy." Howie had not yet noticed the Greens beginning their search. "It's perfectly within her character."

"But it's my moment!" Pen threw his script. The crack as it hit the floor stopped the Greens short. Eleven heads swiveled toward their leader.

"You think every moment's yours!" Tua retored. "Whether it's in the script or not!"

Howie's hands made swimming motions. "Let's talk this over quietly."

Tua gestured rudely. "He couldn't play a quiet scene if his life depended on it."

Lucienne and Tuli burst into high-pitched giggles, like teenagers overreacting. The Eye was moving about without really moving. The patrol captain's head jerked toward them and back as Pen began to pace in tight, angry circles.

"Is this part of the play?" she demanded.

"Not last time I checked the script," Liz replied.

"Little Miss Jealous Nobody!" Pen barked. "Trying to undermine me from the begining, but I'm putting a stop to it!"

Mali rose from the floor, every muscle intent on Pen. I expected Sam, his peace-keeping strong-arm, to follow. But Sam stayed put, edging closer to Ule, murmuring with Moussa. The Greens flicked silent questions at their captain, drawing closer to the light from the windows, away from the shadowed perimeter of the hall.

"You'll do what your director tells you," Mali rumbled.

Howie stepped in front of Mali. "Please. Let me handle this."

Pen shoved past him. "Who are you, telling me what to do?"

"Your elder."

"Please," Howie begged. *"Please!"*

"Elder?" Pen snarled in Mali's face. "Useless old man!"

A collective growl erupted from the sidelines as the other actors scrambled up in protest. A soft ululation began, Lucienne and Tuli holding hands and chanting, louder and louder until Omea joined them. The Greens' eyes widened. Something nudged my elbow. A script lay on the table where there'd been none before. Sam stood a few paces away, watching the fracas.

The patrol captain shook Liz's arm. "Aren't you going to stop this?"

"They'd be after us in a second if we interfered."

The Green went a little limp and backed up a step. Sam turned, meeting my inquisitive glance head-on. His blue eyes reminded me of the papers they'd been passing, like the pipe, no longer in evidence. My hand stole to the script beside me, easing it under the crook of my arm. Sam's eyes lidded in a half smile. He turned away.

"Goddamn!" Howie yelled. "Can't you people get along?"

He won a silence he hadn't expected. The Eye stared at him.

"Settle your damn differences outside the rehearsal hall," he grumbled anticlimactically.

"Howie," Liz called softly, "we've got another problem."

After that, the search was over quickly. Mali drew himself up scowling before the green-uniformed boy who approached him so tentatively, then laughed out loud. He reached into his jeans pockets and pulled them inside out, spreading his arms. "Help yourself, bro."

Of course, nothing was found. Except the patrol leader's ID card, which miraculously turned up in Sam's shirt pocket. Even Ule was squeaky clean. The suspicious books in Mali's backpack that the skinny Green insisted his superior inspect were revealed to be three novels by Thomas Hardy, all properly signed out of the Harmony Free Library. The patrol leader took Howie's word that this was not subversive material.

The Greens did not search Howie or Liz or her assistants. They did not search me, sitting silent at the production table with my hand resting gently on Sam's script. I was pretty sure where the blue papers had gone, but I did wonder how he'd managed to totally disappear Ule's smoking pipe.

"By the way," Howie asked as the Greens were leaving, "who did you say sent you up here?"

The patrol leader blinked at him. "Why, your office, Mr. Marr. I understood it was at your own request."

"Ah," said Howie, "my overzealous staff again. They know I've been concerned about all this recent harassment of my actors."

The Green leader was young but not stupid. "Sorry for the trouble, Mr. Marr," she murmured, and got on out of there.

When the door shut behind them, Howie growled, "Liz, get Kim on line. I want to know who the hell made that call!"

Sam wandered up to retrieve his script just as I was realizing the Greens would have arrested me if they'd found me with anything suspicious. "Easier to make an elephant disappear than a nickel," he remarked.

"What's a nickel?"

"Never mind."

"What made you so sure they wouldn't search me?"

"Long experience as a person of no color."

That sounded too personal to ask him what he meant. "Do I get to know what they would have found if they had?"

He looked down, tapping the script gently against his palm, then flipped it open, and handed over a thin stack of pamphlets and a sheet of newsfax. The newsfax was a HarmoNet editorial about the Conch. The pamphlets were sky-blue and crudely manufactured. The cover was blank. I pushed them back at him.

"Coward," he grinned. He slid the papers into the script. "Now you'll never know."

HARMONET/COMMENT:

08/03/46

The views expressed herein do not necessarily reflect the views of the network.

WHY SHOULD WE CARE ABOUT THE CONCH?

CITIZEN'S EDITORIAL by Charles E. Pluck, Ph.D.

Many citizens in Harmony have lately found themselves absorbing information about a little place they may have thought was a vid show fantasy kingdom, the Isle of Tuatua in the South Pacific.

What was indeed the stuff of fantasy is turning into the grim meat of old nightmares as the island tumbles into civil war. Why should we in fortunate Harmony concern ourselves with the fate of a far-off speck in the ocean?

Because the issue in this war involves us intimately. The surface issue is to dome or not to dome, a question Harmony has not had to consider since our Founder Families first fought through the rights and wrongs of that question. But camouflaged by that accessible and hoary debate is one much more insidious and far-reaching.

There is no better image of this insidiousness than the elusive anti-domer figurehead, the CONCH.

Read his so-called writings, his speeches, his ultimatums to the legitimate government of Tuatua. Do they sound familiar?

Read the writings of Open Sky leader Ingrid Hibberd, and the connection will be obvious.

Though he masquerades behind the banner of mythology and an indigenous people's understandable if impractical concern for the preservation of an ancient religious tradition, this Conch is clearly an operative for Open Sky. That traitorous organization seeks the destruction of the peace and security and quality of life fought for and won by domer soldiers and pioneers all over the world, those same rights we in Harmony are pledged to maintain.

If the Conch is indeed hiding out among us, as some have reason to believe, we must do all we can to swiftly root him out before he can work the nefarious business of the Open Sky conspiracy here in Harmony, exploiting the weak at heart, perverting the innocent minds of our children, and threatening the end of the world as we know it.

BETRAYAL:

Cris was madly jealous that he'd missed the raid.

"You *know* they were just looking for the guy with the big 'CONCH' sign around his neck," he insisted at breakfast.

Because I went straight to the Arkadie, I didn't see the newest e-mail salvo until mid-morning when Hickey slouched into our dressing room–paint shop. He tossed me a folded paper glider. "You might want to take a look at this."

I flattened it out on the counter.

CITIZENS OF HARMONY! BETRAYAL FROM WITHIN! OUR ADOPTED CHILDREN NOW SHIELD OUR ENEMIES! CLOSE THE DOOR!

Clever, getting in that word *adopted*. The CDL had made both its targets into one.

"Very funny." I crumpled it as if it were nothing, a cartoon, but Jane read my eyes and snatched the paper from my hand.

"But it's a lie! How can they just say things like that!" She threw it away as if it had bitten her. "Oh god!"

Hickey retrieved it, refolded it, and skimmed it into a waste can. "Sticks and stones. Until someone puts their name to this bullshit, it's not going to fly with the people."

"The people will believe it!" Jane exploded. "The people want to believe it, the people who vote, the people who run things, the people who want Harmony all to themselves! Damn Howie Marr!"

"Jane, Howie couldn't have known—"

"He could have thought one second about something but himself and making his big splash! Damn this play! Damn the Eye and their goddamn Conch!"

I was on the verge of saying something Crispinish, like making a big splash is what being an artist is all about. Hickey took the male route. He tried to put his arms around her.

Jane shrieked and struggled free, her eyes showing too much white. "They can't just come in here and wreck our lives like this!"

There were voices down the hall. I grabbed her and shook her.

Hickey padded to the door, his finger to his lips.

"There's no need for such extreme action," Howie was insisting. "We do that, we play right into this Close-the-Door thing."

The other voice asked, "But just between you and me, any ideas which one of them it might be?"

At the door, Hickey mouthed: "Cam Brigham."

"Which . . . ?" The approaching footsteps stopped. "Cam, I am doing an important play with ten very talented actors, you hear? We are not harboring any felons, we are not involved in political intrigue, we are doing a play!"

"Are you absolutely sure?"

"Fuck me, I don't believe this!"

"Howard, we need to think of the safety of our staff. These Open Sky types are dangerous."

"They're not . . . damn it, Cam, I won't do it! I will not buckle in to this cowardly anonymous pressure! I will not close my show down because of some smear campaign before my actors get a chance to prove themselves! Cam, Cam, what's the matter with you? I know you didn't like this project, but are you really going to let your theatre get pushed around by some two-bit coffee-klatsch without even the balls to identify itself?"

Silently I applauded. Hickey offered a grudging nod.

Brigham was calm to the point of condescension. "It's the Arkadie's reputation I'm trying to protect. We don't want ourselves identified in the marketplace with sedition and anarchy."

"Our reputation is made by the quality of our Art!"

"Howard, what's lost but a few tickets if we send these people on their way? I can square it with Reede, and Reilly can get on with finishing *Crossroads* the way it should be."

"Crossroads!" Howie spat. "You haven't even been near my rehearsal hall! You haven't a clue what you're trying to shut down!"

"He's right," Jane hissed. "They should close it down!"

I glared at her.

"Censorship is bad enough!" Howie let rage shove his voice down into his diaphragm where great performances are born. "But censorship based solely on preconception and innuendo . . . ! Have you forgotten where you are?

Have you forgotten the principles your own Founder Father helped to frame?"

"Oh rubbish, Howard. This is not censorship, it's business sense. All this crap about risk taking. People don't want risks. Times are hard. They want to feel safe in the theatre."

"Times were one hell of a lot harder when Harmony was built in order to protect the right to take risks!"

Brigham chuckled tolerantly. "But we're not that little enclave of wild-eyed idealists anymore, are we, doing Art to please ourselves? Harmony serves a wider public now. The Arkadie needs to stay alert to the changing times if we expect to hold on to our share of the trade."

"Why do you think I put that piece of shit *Crossroads* on the schedule? Your needs have been satisfied, Cam. Leave me to mine. And no more sneak-search orders coming out of your office with my name on 'em! You want to muck around with *Crossroads*, that's between you and your buddy-buddy Bill Rand, but keep your fucking hands off my show!"

Howie stormed off toward the theatre. Brigham continued in our direction, glancing automatically through the open door as he passed. He was scowling and barely seemed to notice us.

When he'd gone on down the hall, Hickey sagged against the doorframe. "Collaboration . . . the very soul of Art."

"This show is going to be the death of us," Jane moaned.

"Oh, Jane!" I snatched the crumpled e-mail out of the trash and shook it in her face. "These CDL people have already decided against us! We've got to help the people who're on our side!"

"Like the Conch?"

"Maybe!" I returned, too hotly.

"I knew it." Her mouth shrank to a pucker in her face. She swallowed her next thought and bent her head over her work.

"Well, I think I'll go watch some more shit hit the fan," Hickey drawled morosely. "Any estimate on finishing these gizmos?"

"Get me more paint help and we might make it by opening."

Hickey grunted and left. Jane and I painted in silence for several minutes, then she set her brush down carefully and walked out. Half an hour later she was back, red-eyed but, I hoped, recovered. We worked without speaking until Micah arrived at noon for a promised conference with Sean.

He also brought the e-mail, carrying it like a piece of garbage he was looking for a place to dump.

I waved my wet brush at it. "Seen it already."

"I'm glad you're taking it so well," he said.

My eyes flicked to Jane. "Some of us."

Micah crushed the sheet in one hand. "It really is time to put a stop to this."

Jane raised her head.

"How?" I asked.

"There'll be a good many people turning up at Town Meeting this week who don't usually bother to go when civic matters are progressing normally."

Jane muttered, "Town Meeting isn't 'til Thursday!"

"And nothing is going to happen until then," Micah returned pointedly. To me he said, "We're meeting Sean in Rachel's office ten minutes ago. You ready?"

Sean seemed weary but in control. He grinned at me and shook Micah's hand. "How are ya, buddy?"

Micah returned his smile. "On my second round of bids for Marin. Hope I look better than you do."

Sean shook his head. "Sweet sufferin' Jesus, this is a ball-breaker! My wife thinks I've left her."

"Bill Rand's very involved in Big," said Micah.

"Ah, Bill's okay. It's Eider who's killing me." Sean sank gratefully into an upholstered chair. "So here's the story."

Rachel ended a phone call and settled in to listen.

"I've got three men busting ass on your show right now. Soon as *Crossroads* is loaded in, I'll break more crew off that. Long as we can keep Howie out of the theatre, we'll be done but the painting by first tech."

"Including the effects and mechanics?" Micah inquired.

Sean's eyes strayed to the powder blue walls with their three framed prints. "Probably have to work some kinks out during technicals."

"I'd like to see a coat of paint on it before Louisa starts setting light levels."

"And pal o' mine, I'd like to give it to you! It's just . . . where *is* Lou? Electrics still hasn't got a plot from her!"

"Amsterdam. I sent her drawings." Micah refused the

diversion: "What would it take to get the necessary paint time?"

Sean offered up a brittle grin. "How 'bout a miracle?"

Rachel stirred within the fortress of her desk. "I think our most pressing problem is that I can think of no way of keeping Howard out of the theatre."

"Whadda ya mean?" said Sean. "Why?"

Rachel shrugged. "It *is* his theatre."

"C'mon, Rache, we go through this every time. He doesn't need it."

"He thinks he does. Howie's not insensitive to your needs, Sean. He's discussed it with me thoroughly, and it's his feeling that in light of recent events, keeping this particular cast within the safer confines of this building is critical enough to risk putting a little extra strain on the technical departments."

"A little?"

Micah leaned forward. "Rachel, I really think Howard must let us have the theatre."

"He is adamant." Rachel arranged a row of paper clips on her desk. "But here's good news. Reede Chamberlaine says he's heard all the way from London how far behind we are. He's agreed to put in an additional sum if we can match it. After some financial gymnastics, I found what we need. I can make this money available to Sean for overhire."

"Oh, marvelous," said Micah.

But Sean didn't look relieved. He looked cornered. "You got money out of Chamberlaine?"

Micah was already gearing up. "This means we can put on a night crew without burning up your permanent staff."

"No, we can't." Sean was shaking his head slowly, as if there was something he could not quite come to grips with.

"Well," said Micah, "however you want to do it."

"I can't do it."

Rachel smiled her smile. "Of course you can."

"Where the hell am I gonna find a whole new crew?"

Micah laughed. "You know every good carpenter in Harmony."

"Yeah, and they're all working."

"And they'd every one kill to do you a favor."

"They're working," repeated Sean.

Micah nodded. "Then we'll find you other people."

"What, some greenhorn kids I'll have to be running after to wipe their noses all the time? People who don't know me or my shop, how we work? You think anything'll get done that way?"

"I'll find you good people." Micah was slow to accept that Sean was actually saying no. I didn't blame him. I couldn't believe it, either.

"I can't do it. I got too many places to be in at once as it is! I'm running two crews, I'm in here eighteen hours a day, I haven't seen my kids in weeks!"

"Sean, I know how—"

"No, Micah, you don't." Sean's eyes were oddly focused, as if at a great distance. His fingers pressed deep grooves into the padded arms of his chair. "I gotta say I'm fucking sick of taking all the shit when this theatre gets in a scheduling mess! You guys are always coming up with these bright ideas—anyone ever ask *me* if it's worth it? Anyone ever thank me or my crew when we kill ourselves bailing you out?"

"Yes," said Micah fervently, "I do. Always."

"We all do," Rachel added, because she knew she must. For a moment I was almost as angry with her as Sean was.

Softly Micah said, "Sean, just get us through this one."

"What's the problem if they play a few previews unfinished?"

"Please. This one is important. I'm asking for your help."

"You think they're all important! Every one, life or death! When is this ever going to stop?" Sean stared at Micah as if he was a stranger. "More crew is not the answer." He rose abruptly and Rachel shrank away as if he might hit her. "The answer is, this one doesn't get finished on time, maybe you'll think twice next time. Answer is, you keep Howie outa that theatre and we might be done by opening."

He turned and walked out.

I learned later from Flick that Micah's friend and hero, the imperturbable Sean Reilly, returned to the shop, walked straight into the crew room, and hurled a wooden chair into tiny splinters against the gray concrete wall.

"If I hadn'ta been there to see it, I wouldn'ta believed it," she muttered. "That Sean, I tell ya, he's in a bad, bad way."

TE-CUCULARIT:

Micah was stunned, of course. He made a few lame excuses for Sean's intransigence, but the pain in his eyes was so naked it might have embarrassed me if I hadn't been equally devastated.

--Rachel straightened more paper clips. "It seems that he has us over a barrel."

Micah roused himself. "No. No. I'll find a couple of good men—if they just show up in the shop, he'll put them to work. But first of all, we keep Howard out of the theatre."

Rachel said, "You'll have to convince him."

"I will."

Micah went home tight-lipped. I scurried back to prop duty, shaken to the core. Hickey tried to calm me with gloomily sympathetic noises and promises that at least his part of the job would be done. But he made it plain he intended to remain clear of the whole controversy. "When this one's all over and done with, Sean and me'll still be here having to work together."

Jane was another problem. She'd retreated to the furthest reaches of the dressing room, practically in the showers, working in silent distraction. I had to watch her constantly, to remind her to keep her colors consistent and her lines clean, the sort of things you never had to worry about with a detail expert like Jane.

I was concentrating poorly myself. That enervating futility was creeping up on me again. I tried not to be short with Jane, but now it seemed that these props, the one aspect of *The Gift* that I had some control over, had to be extra-perfect. The scene in Rachel's office haunted me. I replayed it over and over. How could a long friendship be so abruptly put on the line? Then without warning, Te-Cucularit arrived. I feared if he threw a tantrum about finding his precious totems in the hands of infidel women, it might just send me over the edge with Jane.

But he came in quietly. I held my breath when he stopped at my shoulder to study my work.

"This will do," he remarked gruffly.

Relieved beyond measure and not knowing what else to do, I continued painting. Cu hovered for a bit, examining each prop, checking each color I'd mixed according to his precise formulae. Finally he searched among the brushes resting in my water jar, drew one out, and dipped it in the rich turkey red I'd just used for the outline of a fish. He pulled up the chair next to me, destroying what little was left of my concentration. He was so close I could feel the heat of his body. I was thankful he didn't walk around half naked like Ule or Moussa. Jane eyed us from her corner.

"But," he said, "it could be better done like this."

He edged my brush hand out of the way. In the center of the flattened top of the Gorrehma, he deftly shaped a fantastical bird. What good angel had made me leave that space for last? He laid in the body and head with clean intersecting arcs, then the bird's feathers with quick parallel lines that echoed the crosshatched background. The sure economy of his stroke imparted a mythic quality to the entire image. It was at once the specific bird of his imagining and every bird in the universe.

"Beautiful," I murmured. "Really beautiful."

He settled himself more comfortably in his seat. The tension that shadowed him evaporated as he worked. With a single sweep, he surrounded the completed bird with a graceful red oval.

Beside his, my own birds as well as my fish and lizards and other animals looked crabbed and contrived.

"I've been keeping things a bit too literal," I noted.

"Of course. You lack the resonances of the history to guide your hand."

I laughed nervously. "Like having to recite a poem you've learned in a foreign language." I'd never had to do that, either, but Songh had told us once about singing in Latin.

"Yes." He said it as one placates a child without really listening, filling his red oval with tiny texture lines.

I inched my chair back to leave us more breathing room. This perfect beauty of Te-Cucularit's drew you whether you wanted it or not: the radiant brown skin, the exquisite modeling of his cheek and jaw. He was like an expensive artwork you would never consider buying but could not help looking at. I wondered if he was comfortable with it, or if his sour habit had developed as a defense against a world compelled to stare at him with hunger in its eye.

Now he gave total concentration to the laying in of the ground around his oval. I wanted to ask how the tales were contained within these daubings on the wood. What were the actual mechanics of the telling? What syntax of line and image resolved itself for a Tuatuan eye into coherent narrative? But in my head, all my questions sounded like skepticism.

"You work very fast," I said instead.

Cu rinsed his brush, looking about. "I need the darker brown."

I passed him a cool burnt umber.

He worked from that jar for a while, then set it aside and sat back. "The ease of it will come, even though you lack the sense of it. You see how already you improved . . ." He touched the tip of his brush handle to the precise spot where I had laid in my own first strokes. He drew it lightly to where I had just been working.

"It's that obvious where I started?"

"To me." His shoulders twitched diffidently. "For Mali and Omea, their tales come in words, Moussa's in music, No-Mulelatu and the girls, in the language of their bodies. Mine is here in the lines."

He caressed the Gorrehma's upper bulge, just where it flattened to provide the sitting surface now decorated with his fantasy bird. "You did not start in the proper place. The tale must be born here and grow this way"—he traced a spiraling curve across the shining wood—"or its power will never awake. Now, yours . . ." His finger wandered drunkenly with the zigs and zags of my cross-hatching. He seemed to be fighting off a smile. "No worry that you profane the secrets here. As even you can imagine, your story is somewhat incoherent."

I couldn't help it. I laughed. Cu let the smile curl the corners of his mouth. He wet his brush and used the umber to add a row of dots just inside the oval framing the bird.

"He's like a firebird," I said. "Or a phoenix."

"*She* is Akeua. Her magic is far older than Phoenix and her power is very great. She is Moussa's totem."

I listened as I had as a child to my grandfather's stories of Before, which were as much strange magic to me then as these Tuatuan totems now. *Please, Grandpa, tell us about* . . . "Tell me her tale."

Cu's brush hand stilled, then relaxed. He resumed his rows of umber dots. "That I cannot."

"Oh." It was like hearing an ominous crack when you'd been sure the ice was a good eight inches thick. Lulled by his reasonable mood, I ventured out on it anyway. "How come?"

He sat back, stiffly angry. "To speak it is not allowed. Would you offer up your clan secrets so easily?"

Taboo. I'd walked right into it but innocently, because I was feeling comfortable with him and dreaming about my dead grandfather. I felt my trust had been abused. "I don't know. I don't have any. I don't have a totem. I don't even have a clan. I have a mother and a father whom I'll never see again!" It just leapt out of me after lying dormant for three busy years. I blinked and tried to shove it back where it had risen from, cursing its inconvenient arrival and the tears it brought.

Cu stared at me.

"When you leave home, you've still got it to go back to," Jane accused.

He glanced down the long counter, then back at me. In his eyes was a very normal male horror at the prospect of hysterical females, but beyond was a bleakness that put my small tragedy to shame. "Every time we return, less of it belongs to us. Every time, less of it *is*."

"I'm sorry," I said, and meant it.

He laid the shaft of his brush across the back of my hand in obscure benediction. "You. What is your name?"

I told him.

"Gwinn-Rhys, observe carefully and do as I do, in mirror image, beginning over there." He held the brush poised while I filled my own. "You needn't know the tale of Akeua to help with the proper telling of it."

THE ATTACK:

Cris arrived after studio hours with Mark and Songh and enough purloined dinner for ten of us. We feasted among the drop cloths and paint buckets. I thought he'd come to do something nice for me, but turned out he was mostly curious.

"What happened over here today?" he demanded. "Micah came back, turned up the music full blast, and worked all afternoon without saying a word."

I described the confrontation in Rachel's office. "We need to work extra hard for him now." After dinner, I gave lessons in the rudiments of Tuatuan totem ornament and set everyone to work cross-hatching.

"How's your research coming?" I asked Mark.

He talked as he worked. "Beyond the letter of the contract, there doesn't seem to be a body of apprentice-related law. But there are what we might call some rights of precedent."

"Precedent to what?"

"Actions were taken by apprentices to address certain problems in the past. When those actions were recognized by the Town government, they gathered an unofficial kind of legitimacy."

"What kinds of action?" I asked cautiously.

"Well, the right to petition, for one."

That made me thoughtful, and quiet for quite a while. It was late when we quit for the night and my back was cramping, but Te-Cucularit had approved my work and the elation still buoyed me. "We actually got something done today!" I cheered as we retrieved our bikes from the stage door rack. I tossed Mark a salute. "Thanks for the help, guy."

"Anytime. I like painting." He looked down at his candy-striped bike and ran a finger along the orange handlebar. "Bela and I used to . . ." He faltered, then gave a sad little smile and I was glad he no longer felt obliged to hide his grief. He seemed relieved, too, as he brushed at a nascent tear and laughed at his own discomposure. "Bela would've had a good time tonight."

"I know." I smiled and swung onto my bike.

With the theatres both in turnaround, Fetching Plaza was empty, bathed in the sullenness moonlight acquires when it passes through a dome. The white cylinders of the Arkadie loomed like a ruin. As if catapulted from a sling, I wheeled out in sweeping curves across the spread of coolly shining marble. Cris and Mark and Songh followed, whistling and whooping, while Jane bisected our joyful arcs in a slow, straight line to the far side of the plaza.

Cris swooped near. "What's with Jane?"

"Oh, the usual!" I banked away from him, thrilled with speed and the freedom of open space after a long day in a tiny one. "Is this what it's like to be Outside, do you think?"

"What?" he yelled. *"What?"*

"Never mind!" I sailed across Jane's bow, out of the plaza and onto the market street, broad and tree-lined, with fountains of natural rock murmuring in the middle. The green-grocers and bakers and *boucheries* were closed up for the night. The taller trees rustled as a gust sighed past above, on its way to wherever the weather computer directed it. A small sidewalk café remained lit. People sat in the leaf-shadow, shimmering in candlelight, drinking wine, and arguing aesthetics.

At least that's what I imagined, in my euphoric state. Several of the debates seemed quite heated to one whizzing past at light-speed. My companions raced to catch up with me.

I pedaled harder. I veered off onto a narrow lane that was less well lit but made a more interesting trip home, and nearly ran down two people crossing the street in front of me. I swerved around them and swept past without a second glance. "Signal next time!" I yelled.

"Gwinn!"

Grinning, I glanced around. Cris had used this ruse before to win a race, and I wasn't letting him win anything now.

"Come back!" he shouted.

They'd stopped at the crossing, Songh and Jane and their bikes in a cluster mid-street. Crispin's lay tossed in a dim pool of streetlight. He was helping someone to the sidewalk.

I circled back. "I missed those people! What happened?"

I braked beside Songh. He'd gathered up Crispin's bike and held it ready, glancing up and down the street. Jane supported Mark's bike with one rigid hand as she gazed in horror at the dark huddle on the pavement.

"Get him over here, against the wall," a familiar voice ordered. "No, away from the light! Let him get his breath." A tall silhouette straightened out of the huddle and called to Songh. "Anything?"

"No sir, not yet."

I stared into the darkness. "Mali?"

Songh sniffed back tears. "Sam's been hurt."

I dropped my bike and ran over.

Sam lay propped against a closed shop window, heaving and coughing. Even in the dull moonlight I could see he was spitting blood. I thought I should throw myself down to cradle his head in my lap like women always do in the vids, but I'd never had someone's blood all over me before. Besides, Mark had beaten me to it.

"We were working late over at the Barn," Mali said. "We were on our way home."

"They beat the shit out of him," Cris exclaimed.

I hovered helplessly. "Who? *Who*?"

Mark unzipped his coveralls and tore off his undershirt. With it he blotted gently Sam's battered face. I shuddered. Could a man take such a beating and live?

Cris wiped his hands on his thighs and looked to Mali. "What d'you want to do? Where should we take him?"

"To the hospital!" I gasped. "Where else?"

Mali knelt. "Sam? What do you think?"

Sam palmed blood out of his eyes. His forehead gleamed wetly. "Gonna need doctor's care this time, Mal."

"And you'll get it."

"We'll have to call Security," Cris warned, and finally I understood. They wanted to keep this quiet. My instinct would have been to scream bloody murder.

"Cora Lee's sure to have a private doctor," I suggested. But Cora's was a ten-minute walk.

"Can you make it?" Mali whispered.

Sam's chuckle rattled damply in his throat.

"We'll carry him," insisted Mark.

Mali flicked another glance at Songh, searching the shadows. The street remained still and silent. "Likely they took off when you all stopped." He touched Sam gently. "They weren't planning to leave you alive, bro."

"Hey, I don't kill that easy," Sam coughed.

"Right." Mali's face, caught in a drift of moonlight, could have been carved of jet, if rock can be thought of as angry.

"You're all right?" I asked him.

"They weren't interested in me." The blood on his shirt was Sam's. "All right. Gwinn, fast as you can to Cora's. If she hasn't got a doctor, let her call the cops. If Omea's there, tell her . . . no, never mind. Just go!"

"Did you see them?"

He nodded. "Four. Young and strong."

"And professional," wheezed Sam. "Some vacation, huh?"

Behind me, Jane was moaning softly.

"You think it was the CDL?" I asked.

"Later," Mali spat. "Go on, now. Out of here!"

I snatched up my discarded bike.

Jane dropped her bike and Mark's in a sudden clatter. "Oh god, oh god! It was me! It was my fault! I told them! I told them it was Sam! I told them Sam was the Conch!"

Cris says Jane became hysterical and could not be questioned until Sam was safe at Cora's and her doctor had assured us that he was tough and would probably survive. I was too busy being scrub nurse to notice, trying to stay calm, trying not to wretch at the sight of Sam's blood on my hands.

Dr. Jaeck was a dryly humorous man not much taller than Cora who talked impasto paint technique with her as he stapled and sutured and taped Sam up on the big refectory table in Cora's kitchen. He later observed that it had been a long time and another dome away since he'd treated his last life-threatening case of assault and battery, and what the hell was going on in Harmony?

Mali paced the impromptu surgery like an angry specter, Sam's blood drying to brown on his yellow T-shirt. Mark and I manned the portable autoclave and rinsed towels while Cris kept an eye on a catatonic Jane in the great-hall. The others, when they came home, hung out in the corners of the kitchen, still dressed for the concert they'd been attending. I listened without hearing for a while before I realized their murmur was a nearly ritualistic recalling of past assaults and injuries to troupe members.

"I'm worried more about his inside than his outside," the doctor advised when Sam had been carried upstairs and

Mali had settled by his bed to worry. "That body took a heavy beating."

'It's his hands he'll be worried about." Cora took Jaeck's arm. "You'll come see him first thing."

He nodded, threw us all a final quizzical look, and let Cora see him to the door.

We gathered in the great-hall, where Cris stood watch over Jane. She was hollow-eyed but aware of herself again, curled tightly into the corner of a plush green sofa. Songh dozed in an armchair by the fireplace.

Omea's bracelets tinkled as she shook him gently awake. "Best get home, child. Your people will be wondering."

He blinked up at her shyly. "I called them. I told them I was sleeping over at the dorm."

"You can, you know," said Mark.

Omea stood back. "Did you tell them why?"

"I can't tell them, but if I go home, I can't not tell them."

"You understand that not going will look like taking sides anyway?"

"Yes, ma'am," Songh replied faintly. "I know."

Omea smiled. "Well, if you're sure, then. Welcome."

Ule beetled over to crouch before Jane like a small ogre contemplating dinner. "Now what about this one?"

Jane shrank into the cushions with a moan.

"Oh, Muley!" Omea nudged him aside and eased herself down beside Jane. "You are perfectly safe with us, dear. Do you feel up to telling us about it yet?"

Jane had cried herself dry. Her voice was rough and uninflected. "I never thought they'd . . . I thought they'd just arrest him and send him away. I thought they'd leave us alone, that the harassment would stop when the people knew the Conch was gone from Harmony."

Omea took Jane's hands and held them gently. "You thought Sam was Latooea?"

"My speculation," Cris admitted. "But I—"

Omea waved him to silence. "And who did you tell this to?"

"He said if I told, he'd have me thrown Out."

"He will never know you told, child. That we promise."

Jane was too broken and exhausted to resist. "I told Mr. Brigham."

And that was no surprise to me.

THE RESPONSE:

The Eye kept Jane with them and sent the rest of us home, with instructions to say nothing about the beating. The terror glazing Jane's eyes as we walked out of Cora's greathall in the early hours was equal only to the wonder in them later that morning when she showed up at the Arkadie not many minutes behind me.

She moved in a daze to her spot near the showers and pulled her chair tight to the counter. She took up her brush but made no move to begin painting. "They said they'd take me with them if I'm not renewed."

"How's Sam?" Maybe the Eye was ready to let her off easy, but I was not.

"They said it wouldn't be just like Harmony and I said anything was better than being put Outside and then Moussa laughed at me and said it *was* outside, at least for now, unless the planters have their way."

"Damn it, Jane. How is Sam?" I'd dreamed about him, and Micah, until their images had combined and I was begging forgiveness from a battered, bleeding face with Micah's numbed eyes.

"Oh. Sam is, uh, coming along, Mali said. After the doctor left, they magicked him up a little and he'll be all right soon."

"They magicked Sam?"

"Oh yes." She dipped her brush and began to paint. "And they made a sign. Did you see it?"

This was too weird. I decided her brain was too busy with revision and reconception to be able to handle normal conversation. "See what?"

"The eye, up over the plaza. It's there. They put it there."

I studied her more carefully. "Jane, after we left, did they give you anything, like to eat or medicine?" Drugs, I was thinking, it's got to be.

She shook her head slowly. Her every move was deliberate. "They talked with me for a long time and then they put me to bed. They gave me Mali's bed since he's mostly in Cora's room now. You should go out and see it. It's pretty."

I set down my brush, wondering if it was safe to leave a person alone when they were so obviously in shock. But there was no one around to whom I could entrust her with any sort of appropriate explanation, so I encouraged her to keep working and headed upstairs to see this wonder for myself.

And there it was. An eye, in midair above Fetching Plaza. It was too early for tourists, but the local merchants were neglecting the setting up of their stalls in order to stand about gawking and marveling.

It was almond-shaped, a green outline with a pupil of gold shimmering like a flame through glass. It was the symbol on the Mattalike banner that the Eye had unfurled during their spectacular entry at the Gates, the symbol Te-Cucularit had forbidden Hickey to use. Insubstantial though it was, it didn't shift or fade, and it bent a benign and knowing regard on the plaza and the admiring merchants and especially on the imposing white cylinders of the Arkadie.

That is a really clever hologram, I told myself, truly masterful. The mystery was how the Eye had gotten it up and running so quickly and invisibly, never mind where they'd found the machinery.

Meanwhile I kept hearing Jane, in that awe-flattened voice: "They magicked him up a little and he'll be all right soon."

But not so soon that the attack could be concealed from Howie, and Howie immediately called a press conference. He insisted that the entire Arkadie staff put aside their frantic preparations for *Crossroads*'s first technical rehearsal and pile into Theatre Two, even though he knew he'd be fighting the noise of construction onstage.

"If this is his way of moving into the theatre . . ." Micah went off to buttonhole Howie while the staff filed into the house.

Reede Chamberlaine had flown in from London and most of the trustees were there, Cora, of course, and Campbell Brigham, puffing around, his oh-so-appropriate outrage tempered with a hint of I-told-you-so. Cora chatted earnestly with him, indicating that the crux of the night's revelations remained a secret among ourselves.

The Eye didn't show until Howie pinned on his mike and was about to get things started. As the saws screeched in the background, ten black-robed, black-hooded specters filed hands-linked down the aisle and settled on the carpet in front of the first row.

Ten? I hastily recounted. As the tenth sat down, the sixth collapsed, leaving a flattened nest of black fabric and an empty space in line. Oh, bravo, I thought.

Howie's graphic secondhand description of the assault told me the Eye had omitted our part entirely, and I relaxed a little. I hadn't even told Micah.

"This brutal act," Howie orated, "is the culmination of a campaign of insult and injury aimed not only at this troupe of actors, our guests in Harmony, but at the founding principle of our unique Town, that of the freedom of the artist to do his work undisturbed by people who may not agree with him."

The news service reporters were uninterested in the freedom of the artist. They wanted the gory details. Actual physical violence in their own streets! The brave Chat reporter who asked if the Eye was indeed sheltering the Conch was treated to Howie's comedic version of public ridicule. He fended off all questions about the eye in the plaza with an air of smug complicity and sent the press home intrigued and laughing.

Then he called a *Gift* cast and staff meeting in the greenroom.

The actors' greenroom was luxurious compared to the shop crew room. The ceiling was high and white, the walls were done in tweedy beige fabric, and the comfortable furniture seemed to have all come from the same catalogue, perhaps even recently. Food and drink dispensers hummed amiably in an alcove, and a bank of show monitors offered views of each theatre from left, right, and front of house.

Reede Chamberlaine looked like he'd been dragged away from something more important, but he offered Mali a sympathetic nod and patted Moussa's broad back paternally, then inclined his silver head to kiss Omea's cheek as he took a seat beside her.

Brigham joined them. I watched him for a sign of guilt. But he only shifted his bulk around in a chair too small for him and looked bored.

". . . and because of their high visibility," Howie came

in, exclaiming to Cora, "the Eye's the perfect victim for these lunatic-fringers looking to make a splash."

Brigham leaned over to murmur with Chamberlaine. Insubstantial movement began among the Eye, the same little shufflings and shiftings that had made such magic the day of the raid. Brigham sat up chuckling from his final remark to Reede and found himself surrounded on three sides by dark Tuatuan faces.

I relished his quick battle with panic. So did Mali. He grinned at Brigham ferally. Recalling his sudden rage at the Brim, I had a satisfying vision of Mali leaping with fangs bared at the fat man's throat. But after a half second's recognition of mutual emnity, the two men smiled at each other cordially and turned their attention to Howie as he raised his hand for silence.

"Reede and I have a few things to add that we didn't need to share outside the family."

Sean and Ruth slipped in late and leaned against the wall beside the door. Micah shifted uneasily beside me.

Howie looked us up and down, drenching us all with his sincere disappointment. "This is not going to be my usual pep talk. We're too far gone here for 'fight, team, fight.' I know this has been a long, hard season, but that's never an excuse for the kind of slacking off I'm seeing in this theatre.

"Many of you seem to have forgotten we're doing *two* shows here at the Arkadie. Sure, one's a monster, but the other techs next week and right now we're where we should have been with it a month ago! Let's get on with it!"

Behind him, the door thudded softly, Sean and Ruth leaving.

"Damn," said Micah softly, and Howie paused, looking after them querulously. "And I'm not reserving all my complaints for the production departments! Reede?"

Chamberlaine stood at ease, his hands in his pockets and his patrician chin lifted. "First of all, as the man responsible for bringing the Eye to Harmony, I must say I'm appalled by this betrayal of Harmony's long reputation for hospitality to guest artists. As artists, we should be allowed to be above politics. However, as we'll all admit, there are two sides to every story.

"For instance: I've been hearing reports in London about misbehavior in rehearsal . . . and elsewhere." He caught Pen's glance and held it until Pen looked away, then moved

languidly behind Mali's chair, leaning over him companionably, smiling.

"Really, my dears, this petty squabbling among yourselves is better settled in your tribal councils. It has no place
among professionals on the rehearsal floor and no place in
public. If you won't show yourselves as responsible members of modern society . . ." He shrugged at them whimsi-
cally. "You shouldn't wonder at a few outraged locals
taking things into their own hands. When in Rome, you
know . . ."

The Eye stared at him stony-faced. A few staff members
in the back nodded in unconscious agreement. Sour Jorgen
from Costumes bent to share a whisper with a neighbor.

Howie, like a good bird dog, sensed a shift in the wind.
"Thanks, Reede, for your honesty. Our job now is to work
together to re-establish a good working atmosphere and not
be distracted by the self-serving machinations of the political
fringes." He beamed on us as if we'd all be grateful in the
long run that he'd slapped our wrists and got us back to
business. "We're artists and we've got a play to do. Okay?"

The meeting broke. I excused myself from Micah and
pushed through the muttering crowd of staffers to intercept
the Eye as they stalked out of the room.

Liz Godwin dogged close behind. "Good working atmosphere, my ass! After this fiasco?"

We ran into Howie.

"Are we moving to the theatre or not?" Liz demanded.

Howie sighed irritably. "Micah talked me out of it. He
swears Sean'll never finish otherwise." Micah stood nearby,
talking with Rachel but close enough to overhear. "The old
bastard threatened to take his name off the program if I
insisted on coming in early. Ah, well. The mayor's so worried about Harmony getting a reputation for lawlessness,
she's agreed to assign Security to the Barn."

Mali approached. I tried to catch his eye, but he brushed
past as if I weren't there. No-Mulelatu followed, last in line.
I grabbed his elbow.

"Ule! Is Sam all right?"

Ule pulled me along with him. "Why, right as rain, my
lady."

"Jane says you magicked him."

"Well . . ." He seemed concerned lest I suspect some

lack of faith in Cora's doctor. "Just to hurry him along, you know."

"Sure, I understand . . . uh, the eye in the plaza was great."

The little dance-man licked his thumb and scribed an imaginary point score in the air as he ducked through the doorway.

I tagged along outside in the hallway, wading up-current against the stream of cheerful *Crossroads* cast members pouring in for their first tech rehearsal. "You didn't tell them about Jane and . . ."

Ule resettled his knit cap on his head. "Nope."

"Why not?"

He tapped the tip of his finger against his temple. "Knowledge is power, ladykins."

He misread the little frown I could not repress.

"Don't worry, we've got it all in hand." He lifted the hem of his orange T-shirt to reveal the carved bone handle of a knife sheathed behind his waistband in the hollow of his back. The blade alone was eight inches long.

"Jeez, Ule. Don't let them catch you with that."

Ule only smiled.

Sure, I understand.

What else can you say when a person, while admittedly eccentric but otherwise quite like a normal human being, acts as if magic were nothing out of the ordinary?

"Exactly the contradiction that got to me in the script," I explained to Mark over a machine lunch in the crew room.

"Do you believe in magic, G?"

"Well, not, you know, fairy godmothers and things . . ." Nobody'd asked me right out like that before. "But their kind of magic . . . oh hell, I don't know what to think!"

"Or what to let them think you think." He gathered up our trash for the recycler. "I know I don't believe in magic. But damned if I've been able to admit that to the Eye."

I lounged deeply in my overstuffed armchair. "Skepticism insults them."

"Irrational belief insults me, or at least my sense of myself as a rational being. And because they seem rational, it's hard for me to believe *they* believe it."

"Maybe they are just playing with us," I sighed.

Micah claimed the Eye's manipulative dexterity was the

height of their art. I thought manipulation was condescending and didn't want to believe it of them. Or maybe I just wanted to be special. One of the chosen few they didn't manipulate. "Guess the best we can do for now is just play along."

"Or avoid the issue entirely." Mark held out a hand to haul me out of my chair. "C'mon, lazybones, duty calls."

"Get any further with the constitution?" I said as we waded through the chaos in the scene shop.

His face brightened. "I'm gathering details on those rights of petition." On the spiral stair to the costume shop, he moved aside for a brace of SecondGen seamstresses returning from lunch. "It's complicated. I'll tell you about it later!"

When we don't have to worry about who's listening, he meant.

I waved him upstairs and returned to my chilly white prison, my dressing room paint shop.

Mark had the right idea. The rational route was easier. After all, the Eye's magic was still by implication only. They spoke of tales and power, but only Te-Cucularit actually used the word *magic*. And they hadn't exactly dazzled us with miracles. Their magic hadn't protected Sam. Even Sam's magic hadn't protected Sam. Yet Jane insisted that magic had healed him. "Inside, where the doctor didn't go."

"The eye's magic, too," she said about the shimmering image fading into the sunset above Fetching Plaza. She was as dogged now in her defense of the Eye as she had been critical of them previously. "I saw them make it. We went there at sunrise and they just *did* it."

I called the studio to say I was sending Jane home but I'd be working late.

Cris brought supper and the news reports. "Howie created a real media event. Managed to bury the whole Conch thing very nicely. Damn!" he reflected irritably, "I was so sure it was Sam."

"Jane says they magicked Sam. I think they 'magicked' Jane. They've got some reason to want her really believing in their magic."

"Jane's the weak link," he replied, as if he were privy to all the Eye's reasoning. "She became dangerous. They had all the Eye's reasoning. "She became dangerous. They had to defuse her somehow, without making a public scene out of it." He peeled back plastic. Steam rose in the chilled air, smelling like brown rice and stirfry. He pulled two stolen forks out of a pocket and dug in. "What better way than a quick dose of revelation?"

"It was our speculating that egged her on," I reminded him. "No, it's more like . . . like they took her on."

He was unconvinced when I told him what the Eye had promised. "Sure, that's all they need, Jane hanging around after them."

"I don't believe they'd lie to her."

"Why not, if it gets her off their backs?"

I couldn't say why I was sure. "Mali wouldn't lie."

Cris laughed. "Maybe they've magicked you a little, too."

After we ate, we went up to the plaza to search for the holo projectors we knew the Eye must have hidden somewhere. But the glowing green image had vanished with the coming of darkness, and though Cris carefully worked out all the math to plot exactly where they should be, we never did locate those projectors.
did locate those projectors.

THE MATTA:

When we went back to work, Te-Cucularit was waiting in the dressing room with all four of the women. Hickey nosed about in the back. "Got any empties to mix new paint in?"

"Gwinn-Rhys." Cu's greeting was nothing that could be called a welcome, but at least he remembered my name. "Tonight we will paint the Matta."

"Great!" The ladies were a triumphant riot of color. I felt recharged just looking at them. "You look wonderful! Have you been to a party?"

Omea did a laughing pirouette. The folds of her garment flared wide, then settled around her in a spiral like a flock of landing birds.

"It is for the Matta," said Cu firmly.

Tua tossed her head. "It is to make us happy!"

"Proud!" breathed Tuli.

The drab white dressing room shimmered with life. Each woman wore a seemingly endless length of brightly patterned fabric wound around the torso, tucked and wrapped in ways as magical and mysterious as Sam's sleight of hand and lying loose below the hips. Wreaths of white flowers nestled against bare brown necks and shoulders. Lucienne wore red to accent her contrasting paleness. The headdresses were towering confections of plumes and flowers, woven into the shapes of birds and animals, trimmed with arching wisps of feather and tails of trailing vine.

"We do need a little pick-me-up," Omea conceded, "after today."

"Reede Chamberlaine." I shook my head disgustedly.

"Howie Marr," she corrected. "We don't expect Reede to know any better."

Tua adjusted her flowers in a mirror. "At home, we would go bare-breasted."

Omea sighed. "Yes. But here it would not be understood."

"I'd understand," promised Hickey, slipping his arm around Lucienne's tiny waist. She nestled against him and a most un-Hickey-like grin blossomed on his face.

I smiled on them benignly. So what if he looked silly?

Te-Cucularit muttered over his paint cans, pouring while Tuli stirred. Tuli was barely out of adolescence, with the gawky grace of very young dancers. Her tongue pressed the corner of her mouth as she gripped the stirring stick with both tiny hands. The sorcerer's apprentice. I smothered a laugh.

"Cu does not sanction this dilution of tradition," Omea noted. "But I say if our intention is pure, the Ancestors will approve."

I gathered up the thick folds of the Matta from the counter. "Let's do it out in the theatre where there's room."

"Wait!" Cu barked, then added more quietly, "Let Omealeanoo carry the Matta."

Omea regarded me sympathetically as I surrendered the silky layers into her arms. "Come. The Matta ritual was my husband's favorite. You will enjoy it."

"Your husband?"

"My husband Seluk. Our first director, our first leading man. Seluk played the roles that Mali plays. He's dead now."

I recalled the name from Crispin's early research. "I'm sorry."

"It was long ago." Omea smiled. "Yet he is with us still. Tonight we will dedicate this Matta to him."

I led the women down the hall, feeling distinctly underdressed.

"How's Sam?" I asked.

"Doing well, thanks be."

"Is he in a lot of pain?"

"Mostly he's angry at having been taken by surprise. You know how men are."

Not these men, I thought. They take violence so calmly. As if it was deplorable but nothing unusual.

Theatre Two was dark but for a tight circle of onstage work light. The three blunted triangles of seating faded to dim geometry split by the darker thrusts of the radial ramp-ways. Like roads into the void. You couldn't help but be drawn into that blackness. An empty theatre holds such promise.

Onstage, the skeletal outlines of Micah's set were taking shape. The back wall swept upward in bare ribs of plastic and steel, like half the hull of a giant boat. The steeply undulating deck was a forest of metal legs and cross-bracing. I was delighted to find four of Sean's regular crew at work on the tracking support. A small crew but still hard at work, after hours. Up center, where the deck curled up to blend smoothly with the sweep, Ruth explained shop protocol to three new faces.

"Oh, hooray," I murmured to Omea. "Micah found extra hands and Sean didn't throw them out of the shop."

"That's nice," she replied vaguely, reminding me that the shop problem was one the Eye wasn't even aware of. I did not elaborate. I spidered across the decking framework.

"Ruth! Okay if we paint downstage?"

"Sure." Her stifled yawn became a snort when she got a look at my 'crew.' "They're gonna work dressed like that?"

"Some kind of ritual," I explained.

"Oh. Right." Ruth plucked unconsciously at her own stained coveralls. "Be my guest."

I grabbed a broom to clear scraps and welding debris from the open space downstage. Omea laid the Matta on the floor, carefully restacking its layers to unravel fold by fold. Tua and Lucienne knelt on either side of the stack.

Omea took up one top corner, Tuli the other. At Omea's signal, they began a throaty, conversational chant, like two matrons singing gossip to each other. They swung slowly across the open stage, hauling out the fabric. They walked and sang, paused while the kneeling women chanted an answering verse, then walked and sang again.

Hickey and Cris brought paint and water from the dressing room. Te-Cucularit followed with the unpainted Puleales and two raffia-bound bundles of brushes unlike any we'd been using, slim and soft-bristled. Calligraphic brushes. The singing crescendoed as Omea and Tuli ran out of stage space and laid their end of the fabric on the deck. Their four-way chant swelled into the darkness beyond the work light. Closing my eyes, I pictured as vividly as if I were there the women calling to each other in the coffee fields. Remarkable, since I'd never been in a coffee field in my life, except through the magic of vids and holos.

Up by the back wall, the crew stopped work to listen.

As the women sang, Cu set out paint jars along the length of the fabric. He unbound his brushes. Their handles were like knotty twigs, shiny with use. He laid them out as you would rare treasures, and selected one. The women wove the four voices of the chant into a single drawn-out trill in minor key that ended like a question. Cu dipped the brush into brilliant orange and handed it to Omea.

Omea held the brush high in a heartbeat of pure silence.

From the darkened house behind us, a deep voice rang out. One phrase of solo declaration, joined soon by the rhythmic punctuation of wood blocks. Moussa stepped into the circle of work light, his arm raised like the hunter returning from the night. No-Mulelatu and Pen waited behind him, half in shadow. Ule held the blocks, Pen a small leather drum. My skin prickled. On cheeks and forehead, each wore a neat thumb swipe of vermilion paint. I was grateful for their gym shoes and jeans because a worrisome time slippage was beginning around me. Like gliding down a jungle river, vines and palm fronds whipping past, falling toward an older world of spirits and mysticism, a world I felt a stranger to but, unlike Mark, could not completely discredit. I looked to Cris, crouched beside Hickey. The avid lean of his body said he'd been waiting for the Eye to do something like this. Something *weird*.

But was it really so weird? A little face paint? The heated

glint in Moussa's eye? Cu did nothing bizarre. He continued to behave exactly as I'd come to expect of him. Sober and intent, he settled cross-legged facing the painters across the shining green river of the Matta. He beckoned Moussa to one side of him, Pen and Ule to the other. Perhaps the strangest thing was that for once, the others did exactly as Cu decreed. Ule passed his wood blocks to Moussa, took off his shoes, and drew a set of panpipes from his shirt pocket.

"What's going on?" Mark dropped to the floor beside me. "You can hear music all over the theatre!"

"Shhh!" I said.

As Moussa shed his own shoes, Te-Cucularit began a new chant.

His light tenor was sure and sweet. It played harmonic chase games with Moussa's bass when the musician joined him after a verse. Ule's panpipes interwove a sprightly melody. The women knelt and began to paint.

Rows of symbols flowed out of their flicking wrists. Half letter, half image, they had the look of hieroglyphs born of rock and water rather than sand, the histories of the clan spun out in color and line. The women sang counterpoint to the men as they worked. Their speed and steady rhythm was mesmerizing. Joy informed each stroke, an infectious communal joy that poured over me as I watched. Because it was joy and not terror, I let it in without resisting, let it spiral me up, away, out of the dark, waiting theatre. Drifting skyward, I felt myself smile.

The music stopped. I woke from a daydream of open sky, marveling at how profoundly blue it was, and how inviting. Too inviting. I am not given to drifting off in the middle of things. It made me uneasy. No, more than uneasy. It scared the piss out of me.

"Good, aren't they?" said Mark coolly. "But then we knew that."

The first section of the Matta was completed. The thin, brilliant pigment that Cu had mixed was already dry enough to allow the fabric to be moved. Cris sat next to Moussa in the line of the men. Presumptuous, I thought, but the Eye didn't seem to mind. Hickey squatted tentatively beside No-Mulelatu, as if being included in such activity was only slightly preferable to being left out.

"That was quick." I tried to sound offhand.

Mark laughed. "We've been sitting here nearly an hour. Where have you been?"

I couldn't answer that for the life of me.

A fresh length of fabric was unfolded. The women went back to work, singing and painting. I'll keep my head better, I thought, if I don't listen so hard. But the Eye's music wouldn't stand still for casual listening. It was too full of surprises, of suddenly syncopated rhythms, of shrill atonal ululations swooping up out of close and gentle harmonies while the pulsing support of a bass drone drops away like land at the edge of a precipice. I was drawn back into my sky dreaming when it became too interesting to resist. When I came to myself again, the Matta was nearly done. Mark was nudging me. Te-Cucularit stood in front of us.

"Gwinn-Rhys, your hand is needed."

I stared up at him. He shifted, irritated by my lack of response. I glanced around. The women were still painting, the men still singing and playing. Cris had acquired Moussa's wood blocks and was managing them rather creditably. The shop crew were on break, but Ruth lingered, sitting upstage on a sawhorse with one of the new hands, a big, scrawny kid with a red beard. They were swinging their feet to the music, enjoying themselves.

"We're all here now," Cu insisted. "You're needed to complete the circle of the women."

I hadn't a clue what he was talking about. I looked around again. While I'd been drifting, Sam and Mali had arrived. Sam! Bruised but upright, propped against a stack of flooring, nodding approvingly as Moussa beat out a complicated riff on a small quartet of lap drums. My joy at seeing him alive took me quite by surprise.

"Go on, G," urged Mark as Cu held out his hand.

I took it distractedly. He pulled me smartly to my feet, then released me, and shoved a brush into my fist. I stared at it as dumbly as I'd stared at him. Sunlight gold glimmered on its tip.

"But I don't know what to paint!"

Cu dismissed that with a flick of his head. "Paint your own tale. Paint as I taught you. It will be all right."

My own tale? Why did this fill me with such unreasoning panic? I cast around for support. Cris, Hickey, Mark—all intent on the singing. Their joy now threatened with its single-minded intensity.

"What *is* the matter?" Cu hissed, in the tone of an actor whose colleague has suddenly gone dry on him. The honesty of it shocked me back to reason. How foolish. If I knew how to do anything, I knew how to paint. The brush was weighty and familiar in my hand, and the memory of my daydream vivid enough to reproduce in every detail. It didn't even matter that the color was wrong.

"Nothing," I said, and knelt to paint the confusion of a young woman winging skyward even while fully aware that she is sitting inside a darkened theatre, under a dome.

The formality of the ritual broke down spontaneously with the completion of the Matta. The women tossed their brushes down. Ule pocketed his panpipes. Moussa and Pen drew aside to play dueling drums. Sam groaned to his feet and limped over to inspect the painting.

His face was hard to look at, stitched and swollen and discolored. He mocked his own slurred speech, even as pain cut short every syllable. He wasn't causing rare orchids to appear, but he was there, walking around when he shouldn't have been able to.

". . . *magicked him*," Jane's voice whispered in my head. The women gathered around to make much of him.

Cris tried to formulate an apology that wasn't too abject.

Sam looked up at him. "So, you thought I was the Conch."

"Well, I . . ."

"Me, all by myself? I'm flattered." Shrugging off Mali's arm, Sam eased himself onto a pile of folded masking. "That'll be the day, when they get the drop on the Conch, when they beat the living shit out of Latooea!"

"Oh, Sam!" Omea laid her brown cheek against his black-and-blue one. "You're beating yourself up harder than they did."

"You see where romantic foolery can get you?" Mali rumbled.

Cris shrugged. "Harmless speculation, I thought."

"Listen, young Crispin: spend less time chasing Latooea and more worrying about your Closed Door League adding apprenticeship to its list of felonies."

Upstage, the carpenters came off break and went back to their cutting and hammering. Two of the regular crew began setting up a rolling metal scaffold. The pipe was rickety and the men moved with the dull slowness of the deeply exhausted. I thought, *Someone should send them home*. But if we did, the show wouldn't get built.

Omea swept up to admire my little bit of work, my "tale." I smiled and nodded, convinced there could be no real sense to what I had done. I wasn't sure it mattered. I felt oddly disassociated. A spacy sense of floating persisted from my sky-dream. I watched Mark sit down with Mali and Sam. Soon they'd be talking politics. Lucienne retired with Hickey to the dubious privacy of house left. He put one arm around her neck and buried the other in the flowers on her breasts. Cris eased away from the political discussion to "find" himself conveniently next to Tua as she helped Tuli pack up their paint. But I stayed where I was, cross-legged in front of the gold-flecked green of the Matta.

My eyes, scanning the stage with all the emotional awareness of a remote-sensing device, finally settled on Te-Cucularit, crouched over the Puleales, still hard at work. The unambiguous physicality of paint and brush and the purity of Cu's intent were stabilizing to my unmoored state of mind. Soothed, I watched him paint.

"No use looking at him, he won't have you." No-Mulelatu lounged nearby, packing the bowl of his tiny pipe with dry greenish fibers.

I quickly shed my dreamy smile. "I wasn't—"

"He won't, you know. Saves himself for his pure-blooded woman." Ule shaped a thin curl of rich, acrid smoke to twist around his finger like a lock of hair. "Now, me, I am not so narrow-minded. I see quality where it lies."

The pipe went out and he lit a nearly invisible lighter to heat it up again. My eyes told me his thumb was on fire. My brain said: okay, perfectly normal for a Tuatuan.

"Or you could just keep on looking at him like that."

"You don't understand, it's not—"

Ule chuckled. "No insult, ladykins. They all look at him that way. Even the men. Especially the men."

"You're jealous."

He considered, sucking in smoke and holding it. "Nope," he exhaled finally. "Rather my passionate heart than his glorious body. You think you domers are the only ones he's hard on? He's a stone, Cu is. Dried up inside."

I was grateful for something concrete to focus on. "Nice way to talk about your friends."

"Te-Cucularit is my clansman, for whom I would give my life. But he is not my friend. Now, Mali and Sam. That's friends."

"I see you with Cu all the time."

Ule shrugged. "We're from the same village. Fourth Clan, Earth—Nawki, the Death. Heavy burden, y'know? Somebody's got to keep him out of trouble, with that stiff neck of his, obsessed with tradition and the past. A thing's not real to him until it's straitjacketed into ritual." He smirked. "Sam calls him the Preacher."

"So I hear. But you don't think tradition is important?"

"Not for its own sake. Latooea writes, 'Through the past we create the future.' Cu only looks backward. No, my lady, you're better off with me. I'm the safer bet."

It was hard not to smile back at him. The offer was generously given. "No insult, No-Mulelatu," I replied. "I'm already taken."

"Are you?" He flopped back on one elbow as if to draw more deeply on his pipe, but his glance targeted Cris and Tua, shoulder to shoulder at the edge of the stage. Tua was talking earnestly. Cris was eager and predatory. "More's the pity," said Ule.

Out in the house, Hickey had taken Lucienne's face between his hands and was kissing her deeply.

Behind me, Mark said to Mali, "I got hassled by some German tourists yesterday. If the tourists are picking up on it now . . ."

This seemed a safer conversation. I offered Ule a parting grin and crawled over to listen in.

"Time to air your issues more publicly." Sam struggled the words past his swollen jaw. When I joined them, he nodded at the Matta. "You do nice work, Rhys . . . for a girl." He couldn't quite manage a grin.

Mark chewed his lip. "The rights of petition are clearly in place, but we don't have the numbers."

"Maybe you do." Mali's bony frame was folded up like a mahogany deck chair tossed carelessly on the floor. "You say there's less than two thousand active apprentices, but think a little further: what about those who once were apprentices? Or those living with ex-apprentices, who might be convinced with a little talk?"

"There's also sympathetic Second- and ThirdGens like Songh who'll go with you," added Sam. "If the CDL were sure of their majority, they wouldn't be bothering with these e-mail games. You'd have all been Out long ago."

I was impressed. In Harmony less than a month, if you didn't count their quarantine, and they already had as good a grasp on its sociology as we did. Maybe better. We saw ourselves as helpless chaff in the wind. These two didn't believe in helpless.

"There are more of you than you think." Mali extended a palm and fisted it. "There's power in those numbers and the CDL knows it and wants you to think otherwise. They want you demoralized and distracted. Don't let them fool you with this dangerous-radicals talk. We're just the bait, bro. You are the prey."

Sam frowned faintly. I wasn't sure he agreed.

Mali scavenged a splinter of wood from the floor and stuck it in his mouth. "On Tuatua, we are two minorities— one rich and in power, one poor but"—he smiled—"well organized. We struggle for control of a mostly apathetic majority."

Sam nodded. "There's your job: convince the quiet uncommitteds to speak up in your favor. Write that petition. Start airing your grievances, like the CDL airs theirs."

"Their way's too sneaky," said Mark.

"And so far it's worked," Sam replied.

"We don't really have grievances," I said. "We just don't want to get thrown out."

"Some jerk hassles your friend on the street and that's not a grievance?" Mali spat his splinter into the air behind him. "Ah, Sam, what are they teaching our children? Everything about enjoying the freedom of the artist and nothing about how to hold on to it!"

Mark felt his hard efforts being dismissed. "I suppose you can teach us better?"

"What the hell," returned Sam softly but not particularly kindly, "do you think he's been doing?"

With a rustle of skirts, Omea dropped gracefully beside me. "There! That's done. Except he'll want us to dedicate it properly, but that can wait 'til it's dry." She raised both arms to her hair to undo some complicated fastenings, removed the tall feather headdress, and set it aside as if it were any old hat. She peered at the men's faces. "Problems of the world time, is it? How are you, Sam? You shouldn't be thinking with your head all swelled up like that."

Mali regarded Sam with wry fondness. "The organizer's gearing up."

"I don't take well to being shit-kicked," Sam growled. He leaned forward, swept the floor with his bandaged palms as if scratching battle diagrams in the dirt of some rebel hideout. "Listen, kid: first you have to set your style, right?"

Mark eased back and let go of his sulk.

Sam returned the best he could do for a grin. "Good lad. Now, the CDL's already stolen the media angle. But you have your squeaky-clean image: innocent youth. Very potent. And because it's important for you to represent the constitutional, the legal and democratic side of the argument—"

Upstage, a warning yell rang out, then a metallic groan and more panicked shouting.

"The scaffolding!" I gasped.

Mali turned, rising. "*Pen! Moussa!*" He was already scaling the decking framework. Two tired crewmen struggled at the base of thirty feet of tipping scaffold. Tools scattered from the top walkway where the bearded kid, one of the new hands, hung on for dear life. Sam lurched up to follow Mali, swearing harshly as Omea and Mark held him back. He was too weak to shake them off.

Moussa beat Mali to the scaffold. He threw his solid bulk against the angle of its fall and planted his feet. Pen and Mali hauled on the other end and the scaffold swung back. Cris reached it and grabbed hold as it steadied and settled back on its legs. The crewmen sank to the deck in relief and exhaustion.

The kid clambered down the still-vibrating metal frame. "Piece o' shit scaffold!" He grabbed Moussa's hand. "Saved my life, man!"

"No problem," Moussa replied.

Mali stood over the nearest stagehand. "How long since you've had a night's sleep, bro?"

The man laughed. "Sleep? Who needs it?"

"You do," said Mali. "Go on home."

The men looked at each other. "Well, we'd sure like to, but—"

"He's right," called Ruth from the loading door. Her face was puffy with sleep. "When we start getting that careless, we should call it a night."

Mark relaxed his hold on Sam. "Sorry."

Sam twitched his clothing into place irritably. "Yeah. So am I."

"Mali's always telling other people's workers what to do," I observed as the tall Tuatuan climbed down off the decking and came toward us.

"Don't mind him," said Sam. "When you're the chief's son, you're taught to order folks around." He pretended Mali had not overheard him. "He does okay, considering."

Mali returned one of his complex looks, then wrapped a careful arm around Sam's shoulders. "Time for all of us to go home, bro."

I'd really like, I thought, to see Sam play Horatio to Mali's Hamlet. The dynamic seemed so right just then.

The evening's bizarre and intimate mood was broken. Omea went to see if the paint was dry. Tuli finished gathering up brushes. Hickey and Lucienne emerged from house left, blinking in the glare of the work light. Though he held her hand firmly in his own, Hickey watched the girl as if she might disappear. I helped Tua stack the paint in a caddy, eyeing her sidelong. I couldn't really blame Cris for finding her distracting, but it hurt when he did it while I was still around.

No-Mulelatu roused himself from his smoke-wreathed reverie. He gripped my shoulder, leaning into me unsteadily. He snatched off his knit cap and jammed it on my head. "A little token. For your good work."

I adjusted the cap with a silly smile. "Ule, are you sure?"

"Yeah." He grinned. "I'm never so stoned I don't know what I'm doing. Look at the rest. Anyone else said thank you?"

"Omea. Sam, sort of."

"Oh. Well, they would." He shrugged and wandered off.

Te-Cucularit, who had painted through the entire disturbance, muttered something indecipherable and dropped his brush into the water bucket. He hunkered over the Puleales to review his work. I gathered his paint jars and capped them.

"Those look great," I noted. He had covered each knobby cylinder with an intricate web of interlocking geometry, recalling a Greek key, pale yellow or red against ebony wood. I reached to smooth the lustrous surfaces with an admiring finger. Cu snatched my hand away so abruptly that I let out a squeak of surprise.

"You may not touch them."

The odd evening had worn me out. "Oh, Cu, I've been handling those things for days!"

"They were not painted then," he insisted doggedly. "They are for men's hands only now."

I wasn't going to let myself tear up in front of him again. I picked up his paint jars. "If you say so."

"I know what you think," he said quickly, before I could move away. "But there are true matters about the separate powers of men and of women that must be observed. Else we are both weakened."

I gave up on the notion that if Te-Cucularit was so aware of himself as a performer in these ceremonies he staged, he might be more into the pomp and ritual than the actual belief. "You don't make it easy, Te-Cucularit."

"Easy?" He settled tightly on his heels, urgency replacing his scowl. "Listen to me. Someone in the world must live responsibly. Someone must walk the Stations. Someone must decide to keep the laws. If not I, then who? If not anyone, then where are we? What are we? No better than our enemies."

I resisted the urge to say, "Lighten up, Preacher," as I had the feeling Sam would have. Cu was too much in earnest. Besides, I decided, we each must be allowed to pursue our personal strategies for keeping Chaos at bay. I was eager to develop one myself, now that it looked like I was going to need it.

THE PETITION:

The more I thought about Sam, the angrier I got with Cris.

"Me?" he demanded. "What about her?"

Across the breakfast table, Jane worked serenely away at a double helping of oatmeal. Beside her, Mark scribbled on a napkin, his eggs cooling at his elbow.

"Jane learned her lesson," I said. "You're still at it!"

"And bet I'm gonna watch who I talk to from now on!"

The long, airy dining room was crowded but suspiciously quiet. No singing or boisterous arguments, no food fights. A halo of empty seats isolated our table.

Songh arrived bearing the latest e-mail snatched fresh from his parents' fax. Jane grabbed it. Mark crossed a sentence out on his napkin and started over.

"The petition?" Songh read over Mark's shoulder. "Sounds like civics class."

"Just consider for one minute that they're telling it straight," I pursued. "That they're ordinary people stuck in ordinary domestic politics and that they're not hiding the Conch."

"Ordinary? The Eye? Be serious."

It was foolhardy to pick a fight with Cris. He was so much better at it, able to be incredulous and defiant simultaneously. "You ought to think about what's good for them for a change, instead of being so hot to show everyone how clever you are!"

Jane read the e-mail. ". . . while the League certainly deplores such unconscionable violence, it does wonder how a certain artistic director did not foresee that a criminal element would bring its own violence with it."

Mark crumpled his napkin and reached for mine. "You need this?"

"Maybe it should be more straightforward," suggested Songh.

Mark nodded. "The power is in the signatures, not the language."

Yolanda stopped behind Mark, balancing her laden tray on her forearm, looking as if she wanted to ask me a question.

I edged away from Cris. "There's room over here, Yoli."

"Nah, I can't . . . I, um . . ." She leaned over the table. "What's this about a meeting last night? A petition? Everybody's talking."

Mark laid down his pen. "Would've been better if they'd come."

"With fifteen minutes' notice at midnight? Come on, I was asleep already."

Cris laughed. "Ten people. Not bad for a bunch of amateurs."

"Got to start somewhere." Mark bent back to his scribbling.

Yolanda shifted the tray to her other arm. "You know, guys, some think you shouldn't be raising waves at a time like this."

"They're wrong," murmured Jane into her oatmeal.

"Like that list you put up? You guys put that up, right?"

Mark was very relaxed and deliberate. Dignified, I decided. He was learning more from Mali than political consciousness. "If apprentices are being harassed on the streets, we should be telling each other about it."

It was Songh's idea to write all the incidents down and post the list outside the dining room. Next to it, he pinned up copies of all the e-mails received to date.

Yolanda leaned in closer. "Nobody wants to tell that stuff! Jeez, whadda ya write, some old lady spit on me today?"

"Sam said not to expect a groundswell right off," said Mark.

"Yeah. Well, just thought I'd mention it. See ya."

"Yoli!" Mark let his voice ring through the dining room. "There's another meeting tonight, don't forget."

We'd called a dorm meeting on impulse after the Matta ritual, with faint success. On the same impulse, we'd invited the Eye to dinner at the dorm.

"Anytime," agreed Mali, the evangelist and teller of tales.

"No way," decreed Sam, the strategist. "Last thing we want is to encourage the CDL's apprentice-conspiracy accusations. They are the conspirators, not you."

But he did approve a breakfast planning session at Cora's as being faintly less visible. "Only to the public, you understand. The CDL will be keeping a record every time you fart."

It was morning cool in Cora's cavernous brick-walled kitchen. The high arched windows let in a quiet lavender light through rippled glass. The butcher-block counters were shining and empty, the antique tole-work canisters all in place. Cora's house was what I'd dreamed Harmony would be way back in Chicago.

Cris bounced around the room, then settled with Mark and Mali under the hanging lamp at the refectory table. He had taken to wearing his coverall unfastened to his navel, and today he had braided the long hair at his temples like Pen sometimes did. I thought he looked stupid.

"Where is everybody?" he demanded.

Mali was still damp from the shower and naked but for

a strip of orange linen wrapped intricately around his groin. He was like bones wound in dark leather. Outrage keeps him thin, I thought. "They're asleep," he yawned. "It's an hour yet 'til warm-ups."

"You think they're all as crazy as we are?" Sam was fully dressed, as always. A different kind of man might have shown off scars like the ones I recalled Sam carried. He limped about opening and closing fumed-oak cabinets and pulling edibles at random out of the walk-in fridge. I thought it unfair he should be the one working, wounded as he was. I found plates and mugs and pewterware, then went to help him with the food.

"Only you and me here not used to getting waited on?" He handed me oranges and crusty bread wrapped in brown paper.

"I can't sit at that table. Last time I saw it, you were bleeding all over it."

His laugh was dry and quick. "Worried about me, were you?"

"Oh yes."

He eyed me a little more gently, as if my honesty shamed him. "No need. No need." He flexed his fingers and deftly palmed an egg, to show his hands were back in working order.

I tried to meet his gaze, to take in his livid bruises and his stapled-up lip and brow as if it were nothing very terrible. I might as well have held up a mirror for him.

"Never was much of a beauty anyhow." He grabbed the oranges from me and turned to stick them in the juicer.

"Now, *last* night's meeting was standing room only!" Cris drummed his fists and crowed. "When we read out the petition, nobody said much but . . ."

"Scared of taking their lives into their own hands," said Mark.

Mali listened benignly, one leg hiked up on the table, whose aged planking was as dark and polished as his skin. "Like you were."

"Yes, sir." Mark smiled and flicked his blond hair back. "Like I was."

"But wait!" Cris declared. "When we called for a vote, it was a few hands, then more, then the whole room rising to approve the motion! Wish I'd had a vidcam. What a scene! It was dynamic!"

Mark said, "Those who didn't agree, didn't come."

Sam delivered a pitcher of juice and signaled me to pour. "So let's hear this miracle petition."

Mark unfolded a copy and read.

In the end, he'd left the eloquence to his statistics and framed a simple request to the citizenry of Harmony, in care of Her Honor the Mayor, for a frank and public discussion of the future of the Outside Adoption Policy and of the Apprenticeship Program as a whole. His quoting of legal precedent for petitioning was eased in almost as an afterthought.

"Good," Sam nodded. "Good."

Cris cheered and pounded Mark's shoulder.

Mark fiddled with the edges of his paper. "My, uh, my father always said, in a lawsuit you have to assume the rights you're claiming, so the other side will appear as the aggressor when they try to take them away from you."

Sam looked to Mali. "What more can I say?"

Mali laughed. "Writing's the easy part. Now get out there and drum up those signatures!"

TOWN MEETING:

The first signature on my petition sheet was Micah's.

"It's Town Meeting tonight," he noted after he'd read it over. "Watch it on the vid."

"We're all painting late. Bring us a report."

Micah handed back the petition. "This approach wouldn't have occurred to me, but it's probably the right idea. Positive action. Risky, but right."

"It wasn't completely ours," I admitted.

"I guessed as much." Micah tossed down his brush, settled back on his stool. "I'm missing all the excitement, closeted up here all day. How are they doing, our dangerous radicals?"

"Come to the theatre more. We could really use you there."

"I'll get there. Soon as I get out from under Willow Street."

I caught him up on the details. One detail was Kim Levin buying me a fancy fruit box in the greenroom canteen so she could get me aside to ask what was wrong with Micah, why couldn't he work things out with Sean and couldn't I do something about it?

Another was a scene I'd had that morning with Sean.

I'd gone by the Arkadie early, feisty from our strategy breakfast at Cora's. The *Gift* build was far enough along that some fairly major problems were becoming evident: curves that did not bank as smoothly as the drawings indicated, riser heights that were off by too many centimeters, shapes and surfaces in the backdrop that didn't match the model.

I reported this to Ruth, expecting the usual can-do response.

"Talk to Sean," she said.

I didn't argue. "Where?"

"Over at *Crossroads*. One of our new holo machines crapped out in the middle of last night's tech."

In form, Theatre One was a traditional proscenium house of the sort that has been around for four hundred years. In scale, it was operatic: five tiers of crystal, gilt, and velvet, four thousand seats and not a one of them obstructed view.

The stage was as big as a sports arena. For *Crossroads*, it was tracked and winched and geared and elevatored six ways from Sunday. Not a square inch of deck was left unmechanized. The fly loft was jammed with scenery, lighting equipment, projectors, and FX machines. Both wings were piled two stories high and two whole acts of finished scenery still waited onstage, getting in the way.

The *Crossroads* show carpenter, a slight, dark man in jacket and cravat, paced around muttering into his headset, halting every so often to stare up into the flies, where the scenery was packed so tightly he couldn't see through it to his men on the grid. Six of the paint crew were up on a rolling scaffold, shiny new I noticed, touching up a hanging window wall. Max Eider lurked beneath them.

"*Ja*, Gallia, is good, only more golden!" He was hoarse from shouting over the noise. "No, Rene, you must make this transition better. That is like finger painting!"

"How's it going, Mr. Eider?" I did not stop as I hurried past.

"You see how!" He gestured eloquently at the painters. "I hear Micah is very far behind?"

I nodded and kept going. It wasn't Micah who was behind.

Sean was bent double over a pulled-up section of deck, shouting to the men below. I had to tap his back to get his attention.

"One sec." He leaned further into the pit. "So check every goddamn connection and run the sequence again! Jesus, man, do I gotta get in there and do it for you?" He straightened. "What?"

"Got a minute?"

"Sure, sometime next year."

"Oh, Sean." I made a comic face at him, as if everything were the way it had always been.

"Awright, awright, what is it? Wait, hold it." He cupped his hands to his mouth. "Pedro! Get the vac over and clean this hole out! This equipment won't work sittin' in garbage!" He turned back to me. "So what's this I hear about a petition?"

"Hunh?"

"You involved in it? Must be, I guess."

"How did you . . . ?"

"Good idea to get the issue out in the open." Sean was nodding without looking at me. "I mean, I got my kids' future to worry about just like anyone, but talking, that's what Harmony's about, right? No point pretending we don't have a problem."

"No," I said slowly. Which problem did he mean? "Of course not."

"Right." He dismissed the topic with a wave. "Well, what's up?"

I expressed my concerns about the set.

"Really? Well, you bring in new people, you know, that's what you get."

"Ruth's not new people."

"Sean!" The show carpenter waved his headset from center stage.

"Yeah, what?"

"Bill Rand's on the line here asking can you still make it for lunch?"

"Tell him I'll be ten minutes late," Sean yelled. He turned back impatiently. "Gwinn, look, they're probably going at it a little fast next door, but that's so there'll be something to walk on by Tuesday's tech. They won't notice what it looks like."

"You mean the Eye?"

"I mean actors. They never do. It still bothers you later, we'll go back in and fix it." He looked straight at me. "You think I'd let Micah down?"

Micah and I both knew the chance of an after-the-fact fix. If a remote broke down or a door handle fell off in an actor's hand, it was repaired, sure enough. But if a major piece of scenery was built wrong to begin with, management right away started weighing the costs of labor and materials versus the artistic necessity of the redo. Most often, it became the designer's job to camouflage the error or learn to live with it.

In Sean's shop, you didn't usually have to worry about mistakes.

Micah didn't mention Sean. "Could it be purely coincidental I'm being so heavily pressured right now to deliver Bill Rand's piece for Willow Street?"

On my way back to the Arkadie, some kid threw eggs at me.

I was philosophical as I washed drying yolk off my sleeve in the dressing room sink. "Could have been a gang of homicidal teenagers, like I've been dreaming about lately."

"Or a man with a knife," said Jane seriously.

Like No-Mulelatu, I thought. "Who d'you think told Sean about the petition?"

"Word gets around," said Hickey.

"Not that fast, when it has to do with apprentices."

"What are you suggesting?"

"Nothing. I don't know." Why would Sean care about an apprentice petition when he was so far over his head with everything else? I shut off the water and blotted my still-soiled sleeve on a paint rag, gazing around at the welter of empty or dried-up jars of paint, the skinned-over cans and murky water buckets, the balled-up paint rags, the old food wrappings and drink. "Hey, where are all the finished props?"

"He took them," said Jane. "To keep them Clean."

Hickey rubbed his face disgustedly. "I'm putting up a sign: Unclean and proud of it."

His expression made me laugh. "You really got to start getting some sleep, Hick. All this burning the candle at both ends'll do you in . . . you *are* going to Town Meeting tonight?"

"They want me at the *Crossroads* dress. Special request from the director."

Bill Rand again. "Are you going?"

"To Town Meeting? You bet. Wouldn't miss this one for the world."

It felt like a game until then, these urgent dorm meetings and petition signing and street harassment, a real-life variation on our armchair survival exercises. Like the sparring of young cubs as they learn the moves that will feed and protect them when they're grown: serious, but lacking the sharp cut of reality. It was not the Eye's fault. Mali and Sam did their best to wake us from our dreaming.

But in the theatre, the unreal is life-critical one moment, the next, a poster on the wall and a recycler full of scenery. No wonder we continued to laugh and go about our work as if it would always be there tomorrow, no matter how much we claimed to feel threatened. If we'd truly understood what was happening, we'd have been glued to Video Town Hall.

We were all hard at work when Micah appeared in the dressing room that night. I was overjoyed to have him finally in the theatre. But he hadn't come to talk about the show. Hickey slid past him, threw his shambling body into a chair, and sat massaging creases into his forehead.

Immediately I worried for the Eye. "You just got out? It's very late."

Mark and Jane set down their brushes nervously.

"The Closed Door League came up for discussion tonight," said Micah tightly.

"Uh-oh," breathed Songh.

"The meeting went on a bit," Hickey muttered.

"How'd it go?" asked Cris.

Micah was very calm. "Half the town was there."

"The wrong half," said Hickey.

"When the subject of the League came up, Cora Lee and myself and some others called for the members of this secret organization to declare themselves and what they stood for." Micah leaned heavily against the doorframe. "I've never heard a packed arena so filled with silence."

"A regular graveyard," grumbled Hickey. "Some woman behind me said she'd heard the CDL was formed to protest the Francotel deal."

"Got a little sidetracked, didn't they," I muttered.

Micah said, "So we made our pretty little speeches about anonymous harassment undermining the democratic principles of Town Meeting, etc., etc. The mayor nodded and clucked and agreed that the matter must be investigated. A committee was appointed, including most of us who'd spoken up, then the mayor insisted we not waste discussion time before the new committee had thoroughly looked into the matter and presented their findings. A motion to table was seconded and voted on faster than you could take a breath."

Hickey nodded. "You catch who seconded that motion?"

"Campbell Brigham."

"You see how he looked at us?"

Micah shrugged. They brooded in silence for a while.

"Well, you tried," I said finally.

"There's more." Micah's head dipped as if in shame. "Next on the agenda was a proposal from 'a coalition of concerned citizens and parents,' who feel that Harmony's 'valued apprentice resource' is under threat from 'Outside influences,' and the best way to assure its safety is a nightly curfew."

"Curfew!" Cris yelped.

Mark said, "You mean they'd lock us in the dorms at night?"

"Like little children?" I muttered.

"Like criminals," said Jane.

"Off the streets for your own good," confirmed Hickey.

"But we do half of our work at night!" I protested.

"That's what kept the discussion going for so long." Micah shoved at a paint rag on the floor with the toe of his shoe. "Until someone pointed out that the curfew would only apply to apprentices, not resident trainees."

Songh groaned.

Cris was incredulous. "But it couldn't have passed!"

Micah's eyes were clear and cold and very angry. "It passed. It goes into effect tomorrow."

CURFEW:

Our petition raced like wildfire through the eight apprentice dormitories. Then we took it into the workplace.

Howie signed eagerly enough. He even dragged me into the main lobby to do it in full view of the citizens lining up to buy tickets for *Crossroads*. But about the curfew, he just rolled his eyes.

"Ah, it'll never stand. Wait 'til the restaurants start feeling the loss of apprentice business at night. Wait 'til their theatres are half empty."

"We can't afford the restaurants anymore, Howie. And we don't buy our tickets." Except for Mark's recent difficulty at Willow Street.

"Look. You are asses in their seats, too many of which would otherwise be empty, especially at night." Heading off to rehearsal, he threw me a wink. "Who'd pay to see some of the shit they produce in this town?"

I looked down at the petition, hanging limply in my hand.

He stopped in the sunlight flooding through the lobby doors. "Hey, tell you what. Just let me get through this show, then I'll get out and do some campaigning for you kids. Maybe it's time to do a play about apprentices, what do you say? There's a good young writer working with the RoundHall I could put you in touch with. Think about it."

I blinked into the darkness of his silhouette framed by the too-bright doorway. "I don't think we've got that kind of time."

"Relax, Gwinny. Nothing happens that fast around here."

Louisa Pietro, freshly arrived from lighting the Ring Cycle at the Amsterdam State Opera, was not so sanguine. "You mean my assistants can't work in the theatres after nine? Gimme that petition!"

Micah and I paced her through the lower lobby after a

winey lunch in Fetching Plaza. "Songh's off with Mark getting signatures," I told him. "That all right?

He nodded. "Push now, while people are angry about the curfew."

I described Howie's response.

"Howard has no apprentice help," replied Micah. "He sees the whole issue in the abstract. The strategy of course is to force us to fall back on our homebred assistants."

"Never had one worth their salt," said Louisa.

We rounded the corner into Howie's spruced-up gallery. Properly hung and organized, the photos had an earnest, important look.

"We might be partly to blame for that, you know." The cooling of Micah's outrage had left him deeply thoughtful. "If we'd given our SecondGens a better chance, treated them more equally—"

"Nonsense!" Lou declared. "It's what comes of prosperity. The pressure's off, you realize you're not going to starve, next thing you know, you're bored and greedy and inventing enemies where there are none! It's as bad as this Open Sky paranoia! I heard Ingrid Hibberd speak when I was doing *Werter* in Stockholm. What she said was basic common sense: now the Dissolution is under control, we should put the same brilliant resources that saved humanity to work saving the world."

Micah eyed the walls as if they might be hiding vidcams and recording devices. He offered an arch, conspiratorial grin.

"Oh balls!" said Louisa. "It's not sedition. Hibberd's only asking do we want to live under glass for the rest of whatever?" She halted in front of a panoramic view of a Tuatuan plantation house, bright white against green. "I don't. Do you?"

Lou Pietro was in the prime of middle age, solidly built with a round, unlined face. Her silvery blond hair was always cut to the latest fashion of whatever dome she had worked in most recently. Now she wore it curling smoothly under at one shoulder, clipped close to her ear above the other. Her gestures were full of stabbing fingers and clenched fists. When Lou and Micah worked together, they chattered spiritedly about Art, life, everything under the sun except the show, and managed in the end to produce work that flowed together as seamlessly as if it had come from a single hand.

"It's a sane, forward-looking question!" Lou continued. "But it raises the issue of common good, of sacrifice by the few for the many, and nobody wants to hear about that these days."

"Taking down the domes is a long-term question. Our problem is short-term: population." Micah studied a black-and-white portrait of a naked Tuatuan carving a dugout canoe and played devil's advocate. "Our space and resources are finite. How long can Harmony afford to add population from without?"

"Let's have fewer children! Or no children! Or, for the short term, let's build a new dome!" Louisa yanked open a door and shooed us into the theatre. "Why is no one talking about that? This town's one of the few that could afford it!"

"That's what the petition is for." I shut the door behind us. "To get them talking."

"For the first time in forty years, one of the founding principles has come up for question," said Micah. "People may be reluctant to face it for fear the whole structure will crumble."

"They're reluctant to face their own greed," Louisa snorted. "Or the fact that the long term may be here already."

Work noise was subdued in Theatre Two. The upstage loading door was cracked open. I could hear the murmur of the shop intercom broadcasting the *Crossroads* dress rehearsal from next door. Louisa marched down the aisle, scanning the equipment-laden booms right and left of each seating section, then the catwalks overhead, where electricians clambered about adding and repositioning instruments in preparation for her focusing session. She slowed when her gaze reached the stage. "I hope you're going to tell me the rest of the scenery's waiting in the shop . . . where *is* everybody?"

I counted four carpenters onstage, only two of them from the regular crew, laying surfacing material across the undulating support framework of the deck. The woven plastic mat was pliant, easily cut, and shaped at room temperature until treated with a curing spray. A chemical reaction hardened it to an early resilient toughness, not like a solid floor at all. More like walking on flesh. Actors loved it.

But the great sweep of backdrop was still a barren skeleton.

"Why are we so far behind?" Louisa demanded. "Damn, Micah, I thought at least here I could count on having a set to focus on!"

I couldn't help feeling responsible. It was my job to oversee progress in the theatre. "Sean says the shop's too busy."

Louisa jabbed her whole arm at the stage. "But four men, when we tech in three days? Let's go have a word with the guy. He always says I'm his favorite harridan."

"I don't think so, Lou."

"C'mon! Sean's used to me sticking my nose in."

"You go. I . . . can't."

"Can't what?"

"Can't talk to him right now," said Micah.

"Can't talk to Sean? An-example-to-us-all Sean?"

"Not right now."

"I don't get it. Are you two fighting?"

"Well," said Micah, "let's just say Sean's made some priority choices I can't agree with."

"So tell him."

"I did. He told me to fuck off. Basically."

So. It wasn't just overwork that had kept Micah away from the theatre.

Lou planted herself mid-aisle and folded her arms. "You guys have been through hell together and suddenly you can't talk to him?"

"Not until I can manage to be civil," Micah replied.

"Jesus, Micah, how're you going to get a show built if you won't talk to your master carpenter??"

Micah chose a seat at random and lowered himself into it deliberately. "That's what assistants are for."

Lou jammed her hands onto her hips. "This is very bad, Mi. Very naughty. This is unworthy of you."

"It's unworthy of Sean to drive me to it." He was almost sullen. *Sullen*. My wise and temperate boss and mentor. "I did my best for him. I can't go in there begging again."

Louisa stared at him. "Well, if you can't, I can."

She strode off to take matters into her own hands. I stood awkwardly in the aisle while Micah stared at the back of the seat in front of him. Finally he pulled himself heavily to his feet. "All right. Let's go down and take a look."

The problems onstage were concrete and easier to talk about. We stepped around a gaping hole center stage, the hole where the vanishing trick would play, and climbed the slopes of the deck. About half the underlayment was in place: upstage where the drop swept down to blend in, and under the curved path of the tracking. I showed him where the elevations of the deck deviated from the drawings, where the changes of level seemed too sharp or angular for the age-worn stone-and-sand quality he was after. But Micah's eye was drawn to the backdrop. His arm scribed an arc in the air, the correct arc, the arc it should have had.

The intercom blared the *Crossroads* rehearsal: deep male voices proclaiming, silvery female laughter. Music. Trumpets and drums. The carpenters watched Micah pace the unfinished deck. The bearded kid who'd nearly taken the fall off the scaffold smiled at me as he hauled a long sheet of surfacing material into place.

"I'm Peter."

"Gwinn." I gestured. "You know Micah."

"No, actually. I'm here 'cause a friend told me he needed help. I . . . really admire his work. Hey . . ." He beckoned me closer. "I saw your petition." He gave me the thumbs-up sign. "But you oughta know, most of the shop's not too happy about it."

I nodded. "Thanks for the warning."

An older woman, thin and muscular, greeted Micah familiarly as he turned away from his study of the drop. "I've seen that look before," she noted. "Don't quite like what you see, eh?"

Micah shook her hand warmly. "I never could fool you, Margaret. Thanks for coming in to help. I wonder, is the model around?"

She shook her head significantly. "But I sneaked upstairs for an eyeful, and let me tell you, if I were building this sucker, I'd tear it all down and start over. But your man Sean, he's in a tough spot time-wise, so I'm just here doing what Ruth tells me. Listen, Micah, it's none of my business, but did you and Sean have a bad fight or something?"

Micah looked down at his feet, then away upstage at the skeleton of the drop. "Without a cross word being spoken, but yes, I guess we did."

"Time to make it up, then."

"So everyone seems to think," he replied with a trace of irritation. "But I don't seem to have it in me just now."

Louisa Pietro bounded up the escape stairs at the back of the deck. "Sean's over at *Crossroads* and there's no one in the electrics shop. Has the entire theatre stopped dead for that other damn show?"

"So it would seem!" declared a voice from the house.

"Marie!" Lou surged downstage to meet her.

"Hiya, Lou. Long time. Look at your hair! Ohh, I love it!"

Marie enfolded the shorter woman in voluminous purple sleeves. Her own dark hair was wrapped in a scrap of glorious floral fabric.

"Hold it, get a camera," murmured Margaret. "All three designers in the same room at once."

Marie draped an arm about Louisa's waist. "So, you want to hear the latest? First this morning I have little SecondGen stitchers refusing to work on our show because it supports 'enemies of Harmony'—a phrase right out of the latest e-mail abomination! Have you read the play? says I. No, says they, but . . ." Marie released Lou to wring her arms wildly. "Next thing I know, Jorgen's bringing in all the skirts from *Crossroads* and throwing them all over the worktables because they have to be shortened by an inch and a quarter, every damn skirt and every damn petticoat, and do you know there are twenty-three women in that cast! Bill Rand says he can't see enough of the ladies' ankles! My god! And of course I had to let Mark off to take his petition around. Oh, Lou, you wouldn't believe it! *The Gift* was a simple import when I took it on, and all of a sudden I'm fighting to get it done!"

" 'Enemies of Harmony'?" repeated Lou. "What *is* going on in this theatre?"

"We're under siege," said Micah pensively.

"Because of this little play?"

"It's not the play, it's the company," said Marie.

Louisa brightened. "Oh, wonderful! I can't wait to meet them!"

Over the shop intercom, a full-orchestra music cue died in mid-phrase, drowned out by a screech that devolved into a hair-raising grind. "Hold it, hold it, hold it!!" someone yelled.

"*Stop, please,*" intoned the stage manager's voice.

The carpenters in Theatre Two froze automatically, listened to the hubbub drifting through the loading door, went back to work.

"Trouble . . ." gloated Marie.

Doors slammed in the shop. Voices shouted orders. Winches hummed. Loading doors rattled and slid apart.

Sean stuck his head though the widening gap upstage. "Donny! Andre! Need you next door, on the double!"

Two of our crew put down their tools and quick-stepped into the shop. Sean squinted at Margaret and Peter.

"Whacha say, Meg? And you, what's your name, redhead! We need every hand we can get!"

Louisa pushed herself forward. "Hey, wait a minute!"

"Yo, Lou! Finally decided to join us?"

"That's our crew you're stealing, buddy-boy."

Sean leaned stiff-armed against the doorframe. "Only 'til we make the repair. Program glitch just blew a whole board of remotes. Open dress tonight. Only way we'll get through it is to hump the damn scenery by hand!"

"What about this dress?"

"A week away. Right now, that's forever." He beckoned impatiently. "You guys coming?"

"Uh, I guess . . ." Peter looked from Micah to Sean and back again.

"Nope," said Margaret.

Sean cocked his head at her. "Suit yourself."

Micah stared after Sean as he stalked into the shop. "All right, then, I'll close down the studio. If he won't do the job, we'll have to do it for him."

"The curfew," I reminded him.

"I don't have a curfew."

"Me neither," noted Margaret.

Micah nodded, brusque and badger stubborn. "Whatever the fucking hell it takes."

Later, by the great stone fireplace in Cora Lee's fairy castle, we held another secret strategy session. Mali wandered the room restlessly while Sam talked.

"You need to present it publicly, not just to the mayor so she can shove it in a drawer."

"Like, at Town Meeting?" I suggested.

Sam nodded, stiff-necked. He was still moving like an old

man, very carefully, as if his muscular body were a sack of loose parts. But he had the full use of his jaw back. He glanced at me speculatively as if pleased to note I was capable of creative thought. "Town Meeting. That'll do."

"Town Meetings are Thursdays," said Mark. "Gives us a week."

Mali twitched tapestried drapes across the leaded panes to block the glare from Cora's new yard lights. "Do it at curfew time."

Sam grinned. "Absolutely right. Oh, absolutely."

"We have our first dress rehearsal that night," I pointed out.

"So?" said Cris.

"Yeah. I guess you're right."

Sam looked to Mali. "I'm not sure I want to miss this."

Mali chuckled softly.

"Have to do it sooner," said Sam. "There'll be a lot of people working that night."

"Monday's our dark night," I reminded them.

Mark weighed his thin sheaf of petitions, nibbling his lip. "The Town Council holds its executive board meetings on Mondays, but I don't know . . ."

"Monday. The day off. Perfect." Sam seemed given to self-deprecatory asides, but he had yet to show an iota of doubt in the rightness of his strategy decisions. "The surprise will give you an edge. They know about the petition, but they won't be expecting you to hit them with it so soon."

"But can we get the numbers that soon? In three days?"

"Well, that's up to you now, isn't it?"

Mark nodded, sitting up a bit straighter. "Yes, sir. It is."

WORKING LATE:

Micah arrived the next morning in the closest thing he owned to work clothes: a pair of thick denims saved for the few chilly days in the weather program, and an old paint shirt that had hung behind the studio bathroom door for at least as long as I'd been around.

It wasn't exactly illegal to close your studio, but it was

assumed that the Apprentice Administration had granted
you a sufficient number of assistants and that at least one
of them should be available during open hours to man the
fort. Some high-handed tourist was bound to complain. So
Micah's gesture was more than just moving his labor force
around. It was a public protest that could cause Sean some
real professional embarrassment.

Margaret laughed when Micah demanded to be put to
work. "Promise you'll do exactly what I say?"

Peter was ecstatic. The idea of having the Great Man
around all day where he could talk at him sent him into a
high-energy buzz that lasted the morning. Micah put up with
it. It got things done.

"Peter and I'll get on with the building," Margaret
decided. "You all put those artist eyes to work texturing
the backdrop. Do a little fix-it along the way." She pressed
her work gloves into Micah's studio-soft hands. "No buts.
Just wear 'em."

"Those hands are too valuable, Mr. Cervantes!"
seconded Peter.

Micah tried the gloves, flexing his fingers. Margaret's
long, rangy hands were as big as his own. "Perfect," he
said, then slipped them off, and stuck them in the pocket
of his shirt.

"Knew you couldn't follow orders," Margaret grinned.

She sent Cris and Songh up the curve of the drop to
smooth out the awkward bumps and seams. Both were
delighted to be out of the confines of the studio. Songh
surprised me, clambering easily about on the sweeping
metal skeleton. He might have a tough time speaking up
for himself, but he was no physical coward. His agility
goaded Crispin into showing off. I was sure one of them
would break his neck.

Jane and I cleared space downstage to prepare materials
for the finish layer. Plastic, foam, and fabric must become
the pebbles, cracks, and craters in the model, and reproduce
the parallel incising of lines that echoed the cross-hatching
painted into the props.

The whole day, I waited for Sean to appear, hoping he'd
find Micah hard at work, see the error of his ways, and
immediately assign a crew of fifteen to finish up the job.
He showed up late in the afternoon, slipping in from the
lobby to stand in the aisle, out of the circle of work light.

If he was fighting any inner battles, his face gave no sign of it.

Micah didn't notice, locked in his own battle with the misshaped backdrop. Sean watched silently for a while. When I looked again, he was gone.

No one said anything. We all kept working. But I felt closer to despair than I had in a long, long time.

Building scenery can be brutish work when you're not used to physical labor. I went looking for work gloves by the time we broke for lunch. The plastics needed hot water to make them pliable enough to mold, the fabrics required a glue that sucked all the moisture from your skin, and the rough edges of the foams scraped and cut like sandpaper. I expected Jane to wimp out early, but she kept at it, slow but steady, refusing to give up on a detail until she was sure it matched the model.

Micah tired quickly from all the lifting and carrying, though he fought not to show it. His long hours were spent sitting at meetings or at a drawing board, and the enormity of the physical task in front of us daunted even him. "They haven't started those tracking units," he noted late in the day. He lowered himself into a seat in the front row with a wheezy grunt.

"No." It was still a question whether the additions Howie had required would work with the rest of the design.

Margaret watched him worriedly. "You go home. Make Rosa a nice dinner."

He squinted up at the backdrop. "Rosa's doing readings in Dakar 'til Tuesday."

"Go home anyway. Go next door to the *Crossroads* dress. Watch 'em stumble all over themselves. I'll see the kids to the dorm if they work after nine. Anyone challenges me, I'd relish the chance to give 'em a piece of my mind!"

Micah tilted his head at her. "Taking sides, Margaret?"

"Oh, Christ, those people! If they want to stop new kids coming in, that's one thing, but it's no fair penalizing the ones already here!"

"Sensibly said." He rose to stretch cramps out of his back. "I'll do better tomorrow night."

"Go on, outa here. If they start canceling previews, it won't be because of the set."

Micah retreated gratefully.

Songh went home when we broke for dinner. The rest of us pooled our pocket change to buy a group supper at the cheapest café in Fetching. But even this onetime piano bar had come up in the world since last we'd been there. A coat of peach paint, some floral-print tablecloths, and suddenly the waiters were looking askance at our apprentice coveralls. Cris was ready to mouth off. I held him back. Peter and Margaret straightened their civilian work clothes and fast-talked the maître d' by dropping Micah's name a lot.

"It's happening overnight," I mourned when we had been conceded a rickety table next to the kitchen door.

Cris glared at the waiter, who was ignoring us. "That only means it's been lying in wait."

Margaret was from funky Franklin Wells, the jazz-crazy, pseudo-urban anachronism directly across the dome, occasionally referred to as the Underside of Harmony. "Fetching's a snob town. If it were me alone, I'd hop the Tube to the Maple Leaf. Nikos there was an apprentice. Oboist. Didn't quite work out for him career-wise, but he runs a great pub."

Halfway through dinner, Songh appeared with a sandwich and sat down. "I am in deep shit at home."

I laughed. He'd said it so seriously, but with this satisfied glint in his eye.

"They want me home right after work every night. They said no hanging out after dinner, no more staying over at the dorm. They said, stay away from *those* actors."

"What did you say?" Jane asked mildly.

Songh flicked his head, very Mark-like for a moment. "I told them that's fine with me, maybe I'd see them around sometime, and I left. My mother's probably still yelling at me."

"Cool," said Peter. "I'm always fighting with my dad."

"I never did," said Songh. "Before."

Margaret clucked her tongue dutifully. The rest of us cheered. Our waiter swept over to tell us that if we couldn't behave ourselves, we'd have to leave.

We went back to work still hungry. It didn't help our grim mood to have to fight our way through the white-wigged and panniered *Crossroads* chorus filling the halls with high-energy chatter and vocalizing. The first act blared over the shop monitor. The evening cleanup had been forgotten in the mad dash to be ready for their first audience. Every drawer gaped open, every cabinet had been plundered of its tools. I found Donny, our erstwhile crew member, sitting on a worktable drinking coffee.

"How's it going?"

"They're gettin' through. Audience seems to like it."

"You coming back to work for us?"

Donny scuffed his palm through a pile of sawdust. "Not tonight. Got a big shift coming up."

"So I guess the remotes aren't fixed."

"Not yet." His glance swung toward me, then away. "Some're saying it's a voodoo curse on it."

Later, I overheard Songh and Crispin having an actual conversation-between-equals, maybe their first ever, about parental oppression. Interesting, since Cris had never offered me anything but the highest praise for his father. Jane rattled on dreamily about what her life would be like on Tuatua, with the Eye. What could I do but listen? She'd let float a major sector of her reality, like a balloon on an endless string, and was happier than I'd ever seen her.

Margaret pulled the boys off the back wall when they started dropping heavy tools onto the deck. "No accidents on my crew," she declared. Too weary to argue, they settled in with Jane and me on the sculpture brigade. When the nine o'clock curfew arrived, no one mentioned it.

Conversation lagged as the hours wore on, and neither the steady tap-tap of Margaret's hammer nor Peter's tales of disasters he'd worked on in other theatres could drive the stillness from that empty, half-dark space. But for the patter of voice and music over the monitor, it was hard to believe there were nearly a hundred people watching a show right next door. There were people busy up in Costumes, and Hickey's crew was still working in the Cage. There were probably people working late in the box office and up in the offices. The *Crossroads* crew banged around in the shop from time to time, going in and out of the rehearsal. No one came to say hello or check up on our well-being. A system going about its business. Within it, our isolation was profound and complete. As if its business didn't include us anymore.

I really didn't understand it at all.

Just when our mood hit bottom, the Eye arrived.

They came trouping down the aisle from the lobby, the

women a rainbow of bright batik wraps, the men in long, loose-fitting patterned robes except for Sam, in black head to foot like a street mime. Mali loped across the back of the theatre to catch the orange that Sam lobbed his way and toss it back again. The throw was mischievously high. Sam leapt, snagged it easily, as if he'd been nowhere near death's door five days before.

"It was him, I tell you," Ule was insisting. "In the lobby right next to the Fat Man. Talking up a storm, they were."

"How could Deeland be here?" Tua scoffed.

Sam frowned at his orange, both discounting and thoughtful. Suddenly, there were two. He looped one backward over his shoulder. It landed in Mali's hand.

"You're saying I don't know what I see?" Ule complained.

"You might have said something," Sam replied.

"Ha. You were too busy taking sympathy calls from the ladies."

The Eye circled and settled among us like birds lighting in the corn. Te-Cucularit knelt to inspect a particularly detailed bit of rock texture that I'd just given up on. Mali wandered about, peeling his orange, testing the solidity of the sloping deck. Omea paddled her legs girlishly in front of her and sent a long look at the backdrop where Margaret was doggedly banging away.

Jane smiled at them as if the sun had just risen in her eyes. Peter charged downstage to greet Moussa. "Hi, I'm Peter. Thanks again, man!"

Moussa and Pen were bickering. Pen held a half-empty wine bottle by the neck, the two-liter kind that caterers use. His arm was around Tuli, hauling her alongside sloppily. Each time the big bottle bumped against her breast, Tuli giggled.

Moussa sank to the floor cross-legged like a giant black Buddha. "Who are you to say what the Work is?"

"The Work," growled Pen, "is not parking my ass in a fucking rehearsal hall week after week, diddling some fool director!"

"It might be," said Omea.

Ule stoked and lit his pipe.

"What are you all doing here so late?" I asked.

"Might ask the same of you," Ule returned.

"The *Crossroads* open dress." Sam drained a paper cup

and tossed it to Pen for a refill. He dropped beside me. His predatory grin seemed out of character and made me uneasy. "We were setting an Eye on the competition."

Lucienne smirked at him. I wondered where Hickey was and what had happened to the Great Romance. I hadn't seen them together the past few days.

Tua flopped down beside Cris. "They could use an Eye or two." She looked ready to leap full-feathered into Moussa and Pen's argument if only they'd fight about something that interested her. "Big crowd for a dress rehearsal."

"Open dresses are a favorite tradition in Harmony," I explained.

"That cast has a lot of friends." Sam's limp and stiffness were gone, the stitched-up scars thin and pink with healing.

"You look so much better," I remarked.

"The fine art of de-lusion." He pulled a ripe peach out of my glue bucket. It had a big bruise on one side. He sneered at it and flicked it aside. Jane caught it and brushed it off. Her thin hands cradled it possessively.

"I mean, you heal very fast," I added.

"With a little help from my friends." Sam tossed back his wine, made a face. "This shit is really bad."

Mali paused behind him. "Then don't drink it."

"I will if I want."

"How was the show?" Cris asked.

"They got through it." Mali bent to share Ule's pipe.

Cris laughed. "Guess you really loved it, huh?"

Holding in smoke, Mali considered. "The show is colorful, detailed, extravagant, rousing, well acted, full of refined grace and totally devoid of content."

Omea took the pipe from him. "Therefore will be a huge success."

"Mind you, it pretends otherwise about the content."

"And therefore is totally boring," Tua finished.

Mali folded himself up beside Sam. "And so, we thought we'd just come by and see where the numberless resources of this great Palace of Art are not being directed."

I hunched up a little tighter and sighed.

"Fuckin' Chamberlaine, anyway!" Pen growled.

"It's not only Chamberlaine," said Cris.

"You just have to see the Fat Man's hand in this," Ule agreed.

"I do question Howie's control of his own theatre," Omea observed.

"Hey, it's gonna be great!" urged Songh. "When it's done."

Omea smoothed his silky hair out of his eyes. "There, child. We're not blaming you."

"I mean, walk around on it a little. It's fun."

"Maybe we should." She rose, held out her hand to him. "Show me around."

Songh scrambled to his feet, still morning-fresh. "Okay!"

Moussa rising was like a mountain levitating. "Show me where I'll sit." Pen followed, dragging Tuli along giggling. Jane trailed after Mali. Tua bent her lovely mouth to Crispin's ear. Beside me, Sam stared into his empty cup. His odd mood leaned on me like a weight.

"What kind of help?" I asked him finally.

"What?"

"Healed you so fast. Can you talk about it?" I watched Te-Cucularit warily as he drifted away to observe Margaret at work. "I mean, is it a secret . . . taboo?"

Sam gave me a bemused look, intimate and faintly mocking. "Help is never taboo."

I decided he was a little drunk. "Sorry. I meant—"

"Miraculous powers of recovery, right? So you can decide I'm the Conch after all?"

"I never thought that."

"Oh?" He laughed harshly. "No, of course not. Not old Sam. Couldn't be him."

"You always think people are—"

"Tch! Don't touch unless you intend to buy."

"I beg your pardon?"

Ule cackled, sucking on his pipe. "It's no use, Sammy boy. I tried already."

Sam passed him a snarky grin. "You mean I gotta stand in line for the privilege?"

I glared at him. "What is with you guys?"

"Sam, Sam, Sammy," chided Ule softly. To me, he sighed, "Just homesick. Domesick. All of us. Sick and sullen."

"*Crossroads* is not my fault!" I declared.

Across the circle, Cris said to Tua, "Sure we could, but I can't get in by myself." He glanced up, looked at me, looked away.

"Sorry," Sam muttered. "We had some bad news from home today."

"Bad news indeed," Ule echoed.

I waited.

"Explosion in a coffee warehouse."

"Eighty-three dead."

"Oh . . ."

Cris glanced up. "What happened?"

"Your WorldNet/News blamed the boiler units," said Ule.

"You think it was . . . ?"

"Always is."

Mali's wanderings had returned him full circle. He crouched, staring as if into a campfire. "Blood of our blood."

"Station Clans?" I whispered.

"Many were."

Sam crushed his empty cup. "And we sit here safe and sound . . ."

Mali tipped his head back, eyes squeezed shut. "The Rock my father rebukes me!"

Ule knocked his pipe out and ground the ashes into the stage floor, humming quietly. Mali relaxed and joined him after a phrase or two, then Sam, then Tua, breaking off her murmurings with Crispin. It was a four-line, keening melody, repeated over and over. What was remarkable was how the Eye had regrouped and resettled around us without my noticing. Pen sat stiff-backed and quiet, Tuli sobered beside him. Te-Cucularit added words to the chant and the others joined him one by one until ten voices sang in unison, filling the dark theatre as our complaints and gossip and hammering had failed to all night.

And then abruptly, the singing stopped.

"*Sa-Panteadeamali!*" came Moussa's ringing cry.

Mali answered as if he were miles away.

"*Pirea-Omealeanoo!*" Moussa called, and so on through each of them. When the last had answered, he sighed with relief and folded his big hands in his lap. "We are ten. We are here."

They sat with their heads bowed. Ule and Omea wept quietly. After a moment Te-Cucularit announced, "The tale that the song tells is this. It tells of times when the clans have not listened to the wild music of Wind and Water, of

Earth our End and Fire our Brother, and in falling out of step, have fallen.''

"If a typhoon comes," Mali translated, "or an earthquake or fire ravages a village, we sing this chant when the dust settles. We sing the twelve stations, then call out every name in the village. Those who do not answer are those who are lost."

"If we knew the names of the murdered at home," said Omea, "we would call them tonight to show that they cannot answer."

"And so the Ancestors will know to welcome them," said Te-Cucularit.

The circle relaxed.

"That is very sad and beautiful," murmured Jane.

"Sad?" barked Pen. "*Sad?* We are sad, that's what, the whole sad fucking lot of us, sitting on our asses doing nothing while the shit hits the fan at home!"

"Maybe we should go home?" Tuli ventured softly.

"Oh no!" I protested.

"You can't do that!" Songh cried.

"Why not?" Sam challenged.

"I . . . the show . . ."

He jerked his thumb at the unfinished scenery. "What show?"

"We'll finish it," I insisted. "It'll be there!"

Margaret ambled over, stowing tools in her belt. "None of my business but it will, you know. Somehow it always is."

Omea rose, hovering like an angry goddess. "For shame, Pen! And you, Sam, of all people! What we do here is not nothing!"

"They don't want us here," Pen muttered.

"My dear, we have always known resistance to the telling of our tale. No matter! We must tell it the truest we know how!"

"It is the actor's job," said Mali quietly, "to make the truth unavoidable."

That is the job of Art, I realized. The hard nut of responsibility at the center of every project and the hardest thing to accomplish, because avoidance of truth is what we are most skilled at, both audience and practitioner. It was a good insight and a lasting one, but it was the the dry sound of Mali's perseverance that stayed with me the longest.

"Time to head home, kids." Margaret dusted debris off her overalls. "Told Micah I'd see you to the door."

Omea rose gracefully. "You've worked a long day. Let us do it."

"Safety in numbers," offered Mali.

"But it's way out of your way," I objected.

Sam draped a heavy arm across my neck and smiled at me lazily. "Nothing like a little exercise before bed to help you sleep."

Tua took Crispin's hand, hauled him to his feet.

Margaret swallowed a yawn. "Makes sense to me."

Sam was making me nervous. I was delighted to make friends with the Eye, but I hadn't thought of getting physical with them. I tried to slip out from under his arm, but as I rose, he moved with me. He pinned me in the crook of his elbow and hauled me in a crooked line across the stage, laughing a throaty man-laugh when I resisted.

He was drunk and I didn't want to embarrass him. I aimed a subtle jab at his bruised ribs. He winced and drew me tight against his side. "Hey. It'd help if you played along a little."

I eased my struggles. "Hunh?"

His winey breath was warm against my cheek. "Trust me."

In the shop, the crew was wheeling in *Crossroads* scenery to be repaired in the morning. A shipment of pipe and fabric had arrived in the vacuum-tube bay. Drawers and lockers slammed. Sam backed me up against the half-open loading door, under the curious stares of the entire shop. He leaned in close, listing, his balance insecure.

I pushed uselessly at his chest, too aware of the comfortable fit of his body against mine. "Sam, what are you—"

"Hush." His fingers toyed clumsily with the fastening of my coveralls. I shoved his hand away. The crash of fresh lumber being racked behind us hid his quick murmur and the impatient spark in his eye from all but me. "Okay, okay. I need a key to Micah's studio. I hear you have one."

"Key?" I echoed stupidly.

"We need a terminal. With guaranteed privacy." He dipped his head and left a line of butterfly kisses along my neck with a finesse no drunk should be capable of.

My breath caught as biology betrayed me. "Why?" I demanded, too loudly. Over his shoulder I saw one of the men jerk his thumb in our direction with a leering shake of his head.

"To send the citizens of Harmony a message." He drew back to look at me, his stance unsteady, his eyes amused and speculative.

"What kind of message?"

"Call it a . . . a counter e-mail."

"On Micah's line?"

"No one will know. That's a promise."

His half smile made me angry. "Why didn't you just ask me? Why the damn charade?"

He tiled his head toward the busy shop but kept his smile on me. "Wouldn't want them to think you *like* me here whispering in your ear . . ."

Mali and the others crowded through the loading door. Sam pulled away, grinning. I stared at my feet. Peter and Margaret passed, called out their good nights.

Mali eased up beside us. "How's it?"

"I think we have a team player. What do you say, Gwinn?"

"I don't want to get Micah in trouble."

"Nor do I," Mali returned.

Cris nosed in behind him, trying to appear nonchalant. "So. We gonna do this now?"

I felt trapped. I didn't know how to refuse them, or why, if Micah would truly not be compromised.

Mali absorbed my sullen confusion. "You needn't worry. It'll look just like we were walking you home."

Ruth trotted into the shop from the big theatre. Sean came after her, shouting orders to the crew.

"No time like the present," urged Sam.

As he snaked an arm about my waist, I stepped aside. "I can manage by myself, thank you."

He backed off, but the half smile remained, mocking me obscurely.

It was Mali and Sam, Cris and Tua and myself by the time we reached the studio. A gang of school kids yelled at us from a brightly lit soccer field along the way, but the dark presence of the Eye discouraged pursuit. Moussa escorted Jane and Songh to the dorm. The rest doubled back home to Cora's. In the dense shadow of Micah's guardian beech, Sam produced a tiny penlight and I unlocked the studio gate. I half expected to find Micah hard at work, but the courtyard was fragrant and still, the windows dark. The thick stones of the stoop shone from a recent shower. A cricket chirped in the bougainvillea.

"Nice place," said Sam as I unlocked the front door. He brushed my hand from the switch plate. "Better not." He passed Cris the penlight.

Cris hesitated. "You're sure this is safe? Micah's not going to . . ."

Scanning the dark room, Tua located the silhouette of the console. She squeezed Crispin's arm. "I'll tap into the public network, leave our message in Monday's e-mail, and get out fast before anyone notices."

Cris blinked at her as before a glare. "You will?"

"Cover my tracks completely."

Sam nodded proudly. "Never seen the like of her."

"But if they catch you—"

"They won't." Tua smiled into his eyes, drew him through darkness toward the console. "You want to watch?"

"Oh yes, you bet I do."

She slipped into Crispin's chair while he held the light for her. Her fingers settled to the keypad as if no machine could be unfamiliar or keep its secrets from her. Cris hovered to one side, Mali to the other. I shut the door and stayed by it. Sam waited beside me, as if guarding both the door and me but so close I could hear him breathing. Would he grab me if I moved away? I wondered if I should be afraid of him.

"What kind of message?"

He stirred as if he'd forgotten I was there. "Just a little something to give them pause. Something they must never know came from anyone's console anywhere. Something that should seem to appear in their lives like"—I started as his shadow reached for me, but it was only to pluck a rose from the breast pocket of my coveralls—"like magic." He offered the rose in formal presentation. Its pure whiteness glowed in the faint light from the windows. "The charade was for me," he murmured.

"We're there," Tua announced from the console.

Cris gave up little sounds of amazement. "Teach me to do that!"

"Maybe later." She leaned into his shoulder to give up the keypad but kept her eye on the screen. "You ain't seen nothing yet!"

Mali bent to the console without hesitation. His fingers worked the pad as smoothly and familiarly as hers. They've done this before, I realized.

And beside me, Sam said with something approaching gentleness, "Because even the magic needs a little help sometimes."

LESSONS:

"I'm going on to Cora's," Cris said to me at the turnoff to the dorm. An antique gaslight stood sentinel among the oak trees. Tua moved ahead along the shadowed lane to wait with Mali and Sam. He jerked his head in her direction. "Staying the night."

I stared at him, too astonished to be angry.

He shrugged. "Just something I gotta do. It's not every day, y'know . . ."

"You are welcome to join us." Mali's voice floated out of the darkness. What did they have in mind? I glanced down the path at Sam and then away.

"No, thanks. I've got an early call in the morning."

"Tomorrow's Sunday," said Cris.

"I'm going in to work on my *Lysistrata*."

The harsh gaslight exposed the heat of Crispin's eagerness. "Okay, then. See ya."

"Just like that?"

"We'll talk about it later."

I felt performance pressure there, facing a domestic squabble in front of three waiting shadows, and found I hadn't the heart for it. Beneath the burn of embarrassment lurked relief. "No, I don't think we will." I turned on my heel and took the brick-paved footpath to the dorm.

It was only a few hundred yards to the door, but the path was an S-curve hedged with tall boxwood. I used to find this quaint and comforting. Now the hedge was dark and every bird a mysterious rustling in the leaves. Besides, if I walked a little faster, maybe I could outrun my humiliation. I was practically running by the time I rounded the last curve, a lucky accident. Five teenaged boys lounged against the pillars and railings of the Gothic porch. Light shone in the window of the closed door, silhouetting the head and shoulders of a person inside.

"Here's one coming now," said one of the boys.

"And it's a girl. I get her first."

"No way, man. I saw her."

I kept running, anger displaced by terror. My momentum broke their ranks as they closed around me. One grabbed my arm. I yanked him with me. He tripped and fell hard on the stone steps. Hands snatched at my clothes. I yelled at the shadow behind the door. The door flew open as one tough plastered his hand across my mouth. A small horde of hollering apprentices exploded through the door to shove the boys off and bundle me in to safety.

Yolanda caught me as I tumbled into the entry hall. "Gwinny, Gwinny, you okay?"

"Yeah, I . . ." I looked back at the door. Someone had fashioned a crude bar bolt to secure it against ramming.

"You're the fourth one we've rescued tonight. Jeanie was the first. She got beat up pretty bad." She consulted a list taped to the wall and checked off an item. "Mark's got us counting heads, so looks like . . . where's Cris?"

I sighed as I headed for the stairs. "You know, Yoli, I don't really want to talk about it. Take my word for it, he's all right."

Mark had left a note on my door. "3,200 so far. Like magic. If we get 5,000, we do the T. C. exec. board meeting Monday. How are you?"

I went up to his room to tell him, but he'd hung his "GONE FISHIN'" sign on the knob. I went back to my empty bed, hoping he was having a better time than I was.

Sunday morning it rained, the longest continuous rain I'd ever seen in Harmony. I got drenched biking to the studio, but at least the rain kept the teen muggers indoors.

Micah was in before me, sitting at his desk with his shirt stuck to his back, shivering in the damp. I made him exchange the shirt for his dry smock. The warm olive of his skin was sallow, his eyes dark and tired. For the first time I worried about his health. I wished Rosa would hurry up and come home, to bully him into taking care of himself.

"Crispin's not joining us this morning?" he asked. "Or Jane?"

"Cris is at Cora's." I did not offer an explanation. Micah raised an eyebrow, then let me work in peace.

It was strange to be back in a cramped white space after so many long days in a big black empty one. The studio was so clean. The drafting tools seemed too small for my work-roughened hands. My fingertips were sore. After working with such intensity in the scale of the *The Gift*, I found myself thinking bigger on the drawing board. And without Cris around making me self-conscious about what he'd think, several problems that had plagued me about my *Lysistrata* design simply melted away in the face of this broader vision. It was like, well, magic.

This being the first good thing to happen in quite a number of days, I let the joy of it overtake me. "I can actually *do* this!"

"Good," murmured Micah absently.

"I don't mean just *Lysistrata*, I mean all of it!"

He must have heard something special in my babbling. He put down his own pencil and came over. "Well, let me see."

I flattened my palms across the glowing sketcher. "Oh, there's nothing here, it's . . . I mean, I'm beginning to see how it works. How it works for me, how to put it together, all of it! It's there, in my head!"

"Then say a prayer right now that you hold on to it," he said dryly. "Revelation is a slippery thing."

I gazed at him, inarticulate with all the pushing and shoving going on inside me.

He smiled. "Well, it is."

"Oh, Micah, I've felt like such a failure."

"Why?"

"I couldn't make this project work right and I couldn't help with Sean or get things going for you at the theatre and—"

"Wait. What's going on at the Arkadie has nothing to do with you," he said sternly. "It has nothing to do with *Design*. That's Execution, or in this case, the failure thereof. Design is here"—he tapped the drawing board, then pressed his hand to his chest—"and here. In theory, Design and Execution should never be considered separately. In practice, you must separate them on occasion or the conflict will . . . break your heart."

I reached over and hugged him one-armed. "Micah, you're amazing. Thanks so much. For everything."

He patted me awkwardly. "Don't thank me yet. Revelation is just the beginning."

At noon, the Master and his apprentice put Design away and readied themselves for Execution.

I told Micah about the gangs at the dorm, and he insisted I walk with him as far as the Barn, where he was due for a run-through. We said we'd walk in order to stretch muscles aching from the previous day's physical labor. In truth, even Micah, as articulate as any about the need for tourism and the Open Studio policy, could no longer bear to ride the Tube during weekend tourist hours.

It rained on and off the whole way, in ten-minute, angry downpours. The dome was the sullen color of lead. Beyond it I could see sun and blue sky Outside. The stingy gray light did nothing to improve my mood as I told Micah about the Eye's ritual mourning and their disillusionment with the Arkadie. "I bet half of them don't even show for rehearsal."

In a particularly vicious pelting, we took shelter under the branches of a spreading magnolia outside some citizen's quaint wickerwork gate.

"Do they do things by halves?" Micah mused.

"They're fighting a lot among themselves lately."

"Performance anxiety, now that we're getting close to it?"

I shook my head. "They know they're getting the shaft here."

Micah looked unhappy. "Is that what they think?"

"Well? Aren't they?"

Half the Eye was missing when we arrived at the Barn.

This time the game was circle catch with a giant ball of wadded-up white paper. The object, at least in Pen's mind, was to lob this missile as hard as you could at the person opposite you. We watched as he juggled the melon-sized wad on his palm and sidearmed it viciously at Cu. Cu caught it against his belly with a soft explosion of breath, then slammed it down in disgust. Pen's catcalls followed him as he stalked away from the circle.

At the production table, Liz and her assistants paged madly through their scripts. Smaller wads of paper littered the floor around them.

"Dead pages," said Liz wearily. "Howie's been doing cuts."

"Isn't it a little late for that?" I asked.

Liz shrugged. "Panic sets in . . ."

Howie was walking Louisa around the ground plan taped out on the floor, spieling eloquence about the evolution of his new production style. Hickey had sent over the little dark-haired woman who would be head of *The Gift* running crew, which was reasonable except Hickey usually came to final run-throughs himself.

Micah sank into the chair beside Liz. "I'd better get those cuts from you."

Mali and Ule sauntered in, not at all concerned about being late. They joined the circle catch immediately. I smelled coffee brewing in the food corner and headed over. I poured one for Micah and stuck a second under the spout for myself.

"So, you get any work done this morning?"

Hot coffee cascaded across my wrist. Clumsy fool. Really, I thought, I should be handling this better. "Sure did."

"Congratulations."

I knew it was significant that I couldn't bring myself to look him in the eye. "You're a mean drunk, Sam."

"I was not drunk."

"Then you're mean sober."

"Hey, I was working. A job needed doing."

Angry, I could look at him. His scars were pale lines against his tanned skin, his bruises fully healed. Amazing. "I don't like being part of your job, whatever it is."

He poured himself a large tumbler of fruit juice. Behind us, Tua ran through the hoots and trills of her vocal exercises. Liz tried to call the company to order and discovered she was still a few short. Sam sipped at his brimming glass. "Okay, if it helps, I apologize."

"You treat us like children."

"No—"

"Yes, you do! Hopeless, ignorant children!"

"Innocent," he corrected. "And that is never hopeless."

"You know, when Mali says that sort of thing, it doesn't sound pretentious."

"Now who's being mean?"

"I'm tired of you looking at me like you knew something I didn't."

He smiled into his juice. "Probably do. A few things."

"I mean—"

"About the world, maybe, how it really is. Other things." He set his juice down casually. "Like, why you let the kid off the hook so easily last night."

This was not a conversation I wanted to have. I moved away, he blocked me. His hands were free, mine full of steaming liquid.

"You let him go because he's a self-involved young snot and you don't need that kind of shit anymore."

Oh, how right he was. "Please, I'd like to take Micah his coffee."

He stood aside, then stopped me with a murmur as I passed. "I lied to you last night. The charade was nothing. Habit. But I learned something from it."

I glanced up, curious in spite of myself.

"Forget the kid. It's me you want, whether you know it or not."

HARMONET/CHAT

08/10/46

Just keeping you up-to-date, and we know you couldn't bear to be otherwise when Mr. Just-moved-to-Lorien CONAKRY sees you coming out of the fitting rooms in your newest DeClara frock. His latest love-chick is in the room next door, but this is Harmony!

***But seriously, folks, and things *are* getting serious in Town lately. Hey, let's have more *fun!* These nasty muggings and all this dreariness in the public e-mail, and what's with this PETITION stuff anyway? Just because the kiddies have to go to bed a little early? Aww . . .

***Must say we agree avidly with the mayor's decision to authorize a Security sweep of the markets, checking on all these so-called visitors come to sell their wares without paying a good citizen's taxes *but* we do hope they won't kick out the ladies we buy our favorite imported handmade jewelry from! *Really,* sometimes our own crafters are just too *ARTY.* Never mind expensive!

But listen, if they're letting in all these peddlers, who KNOWS what else is walking our streets? Is this how we explain the recent wave of nighttime violence?

***Another thing we want to know: is everybody on Tuatua coming here? Does CAM BRIGHAM's dinner guest on Friday know it's not so safe for Tuatuans on Harmony's streets? Or maybe that just applies to the ones who are rumored to be on the *left* side of the law? We're sure that doesn't count Mr. IMRE DEELAND, who looked extremely pleased after feasting at length with Cam and visiting Francotel exec LOUIS ARMANDE. Now there's a Tuatuan who knows how to dress.

***And haven't we all just HAD it with the weather, f&n? Rain and hail and gloom and more rain? Is this all part of the Founders' *Long-Term Program,* or does our dear computer maybe need a bit of a tune-up? We all do, now and then!

***On the cheerier side, log on to the advert campaign for the new MARIN SEADOME. We have, and we're booking our tour tomorrow! Now there's a *creative* entertainment idea! Maybe we should be thinking along those lines here in Harmony. Any entrepreneurs worth their salt out there?

Remember, you DIDN'T hear it here!

MICAH'S DILEMMA:

Micah returned to the Arkadie mid-afternoon. "They really *are* unhappy. I certainly hope Howard can get them back on track."

I smoothed plastic sealer over a freshly carved rock. "The run-through?"

"Awful."

"Even Mali?"

"Like a black hole, sucking up all the energy in the room. The emotional arc collapsed before the end of Act One and the play never made it out from under. One thing for sure: if Mali doesn't perform, the piece will never get off the ground. How's it going here?"

"Slowly." We'd done the best we could to fix the curve of the backdrop, and Margaret and Peter had nearly finished surfacing the deck. The pinkish natural color of the material made the undulating rise from front to back resemble a patched-together human body melting into the stage. But the vanishing trick was a gaping hole downstage center. Two days before our first technical rehearsal and Sean still hadn't sent back our regular crew.

Micah put on his work clothes and settled in beside us.

I always looked forward to the week or so spent in the theatre opening a show. It was a tense, exciting time of high energy and quick camaraderie; a time of miracles, of watching a show unfold like a hatching butterfly and take flight.

Not this time. I took up a new block of foam, cutting in the steplike layers of broken shale. What a sorry group we were: Micah and Margaret working with the concentration of the dead, Jane no conversationalist since her breakdown. Peter had finally abandoned his run-on stand-up comedy due to lack of response. Cris was unsure whether or not he should talk to me and was therefore talking to nobody. I certainly wasn't talking to him. A grim and silent crew indeed. Only Songh remained cheerful, humming tunelessly as he shaped plastic mesh into rock forms for the back wall. But then, Songh was probably a little in love. When Mark walked in, Songh's whole body reoriented itself like a blossom to the light.

Mark trotted down the aisle, a sheaf of papers under one arm, a pen over his ear. He headed straight for Micah.

"Micah, I need a favor."

I recalled a certain boyishness in Mark and wondered where it had gone. We'd called it charming, but when it left, the charm was still there, a kind of golden light about him. Weary, frowning Micah thawed visibly as Mark presented his case. This guy, I decided, was born to convince people of things.

"Yes, yes," replied Micah. "I shouldn't be asking any of you to work extra hours at a time like this."

"Oh yes, sir, you must. And they will. Otherwise I'd ask you to me lend all of them." Mark held out his hand.

Micah shook it, then watched after him bemused.

"Songh! You're reassigned. Let's go!" Mark stopped to ruffle my hair. "Taking one of your workers, G."

"We should be out there with you."

"I got enough. Micah needs you more."

"What's the count?"

"Forty-one hundred. We've posted every possible notice board, every greenroom and gallery that'll let us, and I've got nineteen people out there working it door to door. Even, can you believe it, Yolanda!"

"You're amazing. Hope they're being careful."

"They are. Security's threatening to arrest curfew breakers now." He squatted close beside me. It was like having a whirlwind settle down for a chat. "Listen, there's, um, some nasty gossip about. You all right?"

"Kinda confused, but actually, I think I am."

"Good. Got to tell you something Sam said to me."

"Sam?" Even the name made me start.

"About the Outside." Mark hugged my shoulder and rose. "When we have time."

"When's that going to be?"

He laughed and hurtled away with Songh in tow.

During a break, I checked the petition we'd posted on the shop notice board. It was gone. The corner pins imprisoned two ragged scraps of paper. I hurried through a hall full of laughing ladies and gentlemen in powdered wigs and gold embroidery, so cheerful you'd have thought there was a party going on instead of a final dress before the night's first preview. In the greenroom, I nosed around the actors' call-board, pretending interest in the monitors broadcasting the rehearsal. This petition was still in place. Even had a few names on it, over which someone had scrawled in red, "CLOSE THE DOOR!"

It no longer scared me to find this so close to home. It made me angry, the deep, slow kind of rage that fuels determination, that rises when a longtime dream is being threatened—no, defiled. My Harmony. My artists' sanctuary. I stalked back to the shop and pinned up two new petition sheets where the old one had been.

Back in Theatre Two, Louisa Pietro's manic energy was stirring up the emotional murk. She perched on a crate and shook her fists while Micah worked. "Howie can talk concept all he damn wants, it won't do a bit of good without a set to focus on!"

Micah nodded, fastening a bit of flooring into place.

Margaret laughed, deep and cajoling, her arm sunk up to her shoulder in a slot in the deck. "C'mon, Lou, you've focused just fine on less scenery than this." She tightened a bolt, then extricated her arm and the tool. " 'Course, you swore about it like a damn Outsider—"

"And I'm swearing now. Enough of this gloom. Micah, I'm taking you to dinner. Maybe get you drunk enough to make it up with Sean."

She didn't understand. Nobody did. *I* didn't.

Micah had done everything he could. He'd found extra money for more labor. He'd called in markers to supply that labor. He'd kept Howie out of the theatre, closed down his studio, dedicated his staff and the labor of his own hands to getting the show built. None of this made any visible impression on Sean, and without Sean behind you, things just really didn't happen in the Arkadie shop. The only move left to Micah was to stop short, declare that he could not work this way, and threaten to quit.

Why didn't he?

Because Micah could never desert a show.

And it seemed that's what Sean wanted, for Micah to make himself the weapon with which Sean could bludgeon the Arkadie's management.

So Micah, badger stubborn, kept working, waiting for the confrontation that never came. For his sake, so did we.

Downstage center, the empty hole in the deck drew things into itself like a whirlpool: tools, stray materials, too often nearly one of us. We finally dragged an old platform out of stock to cover it up. Sean wasn't even bothering with basic safety.

Sean.

What would it take to turn him around?

Micah reappeared very late from his dinner with Lou, having shared at least one good bottle of wine. He watched us sculpt for a while, then paced upstage to stare with restless melancholy at the backdrop. When I looked for him next, he was down center, gazing at the platform over the hole in the deck as if it concealed the blackest sort of void.

I wiped glue off my hands and went to join him. "Good dinner?"

"Delicious."

"Where'd you eat?"

"Fishko's, on the square."

"Hope you two didn't talk about this the whole time."

Micah laughed, a short, unamused burst. "Lou saw *Crossroads* last night."

We stared at the covered hole together for a bit. Finally I decided, no point in small talk here at the chasm's edge. "Why's he doing this to us, do you suppose?"

I didn't catch him by surprise. I never caught Micah by surprise. Only Sean had managed to do that.

"I don't know," he replied sadly.

"Couldn't you . . . I mean . . . isn't there something?"

Micah looked at me gravely. "Not you too."

Shamed, I murmured, "No, it's just . . . I should be helping better but I can't, if I don't understand why."

"Why." He made a sound like something brittle breaking. "It doesn't matter why! He's rationalized it to himself and everyone else—scheduling, time, money, men, whatever, the final straw—but the truth is that he's chosen to desert an ongoing production because of some agenda of his own and that's wrong. Not lazy or pragmatic. Just plain *wrong*."

"Yes, but what if—"

"No. If we give in and smile and cajole, and accept that this is the way things work, we make a mockery of the whole idea of right and wrong. What are we left with? He who shouts the loudest wins the day, Art and Quality be damned? There goes civilization down the drain."

"Micah, what if it gets the show built?"

"*We* can get the show built!" His whole body tensed with conviction. "If we have to become like him to do it, what's the point?"

I thought of Te-Cucularit then and his stubborn keeping of the old laws, even in the face of risk and ridicule.

Micah said harshly, "All right, I lied! I do care why he's deserted me! I don't understand what makes a man like Sean overturn the habits of a lifetime, desert a show, throw a friend to the wolves . . . !"

I waited while he fought through his outburst and grew

grave again and thoughtful. I could offer him nothing, since
I didn't understand, either.

"Sean's tired," he mused finally. "We all get tired, I suppose. Burned out. And then the battle no longer seems
worthwhile. And that makes us scared, because if it's not
worthwhile, what the hell have we been killing ourselves for
all our lives?"

"Do you ever wonder if it's worth it?" I asked him
quietly.

"Every day of my life and oftener, the older I get. So far
the answer's always come back yes. I guess for Sean, it
finally came back no."

SAM:

We decided to sleep in the theatre that night, Cris and Jane
and I, to avoid the alternate threats of arrest or mugging
on the doorstep of our own dorm. Jane bundled up some
musty masking velours for bedding and dragged them into
the corner of an empty dressing room.

"We'll curl up like a pack of Outsider dogs," I remarked
lightly.

Micah frowned. "This is not good. Not good at all."

"Oh, it'll be fun," said Jane dreamily.

After everyone left, I watched Jane make methodical
preparations for bed: washing, brushing her teeth with her
finger, stripping to her underwear, and hanging her coveralls neatly on a costume rack. Cris came in and hauled a
length of velour from the pile.

"I'm crashing next door," he announced. "Night, all."

Jane barely seemed to notice.

"Think I'll just work a little while longer," I said dis-
piritedly.

"Don't stay up too late," she said, as if she was my
mother.

It is definitely not healthy to work alone in an empty
theatre. You start remembering every story you've heard
about theatre ghosts, and there are a lot of them, though I
couldn't recall ever hearing one about the Arkadie. You
find yourself trying to work very quietly so you can hear

the little noises you don't want to hear. You can't even look into the cavernous darkness of the house, in case you should spot the shadowed figure watching you from the balcony or the silhouette lurking in an open lobby door.

But my alternatives were bedding down with a madwoman or having that fight with Crispin that would officially end our relationship. The end I was ready for. The fight I was not. So I went back to work on that rock I hadn't finished and terrorized myself, listening too hard, keeping my head safely down.

A quiet plop in my water bucket sent my knife skittering across the ragged foam. I held my breath until I was collected enough to look up. A white rose bloomed among the brush handles. The stage seemed as empty, maybe emptier than it had a moment before. The house was dark as well.

"Damn you," I said aloud.

Sam laughed and emerged from behind the base of the cherry picker. "Only woman I ever met who doesn't like getting flowers."

"You scared the shit out of me."

He dropped to the deck in front of me, sprawling comfortably with his head propped up on one elbow. His gray sweats were well worn and damp, his face faintly flushed. "Sorry."

"You look like you've been running."

"Have been. Oh, don't worry. Nothing chasing me tonight. It's part of the company regime."

"You do this every night?"

"Ule'd have my head if I didn't. Been off it since I got myself shit-kicked. You ought to come with me. It's only six, seven klicks. You domers don't get enough exercise. I was just heading in when it occurred to me somebody here might need an escort home."

"I'm not leaving."

"To your dorm, woman. Safely to your dorm. I'm not an idiot. I can read the signals."

I turned the block of foam over and resumed work on it. "No, I mean I'm staying here. We all are, 'cause of the new arrest order. The others are already asleep."

"Oh?" Sam stretched out on his back, arms folded behind his head. He studied the grid thirty meters above. "I passed your asshole boyfriend ten minutes ago on his way to Cora's."

I stared at the foam for a bit, then let go of the breath I was holding for no particular reason. "And you just had to come by and tell me about it."

"What are you mad at me for? It's him being the jerk." He rolled onto his side to look at me, and the work light threw his face into shadow. Only my cursed memory placed blue eyes in that darkness. "I liked us better before you figured out I'm hunting you."

"Is that what you're doing?"

"Sure is. Hot pursuit. Now if I can just keep Tua interested in the kid, though I don't know, with her attention span . . . ha!" He jabbed a triumphant finger at me. "Almost. Almost a smile. Damn, woman! Why do you fight it so hard?"

I'd been gripping my chunk of foam as if he'd threatened to steal it. I eased my hold and isolated a particular detail to chip away at with great concentration.

Sam swiveled up to face me, cross-legged. "What is it?"

"What's what?"

"What is it that bothers you? About me."

"Um."

"Come on, I can take it."

Chipping away, I said, "You frighten me."

"I . . . ?" He rocked back with a surprised little laugh. "Why?"

"I don't . . . know what you are."

He was silent a moment, pushing wood scraps around on the floor in front of him. "That's something two people usually spend awhile finding out together."

"I don't mean who, I mean what."

"What. Hmmm. Well, I'm male, Caucasian, thirty-four, five foot eleven, hundred and seventy-two pounds . . . ah, let's see . . . actor, mostly character roles, reliable company man, blood member of the Clan of the First Station—"

"Sam, that's not what I—"

"Why do you need to know ahead of time? Ah, stupid question. I forgot where I was." His eyes raked the ceiling beyond the grid and the invisible ceiling of the dome beyond that. "The Land of Borders and Limits."

Goaded, I let it out at last. "Does Te-Cucularit really think the world will end if the Clans can't walk the Stations?"

Sam looked annoyed. "Is this about the Preacher or me?"

"Well, does he?"

"Probably he does. TeCu needs his reality tightly structured."

"And you?"

"Do I believe? That depends on your definition of the end of the world." When I frowned, he said, "Not the right answer, eh?"

"Sam, I need to . . . when you were hurt . . . what healed you so fast?"

"Again?" His mouth quirked. He settled back on one elbow and grinned at me. "Ah. Is that it, love? Spooked by a little garden-variety magic?"

"Was it?"

"Magic?"

"*Was* it?"

"Is that what you want?"

My hands clenched. "I want the truth!"

"The truth. Hmmm." He nodded, sat up. "Easier said than done in this world."

"Something that is not an act or a lie, not a manipulation, not a subterfuge, not a—"

"Hey!" He caught my pinwheeling arms. "Easy now, come on. In my experience, the truth is as slippery as everything else. But I'll make you a deal: the truth between us, or the closest thing we can come up with." He released my wrists. "But just between us."

"You mean, don't tell anybody."

"No one." He watched me carefully.

"Why?"

He shrugged. "We like to play our cards close to the chest."

I'd agree to anything to get a few answers. "Okay."

He slid closer, picking at the loose threads on the cuff of my coveralls. "What healed me. And yes, I know you're going to ask, Tuli also. Omea is Third Station. Her clan has practiced for centuries a kind of earth magic that is nothing more terrifying than the homeopathy the frontiers of medical research have been struggling toward for the last hundred years: the body repairs itself notably faster in a certain kind of deep trance where all the energies and processes can be dedicated to the healing. Omea can induce this trance and encourage its efficiency with the herbal pharmacopoeia that is the heritage of her clan. It's magic that can't end or begin a life, but can certainly help save it, as it has mine on more than one occasion."

"You mean, once the physical repair was done . . . ?"

He nodded. "Dr. Jaeck glued together what he could, the trance state did the rest. Helps if you're good at holding trance—Mali and the Preacher are great at it, I'm only so-so—but it's pretty simple. Is it really magic? Omea says yes. I say, depends on your definition."

Lacking a definition was precisely my problem.

"You're disappointed."

"No, I—"

"You are." He grinned sourly. "Bet you'd hop right into bed with me if I were the Conch."

"You don't understand."

His voice gentled. "Yes, I do. I went through it, too. I wasn't born to this blood, remember." His finger traced the seam of my pant leg up to my calf, heading for my thigh, but stopped at my kneecap, tapping gently, once, twice. "Gwinn, don't think less of magic for being the product of a human skill. Magic makes you question. It teaches you awe and reverence. Our ability to make magic is our only true claim to divinity. You want that lecture, too?"

I smiled at my block of foam. "And I thought Mali was the talker. Yes. The lecture, please."

"Rightio. My own magic, for instance." Sam sat up, elbows on his knees. "I run my routines every day in front of a mirror, without fail, wherever I am. I know I've got it right when a trick is magic even to me. Just that split second where the sleight works so well that I believe it entirely."

It was like when he talked politics. His concentration gathered. The woman beside him, an object of trivial pursuit, fell out of focus before his passion for his craft. His hands sketched deft and complicated sequences in the air. His eyes and body placed his ideal audience somewhere out in the dark pit of the empty house. I relaxed in my obscurity, riveted.

"In your theatre, your effects tech can make anything seem real. Your audiences ooh and ahh, but in admiration, not in wonder. They know they're surrounded by machines.

"In my theatre, there's only my hands and my ability to distract you from what those hands are really up to—to misdirect, as we say, from the actual business. Magic is creating in someone else or even yourself that blessed will-

ing suspension of disbelief, that conviction for the time or
forever that there's absolutely *no other explanation* for what
they've just seen happen. No holos. No lasers. No projections. Not even the old-fashioned traps and mirrors. Just
me. Magic is where you find it . . . or in my case, where I
make it. And I don't always need or want a theatre to make
it work."

He turned his eyes to meet mine. I felt his focus swing
back like a ray of heat. "You want to know what I am? I'm
the best sleight-of-hand man you'll ever hope to see." He
smiled and his finger drew circles on my knee. "What are
you?"

I gripped my stone again, easing away from his touch.
"Oh, nothing so exotic."

"Un-unh," he warned.

"Maybe an innocent shouldn't answer that."

"Smartass replies don't make it, either."

I really didn't have an answer, and that troubled me.

Sam leaned toward me. "Not so easy, is it? You want
neat little explanations? Fine. When you can shoehorn
everything you think you are into a convenient three sentences, maybe I'll have some answers ready for you." He
levered himself brusquely to his feet. "You're an exasperat-
ing woman, you know that?"

Which of my tacit refusals had put him off so suddenly?
"I'm just trying to understand."

"Call me when you do."

"Sam, I . . ." I was surprised it mattered so much that
he not go away angry with me.

"Remember our deal. **Truth** for truth. You owe me,
Rhys."

When he'd gone, I picked **the** rose out of the bucket and
stared at it for a long time.

E-MAIL:

The theatre maintenance crew showed up early to clean the
dressing rooms and rousted Jane and me out sternly but not
unkindly. Even they could see that all was not as it should
be, with the set so unfinished and the cast due in the theatre
the next day.

They let us wash up, even loaned us a towel from their
actor stock. I smiled at them and pretended to feel fully
refreshed. Jane stood contemplating yesterday's wrinkles in
her coveralls. Sleep lines marked her face like a child's.
Unwilling to miss a free meal, she volunteered to bike back
to the dorm and cadge us some breakfast.

I wandered muzzily into the theatre. Sam was right: Cris
was nowhere to be found. Faint echoes from the shop—
tired voices raised in irritation, tool cabinets being unlocked, buckets being washed and tossed about impatiently.
The morning crew showing up for their six A.M. call.

At the loading door I blundered into Sean, hauling in a
four-wheeled dolly stacked with tools and vacuum-transport
boxes.

"What in hell are you doing here?" he demanded.

"Worked late."

Sean jerked at the laden dolly to muscle it over a thick
run of power cable. "You didn't hear there's a curfew on?"

"That's why we stayed over."

"Get back to your dorm and get some sleep."

"Well, uh . . ." I began.

Jane came up behind me. "Are you throwing us out?"

Sean braced his legs against the dolly's weight. "Come
on, you mother," he snarled.

Jane's boldness shamed me. "Are you throwing us out?"
I repeated. "Because otherwise, we've got work to do."

Sean stood free of the unmoving load. Freshly shaved and
showered, he still looked worn as an old shoe, exhausted
beyond understanding by this anger he could not let go of.
Give it up, I begged him silently. Then maybe we could all
laugh and get on with it. I missed his sleepy-eyed laughter

and his ribald joking. The shop was an uneasy place without it.

"Fuck it," he growled finally. He redoubled his grip on the dolly's hauling bar. "If you guys wanna bust ass for a turkey like this, it's no business of mine."

"It's not a turkey!" Jane shot back.

Cris stuck his head around the loading door. " 'Bout time you guys woke up."

"You here, too? Christ, gimme a friggin' hand, will ya?" Sean readied himself for another heave. Cris and I pushed from the hind end and the load bumped over the hump. "At least get some coffee in ya," Sean yelled as he threaded the dolly around the decking supports. "Don't want any accidents in my theatre!"

"Sleep well, Cris?" I asked sweetly.

Jane eyed me and, being morning-lucid, said she thought she'd just skip coffee and go right away for food.

Cris stopped her. "You don't want to check the e-mail?"

"E-mail! Right!" Differences shoved aside, we beelined for the terminal in Sean's office.

"Don't think Sean wanted us to see he's actually working on the show," Cris observed as we scurried up the stairs.

Sean's door was shut and the lights off.

"Jane, keep a watch." Cris went straight to the console and punched up the morning's public messages. "Nothing, nothing . . . wait. Here it is. Goddamn! She pulled it off!"

I peered over his head at the screen, blue as sapphires, white as snow: FASCISM IS THE DEATH OF ART. OPEN ALL THE DOORS.

"That sounds like Mali," I noted fondly.

Jane deserted her post at the door to stare at the message silently.

"Magic . . ." I murmured.

"Very close to it. She's good, the girl is very good." Bent over the screen, Cris began his habitual morning scan of the news. "Oh," he said suddenly. "Wow."

It was a small bit toward the end of the WorldNet report, where the items of minor interest get tossed: OPPOSITION LEADER RETURNS.

Cris read aloud. "Tuamatutetuamatu. Sunday, August 10. A locally broadcast inspirational message from the Anti-domers' fugitive figurehead contradicted recent reports that the Conch had fled and set off tribal celebrations across the island . . .' "

"He's back!" marveled Jane.

"He never left," I said, ashamed that Sam had been savaged for nothing and that it had been our fault.

But Cris had seen Tua at work. He thought in terms of the world computer network more instinctively than I, a daughter of isolationist Chicago. "Or he's Mali, after all. It's gotta be!" Then, angry at his own impulsive tongue, he glared at Jane. "But this time we're keeping it to ourselves!"

Jane's eyes widened reproachfully. "I wouldn't do anything to hurt Mali. I'd rather die first."

DAY OFF:

When Sean decided to do a thing, he did it, for whatever reason.

When we came back from breakfast, Ruth was starting a crew on the tracking units. In the theatre, five men clustered downstage center, banging and muttering and lowering equipment into the hole in the deck.

Sean stood by watching. His beer gut had swelled during the past few months. He eyed us sidelong with a trace of his old humor. "There goes most of your budget, into the pit."

None too soon, I almost said.

"Howie and his goddamn gimmicks." He grinned. "Shit, if your native pals can voodoo my remotes broken next door, I oughta just leave all this to them."

I did not grin back. "Think it'll work?"

"Fuck me, who knows?" he said tiredly. "Yeah, I guess." He threw his shoulders back, surveyed the stage. "All right. Let's get this joint in shape for actors to walk on." He glanced at me slyly. "Or we could leave it messy. Probably more what they're used to, eh?"

He'd moved away before I could respond.

But there was no way the set would be finished by noon the next day. While we built and carved, our foam scraps and sawdust and metal shavings were swept up behind us.

The gaps between the decking sections were plugged. Spongy spots were shored up. Hickey slouched around with his crew, placing prop tables and being told to move them the hell out of the carpenters' way. He'd nod and shrug morosely. He wasn't saying much. I wondered if the Great Romance had ended with him still pining after Lucienne.

Liz Godwin bustled in to check out the safety railings and escape stairs and the installation of running lights where actors had to make entrances and exits in the dark. She edged up to the down-center pit and peered in. "This gonna be ready?"

Sean ran his tongue along his teeth. "Hope so."

"Think it'll work?"

"All right," Sean bellowed to the entire theatre. "Any other asshole wanna ask that question?"

Liz backed away. "Howie's bringing the cast in at five."

"On their day off?"

"Howie wants them familiar with the layout. He doesn't want them thrown by any surprises tomorrow."

Sean sniffed, rubbed his belly. "Five it is, then. But not an an actor on this stage before."

He stayed in the theatre all day, giving orders and assignments, avoiding Micah when he came in to work, taking battle reports from Ruth, who'd been stationed next door at *Crossroads*. In another era Sean would have commanded armies.

At five, Micah stood with me in the house as Howie ushered the Eye around a set they'd already spent more time on than he had.

"Why'd Sean let it go so long if he was going to do it anyway?"

"He's done part of it," Micah corrected. "The technical part."

Yes. Sean had stormed in to save the day at the last minute and covered all his bases except one: the design. The set loomed like Frankenstein's monster, patched and seamed, a functional but ungainly wreck without grace or conviction. Hardly the stuff of atmosphere and illusion . . . or magic. It seemed over-large for the space, raw and out of place, as if Micah had made some sort of horrible mistake.

"Hey, how 'bout this!" Howie waved a sheet of newsfax, then thrust it at Omea like a captured flag. " 'Fascism is the death of Art,' huh? Somebody finally had the guts to respond to those jerks!"

The Eye passed the e-mail among themselves, murmuring as if it were a welcome surprise. They were grumbly today, sticking close together, moving as a unit. Moussa complained that his "spot" was lumpy and uncomfortable, even though he'd not actually be sitting on it but on his Gorrehma. Tuli and Lucienne thought the deck might be too pliable for dancing. Ule found places that were too hard. Te-Cucularit snarled at the two prop boys swapped off *Crossroads* and threatened to walk because they were not handling the ritual items with proper respect.

Mali drew a shell up around himself and broke away to work his blocking in a private dance around the stage. I considered warning him of Crispin's latest speculations, but didn't want to seem a part of this Conch obsession. I no longer cared who the Conch was. I hoped it was none of them. I thought that would keep them safe.

While they circled and groused, I slouched in my seat and studied Sam. Not the sort you'd normally bother to watch. Even his tricks were about *not* watching him. Without his face in front of me, I couldn't call it to mind. Only his blue eyes and a memory of hardness. A serious disadvantage for an actor, this unobtrusiveness, but a talent in magic, perhaps also in politics. Unobtrusive but somehow always there. Mali might claim his father was the Rock, but I identified him more with Fire. Sam was the one whose feet seemed anchored in the very core of the Earth. I couldn't help but find that attractive.

I noted also the Eye's pattern as a group: Omea always in their midst, touching, smiling, soothing over the rough places; Mali apart, listening, digesting, dispensing policy; Sam and Moussa circling the perimeter, each going about his actor-business with a part of him removed and on alert.

Now Sean approached Howie center stage, hands in pockets as if for a chat about last night's dinner or the soccer scores. "I got the lift and the slit-drop working okay, but the field generator's not installed. We'll keep on it but my guess is, you'll have to fake it for tomorrow."

Howie frowned. "I see."

Beside me, Micah sighed. Another day of waiting, plus the spectacle of Howie bounding up the aisle toward us.

"Our trick's not ready," he announced querulously.

Micah glanced up at him, nodded.

"C'mon, Mi, you knew that was the one thing I was really going to want to work with! He won't have my moving units ready either."

"I know, Howard."

"Well, Christ, maybe you ought to work your shit out with Sean and get him back on our team! I don't see Max Eider having trouble convincing him to work nights."

The soft weight of Micah's body seemed to slim and lengthen with the lifting of his chin. Six hundred years of aristocratic heritage fighting to reassert itself. "I'm working on that, Howard."

"Well, work harder. We're running out of time."

Mark startled me, appearing suddenly at my shoulder. "Time to check in with them."

I let him drag me up out of my seat, away from Howie and Micah. "They're not in the best mood . . ."

"Who is?" He nudged Songh, damp and eager beside him. "Get Cris."

"In the shop," I called as Songh raced off.

"Got chased on the way over," Mark panted. "Broad daylight. Some kiddie ball team. Didn't like the color of my coveralls."

"You should have called Security."

"You gotta be kidding. Security are their older brothers and sisters." Mark steered me to the front row and pulled up short in front of Mali. "Got a minute?"

I expected the worst, a flash of that hidden temper, as Mali frowned down at him, this slim blond with the determined jaw. But Mali asked, "How many?"

"Enough, sir. I think."

"You think? Numbers, bro."

"Six thousand."

When Mali smiled like that, it was like watching the sun come up. "Well done, young Mark." He reached behind him without looking and snagged the shoulder he seemed to know was there. "Sam! We're needed. Time to go to work!"

NIGHT MEETING:

It was hard to paint, knowing what was ahead of us that night, but I insisted we work until the very last minute. Cris bitched a lot, but I think even he felt guilty about leaving a job unfinished when the boss is working right alongside you.

"What if we present the petition and they arrest us all on the spot?" I'd worried to Mali while Sam ran through our plan with Mark and Cris.

"Unlikely," he replied. "Too precipitous for domer folk." His long legs were crooked over the seat back in front of him, his elbows rested on the cushions to either side, his head rolled back until I thought his neck would break. Theatre seats were not made for a man this shape. "But there are worse things than jail, you know."

"Yeah, they could put us Out."

"Worse things than that."

I couldn't imagine.

"People do live lives out there."

"Half lives."

Mali sighed, patience and exasperation in the same sound. "Infinitely harder than yours, infinitely freer."

"One kind of freedom I don't need."

"Oh?" Mali raised his dark, thin arms to scribe an arc, aport de bras above his head and I saw blue sky, that profound open blue, the blue of Sam's eyes, and felt myself begin to float. I coughed and sat up and planted both feet flat on the carpeted floor, breathing shallow and fast.

"Never having had this freedom, you can't know how much it might mean to you," he said quietly.

I struggled to deny my disorientation, to refuse the possibility that he'd caused it. "It's not fair to use your life on Tuatua as a parallel for the Outside, just because you haven't got a dome."

He rolled his head sideways to look at me, privately amused, challenging. "What makes you think I was?"

*   *   *

A half hour before curfew, we laid our brushes down. Micah got all formal and shook our hands, Songh and Jane and Crispin and me, one by one.

"Be back to paint soon as we're done," I promised.

The main lobby was a blaze of light for the *Crossroads* first preview. The little SecondGen ushers were tarted up in new maroon uniforms with smart white buttons and trim. They roamed the acres of mauve carpeting and picked up discarded ticket stubs, regarding us with suspicion while we hung about waiting for Mark. Champagne glasses clinked in the upper lobby as the concessions prepared for intermission.

Mark came bounding out of the office door with two women from Administration. SecondGens, both of them, looking worried but determined. I was both encouraged and guilt-ridden. I should have been doing more over the past few days to recruit support. I'd let our problems with *The Gift* absorb me totally.

Four other apprentices trotted down to meet us from the upper lobby, Max Eider's three assistants and a stranger. Roly-poly and spike-haired, the new boy introduced himself as the *Crossroads* sound apprentice. "There's twelve more coming from Music, Costumes, and Lighting." He offered Mark every protocol of respect but a salute. "Maybe a few from Special Effects, 'cept they've really got their hands full."

"Where's the rest of you?" asked Eider's number one.

I laughed bitterly. "This is all of us."

She rolled her eyes. "Boy, everybody's heard *The Gift* is understaffed, but golly . . ."

The professional chitchat covered our nervousness, but it wore out fast as we padded the winding kilometer-long path through the thick leafy twilight of Founders' Park. The flagstone walk narrowed to allow no more than three abreast as it snaked around oaks as wide as double doorways. We picked up strength as we met other pathways, moving inward toward the center of the dome. Cris counted heads and kept revising upward. Over a hundred, he claimed, in our group alone, and when we emerged from tree shadow into sunset, crossing the wide white ring of plaza surrounding the twin spires of Town Hall, crowds were streaming in from all directions.

My birth-dome is a city once known for the quality of its

high-rise architecture, but those buildings were all from Before and Harmony's dominant styles were archaic or at least nostalgic and until recently, under three stories tall. The children's block geometry of Town Hall was the only contemporary large-scale building I'd ever seen, and it never ceased to amaze me: two shining glass cylinders rising sixty stories from the sloping sides of a massive glass cone, set on eight thin stacked discs of white marble. A clean, abstract physicalization of a clean abstract idea: Athenian democracy. The towers housed Business and Administration. The transparent twenty-story cone held the Meeting Hall, its vast curve of glass opaqued only for Town Meetings. It sat thirty thousand people, the heart and soul of Harmony's political life.

"I can't believe we're actually doing this," I exclaimed as the towers rose up before us.

Mark smiled nervously. "The mayor's not going to believe it, either."

Streetlights glimmered sweetly in the wall of glass, like the stars we read about but never saw, their tiny sources being diffracted into invisibility by the energy dance of the dome. The undulating panes scattered golden shards of artificial dusk across the white pavement. Hudson River School. A heroic kind of light. I thought Louisa would approve. Desk lamps glowed here and there through the reflection of Founders' Park and several floors were lit up in the South Tower, where the mayor's office was. Above, behind, the dome was velvet black. Outside, it must have been storming. It was already darker than it ever got in Harmony.

A single Security Green sat by an open door at the marbled entrance to the South Tower. She'd been laughing at some program on her portable vid, but she thumbed the volume down as she watched the inexplicable crowd swell in the plaza. She listened to the unnatural quiet, the murmurs and foot shuffling, the absence of laughter, got up and went in, dragging her folding chair with her.

"Putting in a call for reinforcements," Cris gloated.

"Or asking what the hell to do," said I.

"I don't blame her." In her first sign of anxiety in days, Jane was wringing her hands like Lady Macbeth.

Mark mounted the broad, curving stairs and gathered the apprentice representatives from the seven other villages, a boy and a girl from each dorm, wearing freshly laundered coveralls, brandishing their stacks of signed petitions like a precious but potentially dangerous object. Like I might carry a gun or Ule's knife, I decided, grasping a handful of the BardClyffe stack. I gave some to Jane to keep her restless hands occupied.

Mark studied the irregular ranks still gathering below us, all those expectant faces, raised in a sea of well-worn blue relieved here and there with bits of the brighter civilian clothing. "Crowd estimate?"

"Four thousand, maybe forty-five," said Cris.

"We'll wait a bit longer." He glanced to me for confirmation.

" 'Til curfew," I agreed. "Like Mali said." I looked for Mali in the crowd, but Sam had decreed a low profile for the Eye. "We'll be there if you need us," he'd said.

By nine, the ambers of sunset had muted to lavender and blue. Cris was confidently claiming upward of seven thousand, more than we had signatures. The streetlamps glared. The knot of twenty Greens now huddled in the South Tower lobby had turned them up to full. Somebody's watch beeped, then another.

Mark smoothed his hair back, lifted his chin. "Okay, people. Let's go."

Petitions clutched to our chests, we mounted the white steps and approached the lobby doors. All had been turned off but one, where the Greens stood guard.

"What if they won't let us in?" whispered Songh.

Mark had thought of that, or someone had. He stopped us a few paces from the door, then stepped forward himself, folded his arms, and waited. The Greens conferred behind the glass. One relayed messages from a terminal in the brightly painted tourist-information booth. They all looked young and worried. Their only experience with crowd control was shepherding tardy tourists through the Gates. Finally, one brave boy approached and let the door slide open. "You're all in violation of curfew as of nine minutes ago."

Mark raised his hand, signaled behind him without taking his eyes or his reassuring smile off the Green in the doorway. Songh moved up beside him. A SecondGen girl came up out of the crowd. Mark split his stack of petitions and placed them in their hands. "Not all of us."

"What d'you want?" demanded the Green. He was dark and robust, probably a soccer player.

"We've a petition to deliver to Her Honor the Mayor."

"Give it here and get home. You're violating curfew."

Mark smiled. "Are you going to arrest us all?"

The boy frowned. "I'll take your damn message up to the mayor."

Mark drew a folded paper out of his breast pocket. He walked up and handed it to the Green. "Here's the text. The signatures we'll deliver into her hands only."

The Green scowled at the paper, and a wordless murmur rolled across the waiting crowd, like the wind Outside must sound, or like the growl and sigh of cargo passing through the Tubes underground. The front ranks shifted forward, mounted the first curved step.

"And we don't intend to leave," said Mark, "until we've done so."

"What's your name, fella?"

Mark reached to either side. Songh and the girl were there with the petitions. Mark took a stack in each hand and raised them high. The crowd surged onto the second step. "Our names are here."

The Green backed away. The door hissed shut behind him.

Mark let his arms drop. With his back to the thronged plaza, he clenched his eyes shut and drew a ragged breath.

"You're doing great," I assured him.

"And that was the easy part," he muttered.

"Keep this up, we'll run *you* for mayor."

He gave me a twisted smile. "If we're around that long."

Songh gathered the petitions into his arms. "What do we do now?"

"Play it by ear, Sam said." Mark turned to face the plaza, standing tall. He looked surprised and gratified when the crowd hushed immediately. "Don't know how long we'll have to wait," he called out. "We might as well relax."

We hunkered down on the steps to set the example, and the crowd settled to the pavement in front and around us, whispering, comparing notes. Groups formed, people went visiting. Now there was laughter, relieved and quietly jubilant. Mark's dialogue with the Green was recalled and repeated, passing already into apprentice myth. Even Jane was busy supplying Songh's version with a more exact wording. Cris chatted up a pretty young citizen who reminded me of Tua, telling her what the Green should have said and done if he'd had half a brain.

Mark stared silently at the white marble between his feet. I nudged him gently. "I know it'd be better if he were here with you, but this is a very major gesture in his memory."

"You know what they said?" he murmured.

By now we knew that "they" always meant the Eye.

"They said maybe they could help me find him."

"Find Bela?" I stared at him. "How?"

"They didn't say. You know how they are." Mark raised his eyes, imploring me to give him some reason to believe in this impossibility.

"Gosh," I said.

Hands grasped Mark's shoulders, shook him gently. "Good, kid, good, but remember to show yourself a little so they know you're still here waiting with them." Sam hunkered down between us. His "respectable" high-collared shirt and slacks made him the picture of a model citizen of Harmony, a recycling-plant manager or maybe the owner of a small boutique. I looked for Cris again. The "citizen" he was talking to probably was Tua.

"Get up near the streetlamps so that blond head of yours'll catch the light," Sam advised. "Use that lovely smile. Remember, it's all about performance."

"I'm no performer," said Mark.

"Too late, kid, you're all they've got. Not all elections are official, you know." Sam grinned at him happily, practically ruffled his hair. *Geared up*, as Mali had said. "Go on, now. Give 'em a little touch of Harry." He urged Mark to his feet, watching after him possessively.

"You're really enjoying this," I observed.

"This is the best," he agreed. "This is the climb, where hope is your engine and everything's in front of you, where you watch the potential for power rise like sap out of young people like Mark . . . and you."

And eloquence from their organizer. "Sam, I don't get it. It's not even your issue."

"Is it really so mysterious?" He regarded me with a certain distance. "As Mali says—I quote, so as not to sound pretentious—when you're walking the Stations, you clean up whatever mess you come across. Every situation, even the world itself, has its own set of stations, after all." He looked away, methodically scanning the crowd as it milled about the plaza, restless with waiting. "And we have this habit of resistance, you see. One you would do well to cultivate." His eyes came back to me and he smiled, heavy lidded. "Except, of course, where I am concerned."

I laughed. How could I do otherwise? On the step behind me, Songh squealed, "Here they come!"

The Greens were in motion. Lights flicked on, doors sighed open. Mark hurried up the steps from the plaza. Cris and Yolanda intercepted him. "What now?" Mark hesitated, casting a desperate glance over their shoulders for guidance from Sam.

"Talk to him," Sam urged. "He needs your support." I signaled both thumbs up. Songh raced up with the Bard-Clyffe petitions. A group of citizens strode across the lobby, the mayor's familiar strawberry curls bobbing among them. Mark took the petitions under his arm as Crispin's impatience grabbed his attention momentarily.

"You're on, lad," Sam murmured. When I looked back, he'd gone.

The mayor was a tall, bony woman with a beleaguered, forthright manner and bangs of frizz framing three sides of a long face. The sleeves of her fashionable jumpsuit were bunched up in workmanlike rolls. I was surprised she'd come in person. It was an election year, to be sure, but her own term wasn't up for another two.

She did not cower behind the glass. She strode through the door, gesturing the sixteen members of the Town Council to follow. Cora Lee, as always made less diminutive by her habitual green silk, came last of all. She offered us no sign of recognition.

The mayor halted in the open halfway to the steps. "Would someone care to tell me what the hell is going on out here?"

Our smaller group fell back as Mark stepped forward. This moment we had actually staged.

Mark offered up his old little-boy smile. When he spoke, I envied his steadiness. "Good evening, Your Honor. On behalf of the apprentice population of Harmony, as well as of many of her citizens, the undersigned request a frank and public discussion of the future of the Outside Adoption

Policy, as well as of the future of those already participating in this program."

He stepped back. One by one, he called the names of the eight villages. With each name, two of us came forward to add petitions to the pile already in his arms. When he held them all, he went to stand in front of the mayor like the people's messenger boy.

"My, my," said the mayor. She eyed the stack as if it were an unexpected civic award. "This looks very well organized. Perhaps I should put you to work in my office."

Several members of the council tittered appreciatively.

"We'd like to know if and when this discussion will take place," said Mark.

"Well, we'll certainly look into the matter as soon as we can." The mayor gestured. An aide hurried forward to take charge of the petitions.

Mark held them tight. "We'd like to know tonight."

"Attaboy!" whispered Cris.

Now the titterers muttered disapproval. The rest studied our delegation, perhaps noting that it exactly matched theirs in number. A mixed lot, this council. One man, one woman elected from each village according to a complicated formula that required seating fifty percent ex-apprentices. Cora Lee elbowed her way to the front. "Under the circumstances, Your Honor, opening a discussion seems a reasonable request."

The mayor smiled pleasantly. "Are these children friends of yours, Cora?"

"Some of them are known to me."

Mark raised the petitions in front of him. "There are six thousand, one hundred and thirty-two signatures here, Your Honor. At least twelve hundred are from citizens."

"My, my. That many."

"The issue really should be put on this week's Town Meeting agenda," said Cora. Mali had coached her well.

"Outrageous!" complained a neat, balding man to the mayor's right. SecondGen, Founder Family, I guessed, from the tight expensive cut of his clothes and the equally tight set of his mouth. "This is unprecendented!"

"With all respect, sir," said Mark, "it is not."

The mayor narrowed weary eyes at him. "Done your research, eh?"

"Yes, Your Honor."

She jerked her head familiarly at Cora. "I take it Ms. Lee is known to you?"

"She is, Your Honor."

"Will you and your"—she waved a vague hand toward the plaza—"the rest of them trust Cora Lee to be your advocate in this matter before this council and the citizenry?"

Mark glanced at Cora. "If she is willing, we'd be honored."

When Cora nodded, the mayor nodded, crossing this item off her never ending mental list. "Then Cora, my dear, we'll let you carry all this impressive paperwork. Just punishment for opening your mouth, eh?" She fixed Mark with a school principal stare. "And you. Who're you 'prenticed to?"

When informed, the mayor looked mildly incredulous. "Theatre, is it? Well, if you've any interest in Administration, come see me in the morning. Now if you'll excuse us, we have a full calendar waiting upstairs and we'd all like to be home by a reasonable hour. You're all on probation for breaking curfew, so hustle on back to your dorms."

As she was turning away, Mark said loudly, "Excuse me, Your Honor, but when did you say this discussion would take place?"

She stopped and looked back. "I didn't, did I?"

"No, ma'am. And there are a lot of people here who'd really like to know."

"Now, Dunya," muttered the balding man, "There's no need to be ruled by the rabble."

That seemed to decide her. The mayor, after all, had been an apprentice once. "Well, I see no point in postponing the inevitable. We'll take it up at the next meeting, how's that?"

"This week?" asked Mark.

"This Thursday night."

His challenge met more fully than he'd expected, Mark looked as if all the possible consequences were racing through his brain at once. "That's perfect, Your Honor. Would you like to tell them yourself?"

"So I can't take it back, eh?"

Mark met her tired smile. "I thought, rather, so that you could have all the applause."

The mayor made the announcement and she did get the applause, and cheering as well, the impulsive, disorganized sort that comes when an outcome is unexpected. Cora Lee twitched her green silk into place and smiled as Mark lowered the thick stack of paper into her arms. He looked relieved to have them out of his hands.

"Now the real fun begins," Cora murmured.

When she'd followed the mayor back into the South Tower, we milled around a bit. We'd made no plan for celebration.

"Guess we should get back to the Ark," I murmured. But Cris pounded Mark's shoulder suddenly and yelled, "We got 'em!" He threw an arm around Mark, an arm around me as if there was nothing awkward between us, and I understood something interesting: as overbearing as Cris could be, he was uninterested in leadership. That sort of responsibility might cramp his freedom of expression as an artist.

But he could celebrate Mark's leadership and his whooping set Songh dancing and broke the stall. The plaza erupted with cheers and excited babble. Mark's co-organizers rushed up to mob him with congratulations. He took it with smiling grace but escaped with relief when they moved on to congratulating each other. He grabbed my sleeve. "C'mon. Our part's done." The blouse of his coverall was soaked through. "Oh god, I think I hate this."

"Being scared doesn't mean you hate it. Like stage fright. Some actors never get over it, but they keep acting."

"That's actors." He brushed damp hair from his eyes. "I remind myself of my father when I'm like this."

"Can't be so bad, then."

"Dangerous. He liked power, my father. Liked it too much. Let's go home."

"Where's that?" grumbled Songh cheerfully, catching up at the bottom of the stairs. "You know, it's gonna be something when you're all winning your citizenships and I'm still locked out of my own damn house!"

"You can sleep in my guest room," said Jane.

"Your guest room?" we laughed.

The crowd was breaking up, spilling onto the paths leading radially into the encircling park. A citizen walking on my right smiled and congratulated me. When I realized it was Omea, I hugged her. "You *were* here!"

"Of course, child. Did you think we wouldn't be?"

"Somebody had to show that ignorant crowd how to

behave," said Ule from my left. He'd piled on more clothing than I'd ever seen him in, and none of it looked good.
As I fought off the giggles, he loosened his high neon-pink
collar, slipped off his pointed white shoes. Ahead of us,
Moussa draped a dashiki-clad arm across Mark's back. Further along, Mali and Te-Cucularit strolled at ease and elegant in gallery-owner tweeds. Cu was turning admiring
heads among the crowd moving homeward with us as we
entered Founders' Park. So much for low profile. Behind
us, sporadic cheering echoed from the plaza. The irony of
it piqued me. Our SecondGen supporters could party on
the steps of Town Hall until dawn if they wanted.

"Well, you did it." Sam had replaced Omea at my side.

I snorted. "I didn't do anything but show up."

"Aw, shucks, 'twarn't nuthin . . ."

"I mean, my head's been completely in the show. It was
Mark and the others . . . and you guys."

Sam chuckled softly. "For a woman who looks like she
spends a lot of time thinking, you aren't real big on self-
aware."

It was dark under the big trees. The wrought-iron post
lights were dim and widely spaced. The homeward stream
thinned, veering off to different paths or hurrying ahead.
Our group sauntered, splitting into twos and threes as the
path narrowed. Talking with Mark, Mali trailed his fingers
through the overhanging leaves as if petting a favorite
animal.

When I said nothing, Sam continued, "You don't see
your place in the scheme of things—for instance, how much
people rely on you. Micah, Mark, Jane, and Songh, even
that asshole boyfriend of yours."

"Cris certainly doesn't rely on me, and I do wish you'd
stop calling him that."

"Asshole or your boyfriend?"

"Either . . . uh, both." A breeze whispered in the
branches. Ahead, Tuli and Lucienne moved through a pool
of shifting pathlight side by side, black and white mirror
images of the same willowy long-skirted girl.

"Well, that's progress. Does that mean you're free this
evening?"

I shook my head. "Micah's expecting us back at the
Arkadie."

"See what I mean? Reliable. I answer to that, too, and I'm proud of it. Why aren't you?"

"I am. It's just—"

"You think it's not enough, but at the right moment it can be everything." He said it lightly, but his face was sober under the post light. He looked away from me, whipping his arm back and forth boyishly as if tossing stones. "Well, I'll walk you to the theatre."

"Thank you."

"She thanks me. Ohh, I am making progress."

"Jeez, Sam, couldn't you just talk to me? About ordinary things?"

Again the invisible stone toss, low and flat. "Yes, ma'am, I could. What kind of things?"

"About your life, about the Eye, no, not even. That's not ordinary. I don't know. Anything."

"Still after that what-is-he?"

I shrugged. "Of course."

"You got your three sentences yet?"

"No," I replied quietly.

"Ah, you'll get it all wrong anyway." A dark nutlike object appeared in his right hand. He rolled it deftly across his palm, under and over his fingers, making it appear and disappear. I was sure if I got a close look at it, I'd find twelve little carved totems. Somewhere away among the trees, cheering broke out again. The dark nut hung frozen between his fingers as Sam stilled, listening. He shrugged, and the nut rolled again, up and around, too fast to be possible. "You're from Chicago, right?"

I was surprised. "Yes."

"Terrible town. Can't have been easy getting out of there."

"I guess." I was wondering how he knew.

"And you obviously couldn't buy your way into Harmony like so many do."

My turn this time to correct a misconception. "That's not how it's done. The computer—"

"Yeah, yeah. About the first quarter are chosen on merit. The rest, well, the world is full of talented youngsters. Why not lean toward those who also happen to be rich?"

"How could you know what goes on in Harmony?"

"I make it my business to know anything useful."

"What about Jane?" Surely she was proof for my side.

"Must have been a slow year."

"You're horrible."

"Hey, love, doesn't it make you feel better to know you're the real thing?"

"I guess." Of course it did, if I could believe him.

He looked at me sideways. "Aw, shucks, 'twarn't nuthin'—"

"Sam, Art is illegal in Chicago. I got out 'cause I had to. Don't make more out of it than it was."

He raised an eyebrow in reply, rolling the nut across his knuckles and shaking his head.

I caved in to the silence first. "Did you always live on Tuatua?"

"Nope." He was listening again, more intently. The cheers in the distance sounded like yelling. "Ule, hear that?"

"I hear," Ule replied from the shadows ahead.

"Moussa?"

"Yah."

"TeCu?"

"Here."

The Eye closed rank. Mali and Cu pulled up short of the next circle of path light. Cris and Tua halted with them. Omea and Pen caught up behind, shepherding Songh and Jane.

"What is it?" asked Songh. Omea hushed him. We stood in the whispering dark, listening. A woman screamed shrilly off to one side. Angry shouting rose and died away, then erupted anew in three different locations.

Sam interlaced his left hand firmly with mine. "Truce for the moment and do exactly what I tell you."

Mali's nostrils twitched. He slid out of his fancy jacket. "I'd call it a bit too quiet in our immediate neighborhood."

Te-Cucularit slipped off his shoes, bundled them with his jacket and Mali's, and stashed them in the crook of a tree. He rolled up his sleeves.

"Up ahead, I'm guessing," said Ule, "at the turn."

Lucienne and Tuli eased to either side of him. Mali drew Mark into Moussa's shadow. The three dancers moved to the front. We rounded the turn.

Where the path kinked around three massive spreading oaks, a clot of young men waited in red and white uniforms, armed with SecondGen insolence and branches torn from the trees.

"My old friends, the soccer team," muttered Mark.

"And several dozen of their friends," said Ule.

"We'll match them play for play," Moussa promised.

Sam considered us quickly. "In addition to the usual, it's Cu on Mark, Omea on Jane, Pen on Songh, Tua on Cris. Moussa?"

"I'll cover." Moussa shifted to group with Cu and Mali. I suddenly understood their constant athletics in the rehearsal hall as another kind of rehearsing, defense and offense, precise coordination and deployment of strength. I got an inkling of why Mali had survived Sam's beating without a scratch.

"I'll take care of myself," declared Cris recklessly.

"Stick tight, pretty boy," Sam growled. "We're safer without heroics."

Cris grinned at him. "Who's gonna protect you?"

"Shut up and listen," said Tua. Startled, Cris subsided.

"Down their throats and scatter," said Sam. "There's too many of them."

Ule and his girls nodded. Pen looked eager.

"Okay. What we need now"—Sam flicked back his throwing arm, covered my eyes with his other hand—"is a little light around here."

I saw the flash through the cracks between his fingers. Immediately he grabbed my wrist and we were moving, all of us, fast and tight together. The soccer boys were blinking and disoriented. The flare burned white-gold on the path like a tiny hungry sun. One boy tried to stomp it out. The odor of burning athletic shoe hit me as we raced toward them. They didn't see us coming until we were on top of them.

Ule and the girls plowed into them, shrieking like Berserkers, ducking under and around, grabbing arms and clothing and more delicate parts, tearing branches out of astonished hands. Moussa and Cu were close behind, snatching the flying branches out of the air, swinging hard and at random, bare feet kicking sidelong while Mali and Mark ran between them.

The boys recovered quickly, but we were halfway through by then. Cu sprinted ahead with Mali and Mark. Ule and the girls doubled back to pull three red-jersied toughs off

Crispin's back. Tua kneed a young one in the groin, but his older, bigger buddy grabbed her around the neck, lifting her off the ground with a roar. She arched her back and flipped out of his grasp, landing on one knee in front of me. I grasped her arm. Sam's driving momentum hauled her up.

"Go!" he shouted. Tua sprang free and forward.

Moussa cleared a path for Omea, who had her hands full keeping Jane from turning back in panic. I slowed to help her.

"No!" Sam dragged me onward. I glanced back. Pen and Songh pulled Jane along with them.

Ahead, Ule held off several branch wielders with his knife. He danced at them in a fury, legs spread, jabbing his eight inches of lethal metal as if it were something more organic. "Come on, you mothers!" he screeched. "I'll slice your domer balls off!"

Tuli and Lucienne marked time in the path, their long skirts hiked up into their waistbands. They closed protectively around Omea and Jane. A soccer boy snatched at Omea's hair. Tuli lunged. Another smaller blade caught the dying light of the flare. The boy yowled and jerked away bloodied fingers. He stared at his hand in shock and backed away as the fight surged around him.

"Go!" yelled Sam again. Tuli and Lucienne leaped ahead. Omea doubled her speed. We were almost past them. A red shirt loomed up beside us, large and angry, clumsily swinging a branch. Sam yanked me, swerved aside. Behind us, Pen caught the blow in the stomach, caved and went down. The red-shirt laughed. It was the big one who'd grabbed Tua. He didn't look much like a teenager to me and I began to wonder about this soccer team. He hauled back his branch for another blow at Pen but Songh flew at him like a wildcat, fingers grabbing, nails clawing. Pen staggered coughing and bleeding to his feet just as the red-shirt flung Songh to the ground. Moussa fell back and picked the boy out of the path as if he were an empty sack. Still another blade flashed in Pen's hand, opening up a long gash in his attacker's chest. Pen ducked back, then plunged in for a second cut.

"Go!" ordered Sam.

"Gonna write my fucking name!" Pen screamed.

"*Pen!* Go!"

Pen backed off, scowling at Sam. The red-shirt bent and fumbled at his sock. His torn shirt front was shiny with his blood. His hands shook. I thought he would topple over but he came up sharp with a knife of his own.

I screamed with what breath I had left. *"Pen!!"*

Pen leaped aside. The knife grazed his shoulder blade, slicing his sleeve. He turned in midair and crouched. "Blade!" he warned as he was grabbed hard from behind.

The red-shirt was no longer roaring or clumsy. Two of his fellows held Pen fast. He shifted his knife in his hand and moved in. "Little Outsider piece of shit . . ."

Sam's blade was in his hand and out of it so fast I didn't see it until it was sunk to the hilt in the red-shirt's back. The man staggered, his teammates gaped in disbelief and Pen twisted out of their grasp. He ran straight for the red-shirt, knocked him down and yanked the knife clear in one smooth movement.

"Go!" he yelled to Sam.

I stared at the man writhing on the ground, at the dampness spreading across his back.

Sam jerked me forward. We ran.

There was no one ahead of us, no way to know if the others had made it out. The path lamps had been extinguished. Terror propelled me through the first several hundred meters of darkness, until I was winded and my legs ached.

"I need to stop," I panted.

"Forget it." Sam grabbed my arm. "Look behind you."

They pounded after us through the trees—eight, ten of them at least. Pen pulled up alongside, running easily though his face and arm were smeared with blood. "Fuckin' assholes!"

"All right?" Sam asked.

"Flesh wound. I'll split off when we get out of the trees."

Sam nodded. "See you at Cora's."

I knew I couldn't make it that far. "Isn't there someplace closer?"

"You name it," returned Sam grimly.

I couldn't. Who would take us in, an apprentice out past curfew and a man who could and would bury his knife in a guy's back from fifteen meters? I told myself, just keep running, the boys behind will tire or give up. But they were young and athletic, used to running. And they were angry.

As we broke out of the park, Pen's swerve off to the right drew three of them after him. I glanced back. Seven still in pursuit, gaining slowly.

Trash littered the dark streets, broken glass crunching underfoot and a strange slickness here or there. We weren't the only ones the soccer boys had gone after. I slipped in a patch of wet. Sam caught me roughly. "Stick with me for a while, love. We're gonna try and lose 'em."

"Don't know . . . how much longer . . . !" A needle of pain inched up my side.

"Long as you have to, you want to be alive tomorrow." He spoke in the easy rhythm of his stride. "Told you you needed exercise. And don't talk. It makes you tense. Breathe deep and slow. Come on, this way."

We pounded around a corner. Sam turned hard left into a narrow alley behind a row of houses, then veered right after the second house. We ran in silence across the soft velvet grass of well-tended lawns.

Sam slowed behind a hedge and looked back. "Good. They split up at the turn. Gets it down to four."

The lawns were full of trimmed bushes and little decorative fences, obstacles to trip the unwary and exhausted. I found them all. Sam led me back to the road, loping along still barely winded. My lungs were on fire.

"Sam . . . I can't . . . it hurts."

"You can. You must." Running beside me, he pressed his hand to the small of my back. I could feel the warmth of it even through the sweat and the pounding of my pulse. "Concentrate. Forget the pain. Think about rhythm. The comfort of repetition. Think about . . . why you've got to keep moving. About how I'll feel if I have to leave you behind."

New strength surged through me. "Would you?"

"Heroics are for the stage, Rhys."

I remembered the blood welling thick and slick from the red-shirt's back. This man *would* leave me to save himself. I concentrated on that, and the knife-cramp in my side eased off to background noise. Then I made the mistake of asking, "How much further, you think?"

"Ten, fifteen minutes."

Panic. Pure and simple. I searched the darkened windows with desperate eyes. Each light in an upper bedroom seemed a distant and unattainable sanctuary. I knew I was done for. "Maybe I could . . . hide somewhere . . . You could—"

His hand urged me forward. "No. Concentrate, damn it! Be somewhere else. Imagine . . . yeah, imagine the roughlands . . . big, open scrub desert, full of red rocks and snakes . . . you're there . . . it's wide to the horizon, the sky overhead so blue it makes your eyes water."

I knew that sky. I'd seen it in my mind already.

The pressure of his fingers never slackened. "Picture it. You've been checking the traps . . . been a good day . . . nothing in 'em too weird to eat, nothing too sick . . . so intent on this good fortune, you don't notice half the Possum gang getting the drop on you. Then it's too late. Can't hide or make a stand. You're small and there's six of 'em . . . can only sling the mess over your shoulder. Try to outrun them . . . 'cause they'd like what you got there, too . . . and they're hungry enough to kill for it. But you've got a head start. So you run . . . it's five, maybe six miles back to the lookout . . . first place you can count on any help . . . and that only your sister, but she's a good shot . . . she can drop 'em from a distance. The sun's still high. Wouldn't be bad but for this . . . load on your back and the stock of your rifle . . . slamming your hip with every step . . . you're gonna just slip around this rock here, then straight on homeward . . . whatever happens, you know you can't stop . . ."

We took the turn flat-out. His voice faded under the rhythmic slap of feet against dry-packed dirt. I was barely aware when the touch at my back fell away. I sweltered in the fierce desert sun and settled the load forward on my shoulder, ignoring the metallic jab of the rifle against my ribs. Alone under the blue, endless sky, I ran, unthinking, inspired by the sudden baying of the hunting pack behind me, caught up in the machine of my body, seeing only blue until something rose up hard in front of me and something softer snatched at me and pulled me through.

Voices, one breathless like me. "She alone?"

"He'll be out there drawing them off."

"Shit."

"He'll make it. You did."

Then the clang of metal, angry shouts behind. My knees caving in. A hopeless warring for breath. Hauled up and pulled along, my numbed legs dragging on wood, fumbling up stepped stone. At last the welcome of a giving surface and collapsing, heaving, gasping, dying from the agony in my lungs, the fire in my side.

Other voices. A woman. She forces liquid into my mouth. Probably I won't die, I think. But I do faint.

I woke up alive, in a wide, soft bed.

A lamp glowed comfortably in a corner of a big, dim room. I was in somebody else's nightgown and my hair was damp. My body was unmanageable. Rolling over was a major effort. I rested after accomplishing it and studied the Gothic groin vaulting overhead until I could actually imagine standing on legs like the ones I had left. I struggled up, groaning, and staggered about on the thick carpet until my knees bent in the right direction, then limped slowly to the window and looked out onto treetops and the night-lit waters of a moat. The nightgown was sea-green silk and much too short for me.

Cora's. I was at Cora's.

Hinges creaked across the room. Sam stood in the tall doorway, balancing a tray on spiked fingers like a basketball. He saw the covers tossed aside, discovered me leaning by the window, and set the tray down beside the bed. "How's my jogging partner?"

I had no reply, having just then understood that the problem was not that I might fall in love with this man, this knife-wielding stranger, but that I already had.

He saw it immediately, read it in my silence and the softening of my eyes, the whole story I'd already written, right down to the deeply tragic farewell in a month's time when he went on tour. He smiled easily, then came over, and took my hands, unfolding the tight fists I'd made. He pressed his mouth to my palms with infinite gentleness. "You know, they always tell actors not to play the end of the play while they're still in the first act."

"They say the same thing to designers." I bent my forehead to his shoulder, fighting the urge to flatten myself against him, to hang on for dear life. I told myself, It's unseemly to want someone this much. "Is everyone all right?"

He nodded, brushing hair back from my ear. "We were last. We got the brunt of it."

"How far did we run?"

"Oh, maybe four or five."

"I can't believe it."

"Told you there's nothing like a little exercise before bed."

I touched the fresh scratches reddening his jaw.

He jerked his head disgustedly. "When it got down to two behind, I dropped back to beat the shit out of 'em. Tripped over some citizen's prize rosebush. Pretty fuckin' dumb. Had to do some fast scrambling then. You made that last mile on your lonesome, Rhys. Congratulations." He eased his arms around me and drew me against him. "How do you feel?"

"Sore. Every muscle, every joint."

"I can fix that."

"You'll teach me the healing trance?"

"I had something more collaborative in mind."

I laughed, desire bubbling at my throat like song. His hands beneath the green silk were sure, his kiss slow and easy. I was relieved to have run out of excuses for resisting the heat between us. Desire is so much easier than love.

"Would you really have left me out there?"

"Well, now, we didn't have to test that, did we?"

I had so many questions. He even answered a few of them, mostly the trivial personal ones, but talking, it turned out, was not the best thing we did together. I'd never had as good as he gave, or given as good as he got. I told him I loved him, that I'd never feel alive again without him inside me, the silly things you say when you've fallen very hard for the first time.

"Hush now," he said. "Of course you will."

Later, I ran my hand lightly over the scars ridging his lower back and thought of Crispin's flawless silky surfaces. Sam's body, like his character, had edges, hard planes, and knots. He was all over sun-browned but for a paler shadow at his groin. "You look like you've walked into trouble all your life."

"In a manner of speaking."

The slick, damaged skin numbed my fingers with sympathetic pain.

"Planter's whip," he said matter-of-factly. "Before I met the Eye. Would have healed clean otherwise."

I gathered my own memories of him torn and bleeding

in Cora's kitchen. I was jealous of any pain he'd suffered before I was there to comfort him. "When was that?"

"Soon after, I met Mali and Ule in a bar down by the port, where you can still smuggle yourself onto the island if you're fast and clever. Mal was talking politics. I was trying to pick his pocket. Ule's knife talked me out of it."

"Why were you doing that?"

His oh-you-innocent look was back again. "I was hungry."

"Oh." I added *thief* to the list of reasons I should be having nothing to do with this man.

"Not that he looked so ripe or anything. It was mostly for the practice. Thin guys like him are the hardest. So while Ule was deciding how many of my fingers to cut off, I told Mali the only reason they'd noticed me at all was because I'd liked what he had to say and listening threw me off my rhythm. Turned out the troupe had just lost someone. They were looking for a quick pair of hands. I thought it sounded better than running shell games on the docks. Mali took me home to feed me and I never left."

"When was this?"

"Ten, twelve, a lifetime ago." He stretched, gathered me into his arms. "Come here to me. What're you doing so far away?"

I nestled happily. "That story, the one you told me while we were running?"

"Wasn't sure you even heard me."

"That wasn't Tuatua . . . ?"

"It wasn't anything . . . a story, to keep you going. Worked, didn't it?"

I lifted my head from his chest and tried to stare him down. He brushed hair from my face as if I were an importunate child, but there was a glint in his eye I didn't understand.

"I'm not sure you're ready for it yet, that's all."

"You've been Outside. I guessed that already."

He chuckled. "You mean like, once or twice? Is that the scariest thing you can imagine?"

"Sam. Please."

"Okay. But don't blame me if you don't like what you hear." He eased me off his chest and turned to rest his head on his elbow. "I needed an image to keep you moving, so I was thinking of times I'd been running scared like you

were, and what came to mind was being six or seven on
what used to be my family's cattle station in the Outback."

"You mean, Before? You're not old enough to—"

"After. Just listen. At first they pretty much left us alone
out there, but the big famine finished that. My dad hung
on as long as he could and when they finally killed him, the
rest of us threw in our lot with the local tribesmen."

I sat up. "Your father was killed?"

"One of the white gangs. I never knew which."

"Gangs? You mean, Outsiders?"

He shoved upright, grabbed my head between his hands.
"Don't talk, listen! Let go of these kiddie bedtime stories!
This is truth I'm telling you. Try to hear it!" He released
my head, aware that he'd frightened me. "The real Outsiders are not those poor fuckers who hang around the domes
for the charity. They're all those people whose lives went
on while civilization-as-we-knew-it crumbled around them:
the farmers, the rural poor, the nomads, the tribal peoples,
people who didn't even know the domes were going up until
they were already shut out of them, people who suffered
and died by the millions but whose lives were so glancingly
connected with so-called civilization that they had a chance
of surviving without it. Or so they thought."

He sat back, putting a distance between us. "And some
of them did. So now there's the people inside and then
there's everyone else out there, trying to put together some
sort of a life for themselves. I never—are you listening?—
never saw the inside of a dome 'til I went on tour with the
Eye. If anyone's an Outsider, Rhys, I am."

I said, "I don't believe you."

He sighed. "No, I guess not. I sort of hoped you would,
but what's one man's word against a lifetime of domer con-
ditioning?" He relaxed against the thick pile of pillows.
"You wanted the 'what,' love, and here I am giving it to
you. All of it."

I was angry. "You think I'm gullible."

"I thought you had an ear for the truth."

"If this was true, we'd know about it! We'd—"

"What? How? You never go out there."

I shuddered.

Sam leaned forward. "Those few who do know keep the
truth to themselves to assure their control of the world's
resources. Think about it! The domes are a mega-cartel's

dream, a perfectly closed system. Nothing goes in or out
without their say-so. Why do the planters want to dome
Tuatua? Why is your power-broker Brigham on our ass?
He and his CDL don't want what's closed to be opened.
The planters want what's open to be closed!" He stared at
me, to be sure I was listening, then smiled, a tight proud
private smile, and in his hand was the little wooden sphere
with the twelve tiny figures, rolling round and round.
"Nonetheless . . . over forty years the system's sprung a few
leaks. The Eye is one of them."

I was not doing what he asked. I was not *hearing* him.
"You told Mark this same fish tale, didn't you? Oh, Sam,
how could you? It's cruel to give him hope of finding Bela!"

He eyed me coolly. "I think we can, if he's alive. Five
years ago, no, but communications are improving out there.
People are getting on their feet well enough to think about
organizing. These days, expelled domers are recruited more
often than victimized. Did you think what's going on in
Harmony is unique? For every event like the Stockholm riot
where we do get the word out into the world, three others
go unreported. It's hard to spread the truth when you don't
own the media and there's impenetrable walls around the
centers of power."

I stilled, caught by a memory of evidence I could not
deny. "There is a world Outside—"

"That's right, Rhys, there is."

"I meant the pamphlets in the vacuum tubes—"

His interest quickened. "What? When?"

I told him about Sean and the recycler.

"Damn! Smack into enemy hands! A delivery like that
takes months to set up." He grasped his knees to his chest,
chewing on his thumb. I could practically hear his brain
ticking away, calculating time lost, contacts wasted. The
Organizer. It was hard not to gaze at him fondly, whether
I believed him or not.

"Sam, why are you telling me all this?"

"You asked, as I recall."

"What if I turned you in?"

"Looking at me the way you do?" The glint was back in
his eye. "Besides, I thought you didn't believe me."

"I don't, I . . . but . . ." My confusion reduced him to
laughter. I frowned stonily. "You're saying there's lots like
you Out There?"

He cupped my breast and kissed it. "No one like me, love."

"I mean . . . you know . . ."

"Two arms, two legs, you mean? No communicable diseases? Normal?" He fell back on the pillows, roaring helplessly.

I was humiliated. "What's so goddamn funny?"

He lifted his head, regarded me drolly. "Well, think about it. You just spent three hours making drop-dead love to your worst nightmare." He flopped back, laughing again, his arm thrown over his eyes. "Ah god, I'm gonna sleep well tonight!"

But we only dozed, and then he woke me with kisses between my thighs and much more after that.

PHASE III

Technical Rehearsals

THE MORNING AFTER:

It was Sam who slept the sleep of the innocent that night, not me. My world was in upheaval. Not since my first day in Harmony had I so much reconceiving to do all at once. People out there, if I believed him, lots of them. Not all criminals and misfits. Normals. Families, maybe whole communities, struggling since before the domes with a dying ecology, poisoned water, deadly air. Children without families, making their way in the world despite all. Orphans. Like Sam. Was this the truth Mali meant to make unavoidable?

I wondered if this was what they'd said to Jane that so disconnected her. It was having that effect on me. Meanwhile, Micah needed me functional. We still had a show to do.

The Eye did not follow the age-old actors' custom of sleeping late. By eight-thirty the next morning, Ule had already run the company through warm-up exercises and a modified barre in Cora's music room. The brick-walled kitchen was as busy as a dormitory dining hall. I wandered in dazedly, following Sam as if he were a magnet, loath to be out of his arm's reach even in this room I'd so admired and felt welcomed in. That morning I saw it as artifice, a careful romantic reconstruction, like one of Micah's castle halls for the Marin project. Comfortable. Charming. Unreal. Like everything else in Harmony.

Cris looked relieved to see me, maybe because I was alive and well, more likely because I'd found a distraction of my own to ease the burden of his guilt, if he felt any. Public newsbox printout was spread across the refectory table. Ule and Tua bent over it, eating papaya and reading passages out loud. Even Cora was up, wrapped in silk the color of new leaves, leaning contentedly against Mali's hip as he talked with Mark in the light from the tall lavender windows.

Jane sat in isolation at the end of the table. I felt a sudden kinship with her and wished for something as steadying as her intense involvement in sectioning an orange. At the other end, Pen reenacted his narrow escape in holographic detail for Tuli and Lucienne. Songh listened wide-eyed, as if he hadn't been there to see it all himself.

"Hey, Jane," I called, "what's up?"

"The news. And this." She pushed a paper toward me.

E-mail: CITIZENS OF HARMONY, BEWARE! WHEN CHILDREN USURP DUE PROCESS, A COUP IS ON THEIR MINDS! CLOSE THE DOOR!"

I patted her shoulder. About all one could offer her these days was reassurance. I certainly had nothing better.

"Here's the announcement." Cris straightened up from the table, trailing printout. " 'At Thursday's Town Meeting, the scheduled agenda will be put aside to allow citizens to consider a special issue: Is Outside Adoption still right for Harmony?' "

Sam read over Ule's head. " 'Outbursts of youthful enthusiasm led to several minor disturbances in and around Founders' Park after a cordial meeting between apprentice representatives and the mayor.' Guess we know what the official line on this is going to be."

" 'Only minor injuries reported.' " Ule grinned. "Squeaked by again, Sammy boy. What they don't know, we won't tell."

"A few kids'll have some tricky explaining to do."

"Yeah, that reminds me," called Pen from his end of the table. Silvery metal arced gracefully through the air past Crispin's nose and pronged into the planking beside Sam's hand. "Thanks, old man."

Ule clucked. "Pen, lad. Cora's priceless table . . ."

The knife was bone-handled and slim, double-edged unlike Ule's heavier weapon. The silky metal was engraved with fine dark lines. Hickey, from his prop master's store of arcane knowledge, would have called it a dirk. Sam gentled the blade free and stowed it I-don't-know-where. It simply was there and then it wasn't.

Ule brushed papaya juice off the printout. "Even if you did ice the guy, we surely won't see it here."

Sam grunted. "Question is, who put him on to us?"

Ule sucked his teeth, nodded. "Brigham?"

"I don't understand," I said.

Sam steered me toward the sink, where Moussa was slicing a gigantic pineapple. "The big guy with the knife was a plant, a ringer aimed at us. Whoever put him there cleaned him out fast and quiet. If he'd really been one of the soccer kids, your news services'd be screaming bloody murder."

"You mean, you think you . . . killed him?"

He looked at me warningly, passing over a chunk of Moussa's pineapple. "Here. Eat. Got to get you to the theatre in one piece." He raised his voice to include the rest of the room. "Time to wear something less conspicuous than these damn coveralls."

"No," said Mark.

Sam had not expected contradiction. "What?"

Mali smiled, pushed himself away from the windowsill. "He's right, you know. Hiding is not the point here."

"Neither is dying.'

"Then we should teach them to take care of themselves." Mark looked to me. "Anyone afraid to wear the blues?"

"No way!" said Cris.

"Great," Sam muttered. "A bunch of fucking heroes." But Mali looked amused and proud.

HARMONET/COMMENT

08/12/46
The views expressed herein do not necessarily reflect the views of the network.

AN OPEN LETTER TO ALL APPRENTICES

CITIZEN'S EDITORIAL by Susan Wakeman Brown

Please! Is this any example to set for our children? No wonder they've forgotten how to behave themselves!

While you are running around raising a fuss and bringing violence to our idyllic streets, does it ever occur to you to be grateful to the Town that has taken you in and given you shelter and training, though it had no obligation to? You weren't born here. Nor were your parents. Yet we allowed you in to share in the richness of our community. And now you presume to tell us how to run our Town?

You have forgotten that you are our guests. Perhaps it is not so wise to abuse our hospitality.

FIRST TECH:

The streets were quiet on the way to the Arkadie.

"Too quiet." Sam left us at the stage door. "Watch yourselves."

Micah and the head scenic artist were setting out the big rolling fans to dry a full-stage coat of paint. He frowned when he saw us. "Where . . . I called your dorm . . . ?" He didn't finish the thought. With a side glance at the painter, he said firmly, "Congratulations. Your voice was heard. The issue's out in the open at last."

Cris raised a clenched fist. "You should've seen us up there! It was great! We were great!"

"I'm sure." Micah noted my graver expression.

I wanted to tell him more but could not for fear of exposing the Eye's illegal weaponry. And Sam. How could I tell him about Sam? If Sam was what he claimed to be, his very existence in Harmony was illegal. I gestured at the still-damp paint. "All by yourselves? The two of you?"

"No, amazingly. Some of the painters dropped by after the *Crossroads* preview and stayed to work. But we outlasted them, didn't we, Jan? All those young folks."

The head scenic returned a yawn and a rueful nod. Paint smeared her cheek and chin and crawled halfway up her right arm. "Okay, Mi, I'm outa here. I can give you an official crew tomorrow morning when that fucker next door is done with."

"You've already saved my life and made this afternoon bearable."

The scenic waved and left. Micah added, "She didn't want Sean seeing her do overtime without his permission. It's only a base coat but . . ."

"But everything."

The set was so much easier to look at, no longer oversized

or ungainly, its intention at last apparent. The bright patch-work of raw materials was muted to a tapestry of greens and browns and gray. The rolling sweep of the deck focused the center of the space like a living presence and sank into the corners as if it had taken root. The back wall soared upward toward the grid like the flank of a rocky hill rising into velvet night.

"Look!" I snatched at Micah's arm, startling him out of a tired reverie. A softly glowing green eye stared at us from the darkness at the top of the sweep.

Micah blinked, then smiled. "The gods watch us from Olympus."

"When did they get the time to do that?"

"This time I'm gonna find out how," Crispin swore.

Micah frowned. "No. Let it be as it's intended. A gift of mystery. We need every bit we can get right now."

The eye in the flies was still glowing faintly when Sean brought his crew in to continue installing the trick. He sent two men out into the house to set up a production table in the tenth row, where the electrics crew was already tuning remote intercoms and running cable for Louisa's lighting console. Sean didn't seem to notice the eye floating above his head, though a few of his men stared up at it with wondering smiles and shrugs. As far as they knew, it was some special effect Lou was trying out.

The tall kid Peter was hanging around, even though he'd worked his usual graveyard shift with Margaret.

"Why aren't you sleeping?" I chided him.

He pointed at the hole in the deck. "This is a real genius idea! Sean won't let me near it 'cause I'm not regular crew, but I gotta see how he does it."

"I sure hope you're right about the genius part."

He moved closer to whisper, "Hear there was trouble last night."

His puppy-eagerness put me off. "Yeah? What'd you hear?"

"Word is, some heads were broken."

I looked amazed. "Really? Didn't see that in the news. Where?"

"Around the park mostly."

"Glad I missed it." I tossed him a cheery grin and retreated to the shop to see how the tracking units were coming along.

I was gazing up at one of Eider's drops that had been hauled in once again for revision when Hickey sidled up. "Are you guys okay?"

"Hick! Where have you been?"

"*Crossroads*, of course." He drew me aside, looking me over closely. "You okay? Really?"

"Sure. Why?"

"Very nasty stories going around. Listen, about this petition thing. Lucienne told me it was all Mali's idea."

"Are you and Lucienne still seeing each other?"

Hickey shuffled. "A pipe dream. Couldn't ever work out." He wasn't going to talk about it. "Gwinn, are you guys sure this is the right thing, putting all your names on paper, making targets of yourselves? Sam and Mali don't know how things work around here. It could blow up right in your face!"

"Hickey, somebody's got to stand up to these people."

"Sure, sure. Just want you to be careful." He draped an arm around me to walk me further away from prying ears. "Look, I got the data on the e-mails. It's no big surprise. My friend says they were all billed through the Willow Street Theatre account, different departments and charge numbers, but the bills were eventually paid out of a private account she traced to Cam Brigham."

"Can she prove it?"

"If need be. Pretty bold. The guy's not even bothering to cover his tracks."

"He figures he's above suspicion."

"Or that nobody would be asking where those e-mails are coming from. Like they're not ready to get up and say it themselves, but they're sure glad somebody is."

The Willow Street connection was a bit of a surprise. I didn't picture Bill Rand as one of Sam's "power brokers," the sort who knew the supposed "truth" about the Outside.

Strolling, we reached a wall. Hickey turned to face me. "Now you know this, you'll see why I couldn't sign your petition. I hate what they're trying to do to you, but if Cam found out I signed, he could trump up some excuse to have me fired." His fingers curled into my shoulders like claws. "Gwinn, without this job, I'm nothing." He shook me gently. "Only one unimportant little name less. You understand, right?"

"Sure, I understand."

"Right." He glanced away miserably. "Well, here comes old Crispin. You two still fighting?"

"Damned if I know."

"Don't. There's enough of that going on." He patted me on the back and slouched away. I frowned after him until Cris moved into my line of sight. I let Cris have the full-bore stare.

He grinned at me slyly. "You and Sam, hunh? I wouldn't have figured that."

"Yeah, well, I had all this extra time on my hands."

"Hey, we're still friends, aren't we? We'll both be here after they've played their four weeks and moved on."

I sensed that Sam's taking me to bed had raised my value in Crispin's eyes, but I didn't want to talk about after. Didn't even want to think about it. "Wouldn't be too sure. Hickey was just explaining how he didn't sign the petition because he's afraid for his job."

"You mean the job he gave up his real work for? Getting him fired might be the biggest favor we could do him."

"Try telling him that."

"I might."

"Cris, the point is, he won't dare argue for us at Town Meeting, either. A lot of people won't, for the same reason."

"You worry like Jane. Speaking of which, you seen her around?"

"Not since after breakfast."

"Micah's looking for her. Never mind, I'll deal with it."

"Yeah?" Could he actually be maneuvering for reconciliation?

He threw back his shoulders. "Hey, this is me. C. Fox, Assistant Extraordinary."

My laugh was flat and dry. "Sure, kid."

"Don't call me that!"

I shrugged at him innocently.

His lip curled. "Sounds too much like Sam."

The Eye stumbled about on the set that afternoon, feeling their way, taking possession of it as actors must before they can stop hating it for not being their safe and familiar rehearsal hall.

The technical rehearsal started off at a decent pace until Howie decided to restage several scenes. He made it clear the set was in the way of his blocking, but he'd just have to live with it. Things bogged down as the actors got bored and testy. Omea began whispering all her lines "to save her voice." Te-Cucularit had a growling match with the prop head after a woman crew member was seen handling one of the Puleleas. Howie had to stop everything for a lecture about respecting other people's values. It was the usual technical-rehearsal tension, but I hated watching the Eye misbehave like normal actors. I wanted them to be bigger than that.

To spare Micah my restlessness, I excused myself for a shop check. Most of the scenic artists were still playing catch-up on *Crossroads*, but the tracking units were nearly finished and Cris had recruited one of the paint boys to throw a base coat on the scenery as fast as the carpenters could build it. My pal Flick thought Jane had gone home to sleep. An odd thing for her to do without asking Micah, but which of us was behaving normally anymore?

I went to the crew room for coffee and found a bunch of the guys in there talking. The room went dead in that stalled sort of way. A few of them greeted me. Most of them looked at the floor or into their coffee mugs. I filled my cup and got out, but not without noticing that everyone there was SecondGen.

So I went back to the theatre and sat house center, immobile with lack of sleep and too much conflicted thought. Wanting Sam, fearing what he stood for. Distracted, pretty much useless. Micah wandered the darkened theatre studying the set from every possible angle. If he wanted company, he didn't say so. Every so often I'd catch him staring at his scenery with an eerily blank intensity, not so much seeing it as willing it to *happen*, to become whole as he sat there, before his very eyes.

Now's when we need the magic, I sighed. Real magic. Would I ever be able to admit to Sam that he was right? I didn't know it until he'd said it, but I wanted the magic to be real.

The only one satisfied with the day was Louisa. Stationed mid-house, oblivious to all of Howie's fits and starts, she happily played with her lighting. Her console gave her control over the color, focus, and intensity of each individual lamp and effect. She played it like a concert synthesizer, improvising entire scenes as she went along. Lou played and the computer recorded. She would edit the program later and revise it during subsequent rehearsals until she had a show she was happy with.

When Liz called dinner break, Howie asked the company to stick around a moment. "Liz, get Sean out here."

Micah joined Louisa and me at the console. "We'll work the break, get some food in here and start doing some real painting. Is Jane back yet?"

I retrieved Louisa's discarded headset and murmured, "Page Jane for Micah, will you?"

Sean showed up carrying a half-gulped sandwich and a beer. "Christ, a man can't even eat around here." He grinned at Liz and did not bother to disguise a soft belch.

"Can you get the trick working over dinner?" Howie demanded.

"Hey, hey, easy does it, eh?"

"Well, can you?"

"Not tonight. Come on, we've got a preview next door."

Howie's script slammed to the deck. "You know what? I don't care about their preview! I've got to put this show in front of an audience in four days! Now, I'm running this theatre and I want equal service from the people being paid good money to get shows built on time! I can't fucking work like this!"

The Eye watched impassively as if refereeing a tennis match. Micah, Lou, and I drifted closer together.

"Ladies and gentlemen," murmured Lou, "place your bets."

Sean jiggled his beer bottle against his thigh. "I didn't make this schedule, pal."

"I don't care who made it! The actors are ready, I'm ready, everybody's ready but you, Sean!" Howie turned, paced away, turned back, punctuating with sharp jabs of his finger. "This show needs its parts together before we know what we have, 'cept we gotta wait for you to get your god-damn shit together! I don't care what your problem is! You're holding up the whole process! I want your men on it, and I want 'em there the minute we're out of here!"

"No can do, even if I had all the men in the world."

"All right! If I give you the damn stage tonight, will you have it up and running by tomorrow?"

"Could be. If you get the fuck outa here and let me work."

For a moment the only sound in the theatre was Howie's labored breathing. Then he bent, snatched up his script, and pivoted away. "Liz, release the company for the evening. The shop has the stage." He swept past Micah on his way up the aisle. "See? You got me doing your goddamn job for you."

I'd had it. When Sean headed back to the shop, I went after him. Sam blocked my way at the bottom of the aisle. "Come home with me."

"I have to work."

"For dinner, then. We'll run back."

"I have to talk to Sean."

"Was I that bad this afternoon? Or maybe it was this morning . . ."

I grinned, even blushed a little. "This is something I really have to do."

He stood close, not touching me. "Look, Rhys, we're not going to have a lot of time together."

My heart quickened. "I know."

Sam sighed, backed off. "Being reliable again, eh? Damnable woman. I may just have to take you with me." When I eyed him wistfully, he shifted, looked after Sean's retreating back. "Hard case, that one."

"He didn't used to be."

"No? What's he so angry about?"

"You, among other things."

"Yeah, I rub a lot of people the wrong way, until they get to know me—"

"I meant all of you."

"Sure you did." He leaned in, kissed my forehead, my neck, my throat. "Please. Come home with me . . ."

"Sam . . ."

"Go. Work. I'll be back for you later when you're too tired to resist."

Sean was alone in his office with his feet up on his empty desk, staring at the wall.

The door was ajar. The only light was the desk lamp beside him. I knocked.

He didn't look around. "Now what?"

I eased in, leaned against the wall by the door, hearing the dry crinkle of *Crossroads* plans behind my head. The office was chillingly tidy. Not even the odd beer empty lying comfortably about. "Nothing. I . . . um, this is none of my business, but are you okay?"

"Yah, I'm just great." His feet, crossed on his desk, beat a jerky rhythm against each other. He had a crumpled sheet of paper in his lap. He was tearing off corners and wadding them up into little balls between his fingers, lining them up on the desktop. He already had a good number of them.

"Sean, you know how Howie gets when he's nervous. What would we all do for comic material if Howie behaved himself?"

He didn't seem to be listening. I perched on a corner of the desk, trying to fit commiseration, humor, and pleading into the same smile. I could see now what he was staring at: the season's schedule, taped to the wall between drawings and other paperwork.

He tossed a little wad at it. "Ah yes, where's our old Sean, that laugh-and-smile boyo? Micah send you up here?"

"No, he—"

"He's taking this so fuckin' serious."

"He always does."

"Well, he wants something, he can come up here himself."

"Sean, Micah's just as pissed at Howie as you are."

"Yeah? And how pissed is he at me?"

Now I was wondering what demon of egotism had drawn me up here to negotiate in a war I didn't understand the nature of. "He's more hurt than anything."

Sean spun upright, scattering the little paper balls, slamming the chair against the desk. "What the hell does he want from me? Haven't I killed myself enough for him before?"

"You're killing yourself now for Max Eider!"

"Fuck Eider! Eider's a lunatic!" He circled the room like the walls were bars. "Look, Bill Rand is a friend of mine. We go back. We . . . our families know each other. You want me to throw in my friend for some guys from nowhere, some friggin' weirdos I don't even know?"

The wall behind me was prickly with the heads of pins holding up all the *Crossroads* drawings. "I thought Micah was your friend. He thought so, too."

"Then he oughta see I got a lot of shit on my plate! He oughta give me a fuckin' break!"

"He has, Sean. He didn't dispute *Crossroads* getting precedence. He found you extra men, more money, gave you all the benefit of the doubt, but now they're talking of canceling performances and Micah's still trying to see what he's got up there!"

"I got men on it, dammit."

"It's you he needs, Sean. Your special energy. Your expertise. Your valued advice and support. He needs the crew to know you're behind him. This show is very important to him!"

"This piece of crap? *Crossroads* is big, but at least it looks like something! You don't mind busting your balls for something you can believe in. What's Micah, crazy? Putting his name on the line for the likes of them? What am I supposed to think, either he's a fool or he agrees with them?"

"Why not ask Micah? Talk to him, Sean. Accuse him, fight with him if you have to, but talk to him!"

"Don't see him going out of his way to talk to me." He moved around fitfully, his hands clenched. "Why's this one so friggin' important, anyway? Those guys don't care about Art, they come here to proselytize. Bunch of friggin' trouble-makers!"

"They're not!"

"Yeah? Look at all the shit's been stirred up since they got here!"

That propelled me off the desk. "You don't know anything about them! You haven't tried! You haven't even been around!"

"I hear, I hear. I hear from Ruth, I hear from Liz. I see 'em walking around here barefoot like they owned the place, making their own rules, jamming their mystical bullshit down our throats, spreading their Open Sky sedition around the place. They don't like domes, let 'em go home! Plenty of people born here need the jobs. We don't need importing subversives in from Outside!"

"The Open Sky aren't subversives or anarchists." I was now on shaky ground, only parroting what I'd heard from the Eye. "They're domer citizens who happen to think the world's wealth should be spread around a little. That's not unreasonable."

Sean pounced. "So you admit these guys are Open Sky?"

"It's no secret the Station Clans are sympathetic to certain Open Sky ideas. Jeez, Sean, you make it sound like some kind of conspiracy."

"What the hell else do you think it is? It's the biggest there is! Christ, it's people like you make us need to take things into our own hands now and then!" My stunned silence must have worried him. "Come on, don't take it like that. We know they're just using you kids, like they're using Micah."

"We?"

His eyes shifted away irritably. "Don't give me that. I know you've been poking around, asking questions." He sighed, rubbed his face viciously. "Aw, Christ, I don't hold with all this secrecy stuff either. Always put my vote in against it, always get overruled. Lot of paranoia building in this town. That's why this petition thing of yours is good, like I said. Gets things out in the open. Things gotta change in Harmony and change is never easy but we need it to survive. Once we get this all ironed out, you'll know we did right. And you'll see we take care of our friends."

"Do you, Sean? Look around. Some people who thought they were your friends are getting fucked, and you're the one doing it!"

Wanting to slam doors, wanting to run, I did neither. I turned and walked out, wishing I had somewhere safe to go, besides the very temporary refuge of Sam's arms. Wading through the shop as through a jungle, I made myself smile cheerily at all the SecondGen carpenters who'd closed me out in the crew room earlier. I thought I had it under control until I reached the theatre and strode unblinking past Micah on my way to begin mixing paint.

"We still can't find Jane," he complained. "Have you seen her?"

I kept walking. "The crew says she went home."

"Gwinn?" he called after me. "Is everything all right?"

I slowed, turned on him. "No!" I yelled. "I just had the fight with Sean you should be having!"

Micah's jaw sagged as if I'd hit him, and I burst into tears.

Micah forgave my outburst readily enough. He said he must be getting old—he couldn't make sense of what was happening anymore.

Later, Sam made me repeat everything Sean had said, word for word.

Mali smiled pensively. "I'd say we aren't quite orderly enough for Mr. Reilly. The specter of chaos haunts so many domer dreams."

"Not turning my back on him," Sam declared. "Probably a major CDL organizer. Could be him hiring the thugs."

Cora's legs were neatly curled up beneath her on a green velvet chaise in her sitting room. "No, Sean Reilly hates the Outside and is very conservative and no brilliant intellect, but he comes to Town Meeting regularly, speaks his mind. He's an honest man who believes in the democratic process. The secrecy was bound to eat away at him sooner or later. I think we're seeing factionalism within the CDL."

I wondered what Cora knew about the Outside. The Eye had made themselves so easily at home in her castle. A medieval madrigal floated up from the music room, as sweet as birdsong. Moussa was running the rest of the company through their nightly vocal exercises.

"Factionalism can always be used to advantage," said Mali.

Cora pursed carefully crimsoned lips. "I wonder if I should have a little chat with Sean . . . ?"

Omea stuck her head in. "Hello. Is Jane with you, Gwinn dear?"

"I think she went back to the dorm."

Omea frowned gently. "Did anybody check?"

"Um, no. We thought maybe she needed some space."

"Perhaps. Well, good night."

Cora said, "In another world, my Sam-uel, you and Sean would be drinking buddies. You'd rely on him and he'd serve you well. I wouldn't be surprised if it was Sean being used, by his CDL."

"I'm still not turning my back on him," Sam muttered.

"Talk to Sean, Cora," I begged.

Sam rolled away from me in the bed. "I want you to do something for me."

I stretched languorously. "Didn't I just do that?"

"Reality time, love." He rolled back, placed his hand between us, palm down on the sheet. "I want Ule to teach you how to use this."

He uncovered a thin, flat-bladed knife. The whole of it

was six inches long at most, and I could tell it was very old. The handle was ebony chased with delicate rings of silver, smoothed to satin by many hands. It could have been a prop out of *Crossroads*, a *marquesa*'s graceful letter opener, but for its keen-honed edge. It was very beautiful and it made me more nervous than I could say.

"I couldn't."

"You can. Pick it up."

The knife nestled into my hand like an incubus taking up residence. The silky metal was eerily warm. I had to remind myself that Sam had been holding it. A knife is not a living thing.

"Work with Ule, half hour a day. He says he'll be happy to find the time. And you and I'll run every day, build you up slowly."

"Sam, I can't . . . carry a knife. I couldn't . . ."

"Kill a man?" he finished savagely. "What if it had been me out there instead of Pen?"

"I . . . uh." Sean Reilly was right to fear these people. They blew into Town like an injection of another reality, bringing their own set of rules and more violence in six weeks than I had witnessed in my entire dome-bred life. Stability just wasn't one of their priorities.

"What if it's you out there someday and me not around to help?"

The little knife assumed a totemic significance. The gift of a piece of Sam's mysterious life. A sign, dare I hope, that I might be something more than a casual bed partner to him. I set it down on the sheet. It seemed to leave my hand reluctantly and my palm felt chill without it for minutes afterward.

I laid my hands on Sam to warm them. "Of course you had to save Pen's life. The problem's not, you know, scruples or anything. It's just, well, it wouldn't feel real. It would feel like *acting*."

"Good, good. Half of life is acting." He smiled at me oddly and his sky-colored eyes had never seemed clearer or more mysterious. "You've been playing those apprentice role games. You know how it's done. So here's your newest role, and it's me going to prepare you for it: Gwinn Rhys, survivor."

SECOND TECH:

I had my first session with Ule that Wednesday morning,
in Cora's parquet-floored music room, the ebony concert
grand pushed into a corner, the silk bokhara rolled up
against the wall.

"Inept," said Ule, "but not slow and not clumsy. Now,
take up your blade, and take it up well. A blade's like the
magic: you use it as a last resort and no messing around
when you do."

Take it up *well*? Sam watched, intent and silent on the
window seat. I slid the little knife out of its sheath and
folded my palm around the smooth, flesh-warm grip. It was
like holding someone's hand.

"Yes!" Ule grinned happily. "This blade tells you how to
handle it. This blade's life is strong." He nodded to Sam.
"Good choice. It likes her."

Sam offered me his blandest smile. "He means it's the
right knife for you."

"When it knows you better," Ule told me confidingly,
"he'll sing you its history."

Ule was not an easy teacher. He yelled at me when I
made mistakes, mocked me when I stumbled with exhaustion. Sam never made a move to stop him. Not like learning
from Micah, but at least I was smart enough to realize it
was part of the training. I put up with it, to please Sam.
When the lesson was done, Ule showed me where to strap
on the soft leather leg sheath. He told me to wear it without
the knife until I got used to having it there. I left it on
under my coveralls when I went off to work, but I felt
utterly foolish.

When I arrived at the theatre, the vanishing trick was in
place and the tracking units installed onstage. Micah was
painting furiously while Louisa ran her edited cues. Light
and darkness played in fast motion across the stage.

"I've a few prop notes Te-Cucularit asked me to take
care of," I told Micah.

He nodded absently. "Jane isn't with you?"

Worried at last, I instituted a search.

The corridor offstage left was stuffed with potted plants. Live ones this time. A long-suffering assistant stage manager and a very grumbly prop runner were hauling them into the Eye's dressing rooms. I found Mark overseeing delivery of the costumes. The rolling racks were a welcome blaze of color against the cold white counters and walls.

"You got Jane with you?"

"No, haven't seen her." He offered a richly patterned batik for my inspection and held it up against my chest. "You look fabulous in this color, G. I should make you something after. If there is an after." He turned away abruptly to hang the costume on the rack. "Can you believe Wardrobe is already complaining about the greenery?" His usually deft fingers fumbled with the cloth.

"Oh, Mark." I put my arms around him. "Scared? You of all people, our fearless leader?"

He leaned his head against mine. "You ever wonder how he's doing Out There? You ever think about *being* Out There?"

"All the time." It wasn't quite a lie. I didn't used to think about it. Now I did. "They told you, didn't they? About the Outside."

He nodded.

"You think it's all true?"

"Yes. But I don't know what it means, for me, for us." He wiped at his eyes. "I'm worried about Thursday, G. I think there's a strong chance these good citizens'll vote us right out of Town."

"I've gone sort of numb about it."

He smiled fondly. "Nah, you're just steady. Really. A rock."

"No. That's Mali."

We both giggled and felt a little better, until Cris came back from BardClyffe to report that nobody had seen Jane at meals and her bed didn't look slept in. "Maybe the Admin took her."

"Her term isn't up for another two weeks," I protested. "Besides, they don't leave behind a whole roomful of your stuff."

"Yeah," seconded Mark faintly.

I'd seen Bela's room after. Gone without a trace, as if he'd never been there. "We'd better tell Micah."

*   *   *

"Missing for *two days*?"

I was appalled myself. "We just now put it together."

Micah dropped his brush into water. "I'm in Howie's office if you need me."

Liz Godwin paged me in the shop just before noon. "Micah's gone off and they want to test the trap. Come and play designer."

I debated rousing Micah from the office, but I hoped he was on the phone to the Apprentice Administration. I trotted out onstage. The crew had cleaned up and broken for an early lunch. Sean straddled the spot where the hole had been, explaining the mechanism to Howie and Sam. The pliant decking material between his feet gave softly as if full of water. The trap looked more like a tear in a taut stretch of fabric than the gaping hole I knew it to be underneath. Mali and Ule stood by listening. Howie was being conciliatory. Sam was being bristly, asking questions.

Sean pushed off one foot and regained solid ground. "Watch this now." He signaled the booth, and the rent in the fabric of the ground tightened like sheet elastic and sealed itself without visible seams. Sean stepped onto the spot where the hole had been.

Liz drooped against me in relief. "Damn thing works."

Howie applauded. "Bravo!"

"What tells you he's through the trap before it closes again?" Sam asked.

"Got a little beam gate in there."

"Is there a fail-safe?"

"Sure." Sean glanced at Liz as if to say, Who is this asshole?

"Let me," said Ule. Sean shrugged and moved aside. Ule whirled and leaped, landing full center on the trap. It held.

"A slider moves in under after the tension's turned off," Sean told him lazily. "It's rated for a ton. Don't be worrying about the weight."

"What should we be worrying about?" asked Sam.

"Acting," said Sean levelly.

Liz moved between them. "Well, I'd like to know a little more, since I'm going to be presetting the thing."

Sean was like a dog with its hackles raised. He turned his back on Sam and showed Liz the tiny pinholes ringing the trap. They formed a circle about a meter in diameter. "The reflector field is weak, but I wouldn't want to get my ass caught in it too often."

"How about a demonstration?" said Sam.

"No problem." Sean draped his headset over his ear and murmured into it. "Stand back a little, eh? This part's never been tested, but what the hell." He stepped into the center of the circle of pinholes. He grinned at his men, winked at me, and for a moment was the jaunty old Sean again. "Good-bye cruel world!"

The field switched on with a bright hum. A dancing column of not-quite-visible force shot up around Sean's body. His image wavered and vanished. The field shut off. The hole in the floor had not quite finished sealing. I looked up to find Micah watching from the house, looking pensive.

"Could have done that with light and flash powder," Sam muttered disgustedly.

"But that wouldn't be invisible," said Howie.

"Is this?"

The trap gaped again. Sean peered up at us, hands on hips. "Well?"

"Needs a little work," said Howie. "It's noisy, you know?"

"It's not worth it," said Sam.

"Well, now," countered Howie, "I can see the potential."

Sam eyed the hole stubbornly. "What do you think, Mal? You're the one who's got to ride it."

"I think we give it a try, bro."

"Damn straight." Sean stood aside for him. "Right over here."

Mali shook his head. "I'd rather run it in rehearsal."

Sean shrugged. "Suit yourself."

Howie let out the breath he'd been holding. Liz clapped her hands. "All right, everybody. This is your fifteen-minute call for Act One."

I joined Micah in the house. "Looks like it'll work. Any word on Jane?"

"They're looking into it."

When the light came up on the set that afternoon, Micah sat up energized. "Ah, Louisa, marry me. You've done it again."

Lou nodded from her console. "It's going to work, Mi. At least our part of it."

The light fell into the space like mist. It touched life into the sculptured contours like an Impressionist's paintbrush. Metal, plastic, and wood breathed in the darkness, coiling out of the shadowed corners, steaming in the green jungle air.

I caught my breath and shivered. This was Micah's magic.

"Looking good, Mi!" Howie strode down the aisle from the lobby, Kim Levin hot at his heels. He bent to Louisa's ear. "Make it brilliant, darlin'. We've got visitors."

Across the house, Cam Brigham bulked into an aisle seat with an audible grunt. Rachel Lamb and Reede Chamberlaine followed with an entourage of secretaries and assistants. Rachel looked nervous. Chamberlaine looked like polished steel.

Micah shook his head.

"He wasn't supposed to be back 'til opening night," I whispered.

"Come to check on his investment. Somebody's been telling tales."

"Oh, Reede," scoffed Louisa. "He ought to be outlawed. Always putting these high-toned projects together, then bitching when they turn out to cost him some small percentage of his profit. I'd sworn never to work for him again, but you talked me into it."

Micah sniffed. "I heard he sent a star package on the road in black velours last year because he wouldn't pay overtime to get the set built."

Through the headset waiting on my shoulder, I heard Liz calling places. I put it on, to be in touch with the prop and automation crews in case of a cuing screwup.

Lou hooked the slim curl of her own wire over one ear. "Well, here we go. Remember that old vid, Mi?" She let her voice get husky as the houselights faded, drawling, " 'Fasten your seat belts. It's going to be a bumpy night.' "

A breeze whispered through the darkened theatre, the scent of salt and damp undergrowth. Micah had been unable to resist these very simplest of effects. The first sound swam up through the blackness like a dream melody: the trill of No-Mulelatu's pipes, followed by an earthy rumble of drums. Light glowed on a seated figure house left, Moussa on his "hill." He wore only a loincloth. His oiled skin caught the light like a prism. Elevated on his narrow promontory, he loomed like a giant out of myth, a jungle god.

"Clever Micah," Louisa murmured.

Downstage center, light burst around Te-Cucularit in full-body paint. Micah sighed and sat forward in his seat.

Cu was zebra-striped in red and yellow. As he moved through the light, his darker skin became the negative space. The vibrant stripes seemed to turn in the air disembodied. He brandished a bright, plume-tipped Puleale in either hand. Floor-length orange feathers trailed from a headdress of brilliant red. With a thrill I recognized Moussa's totem. Akeua the bird of power stalked the stage of the Arkadie.

With a soft explosion of wing sound, a cloud of tiny shadows fled across the stage, vanishing in the darkness overhead.

"What was that?" Micah demanded. "Was that one of yours, Lou?"

I squeaked with awe and delight. Over the headset I heard Sam's background murmur: "That oughta wake 'em up out there."

The show moved along well for a while, through the magical opening music-and-dance ritual at the secret shrine of the Ancestors and through the introductory scenes in the village, the clansman and his wife worrying over the harvest, the clandestine meeting of the young lovers and the visit of the planter to announce the clearing of new fields. Neither Mali nor Omea was in costume, though Omea had worn an appropriate blouse and skirt-wrap from her own wardrobe. Mali slouched around in black sweats, which combined with his own darkness to render him nearly invisible. He was a disembodied voice floating within the deep earthy colors of the set. Lou made rapid adjustments at her console. A moment later, we could see his face.

Marie hurried over. "Don't worry, what he's really wearing is this kind of washed-out gray shirt with a little stripe and mossy green work shorts. They wouldn't give me the dyers until this morning, but we'll have it by tonight. Omea's in dirty pink with a little lemon and his same green."

Lou nodded. "What about whatsisname, the one with the tricks?" Whenever Sam came on, his shiny-new khakis practically blinded you.

"Oh I know, it's awful! He looks like a tourist in the Serengeti Safari Dome! I've scheduled him for tomorrow."

Marie shoved her billowy sleeves up to her elbows. "Maybe I'll do it over dinner break."

Their whispered chatter broke off as the first of the tracking units glided onstage.

It was the public bar unit, a raunchy, broken-down hovel crammed in the most naturalistic way with the sort of dressing Hickey normally threw into the recycler. It came in smoothly, quietly, and on cue. I heaped approval on Automation over my headset as the unit breathed to a clean halt just as Ule and Cu arrived at the door. Cu, out of body paint, looking . . . mortal again. But the bar's perfect entrance was the only thing right about it. Once it stopped moving, it sat there like a lump, a fussy, literal-minded intruder in an alien landscape. Beside me, Micah groaned softly.

The actors sensed the change. Ule dropped a line and asked to start over. Liz made the crew reset and run the cue again. This time Ule and Cu kept the scene going gamely, but the tension had gone out of it. Howie stood up, shaking his head.

"Stop, please," Liz intoned into her mike.

Howie bustled onstage, beaming encouragement.

Louisa sat back, flopped an arm over the back of her seat. "He made you add that monster, didn't he?"

Micah shifted uneasily. "Anything you can do to help would be appreciated."

"At least the entrance timing was nice," I said.

"Perfect," Micah agreed.

Howie turned from his conference with the actors. "Liz, can we get this damn thing onstage any faster?"

That set the tone for the rest of the afternoon. Every excuse for stopping was seized upon, every chance to go back and redo, to fuss with a prop, a costume, an entrance, an exit. After less than an hour, Reede Chamberlaine got up and left, quietly but for the noise his entourage made following him out. Cam Brigham let his seat close up behind him with a sharp report, causing a heartbeat of silence onstage. Mali froze in the middle of a line, Omea's head whipped around, Tuli and Lucienne came to full alert upstage. When they'd relaxed and moved onward, Rachel Lamb watched a moment more, then slipped out after Brigham.

Over the headset, I heard Automation mutter, "It's the

tall one holding things up. Dragging his ass so he doesn't have to try out the trick."

Sam slid into the seat beside me during a break. "Any sign of Jane?"

"None."

Micah said, "The usual practice is to inform the craftmaster of a termination at least a day ahead of time."

"They didn't tell Marie about Bela," I pointed out.

"No. They didn't."

"Could the Admin be terminating people early without telling anyone?"

"Terminating," Sam remarked. "What a way to put it."

"That's what it amounts to," said Micah.

Sam did not dispute him. He twined his fingers in the hair at the nape of my neck, massaging gently. "How're you? Stiff yet?"

"Not yet." I could feel Micah's interest even as he gazed pensively at the stage. How would he feel about his chief assistant learning self-defense with a knife? An Outsider's knife. I pinched the starchy beige fabric of Sam's sleeve between two fingers. "This sure needs some softening up."

He laughed softly. "I don't know. I'd hate to get too comfortable in the enemy's clothing." His lips brushed my ear, the tip of his tongue curling deftly around my earlobe. I clamped my mouth shut so as not to make a lustful spectacle of myself, then he was up and trotting down the aisle as Liz called places to resume.

"I *have* missed a few things lately," Micah observed.

I laughed, embarrassed and delighted. I tried to mimic his ironic tone. "I'm afraid it's all very sudden and hopeless."

"It usually is," he replied, and then the scene started.

"What is?" I whispered.

"Life," said Micah. "Ssssh."

When it came time to sequence the trap into the action, Howie stopped rehearsal and summoned the entire running crew to the stage.

I murmured to Micah, "Backstage they're saying Mali's afraid of the trap."

Our crew was mostly young, entirely SecondGen. They eyed Howie with the dubious sort of respect that mellows with experience into the cheerful cynicism endemic to stagehands.

"The success of the whole play turns on this scene," he lectured them. "This moment is the mystical core of the evening."

"Why doesn't he just let them get on with it?" muttered Louisa irritably.

"All right, then," Liz intoned. "From the top of five."

Act Two, scene five: Cu and Ule as the village elders began their ritual, calling on the spirits of the Ancestors to punish the revelation of tribal magic to an infidel planter.

Their conjuring isolated Mali downstage center in a diagonal shaft of light. His profile was edged in silver, his eyes were bright with tragic comprehension. He welcomed death as an end to the disillusionment and remorse he felt for his wasted sacrifice of the clan's most precious secret. From the surrounding darkness the green and gold of the Matta shimmered into life. Indefinable shapes circled and hovered. A voice spoke, low and inexorable. The clansman knelt as the Matta flowed around to envelop him, seemingly of its own volition.

"Hold it, hold it," Howie yelled. "Do it without the Matta first. I don't want him strangling in the pit!"

Eighty feet of fabric rustled to the deck. Lucienne and Tuli marked through their winding dance without it. The voice—Sam's, though I barely recognized it—chanted while Moussa beat a quiet fury on his lap drums.

Micah was as still as a rock.

Over the headset, I heard Liz cue the booth, a little nervous, a little loud.

A hum, a snap-flash in the reflector field, then nothing. Mali was still there, kneeling on solid ground.

Muttering over the headset. "What happened?" demanded Liz.

Mali stood up, shading his eyes and squinting out into the house.

"Stand back from there, Mal," ordered Sam from the darkness.

"Where the hell's Sean?" Howie complained.

The running crew drifted into view around the edges of the stage. The show carpenter padded down to the trap area, talking to the booth over her headset. "Yeah, try it again." She tested the deck with her boot. "Looks like it's not getting power. Must have jogged a connector loose somewhere." She turned to Howie. "You want to stop and fix it now?"

Howie grumbled and paced. "Liz, how long 'til dinner?"

"Thirty minutes." She handed him a folded paper.

"Fuck it, we'll break early. Everybody back at seven." He unfolded the note, made a face at it. "Reede wants a meeting? Fine. Get him in here."

Chamberlaine arrived with Cam Brigham still in tow. Trustees rarely hung around so much unless they were worried about something. Rachel Lamb followed, nearly hidden among the Londoner's entourage.

Chamberlaine got right to the point. "All the technical delays have taken their toll, Howard. This cast is not ready. Time you thought seriously of canceling previews."

"All our preview performances are sold," said Rachel. "With the extra money we've put into this, we can't really afford to cancel."

"Postpone, then. Reschedule the opening."

"We're on a subscription season," she reminded him. Her hands were tightly clasped in front of her as if she felt herself on the brink of terrible danger. "We're locked into our schedule."

The producer smiled patiently. "If you go before you're ready, you risk bad reviews and your box office will suffer anyway."

"Better not to open it at all than risk bad reviews," put in Brigham.

"And bad reviews could hamper the tour," Chamberlaine added.

"We're not going to get bad reviews," said Howie impatiently, "and we're not going to cancel. We'll be ready. Don't worry."

Chamberlaine smiled again. "Well, let's give it another day."

From our remove at the production table, Louisa muttered, "Where's Sean when he should be listening to all this?"

The running crew opened up the trap with a manual override, then left it gaping while they went to hunt up Sean and grab a quick bite from the machines. Crossing the stage to Sam's dressing room, I heard knocking and puttering down in the hole. I peered in. Peter was nosing around underneath with a flashlight. His tool belt clinked as he moved among the forest of deck supports.

"Don't you ever go home?" I called.

He glanced up, startled, then grinned like a kid caught with his hand in the cookie jar. "Oh, hi. Pretty amazing down here. I'm gonna give Sean some mean competition when the time comes."

"You working tonight?"

"Nah, we're on a day schedule starting tomorrow, to finish up." He thumbed off his light. "Well, I'm off. Hope Sean can get this working okay. It's a great idea." He waved and ducked away under the deck and down the escape stairs into the below-stage trap room.

I knocked at the dressing room Sam shared with Ule and Cu, and stuck my head in. Green jungle air invaded my lungs. Clouds of steam from the shower billowed through the bathroom door, settling in a fine mist on thick rubbery leaves, lacy ferns, and drooping palm fronds. Ivies scaled the mirrors. Purple and green orchids bloomed around the light fixtures. An astonishing amount of plant life had been crammed into the narrow space. Te-Cucularit sat out of makeup at his mirror, writing in his notebook with such concentration that I felt guilty for disturbing him.

"He's in the shower," Cu said without looking up.

Ule was stretched out on the cot, buck-naked and asleep. I leaned against the doorframe. "I love the way it smells in here." Though Cu gave no sign of listening, I told him about my grandfather's "green" room. "I knew he was crazy, but I loved being in there with him anyway. It was like a refuge."

"For him, it was," Cu said quietly.

"Yes. If only I could have understood that then." In the bathroom, the shower shut off with a lingering hiss. "You were amazing in the opening ritual today. I felt like Akeua was in the theatre."

"She was." He flicked me a cool smile in the mirror and bent back to his writing.

"You're not allowed to give the Preacher compliments, didn't you know that?" Sam came in toweling off. "Nobody who looks like that should be allowed compliments."

Cu's perfect body was an abstraction to me now, obsessed as I was with the thicker, more compact body in front of me. "Even if they did something right?"

"He's always right, aren't you, TeCu? Hasn't been wrong since . . . well, I'd hate to give away clan secrets."

Te-Cucularit raised barely tolerant eyes to the mirror. I offered him sympathy and got again the brief, careful smile.

Ule stirred on the cot, turned over. "Oh hullo, ladykins."

Sam tossed his towel at him. "Cover up, man."

Ule winked at me, wrapped the towel slowly around his waist. "Ver-ree possessive, our Sammy. How's the leg feel?"

The sheath on my calf. "Forgotten all about it," I admitted.

"Good, good." Ule rubbed his face. Slumped on the edge of the cot, without his dancer's energy enlivening his body, he looked thin and worn, more like the fifty-three years he claimed and I found hard to believe. "Time to add a little weight, then."

The little knife appeared in front of me, on Sam's palm.

I sighed, took it from him, and knelt to slip it into its sheath. "I have to tell you, this feels really silly—"

"No," said Te-Cucularit. "You must be protected."

Ule and Sam looked at him in surprise.

Cu rose, folding his notebook under his arm. I stood aside to let him pass. In the doorway he turned back to me. "He was not crazy, your grandfather. He was preserving what he thought was right in the only way left to him. Gwinn-Rhys, listen to the voice of your ancestor."

"Uh-oh," said Sam when he'd gone, "Preacher's looking for a convert."

Coming back from dinner and other things, Sam and I met Micah at the stage door.

"The Administration denies terminating Jane," he reported. We slowed behind a clot of *Crossroads* actors blocking the alley with their effusive greetings to one another. Tonight was their press night. "I've alerted Security."

My body was still languid with the pleasure I'd had with Sam. I felt the guilt sharply. "All day long I've been thinking we should be out looking for her instead of . . ."

"Instead of inside doing a play?" Micah held the door, nodded us through brusquely. "They promised an immediate search. We'd only get in their way. The secretary at Admin did ask if Jane had been out after curfew or involved 'in this petition thing.' "

Sam murmured beside me, "Nowhere outside this building without me, you understand? Nowhere."

In the theatre, Sean was lecturing Cris about the trap. Cris was in pirate mode, with his bandanna knotted around his head and his long hair pulled back. He'd stayed to work through the dinner break with Automation.

Micah moved past them, across the stage. "I'll be in the house."

"They've got to sync the drop with bringing the field to full power," Sean was insisting.

"I'd like to edit out the delay," said Cris.

"Nah, let 'em practice. Can't get these timings right the first time, you know."

Sean signaled and the crew ran the sequence. Cris rode the trap. It worked, it was quieter, but it was still not magic. I wanted never to hear how much this device had cost. I wasn't going to think it was worth it.

Howie appeared, Howie who could smile at a man who'd just spat on him if the need was great enough. He hovered at Sean's shoulder. "How's it going?"

Sean dusted his palms together. "Got the sucker licked."

"How about sticking around for the rehearsal?"

"I'll be in and out. A man's gotta eat."

"Eat here. I'll buy you dinner."

"Howie? Need you a minute." Kim Levin stood downstage with one of the Chamberlaine entourage, a thin, young man failing in his efforts to mimic Reede's London elegance.

"Mr. C. sends his apologies," he breathed.

"He's not coming tonight?"

"Since he's leaving tomorrow evening, Mr. C. thought he should take advantage of the chance to see the performance next door. But Mr. Rand has invited your company to be his guests at the press reception in the lobby afterward."

"*His* guests?" Howie roared. "This is *my* goddamn theatre!"

"Yessir, I know, of course, sir." The young man's last shred of polish vanished.

Howie waved him away and threw himself into a seat in the front row, muttering, "Cam Brigham at work again. When this is over, I'm getting myself a new chairman of the board."

He didn't let the cast in on Reede Chamberlaine's desertion to *Crossroads*, but he was edgy all evening. Having decreed a proper dress run-through in full costume and makeup, he then stopped the action every five minutes to dispute a line reading or rework some blocking. It took two and a half hours to get through the first act.

"Just let me play the damn scene!" Ule snarled at him. Sam took him on over the timing of a bit of magical business and told him he had his head up his ass. At the intermission break, Omea walked Howie to the back of the house for a very animated conference. When the second act began, Howie left the actors alone and took notes.

The act glided right along and we were into Two, five, before we had a chance to worry about it. Ule and Cu began the incantation, the matta appeared, the Ancestors spoke, and Mali moved into position downstage center. I didn't hear the field hum; but a quick, hard flash lit the backdrop white and a geyser of sparks shot up as the floor slitted to drop Mali into the trap. He danced back from the widening gap. Sam hurtled forward to snatch him away. Bright pinpoints of fire died in the air above their heads.

Babble roared in the headset. "Kill it, kill it!" Liz yelled.

Actors and crew surged into the wings and the exit ramps. Howie raced center stage. "Everyone okay? Mali?"

Mali nodded, searching himself and his clothing for burns.

"Where's Sean?" Howie was tired of asking.

"Not here," someone called.

"In the big house," someone else added.

Howie shoved his hands to his hips and stared at the floor for a full thirty seconds. "All right," he said finally. "Let's work it through to the end."

"It's not fair," I muttered to Micah afterward. "A whole evening ruined by the failure of one effect."

"An arch would collapse without its keystone."

"Well, that's not fair, either," I returned irritably.

"No, but it's so wonderful when it stays up that it's worth it."

Ever since I'd joined his studio, Micah had been leading me toward an understanding and appreciation of the "wondrous" aspect of risk. Until then, I'd thought he'd succeeded. "Is it?"

"You'd prefer a sure thing, perhaps?"

"Surer than this, I guess."

An ironic smile softened his rebuke. "Then you'd better join Reede Chamberlaine next door."

Howie insisted that we all put in an appearance at the *Crossroads* press reception in the lobby. To my surprise, the Eye gathered willingly to plan another of their attention-grabbing entrances, then went off to change from one set of costumes into another.

Press nights weren't jewels-and-black-tie fancy like official openings, but being the "in" night for the literati, they brought out the most expensive casuals in Harmony's closets. Well-worn coveralls used to be an apprentice badge of merit, but now, conscious of their stains and baggy fit, Mark and I sipped champagne on the sidelines with Songh, and watched the Eye work the crowd. Enveloped in their most exotic finery, they laughed and sang like eccentric sentient birds imported from another planet. Sam moved among them mute and entirely in black, creating minor sensations with his astonishing hands.

Crispin let no apprentice self-consciousness hold him back. He retied his red bandanna to a more rakish angle, split the neck of his coveralls another several inches and plunged into the glittering crowd bearing his arty beauty and his most arrogant smile.

"We should be doing that," noted Mark.

"Yeah," I agreed, with equal lack of enthusiasm. "At least you're good at it."

"With me, it's an act. Crispin *is* the act."

"I just want to do the work. The selling shouldn't have to be part of it!"

"Micah doesn't sell," said Songh.

"Not now that he's famous," Mark and I replied simultaneously.

When they'd done what they could with this opportunity for free publicity, the Eye drifted away, taking us with them.

"That ought to sell a few tickets," I said to Omea on the way to the dressing rooms.

She sighed, untangling orange feathers and blooms from the dark buoyant cloud of her hair. "Just once, though, I'd like to know we sold because we were the best show in town, not just the weirdest. I mean, however we sell is better than not selling, but . . . just once."

"This time," I insisted gallantly.

Omea laughed and curled her arm about my waist. "Of course. What am I saying? Of course, this time."

Crispin caught up with us in the corridor as the Eye dispersed to change into their street clothes. "Did you guys talk to the production manager from Pineland Stage? Guy with a dark beard and glasses?"

This described half the men in the Arkadie lobby. It was press night, after all, and eyeglasses were back in vogue among journalists. "Didn't get around to him," I said circumspectly.

"They're looking for designers for next season. He wants to see my stuff, said to call first thing tomorrow." Cris smoothed his hands down his coveralls as if they were suede and silk. "He really liked what I had to say."

"Good," I said wanly.

"We might not even be around next season," muttered Mark.

"Come on, you guys! We're gonna be here. We've got it nailed!" Cris untied his bandanna and folded it carefully. "So then I talked to this woman from the puppet theatre in Franklin Wells—"

"I, um, left my notes in the theatre. Be right back." I shot Mark a look of apology and escaped down the corridor.

Theatre Two was a lightless cavern at the end of the white tunnel of hallway. Preoccupied with what I wasn't doing to further my career, I was already onstage before I felt the full weight of the darkness, and then it closed around me like a fist. I slowed. Had I heard someone behind me? My hand shot to my pant cuff, fumbling. *Gods, so quick to reach for a weapon!* And then I thought, What good is it if I can't get it out any faster than this?

"Gwinn? Can we talk a minute?"

"Cris! You scared me."

"Sorry. Suddenly got nervous about you being alone in here in the dark." He shrugged. "Silly, hunh?"

I exhaled deeply. "Liz forgot the safety light."

"I'll get it."

He turned toward the red glow of the indicators on the work-light panel against the stage right wall.

"Cris! Shhh!"

When he stilled, there it was again, a faint rustle and thump from the darkness onstage.

"Yeah. I hear it." He felt his way quietly to the panel.

The work lights flared on, revealing an empty stage. The noises continued. I knelt, pressed my ear to the deck, then looked at Cris, and jabbed my thumb downward. Cris moved silently to my side. I was very aware of the knife strapped to my leg.

Suddenly the downstage trap unsealed and Peter rose through it on the elevator, a lit searchbeam in one hand and the little remote operating console in the other. He squinted around in the work light, then spotted us staring at him openmouthed.

"Hi!" He gave us his puppy-dog grin. "Just finishing up here." He switched off his beam, hung his belt. "Man, that Sean is one clever dude. Hey, how was the party? Lots of priceless fizzy?" He stepped aside and thumbed the remote to retract the elevator. The hole resealed.

Cris eyed Peter's laden tool belt. "What's up down there?"

"Oh, she's working fine now."

I went to retrieve my pad from the house. "No call tonight, right?"

"Tomorrow first thing. You got notes for me?"

I laughed. He was so eager. "Morning's soon enough."

He loped over to the work-light panel, looping his long legs over obstacles instead of going around. "Go on ahead. I'll get these." He waited until we'd reached the stage right door, then doused the lights.

"Leave the safety," I reminded him.

"Oh. Yeah." He messed around for a bit, then the overhead safety light glowed on. He followed us out. "Okay, see you in the old A.M." He tossed us a two-fingered salute and went off down the corridor, bobbing and jingling.

"Odd," I said, watching after him. Laughter echoed from the dressing rooms.

"Who, him?" Cris snorted. "He's the kind of techie who figures the more his tool belt rattles, the better his work must be."

"No, odd him being there. I'm sure he told me Sean was keeping him away from the effects equipment."

"Odd who was where?" Sam came down the hall with Moussa and Mali. He was still in his black jumpsuit, looking trim and competent, and I was very glad to see him. He moved between Cris and me, drawing me close. Pen was with them, raucous with a vermilion blossom behind his ear, a little drunk.

"That new kid Peter was in the pit. And . . . wait a minute!" Peter had gone toward the stage door, not the shop. "He took the remote console with him."

Crispin laughed. "Trying to steal Sean's secrets. As if all it took was a look or two."

I turned, met Sam's clear gaze. He nodded, looked to Mali.

Mali dipped his head.

"Moussa?"

"Where?"

"Onstage," said Sam. "Pen, are you with us?"

"Back off," Pen growled. "Just tell me where."

"A look around up here, then the stage door."

I led the way down the back stairs to the trap room, turning on lights as we went. Beneath the stage, a complicated scaffold of braces and posts supported the elevator mechanics and the dark bulk of the field generator, surrounding the access stair to the landing just below the trap. Construction debris had been simply pushed aside to make a pathway to the bottom step. Plastic rod and particle board were piled at random along the way. Portable work lights clamped to the cross beams lit up a hanging garden of abandoned strips of wrapping tape. Wires trailed and silvery cable looped around the slim shafts of the hydraulic cylinders.

"A little man-made jungle," Mali observed.

"Don't get underneath the stage too often, do you?" Cris grinned. "It's always like this."

Sam adjusted his tiny searchbeam, the size of his thumb. It produced an astonishingly bright and directed light.

"What are we looking for?" I asked.

"Anything out of order."

I glanced around. "Order? Here?"

"That's what's going to make it hard to find." He started up the stairs to the elevator access platform.

Cris went up after him, clambering around on the scaffold, following cable runs, checking connections. Mali leaned against a post, content to let Sam do the climbing. "And how is your own work coming in the midst of all of this?"

"Mine? Neglected, I'm afraid. We've been so busy."

He smiled at me. "And so distracted."

"Well, I . . ."

"No excuses. I love him, too, but the Work, that must not be neglected. If it is your Work."

That's how it was with Mali. You'd be talking, casually, you thought, and then he'd drop something like that on you, where you felt the extra weight of the capital letters like guilt or inspiration. "What do you mean, if?"

Above our heads, Cris called softly. "I don't see anything."

"Keep looking," Sam replied.

Mali settled himself more comfortably against his post. "Only that you are young and may not have found your real Work yet."

Did he mean I wasn't good at it? "I don't know what is, if it isn't this!" I remembered the joy I'd felt solving my *Lysistrata*. I clung to that for support. "I've risked my life to come to Harmony, and these three years with Micah have been—"

". . . worthy training," he said soothingly. "But the path to the Work is not always a straight one. Look at Sam, how roundabout it's been for him."

I was sure Mali knew everything that had gone on between Sam and me, every intimacy, every detail, either because Sam had told him or because he just *knew*. An odd feeling, and odder that I didn't mind it. "How do you know when you've found your . . . Work?"

"Oh shit," Sam said quietly, as if he'd stepped into a nest of snakes.

Mali stood free of his post. "What?"

The scaffold shook as Cris scrambled toward him. "What? What?"

"Damn, kid, don't move so hard! Mal, come up but come up easy."

Sam hooked his legs over a sprinkler pipe to hang out beyond the reach of the scaffold. Mali ignored the stairs and swiftly scaled the bracing along the side. Squinting up from below, I saw nothing until Sam's little beam picked it out; three tiny daubs of pinkish gray, stuck like wasps' piles to the inside corner of a steel I beam. A strand of wire fine as a hair passed from one daub to the other, then out around the I beam toward the field generator housing.

"Exactly," muttered Sam, "where I'd put it myself."

Cris craned his neck around the bottom of the I beam. "Ohh."

"Down," Sam said to him. "I don't want you up here with this."

Cris obeyed without argument.

"What is it?" I demanded.

Mali sighed, then quietly let himself down the scaffold. Sam followed, plodding pensively down the stairs. At the bottom he leaned against the legging, arms crossed and his eyes on Mali. "Some vacation, hunh?"

"So. It's me this time," Mali rumbled.

"Please!" I begged. "Will somebody—"

"It's plastique," said Cris.

"Not a lot." Sam was still looking at Mali. "Enough to kill within three or four meters."

I was aware of the darkness again, past the tight glow of the work lights, hanging like smoke among the pipes and posts and looping wires, darkness that rendered the pinkish gray daubs invisible. Three tiny blobs of death.

Sam said, "That kid who was down here . . . where'd he come from?"

"He's an extra hand. He came in to help Micah."

"What d'you know about him?"

Nothing, I realized. "You think Peter put it there?"

"Does kinda look that way," said Cris.

Sam frowned. "Well, that's just the problem."

"Made himself rather conveniently obvious," Mali agreed.

"Misdirection," muttered Sam. "Could be. Question is, who's the business?"

Peter didn't fit my profile of a thug. "Maybe somebody on the regular crew put it there?" I recalled the clique in the coffee room. "They're all SecondGen—it could be any of them."

"What d'you want to do, Mal?" Sam idly flipped his searchbeam from finger to finger until it was spinning so fast it looked like a solid silvery disk. "How 'bout this; let's play the scene out."

Mali shrugged a wordless negative.

"Why not? It's the thing they'd least expect." The searchbeam vanished. Sam's hands smoothed the air in front of him. The beam reappeared. "If we rip it out now, they'll know we're on to them. They'll just find some other place, some other time. If we leave it, my guess is they'll wait 'til there's an audience, for the greatest impact. If we play it right, we'll flush them out and win the sympathy vote, plus all the oohs and ahhs when you show up walking around after all." His hands flicked, empty. "A miracle."

"You want to let it blow?" Cris whispered.

Sam ignored him. "All that with one perfectly timed coup."

Mali wagged his head slowly from side to side.

"It's beautiful, Mal—"

"Does this theatre really deserve it?"

Sam jerked his thumb at me. "No one but these kids and Micah are pulling in our direction around here! We do our play as brilliantly as we know how, this town still won't give a damn. But this would get their attention!"

"This is an artists' town, Sam. Better to reach them as artists."

"Was an artists' town."

"You'd really let it blow?" Cris was grinning. "Wow."

I was horrified. "They can't do that!"

"Make it look like, he means. That is dynamic! That is great!" Cris did his little warrior dance among the pipe legs and cable loops. "That's what the Conch would do! It'll be tomorrow, won't it? There's an audience for the open dress and—"

"Get him out of here," Sam snarled at me.

"Don't blame the boy." Mali shut his eyes resignedly. "Where has he had a chance to learn any better?"

"When has he shown any sign of wanting to?"

"We put it to the others," Mali said firmly, "before we do anything."

Sam nodded, reluctant, but Mali was his final authority, however vehemently he argued. "Either way, we can't leave it like it is."

A dip into some dark recess of his jumpsuit produced a small screwdriver and a pair of wire cutters. Peter's tool belt jangled in my mind. I marveled that Sam could move so silently with all the equipment he carried, or at least could produce on a moment's notice. He scissored the cutters like jaws. "Our pal Reilly might stumble into it in the morning and get himself squashed like a bug. Unless of course he knows what to avoid."

"No," I said, even though I had to consider the possibility, after that scene in Sean's office.

"Not impossible," he countered. "In fact, it's very likely."

"No," I repeated. Not Sean. Not like this.

"Well," said Sam, "we'll see, won't we?"

JANE:

Walking back to Cora's, I lagged behind. I studied the dark trees. I read a poster, hastily printed, hastily tacked to some citizen's bamboo fence. It read: Do We Owe Them the Future Our Own Children Deserve? I didn't bother with the small print.

Finally Sam slowed to walk beside me, hands clasped behind his back. "There's a chill in the air. Disapproval, is it?"

"It's horrifying, what you're suggesting."

"More horrifying than Mali in pieces all over the theatre?"

I moaned and he put his arm around me. "Think of it as just another magic trick—the stuff I do so well."

"But, Sam, with all those people watching? They'll think—"

"Right. Maybe they *will* think for a change. Like, if this is the sort of thing the CDL will do, endangering innocent lives to get at somebody, maybe they don't want to support 'em after all. Rhys, we have to take the offensive now and then, when the opportunity presents itself. Retreat is pointless. We had hoped for a bit of a break here but . . ." He shook his head, rueful and determined. "There's no safe haven when you wear your politics on your sleeve."

"Not even on Tuatua?"

"Especially not on Tuatua. Why do you think we tour so much?"

"What about Outside?" I challenged.

Sam laughed. "Outside, yes. Here or there amidst the chaos, a place of refuge." He grasped the back of my neck and rocked me gently. "You do want to hear about it after all."

I leaned into his side, missing him already.

"There's one spot I'd take you to." He let his head loll back as we walked. His voice eased softened. He was somewhere else. "A bit of gardener's sun in the deep north woods, warm tight homes dug into the ground. We'd wake at dawn and make love beneath a waterfall still pure enough to drink."

"How romantic," I grumbled, while my heart cried out for such a place, as I had once cried out for Harmony.

Sam pushed me away. "You see? You're just like the Planter. I offer my most precious secrets and you won't for one minute consider that they might be true."

"You understand why, or you wouldn't be able to play him so well."

"I understand him better, watching you. You'd never walk out there willingly, no matter what secrets are revealed to you."

I thought: I might, if you asked me. "Sam, each time I decide to believe you, the tale gets wilder. Gardens and waterfalls?"

He gathered up my hand, pulled me back to him. "And I've only just begun. Imagine that."

My next lesson in real-world politics came when the debate over how to respond to the sabotage in the trap barely touched on the morality of terrifying a theatre full of innocent people. Discussion concentrated on the potential advantage to the Station Clans' cause and whether the coup could be pulled off without risk to Mali.

Omea, like Mali, preferred the persuasive potential of the play itself. Te-Cucularit agreed decisively, then left the room.

"We can have both," Tua pointed out. "We do the thing, make a splash, then play our run. What's the problem?"

"It's good, clean work," Sam allowed. "Once I hook our deal to his wire, we can trust it not to blow until he triggers it."

"With the remote," I murmured.

He nodded. "I've disconnected the explosive. Left everything else in place. I'll rig some lively fireworks to work off his signal. The rest is just good acting."

I was worried about Mali. "What if he comes back and fixes it?"

"We keep an eye out for that," Sam returned irritably.

"It could be," said Moussa, "sublimely spectacular."

"It's cruel to make people think someone's dead when they're not!" Songh protested.

Tua stretched her bare legs languidly. "Isn't that what we hope we've done when the lights come up anyway?"

"That's different! That's a play!"

Sam said, "And this is its new third act."

I kept out of it until the decision had been made. "Can I tell Micah? He'd die if he ever thought . . ."

"Let me," said Mali gently. "Micah will understand."

The gate alarm woke us at four. The insistent trilling rushed around me like a cold torrent. In my sleep-logged state, I thought the house itself was screaming at me.

The alarm stopped. I reached, felt empty bed. "Sam? Sam!"

"Hush! Here." He moved away from the windows, a lithe shadow against the lighted trees in the courtyard. He tossed a robe that settled on me like a deeper night. I struggled with it in momentary panic, then threw it on, and met him at the bedroom door.

"Did you see anything?"

"No. Come on."

We met Ule and Lucienne in the dark hallway, gliding silently toward the staircase. Tua joined us at the top step. Eyes and hands and heads did all the talking. At the bottom of the stairs Ule slipped off toward the kitchen, Tua to the music room, Lucienne to the dining room. Sam and I moved into the vast darkness of the great-hall just as Moussa and Mali padded down the stairs behind us.

Moussa slid open the tapestry drapes to let in light from the courtyard. The heavy brass rings made a sound like a cello along the rod. Nothing seemed out of order. Cushions littered the stones in front of the fireplace just as Tuli and Lucienne had left them. Pen snored obliviously on the sofa, covered with one of Cora's handwoven pictorial throws. Sam signaled Moussa to the front entry. Much too soon Moussa was back, waving us to him.

We followed quickly down the stone steps to peer through the single diamond of glass set in the thick wooden door. The drawbridge was serene in the soft light from the wrought-iron lantern. A big pile of blue rags had been tossed against the gate.

"That set it off." Moussa put his hand to the door, hesitating.

"Easy target out there," said Sam.

"Got to chance it." Moussa eased the door open and ventured onto the drawbridge.

"Stay here," Sam told me.

"No."

I shadowed him across the wooden planking. The black water in the moat was a perfect mirror. The grove beyond the gate was still and dark. Moussa unlatched the gate and let it swing toward him. The bundle of cloth fell inward to the ground. The bundle was a woman, lying on her face, limp and mud-stained. I recognized the curly hair.

"Jane! It's Jane!"

Sam pushed me back. Mali grabbed my shoulder.

Moussa knelt and turned her over gently. Her eyes were open, staring oddly.

Mali called behind him, "Get Omea. Hurry."

Moussa put a hand to Jane's neck, then shook his head. Sam made a soft sound of dismay and crouched beside him.

My step backward brought me hard against the rocky cliff of Mali's chest. "Call Security! Get the ambulance!" I turned to race into the house but his arms closed around me.

"Too late. Rest easy now."

Sam looked to Mali. "Omea?"

"Sent for."

Sam drew his fingers across Jane's face. With her eyes closed, she looked asleep and I thought they must all be wrong.

"Think there's a chance?" Moussa asked.

"No." Sam studied the darkness between the trees. "But cause and time might tell us what we're up against."

"Pretty badly roughed up."

"Yeah."

Moussa rose, for once moving heavily like the big man he was. On his way into the house he stopped to touch his palm to my cheek. He had tears in his eyes.

"She's really . . . dead?"

"I'm sorry," he replied, moving away.

Sam joined us in the middle of the drawbridge. He did not look at me. Mali did not relax the tight circle of his arms. I felt like a child among adults.

"A death like this should not go wasted," said Mali.

"It won't," said Sam.

Omea came down, in a silent flurry of filmy cotton. She

bunched the full sleeves of her robe around her shoulders and sank to her knees beside Jane. She laid her cheek against the pallid face, her hands upon the still chest. Doubled up over the body, she stayed that way for long minutes. Then she sat up and drew away. "Dead too long and died too hard. I can do nothing here."

Sam walked me back to the house. Mark stood at the top of the entry stairs. "Is it true?"

"Yes," said Sam curtly. He pushed me at Mark and went upstairs.

He came down shortly with Moussa, Cu, and Tua. All of them had changed into loose, dark clothing. They left without saying a word. Mark and I huddled together on the sofa in front of the fireplace, our arms around each other.

Omea came in. "I think you should wake the others."

When Cris and Songh had joined us, dazed from broken sleep and shock, Omea began to talk. She told us about her husband, Seluk, founding member of the Eye and Mali's older brother. She told us every detail of his murder by a plantation owner for unionizing the field hands. She told us of Tua's father, Bez, a rare Station Clans representative in the Tuatuan parliament, recently the victim of a convenient farming accident, and how Tua had joined the Eye in her brother's place when he was elected to his father's vacated seat. She spoke about death and the need to give it a healing purpose, until our numbness had eased and we could speak to each other. As Mark began to talk about Bela, Omea slipped off into the kitchen and came back with steaming mugs of one of her soothing teas.

"Drink up and no refusals," she smiled sadly.

"I'm going to get the people who did this," declared Songh, "if it takes my whole life."

Nobody mocked him, not even Cris.

Exhausted, lulled by Omea's infusion, I laid my head on Mark's shoulder and fell asleep.

Sam woke me later and led me upstairs to bed. He was cold and damp. I pressed myself against him to warm him.

"You've been running."

"Just for the exercise."

The chill of his skin made me think of Jane, and I shivered beneath the quilt, even though I was warm and dry. "I'm scared, Sam, really scared."

"More than when the soccer boys were after you?"

"That was scared for the moment. This is scared about forever. What's going to become of me?"

"Right now I'm going to make sweet, sweet love to you."

"What do I do tomorrow, or the next day, or next year . . . even if they do vote in our favor? How can I go on as if nothing happened? I can't trust this place ever again."

Sam warmed his hands against the small of my back, smoothed them along my thigh. "Not an unusual lesson to learn in this world."

"Why Jane?" I couldn't bear the thought of how bad her last hours must have been. "Who would have done . . . such a thing?"

"I have my list of candidates." He bent his lips to my throat, kissed my breasts, but I was restless, wound like a spring.

"What did you do with her?"

"Don't talk about it now."

"But I have to!" At last the tears came, for Jane, for myself and my uncertain future, for the day Sam would be gone, even a little for my mismatch with Crispin, and for all the losses we'd talked about that evening: Seluk, Bez, our friend and colleague Bela. My belief in Harmony. My innocence. All the weeping I hadn't done, rushing me in waves like the tide.

"Ah, Rhys, don't . . ." Sam left off his lovemaking and gathered me up as tenderly as a parent. "You're safe, no matter what. I promise."

HARMONET/NEWS

08/14/46

The body of a female apprentice informally identified as Jane Kessler, 28, formerly of Providence Dome, was discovered at five A.M. in front of the South Tower of Town Hall by members of the mayor's office staff arriving for an early start on their lengthy workday.

The coroner's preliminary examination suggests that Ms. Kessler died sometime yesterday afternoon or evening of a broken neck, though multiple contusions indicate additional internal injuries. The possibility of accident or suicide was discounted. According to rumor, a note was discovered in a pocket of the victim's apprentice uniform. The mayor's office has refused to confirm or deny this report.

Mayor Dunya von Hirsch expressed her deep shock and outrage but has withheld further comment, pending further investigation. However, an unnamed source quoted Her Honor as speculating privately that the blame may lie with the same disaffected youths responsible for the considerably more minor disturbances after Monday's Town Council meeting. Chief of Security Bean Walker has issued new warnings to all apprentices to observe the nine o'clock curfew, and promises that the utmost will be done to find and bring the killers to justice.

The mayor said the chief's suggestion to roll the curfew back to seven P.M. would be taken up when the Outside Adoption Policy is offered for review at tonight's Town Meeting.

Ms. Kessler's craftmaster was the eminent scenographer Micah Cervantes. Contacted at his home early this morning, Mr. Cervantes described his former assistant as "a model apprentice, a hardworking and sincere young artist who looked forward to receiving her citizenship within a matter of weeks." When questioned about Ms. Kessler's involvement with the Apprentice OAP petition, Mr. Cervantes said he could not speak for Ms. Kessler but that he himself had signed the petition. Though he favors a balanced and immediate review of the policy, he stated that to "deprive Harmony of the creative lifeblood that our apprentices provide would be folly."

In other developments, Lorien's Campbell Brigham held a breakfast press conference at his elegant gallery to announce the formation of a new lodging and entertainment consortium. Members so far include Mr. Brigham, the hotel giant Francotel, investment groups from Paris, Montreal, and Stockholm, and private inter-dome entrepreneurs Imre Deeland and Genvieve Pratt.

When asked if the consortium's plan to provide comprehensive luxury entertainment services to at least ten major domes might reduce the world's need for leisure travel, thus threatening Harmony's lion's share of the tourist industry, Mr. Brigham laughed expansively: "After our long and difficult struggle to survive, surely we domers have appetite enough for leisure to make us all rich."

JANE'S LEGACY:

It no longer seemed so foolish to be circling with a nearly naked grinning little black man on the golden waxed parquet of the music room, a knife poised in my hand. Mark joined us that morning at Mali's insistence, though he had no knife and refused the loan of Ule's, even when it was safely shrouded in its plaited grass sheath.

"I don't, um, trust my hand with a weapon in it." Mark stroked his palm across his chest. "Too much rage in there."

"Me too." Mali spread his own weaponless hands. He gave Mark a cryptic smile. "I knew I'd chosen well."

"Mali never carries," Sam explained.

"Two toothless babes!" Ule's grin turned wolfish with disgust.

Fleetingly I regretted having caved in so easily to wearing a knife. Sam's fault, my weakness. But I'd grown to like having it there, and that was more disturbing than the little blade itself.

Mark flicked his hair back. "I do have some hand-to-hand training."

"You do?" I glanced up from my warm-up exercises. Mark was forever proving himself to be other than his surface indicated.

"My, um, father insisted." He traced the pattern of the parquet with his foot. "Leningrad isn't quite as orderly as

Chicago, G. There was this rash of ransom kidnappings for a while."

Mali laughed delightedly. "Then this um-father of yours is a very rich man. Very rich or very powerful." He strutted a little, exactly like Pen. "Mine was Headman of the First Station."

"Was?"

"Ah, yes."

"Sorry. Mine too. Was, I mean. He was assassinated by his political enemies. I . . . was there."

"So was mine. So was I." Mali offered his Pied Piper smile. "The pressure they exert, these fathers, ha? Even from the grave."

Mark's composure faltered. He dropped his eyes to the floor.

"Enough of this lazing about!" Ule clapped his hands like a ballet master. "To work, ladies, to work!"

Mark's awkwardness fell away like a discarded garment. He was trained, all right. He was fast and agile, and though he was two years out of practice, he made Ule work to get past his defenses. I was proud of him and glad for another target to share Ule's banter and screeches and dismay.

"You're concentrating better," nodded Sam from the window seat. I leaned against him, panting for breath, as Mark stepped deftly aside of Ule's howling advance. "Intimidation," Sam noted, "can be very effective if you're really convincing. Watch."

As he said it, Ule sprang up, twisted mid-air in an extraordinary stiff-legged leap, and landed behind Mark, who whirled off balance to meet this attack. Ule stared at him coldly and bared his knife, flipping the sheath away. Mark's eye instinctively followed the sheath. Ule's foot shot out. Mark stumbled backward and was on the floor in seconds with Ule's blade at his throat.

"Ha!" Ule roared.

"See what I mean?" approved Sam.

"I remember." Ule had humiliated me likewise the morning before, with a lot less effort.

Ule bounced to his feet, hauling Mark up by his elbow. "These puppies think it's gonna be easy with an old man like me!"

Mark jerked free of him and brushed at his coveralls,

though Cora's floors were never dirty. He combed his hair back brusquely with both hands. "Next time it might be!"

Mali laughed and sidearmed the discarded sheath at his chest. Mark caught it angrily. Then he looked at Mali and his shoulders relaxed. He went over to present the sheath to Ule with a courtly little bow.

"Good lad," said Ule, and slapped him on the butt with it.

Cris and Tua came in with handfuls of printout from the local public newsbox. "It's raining like piss out there," Tua announced.

Ule chuckled. "Must be the Preacher's stormsongs again."

I heard the antique doorbell chime in the great-hall. Cora called out casually, "I'm getting it," as if seven A.M. were a normal hour for visitors. Mali and Sam lunged out the door after her. "Cora! Be careful!"

Cris spread the damp newsfax across the silky ebony of the grand piano. There in full-color pictures was our Jane crumpled on the marble steps of the South Tower of Town Hall, exactly where we had stood to present the mayor our petition.

"Look at this: the Chat runs a special bold-print headline, 'Murder in Harmony!', then gives us all the gory details of the seven other murders committed in town over the past ten years, all crimes of passion." He grinned at me crookedly. "Jane would be scandalized to know the company she's keeping."

I reached for the more sedate and reliable HarmoNet release.

"A new message in the public e-mail," Mark noted. "VOTE NO TO THE OAP OR WE'LL PICK THEM OFF ONE BY ONE."

"Brilliant," said Cris. "Sounds just like 'em."

"Yours?" I asked Tua.

She shrugged amiably.

At the door, Cora said, "Could you all come in here, please?"

Micah was in the great-hall, sitting alone in the middle of the big couch facing the fireplace. His clothes were rain-damp, his shoulders hunched, his hands pressed tightly between his knees. I'd never seen him look so vulnerable and disconsolate. Omea perched on one arm of the sofa while Mali paced, explaining a thing or two.

We slipped in quietly, greeting Micah with our eyes. Songh sat in a corner, looking like he'd cried until morning. Mali moved about with rare unease. I listened carefully for what he was leaving out, which was everything about where Jane had been first deposited and what the Eye had done about it.

". . . but she persisted in her delusion," he was saying, "that one of our company was Latooea, the Conch."

"Yes." Micah glanced at me, so weary, so infinitely sad, so old. "I'd heard something of that."

"It's possible someone believed her and thought she had information."

"More likely someone intended her as an object lesson," Omea put in. "Unstable as she was, poor dear, Jane was easy prey."

"Yes." Micah released his hands and sat back limply. "I called the mayor. She's very upset—asked if Jane had any enemies. I said: yes, the Town of Harmony. I don't think she understood." He raised his copy of the morning's e-mail from the cushion beside him. " *'Pick them off one by one?'* What kind of monsters are we dealing with?"

"That one's unsigned," said Sam. "They'll deny it."

"Might be traceable to them," Tua suggested blandly. "Like all the others."

Micah straightened. "Traceable?"

Mali explained and my heart went out to Micah. Even he walked innocently into the Eye's manipulations.

"Cam Brigham?" Micah looked to Cora. When she nodded, his jaw clenched. "Doesn't he know his damn gallery shows only ex-apprentices?"

"He's moved a lot of his money into the tourist industry lately. Voting out the Apprenticeship Program would leave him more room for paying customers." Cora smoothed the pine-dark green of her housedress. "I'd been saving the e-mail connection to use against him in case things get sticky at Town Meeting tonight. It never occurred to me he'd stoop to actual murder."

"No. Who'd have thought the danger was so . . . immediate? I've been so preoccupied with the show."

"We share the burden," Mali said.

"There must be evidence enough to turn him in . . . ?"

"For sending e-mails? Would you ask the law to curb free speech?"

"Nothing ties him directly to Jane's murder," said Mark, the lawyer's son.

"We can't let him—"

"Micah." Mali stopped pacing. "We won't."

Micah heaved himself to his feet as if the comforts of Cora's furniture insulted his agitated state of mind. "To be caught so by surprise, after forty years of actual . . . well, *harmony*, to lull us into trusting the basic decency of our fellow citizens!"

"Decency!" spat Sam.

"Don't," I begged.

Mali was pacing again. "When you raise an entire generation to be sick with fear of the Outside and sanctify in the name of artistic purity the expulsion of all adoptees who don't perform to standard, you have to expect some perverse definitions of decency!"

Micah regarded him evenly. "Jane's death will be propaganda for both sides, I see."

"Better than an anonymous 'termination,' " said Sam.

Micah sighed. "Yes. Yes, of course." He sighed again, deeply, and dropped his head into his hands.

Omea eased off her perch and settled beside him. "What, Micah?"

"I fear this opening up you will bring us," he replied hoarsely. "Oh, be careful. It must be a gradual process, or there'll be chaos at the door once more."

"There are worse things," said Mali.

Micah looked up. "Are there?"

"There is the death of the world." Mali dropped cross-legged to the floor in front of him. "This quarrel is not between us, Micah Cervantes. I am only the messenger and you are a man who listens in spite of himself. I bring the tale of truth and fling it here and there until it falls on fertile ground, someone like you or these children, who will take that truth and act upon it, while I move on to scatter it on other gardens. Micah, I deal in the *what*. The *how*, even the *when*, is up to you."

HARMONET/CHAT

08/14/46

SPECIAL RELEASE

***Just keeping you up-to-date, friends and neighbors, and on this terrifying morning, we know you want to be up-to-date 'cause you want to be *safe.* We know that and we sympathize, so we'll be going back to press today each time we have new information to give you about the grisly TOWN HALL MURDER.

***First, here's a press-conference quote from CAMP-BELL BRIGHAM, a pillar of Harmony and an honor to his Founder stock: "We have been lax about who and what we let into our Town. Too many people without talent and resources, without a stake in the security of our dome. Unless we tighten our gates immediately, this street killing is only the beginning! The integrity of our dome is threatened. Severe measures are called for to assure our future survival."

***The MAYOR'S OFFICE still isn't saying much about the killing, but our deep throat in Town Hall tells us there *might* have been a NOTE left with poor Janie's body, the general rhetoric of which *might* be reminiscent of the recent e-mail campaign. Don't we want to know about this note, f&n? Don't we want to know if the alleged CLOSED DOOR LEAGUE has raised the stakes from agit-prop to murder?

***Funny you should ask, f&n. The CDL must use the same deep throat we do. What should appear on our newsflash board but a hasty disclaimer from none other. In case you're avoiding the public e-mail these days, we'll send it along on our own time:

   The Closed Door League hereby makes its first and final public announcement. We are a group of citizens like yourselves, concerned about the future of our Town. We intended only the best for Harmony, but our experiment in consciousness-raising has backfired and left us vulnerable to a campaign of slander being waged by the very enemies we sought to reveal. It is surely they who have perpetrated this horrible crime, in order to discredit our honorable intentions. *We did not kill the apprentice Jane Kessler*, but only time will prove our innocence. Therefore, the Closed Door League sees no alternative but to disband as of this announcement. Any subsequent opinions, statements, or actions attributed to us will be known to be the work of our enemies, and the enemies of Harmony.

***Now they don't sound like such bad folks after all. So this time, friends and neighbors, remember where you heard it. Think about who you want to believe. Help keep our streets safe.

FIRST DRESS:

Micah brooded as I paced with him through the rain to the theatre. "He doesn't know what you did for Jane, keeping her on and all."

"Ah, Mali's not short on compassion," he allowed. "He's just abnormally long on perspective."

I picked up the latest Chat from a handy newsbox. It went limp and soggy in my hands. "Here's the CDL's denial. Didn't take them long." Would Micah feel better or worse knowing how fully the Eye had exploited Jane's murder, he who so appreciated their manipulations of reality?

The corridors of the Arkadie filled with condolences as we passed through. Fifty-four versions of how-awful-I'm-so-sorry, some of them sincere, most of them only horrified at such a turn of events in their own backyard. We found Howie in the theatre, yelling at Rachel Lamb.

" . . . I don't care who he is, he's using this horror as an excuse to grind his own personal ax! I won't have him shooting off his mouth in the name of the Arkadie without consulting me!"

Rachel murmured something unintelligible about trustees, hotels, and single ticket sales.

"Fuck him and fuck his goddamn hotels! We're better off without him!" Howie stopped when he saw us, and Rachel escaped across the stage. "Ah, Christ, Mi, what a thing, eh? Poor little Janie. Still can't believe it." He flapped his arms uselessly. "I was telling Gwinny before, it's time we did a piece about the apprentices. Never thought we'd have something so dramatic to build it on! Just so's you know, we're announcing a special apprentice dress this afternoon—over my head trustee's objections—to make the point that the curfew keeps them from attending evening performances. And we're rushing out a memorial insert for the program. Betcha we have a full house *this* afternoon." He raised a clenched fist as he headed up the aisle. "See you at noon. Talk to Kim if you want to add anything to the insert."

Micah and I traded helpless glances.

"Best way to survive this day is to get on with business," I declared. I worried about this sudden audience in the afternoon and cursed Cora Lee for refusing a communications hookup. What if Peter triggered the trap before the Eye was ready? I sent Songh off to Lorien with a warning about the apprentice dress, then went about taking care of my notes as if nothing were out of order. When Songh returned, he told me his mother had been at the theatre looking for him. He watched for my reaction.

"She's worried, of course. She's thinking it could have been you sprawled on the steps of Town Hall."

He gazed at me tearfully. "But it never would have been. That's what's unfair!"

"Maybe you should go home and tell your parents that."

He looked scared. Like me, when it came time to tell my parents I was going to Harmony. "It's not so hard to stand up to your parents if you really believe a thing," I said.

"That's what Mali would say, isn't it! That's what he'd want."

"I'm sure it is."

Songh shoved his prop notes into his back pocket and slipped away, grave and thoughtful. I hunted up Cris to deliver a few set notes, mainly so he could look busy while he kept an eye on the trap.

Peter and Margaret were in the shop, finishing up the final details on the tracking units. Margaret shook her head sadly when she saw me. Peter followed me about dog-like,

with run-on condolences in the awestruck manner of one
who can't believe he's had the good fortune to know someone who was actually murdered. He pressed for details. I
wanted nothing more than to be away from him, but Sam
would expect me to perform my assigned role properly. I
assured Peter I knew nothing but what the news services
had provided, then got out of there as fast as I could. But
not before I'd noticed the faxpix of Jane pinned to the shop
call-board, with the e-mail threat right beside it. Some asshole had drawn a red bull's-eye around her head. How
could Sean allow this in his shop? The suspicion that Sam
might be right about him penetrated a little deeper.

Onstage, our show carpenter Jilly had kicked the painters
out of the trap area to work on the closure mechanism. She
fiddled above and fiddled below, then ran it a few times.
Sam had said the plastique would not explode unless triggered, but what if Peter had rearmed it already? I found
an excuse to draw Micah upstage. I watched Jilly's slight,
muscular body bob in and out of that hole, her mouth set
in earnest determination to make the damn thing work. I
could not believe we had walked away last night leaving
death hiding in the basement. I marveled at the Eye's power
to convince, to draw the uninvolved into their machinations.
I should warn her, I told myself, even with Jane lying in the
town morgue. I should conveniently discover the mysterious
added parts. Surely Jilly was innocent and didn't deserve to
die in a trap meant for someone else.

I approached cautiously. "Sean in yet?"

"Not as far as I know." She signaled the booth and
watched the floor seal itself perfectly. "Looking good. By
the way, you seen the remote for this thing around
anywhere?"

My decision was unmade in an instant. "Uh, no, I
haven't."

And then, of course, it was too late. Because I understood that Jane's murder had forever altered my moral landscape. Now I too longed for this confrontation, now that
my planned and ordered life had turned into something I
didn't recognize or understand.

People, too, were less familiar by the minute. Hickey, for
instance, who was clearly avoiding me, slinking about with
Songh, taking care of my notes but never catching my eye.
Until later, when one of his passes across stage brought him

close by. He whispered, "I'll be there for you guys tonight, don't worry," and moved away immediately.

I stared after him. Hickey was scared even to be seen talking to me. Now the premature end to his romance with Lucienne was explained. I wondered what he heard in the shop these days when there were no apprentices around. Avoiding the hostile territory of the crew room, I went to the greenroom for coffee. Cris was there keying up the monitor that carried the news services.

"What's up?"

He made sure we were alone. "Want a look at Brigham's press conference?" He tapped in the file request. The clip came up quickly, and there was the fat man, smiling and joking, toasting the press with his breakfast champagne. I felt nauseous just looking at him but watched it through anyway. Know your enemy, Sam would say.

The clip ended. "Yuck," I said. "Well, back to work."

"Gwinn, wait . . ."

"Not now, huh?" How could I explain to him how little he mattered anymore?

"Just don't be mad at me. It's a temporary thing, for both of us."

I turned away, and there was Sean in the doorway, eyes fixed on the monitor with an expression I could not quantify. Dismay, or just as easily, guilt. Disgust, or perhaps agreement. Whatever it was, its intensity frightened me. Scared of Sean? Oh no. Then his eyes slid toward me. *Oh yes*.

"Excuse me," I murmured by the door, feeling my throat tighten. His work clothes were filthy. He looked like he'd forgotten to shave that morning.

"I'm so sorry," he croaked, "about Jane."

I couldn't help it. I glanced at him accusingly as I ducked past him through the door. He grabbed my arm.

"Gwinn, what . . . ?"

I jerked away. His face went slack with surprise as I bolted down the corridor.

"Gwinn!" he yelled. But I kept running. All the way to the theatre. I could avoid him there as long as I stuck close to Micah.

I dived back to work on a request from Moussa to make his hill a little more comfortable. A small price to pay to keep the music going, said Micah. Jilly assigned me one of the older crew, a rough-voiced fellow who sighed a lot to show how patient he was, taking orders from a mere apprentice. When I made him pull up two square meters of neatly laid surfacing to add padding underneath, he muttered crossly, "He's just got some damn rock to sit on where he comes from, right?" Even then he wouldn't let me help him. "If the job needs two, let Sean put another man on it."

But I wasn't going to be able to face Sean again real soon.

I sat and gave directions, whole paragraphs of inadequate description, when my hands could have showed him in seconds. I hated him. Maybe it was you, I thought. So much easier to imagine this man's beefy, work-scabbed hands around Jane's neck rather than Sean's.

The Eye drifted in one by one instead of swooping down all at once at noon with their customary flourish. First there was Te-Cucularit grilling a nodding, openmouthed Songh about the prop revisions. Then I noticed Sam talking with Cris in that touchy, aggressive way they related to each other. They headed for the shop together. Soon after, Moussa sauntered over to test his spot. He sniffed out the situation right off and stuck out a hand to my bluff crewman, thanking him for this fine work that was going to add so much to his performance. The man seemed more impressed by Moussa's size than anything else but found himself kneeling side by side with this cheerful giant, detailing the mysteries of the surfacing material with a willingness he couldn't quite explain.

I wanted to kiss the top of Moussa's curly head, but that might break the spell. I left him to work his gentle miracles.

Mali was standing alone in front of the trap, watching the painters touch up the scrapes and scars left by Jilly's repairs.

"Did you hear about the audience this afternoon?" I murmured.

He did not reply. He was gone somewhere inside his head. Something fierce and angry in the set of his back compelled me, instead of moving on and leaving him to his musings, to take his hand and lean against his arm. It was only when his fingers tightened around mine that I recalled standing like that with my father, on evenings when he came home from work silent with mysterious unease.

"Stay with him, if it happens," he said.

"If what? . . . Mali, nothing's going to—"

"He'd never ask it."

"Mali . . ." I shook his arm gently. "You're scaring me."

He looked down at me, as if from miles away. "Night terrors, child."

"All ready below, Mal," said Sam from behind us.

Mali nodded soberly, then grabbed Sam's hand as he came alongside and folded it around mine, pressed between his own. He held us like that for a moment, then turned and walked away.

Sam frowned after him. "What's with him?"

"I don't know."

We let our hands drop, awkward with Mali's gesture and with each other. I searched the floor for places the painters should take care of. Sam studied me.

"This has," he said quietly, "become something I did not quite expect." His even tone would not admit if he thought this good or bad. "What do you think they'd do if I made love to you right here in front of them?"

"Cheer us on, I guess." Laughter was the only way to keep from saying what I shouldn't.

"Get back to work." He pushed me gently away.

Downstage, Mali had invited Micah to step aside with him into the house. They strolled side by side up one long aisle and along the curved rear wall, heads bowed at matching angles, their hands clasped behind their backs like two professors debating an arcane point of logic.

Peter wandered in from the shop as the last of the tracking units was being wheeled up a long ramp onto the deck. Sam immediately drew him into some jocular exchange I couldn't hear. Nothing in Peter's manner suggested he was aware of being subtly interrogated, but then, nothing in Sam's manner suggested that he was extracting any useful information.

Howie returned at noon. "Liz, we'll start with a curtain call and here's how we'll do it." His elaborate staging not too subtly isolated Mali as the star of the evening.

Mali said, "We always do company calls."

"In our blacks," Omea added more gently. She meant the anonymous black robes they'd worn for their first entrance into Harmony. "Always. It's our signature."

"Not too much fun for your audiences." Howie always

said staging the curtain call was his favorite part of being a director.

Omea smiled. "You mean, not allowing them to play favorites?"

"You could put it that way."

"That's the way we see it," said Ule.

Howie sighed and slumped in his seat.

Omea sat down next to him. "Dear Howie, we've had to work very hard to maintain our unified public voice. Audiences always want to divide and conquer. By making one performer a star, they take power over that life. They have made it and can unmake it whenever it pleases them."

The canny producer in Howie was locked in battle with the more empathetic director. "But it gives you equal power over them. They'll offer themselves body and soul to a star they've created."

"For a time."

"A short one," said Ule.

Omea squeezed Howie's arm. "We'd prefer long and fruitful lives in the theatre. There's so much work to be done!"

"All right. As long as it's as spectacular as you can make it. We'll have been serious with them all evening. You gotta give them a chance to love you."

"But of course," she replied, and that was the end of it. Or so we thought.

The house was full by two o'clock.

"Like being at a wake," Micah remarked.

In Chicago, I'd heard wakes described as a barbarous custom but Micah made them sound quite civilized, and indeed there was something soothing about the steady flow of condolences past the production table, cast members from *Crossroads*, musicians and backstage staff, apprentices we knew and many we didn't, all offering sympathy as if Jane had been our relative. And it wasn't just Jane. It was what she stood for. With one masterful stroke the Eye had turned a messy death into a noble symbol of apprentice resistance. I hoped they'd be able to do the same with their play.

It was not your usual lively apprentice audience, with chatter and row-hopping until the lights went down. Too worried about the evening's Town Meeting and whether it would decide our fate. I was glad for the *Crossroads* folk, even though they'd probably come just to check out all the nasty rumors they'd heard next door. No matter. They were a cheerful lot, and devoted enough to the art to be willing to spend their first afternoon off inside another theatre.

Micah sent Songh and me to Moussa's side of the house to check sight lines. He'd said nothing of his conversation with Mali, but as I was leaving, he remarked, "If anything happens, you'll be by the pass door and can get backstage as quickly as possible."

So Mali had talked him into it. We exchanged a look and I nodded gravely, wondering what use he thought I could be. Poor Micah. Matters had gotten so out of his control that even a futile gesture seemed better than none at all. But just as well. As Liz was calling places, Reede Chamberlaine oozed in with his retinue and filled up all the empty seats around the production table. I'd have been asked to move anyway.

From where we were sitting, the curved backdrop towered in profile to our left, shadows of moss and stone. When the lights went down, the audience settled immediately into the rapt waiting that thrills the heart of a theatre practitioner. Bird shapes flitted past, winging out into the house above our heads. Odors of jungle and sea tinged the stirring air. Songh shivered delightedly. He'd been too busy with props and petitions to see any rehearsal. He leaned forward in his seat as if expecting miracles, and by halfway through the first act, I was convinced that's what we were seeing.

The show was working. I mean, really working. Not just technically, with everyone remembering their lines and blocking and all the effects going right. For the first time since that rough run-through five weeks earlier, the characters and story came to life.

Mostly it was Mali, with his performance at last fully unleashed. He started wooing the audience on his very first entrance. Once he'd hooked them, he played them like an expert angler. He shared with every eye the same intimate contact: only you understood, only you were his ally. You must therefore love his wife and children as he did, worship his gods with his same devotion, and suffer his pain and confusion as together you sought to reconcile clan tradition with his innovative vision of the future. And with those anguished eyes and radiant smile, Mali drew his fellow actors into the spiral of his energy. They bloomed in his light as if he were the sun they'd been waiting for all along.

Applause broke like thunder at the first act curtain, long and enthusiastic. I pushed across the crowded house to congratulate Micah. Howie looked as shaky as I'd ever seen him, so painfully hopeful in the face of real evidence that the long, hard weeks and all his struggles and political maneuvering might actually have been worth it.

Reede Chamberlaine stretched discreetly and sent a subordinate backstage for coffee. "Excellent work, Howard. Let's talk later about what your publicity department has planned for Mali."

Howie looked uncomfortable. "You know, Reede, he's not going to like it."

"Ah yes, the company identity number."

"Pretty sure he means it."

Chamberlaine's laugh was like the rustle of silk. "He thinks so now. But all great actors have great egos. The humble act never lasts once they've seen the possibilities. I'll buy the three of us a little chat over an expensive dinner. Give him a taste of things to come. Always works. Trust me."

I didn't, not for an instant. But I was only eavesdropping, and after all, if Howie knew Mali's father was the Rock, he'd listen to Chamberlaine with a more skeptical ear.

Onstage, the assistant stage manager stalked around checking the preset. As she crossed down center, I started. Mali had made me forget even that. As the lights dimmed for Act Two, Cris hauled Songh out of the seat beside me and sat down.

"Did Sam have time to . . . ?"

He nodded. "But I can't find Peter anywhere. Shop says he went home. Looks quiet underneath, though."

"How far can the remote signal carry?"

He chuckled evilly. "How're you going to manage without me if you don't learn these things?"

"Cris . . ."

"He won't be around either, remember."

My jaw tightened involuntarily. "How far?"

"No more than fifty meters. Otherwise we might trigger a few surprises next door in *Crossroads*. He's got to be somewhere inside this theatre."

I surrendered the knots in my stomach to Mali as soon

as he reappeared onstage. He was a stealer of souls. He imprisoned you behind his eyes while he labored to impress the Planter with the mystery and rightness of the ancient magic.

I had a new insight into the play that afternoon. Our tragic hero's real crime was not the revealing of clan secrets without consulting his clansmen. The Ancestors might have forgiven that. What they could not forgive was his innocence: he believed that a rapprochement between opposites could be reached, even though the Planter, as the one in power, had no need for rapprochement, no need to see any version of reality but his own. To be innocent and well-meaning in such a world, the play was saying, is to be fatally vulnerable.

No wonder Sam gave my own innocence a hard time.

Meanwhile, Two, five rushed toward us. The outraged elders gathered in the ritual clearing and fell prostrate before the materialized image of the Ancestor. The shimmering green of the Matta floated out of the darkness like water filling a void. Gold symbols flickered and danced. Sudden double vision dizzied me as I picked out the tale painted by an apprentice scenographer in a place very far away from that jungle glade. I was Mali and I was myself. I watched with growing dread as he gathered the Matta around him. Cris and Songh tensed forward at the same frightened angle.

The elders' chant crescendoed, the ghostly ancestor raised his arms. A soundless impact shook the air, like a giant bubble bursting. Faint diamonds sparkled in the water-green of the Matta. I blinked and Mali was gone.

"My god," Cris whispered. "It worked. It fucking worked!"

"And," I murmured joyously, "that's all it did!"

There were snuffles behind me in the silence, and solemn sighs further down the row. When the grieving widow received the Planter's funeral gift of a basket of the fruit she had picked herself, the sighs turned to weeping. The standing ovation began in the final blackout and lasted through the swirling, triumphant curtain call, until one of the black-robed figures danced forward and raised a palm.

The silence was immediate.

"Dear friends in Harmony," Omea's voice sang out from beneath her hood and veil, "this performance is given in memory of Jane." She whipped her arms down and around. Nine pairs of arms followed. Ten trailing black robes became a glowing sky blue. A flight of white doves burst from the catwalks overhead and swooped low as the company made a final deep ensemble bow.

Applause broke again, a cascade of cheers and stamping. Here and there a *Crossroads* company member sat frowning in his seat, but many rose to their feet with everyone else. Out of the sober telling of a tale of death came a cathartic reaffirmation of life. The Eye sent their apprentice audience out of the theatre to face the evening's uncertainties with energy and resolve.

I didn't wait to report to Micah. I ran straight backstage, into a tumult of relief and celebration. I've never been the sort who'll hug and kiss just anybody, but it was in the air back there, and even Te-Cucularit and the girls got their share from me. The office staff, stage managers, apprentices from *Crossroads*, mobbed the dressing rooms. Omea reigned as queen of the corridor, with Ule as her jester, gathering compliments like flowers. The crowd thickened outside the room Mali shared with Moussa and Pen. Everyone knocked and called for him, but one of the dressers had been posted to keep people out. I fought my way around the corner to Sam's room and there was Mali, slumped on a stool while Sam's strong hands worked on his neck and shoulders.

"Thank god we made it through without . . ." I shut the door behind me.

"He's going to need a full-time masseur before he's finished with this place," Sam remarked.

Mali grunted and closed his eyes.

Sam pummeled him harder. "And this lovely young woman wants to know why I don't just go down there and rip the whole thing out instead of putting you through this."

"The show," I said breathlessly, "was wonderful."

"We knew it would work," said Sam.

"No, we didn't." Mali lifted his head like a tired prince to acknowledge the awe and admiration I could not keep out of my eyes. Mali knew but would never say that unlike the Eye's earlier ensemble work, this piece was his and his alone. I barely recalled anyone else's performance. Even Sam's.

The door cracked open. "He's in here, for chrissakes!"

Howie burst in. "Inspired, gentlemen, truly inspired! Why are you hiding out in here? It's everything we hoped it would be!"

"Oh good." Sam gave Mali a final slap. "Does that mean we can go home now?"

Howie laughed boisterously. "Only after you've finished taking the Town by storm!"

Liz knocked at the open door and handed in a creamy stiff envelope. "For Mali. And Reede would like a word with the company in the greenroom as soon as they're out of makeup."

"Sure, sure. Little party he has planned." Howie passed the envelope along.

Mali stripped it open, glanced at the few lines of elegant scrawl, and tossed it aside. To Liz he murmured, "Send him my apologies. I already have dinner plans."

Howie rubbed his hands. "Should have seen old Reede afterward. He was knocked out. Even looked a little pale, the limey bastard!"

Reede Chamberlaine was always a little pale, I thought. His pallor had that cultivated look. I imagined him carefully bleaching his skin so it wouldn't clash with the icy silver of his hair.

He was not in the greenroom when the company straggled in from their showers, still dressing and celebrating. One of the sycophants kept watch by the door until Tua trotted in, tying the sash of her sky-blue kimono. "Oh, am I the last?"

The sycophant simpered and leaned out the doorway. Reede strolled in, gray-suited and smiling.

"I shan't keep you long, my dears. You've worked hard and I know you're eager for a break." He paused faintly to offer Mali a sly glance of complicity. "To that end, we've arranged for a lovely dinner to be brought in, so you can relax between shows—we've a real, grown-up audience tonight, remember." Two of his assistants came in behind him bearing champagne and glasses. I recognized the silver trays from *Three Sisters*. Reede mimed delighted surprise. "Ah! This should get you through while I bore you with a few necessary matters. I'm back to London right after, you know. Time to get the tour machinery rolling."

The acolytes poured and passed glittering crystal alive with tiny bubbles. Reede did a room scan that rivaled Sam for subtlety and efficiency. "Before we start, perhaps it'd be best if anyone not directly associated with this project gave us a few moments to ourselves."

It was the cast and the stage managers only. And Howie. Typical of Reede Chamberlaine not to think of inviting the designers to a company meeting. Being the only apprentice in the room, I gathered myself to leave. "Don't you dare," Sam murmured, easing me back against the wall beside him. Chamberlaine smiled his smooth, frosty smile. "All in the family, then? Well, first let me say I was enormously impressed this afternoon. This is a remarkable piece of work, and it proves without a doubt that your company can look forward to much expanded horizons."

He accepted a glass of champagne and sipped at it delicately. One of the male acolytes brought an old wooden chair from against the wall. An uncomfortable choice, but its stiff back and higher seat allowed Reede to sit and still look down on the rest of us. Omea and Tuli sank into the cushiony embrace of a loveseat. Mali lounged in a deep armchair, his long legs stretched out in front of him as if he was ready to doze off any minute. The others sprawled on the carpet or leaned against the padded furniture. Ule lay flat on his back at Omea's feet. Howie commandeered the arm of Mali's chair, beaming at them all like a proud father.

"Here's the question." Reede held his glass out to the side and an assistant whisked it away. "Whether *The Gift*, marvelous as it is, is appropriate for our tour as I've laid it out. It might be advisable to wait before adding this piece to your regular repertory."

"Wait for what?" Pen muttered.

"Oh, I don't think so," said Howie. He smiled down at the top of Mali's head.

Chamberlaine nodded as if Howie had agreed with him. "There's another possibility, and that's to rethink the way we sell the piece. Now as I've said many times, I'm not in this one for the money, but the tour will be expensive and I'll need full houses every night just to pay back my investors. A new play like this, intellectual in content: it's a very hard sell."

"Easier with the reviews you'll be getting here," Howie noted.

"Very true, and I could write those reviews word for word after this afternoon. Which is exactly what encourages me to suggest a further break from the Eye's past traditions, that you let my agency sell *The Gift* on the basis of Mali's virtuoso performance."

"No," said Mali from the depths of his chair.

"Hear me out, now."

"No."

Reede shrugged gracefully. "We could have discussed this a little more privately, my dear. It's nothing very much, you know, just the usual biographical profiles, exclusive interviews, photo essays. Not so painful, given the benefit to the company in the long run."

"You do it for me, you can do it for all of us."

"Tut. Are we going to be stubborn about this?"

Mali glanced at Omea. "Round two."

"No way, man," said Pen.

Omea hushed him. "We don't think singling one of us out will benefit the company."

"But I know it will benefit the tour, and that will benefit the company. Omea, this is your premier first-class engagement. The only fiscally responsible choice is to sell Mali for all we're worth. Either that or leave this piece out of the repertory."

"Oh, Reede," Omea pouted prettily, "must we be fiscally responsible?"

"Yes, my darling. That we must always be." Chamberlaine sat back and crossed his legs. "Well, what do we think?"

Howie stirred. "Reede, I don't get it. You read the script, you knew what it was, you were excited by the possibilities. The whole point was to add something controversial to contemporize their traditional repertoire."

A fresh glass of champagne appeared at Chamberlaine's elbow. He shook his head, then braced his arms elegantly on his knee. "Howard, you insisted on artistic control and I gave it to you. We both knew the risk. Personally I admire this work, but it would be easier to sell if you'd made a few different choices. Why, for instance, in a play about magic, have you ignored the potential for glorious special effects? Why waste our master of romantic invention Micah Cervantes on a production style that's so somber and plain? And that funereal curtain call! The people like their spectacle, Howard!"

"The people, Reede, just gave us a standing ovation!"

"A standing ovation from a young and especially sympathetic audience." He bent a regretful eye on Omea. "Getting yourselves embroiled in local politics was perhaps not the wisest thing to do, my dear."

"The local politics embroiled us," Omea replied. "We came here to do our work in peace."

"Besides," added Sam, "our politics are none of your business."

"Ah, but my good magician, business is precisely what they are. Bad business. Oh yes, I know what's been going on here. You think people are going to be eager to invite into their domes the architects of Harmony's peasant rebellion and then sit still for a lecture on their own greed and inhumanity?"

Mali unfolded slowly from his armchair. Chamberlaine was a tall man, but when Mali drew himself up to his most regal bearing, the man in gray had to crane his neck or take a step backward. Chamberlaine did both and seemed somewhat less elegant in retreat.

"A judicious producer wouldn't mention what has happened here," Mali said. "A courageous producer would not care. A visionary one would put it to profitable use."

"Oh, excellent!" Reede offered his smile to the others. "See how marvelous he is? What presence! You're no stripling youth, Mali, but you've still a major career ahead of you if you play it my way."

"You can *make* me, is that it, Reede?"

"It would be a pleasure."

"And the rest?"

"Will bask, and profit, in your glory."

Mali stared at him coldly, then turned away.

"Whoa, whoa, let's back up here," begged Howie. "This problem can be resolved."

Mali stalked past him. "Then resolve it."

Howie said, "Reede, why don't you and I step up to my office so we can talk this out?"

"I'd say it was out of your hands, Howard, unless you've more control over this headstrong company than it appears you do."

Howie looked after Mali helplessly as the Tuatuan began a long slow circuit of the room.

"While we perform at the Arkadie, we abide by the decisions of its artistic director," Omea said. "But the future of our company must remain in our hands."

Mali's tiger walk took him along our wall. Sam touched his arm. "Back off, Mal. The man is baiting you."

Mali brushed past abruptly.

Uh-oh, I thought.

"I would never argue with autonomy," Howie argued, "but—"

"The future of a company is in the individual success of its members," said Reede. "You hold one back, you hold back everyone."

"No, Reede!" barked Mali from the back of the room.

"Ah shit," Sam muttered, "here it comes." Ule sat up. Omea's mouth tightened warily.

"Ignorant savages, hah?" Mali sneered. "Just don't understand the grown-up world of business? Listen to yourself, Reede! You sound like a fucking cliché!"

Howie's glance to Omea asked, Should you stop him or should I?

"Now, Mali, there's no need for raised voices."

"This is a need, Reede, because I'm likely to puke if I sit here listening to you another second! How about you listening to me for a change!"

"With pleasure." Chamberlaine resettled himself in his chair. "I'm all ears."

Mali did not bother to conceal his loathing. "We have put, some of us, fifteen years into evolving a working company consciousness. That rare and precious understanding is what allows us to create work like *The Gift*. Do you think we'd throw all that away like the foolish virgin on a promise of fortune? Do you understand anything about us at all? Do you think we are like *you*?"

Howie stood. "I'd like to say something here—"

"I understand one thing very clearly," Chamberlaine drawled. "Your ingratitude. This company was the ten A.M. booking at mass admission dance festivals when I picked it out of the gutter! Four months later, I've got you a production in Harmony and two-week exclusives at the best theatres in the world and you can't shake yourself free of your mystical claptrap long enough to keep your part of the bargain!"

"*Our* bargain, Reede, and *we* have kept it!"

"I don't need your 'company consciousness'! I live in the

modern world and I need a star! I need you, out there
acting!"

"You want a star performance?" Mali yelled. "I'll give
you one, right now. You alter a single term of our contract
and I, Sa-Panteadeamali, the individual, will consider it null
and void. You can take your tour and your fucking domer
contempt and shove it! I will not perform under such
conditions."

"Well, well, well," murmured Chamberlaine. "I'm very
sorry to hear that."

"He doesn't mean it," said Howie quickly.

The producer slid his hands into his pockets and regarded
Mali with satisfaction. "I'll need to hear that from him."

Omea rose, just managing to keep resignation out of her
voice. "If you cancel *The Gift*, I will not perform, either."

"No, I expect not," Chamberlaine allowed.

"Nor I," said Moussa.

"Me neither."

"Nor me."

When the rest had added their agreement, Pen shook his
head. "And I gave up good money for this."

Te-Cucularit said, "This is what comes of domer
dealing."

Chamberlaine surveyed them calmly. "So it's unanimous,
then? Follow the leader?"

The Eye stared back at him stonily.

"Guys . . ." pleaded Howie. "He'll do it, you know. He'll
cancel the tour right out from under us. Reede, look, we've
got a whole month here. We'll work on the piece in performance. It's the best way to evolve material like this . . .
organically."

"What they don't want, we can't force," said Chamberlaine. "It's a shame, but . . ." He shrugged. I really hated
the smug gleam in his eye.

"We've been outmaneuvered," said Sam disgustedly.

"I don't believe this!" Howie exclaimed.

"There, there, Howard. Don't take it personally. They're
not refusing to play out the run here." Reede smiled down
at Omea. "Perhaps it's all for the best, my dear. We'll agree
on a little statement for the press citing irreconcilable artistic differences and hope to work together another time.
When the climate is more favorable, eh?" He raised her
hand lightly to his lips, turned away, then turned back as

with an afterthought. "And, Mali, when you come to your senses later and want a proper high-power agent, call me. I know just the man."

"Fuck you, Reede."

Chamberlaine gathered his staff, champagne glasses, trays, and all, then took Howie's arm and steered him toward the door. "Now we've settled this issue, let's leave these hungry people to their dinner and have that little chat in your office. I'd like to lay out for you the plan Rachel and I have put together for a world tour of *Crossroads*."

FINAL DRESS:

"*Crossroads??*" Mali spat.

Howie threw back a despairing glance. "I'll deal with this!" The last of the retinue oozed out and shut the door behind them.

"Sure you will!" Pen hurled his champagne glass at the door. "You could have left the fucking bottle!"

"Sonofabitch!" Mali's regal posture collapsed. He looked to Sam. "You did warn me."

"I did," Sam agreed.

Mali sagged into the nearest armchair. "What have I done?"

"I'm not sure yet," Omea replied. "Let me think about it."

Sam pushed away from the wall. "If it were only local politics, he wouldn't care. When they start connecting us to Open Sky, it gets too radical for Reede. Even if you hadn't given him the excuse, he'd have found some way to dump us."

"Poor Howie," said Omea. "He goes partway down every road, then retreats in confusion when he runs into real resistance."

Ule nodded. "All show and no go. Harmony in a nutshell."

Liz and the assistant stage managers emerged from their back corner. I'd forgotten they were there. One of them went straightaway to clean up Pen's shattered glass. Liz said heartily, "We still have a show tonight, so let's get you guys fed."

She was blocked at the door by a dolly full of vid equipment. Liz held the door open. "What's all this stuff?"

"We need an extra monitor in here tonight," Cris announced from behind the pile. "For Town Meeting."

"Oh, no. The first cue that gets missed in *Crossroads*, Wendy'll yell at me for allowing distractions in the greenroom."

Cris straightened, with Mark alongside him. "Liz, don't you think this meeting tonight might be a little more important than *Crossroads*?"

She thought about it but not for long. "Sorry. Of course it is. Bad enough any citizen has to work tonight."

Mark left Cris to do the hookup and came over. "Something's up," he guessed.

I groaned. "Reede just canceled the tour."

"What? After a performance like that? Is he crazy?"

"No. Only greedy," said Tua. "We're the crazy ones."

Mark threw his head back. "What, he's afraid he'll ruin his rep if he's associated with real Art for a change?"

Omea laughed. "Nice, Mark."

I knew it wouldn't do to demand how they could take it all so calmly. "What are you going to do?"

Ule chuckled. "Hey, we've been out of work before."

"Rest easy, child," Omea said. "Perhaps we understood the risk of Reede Chamberlaine better even than Howie."

"Didn't expect it to happen quite this fast," admitted Moussa.

"What it really is," Omea sighed, "is the fortune he'll make touring *Crossroads*. Too much for him to resist."

I was glad when the food arrived to distract them. The stage managers set up folding tables and set out trays of fruit and bread and cheese. Sam and I took our plates to a corner sofa.

"If you saw what Reede was doing," I ventured, "why didn't you stop Mali before he blew?"

"I can't 'stop' Mali. Mali does what Mali does. I can try to convince him, but I can't stop him."

"You could if—"

"No," he said sternly. "That way lies tyranny. You don't try to make somebody else's decisions for them."

"It was your decision, too. What he's done affects all of you."

"And we'll all deal with it, individually and together."

What Mali had said homed in on me. *He'd never ask.* But if he wouldn't ask, how would I know if I had a decision to make? I'd have to do the asking myself, or lose him without ever knowing.

"What is it?" he asked, so gently that for a moment I thought he knew. "The tour? It's nothing. The real proof of our success here is what happens tonight at Town Hall."

I was too preoccupied to think of challenging his obvious inconsistency. For if coercing your friend into risking his life once a performance wasn't making a decision for him, I didn't understand Sam's definition at all.

Songh barreled into the greenroom. "There you are! Micah says if there's enough food, will you bring him some?"

"You don't do food?" I teased.

He stopped at Mark's elbow, his dark eyes bright and nervous. "I'm going home. I'm going to talk to my parents before they leave for Town Meeting." He turned back to me. "Mark says I was maybe staying away to avoid confrontation, but now I'm going to tell them everything about how I feel and I'm going to make them listen!"

Mark smiled down at him. He gave the boy a quick, supportive hug. "Good luck."

"Yeah," I seconded. "Don't be too hard on them."

"Do it for us," called Cris, as he tuned the new monitor to Video Town Hall.

"For Jane!" Songh hunched his shoulders tight around his neck and let them drop. "Well, see you later, if they ever let me out of the house again!" He winked and sprinted away.

"How long since he's been home?" asked Sam.

"Oh, about a week."

He nodded. "He'll do all right in life, that kid, once he grows a little."

"Grows, or grows up?"

"Well, in his case, it'd better be both."

"You're very cheerful for someone who just lost a job."

He smiled sleepily. "Must be the company I keep." He leaned in and kissed me, and for a moment we both forgot where we were, until I nearly lost my plate off my lap. Sam caught it, laughing, and we looked up to find Mali watching us, both critical and possessive, as if we were a work he was still in the middle of creating.

I left reluctantly to take Micah his dinner, then got caught telling him about the cancellation of the tour. I couldn't get backstage again before curtain. Micah and Lou were running cues so he could man the lighting computer during the dress, leaving Lou free to go to Town Meeting. Marie had already gone, declaring that Mark took all her notes anyway, so why sit useless in the theatre when she could be yelling at the mayor? Lou left soon after with Micah's proxy, in case it really did come to a vote. I didn't see Hickey around once the preset was in. I hoped he was keeping his promise.

Then it was Micah and me, alone behind the production table as the theatre filled for the open dress rehearsal.

"Not much of an audience tonight, with everyone at Town Meeting."

"The dregs." Micah surveyed the house. "Tourists with shopping bags, SecondGens too young to vote, and all the geriatric subscribers who wouldn't miss a paid-for ticket if it were doomsday tomorrow."

He was right, and the shopping bags were going to be a particular problem. I let myself be transfixed by the amber numbers glowing in the bank of tiny monitors on Lou's console, as if they were the excuse for my silence.

"You're worried about tonight?" Micah asked kindly.

"Micah, you're worried. How could I not be?"

He smoothed the ends of his mustache, gazing into the emptiness downstage center. "There are so many things to worry about."

We sat in silence a bit longer.

"Do people ever leave Harmony?" I asked him finally. "Willingly, I mean. On their own?"

"Some do, if assured of a welcome in another dome. Harmony is not everyone's idea of utopia, no matter what we try to tell ourselves."

It was mine, I thought sadly, once upon a time. "Why do they leave?"

"They're seeking a plainer life-style, or they can't stand the tourists. It's the tourists, mostly. Writers especially find the open studio policy intolerable." He chuckled privately.

"Rosa's forever finding places she thinks we might like better than here."

"What would you do if she found one?"

Micah's look was a gentle warning.

"Sorry." I glanced away. "It's just, well, these people who leave . . . do you ever hear from them again? Do you see their work?"

"Do they manage to succeed, do you mean? Certainly. Harmony is not the only place to build a career. London is a thriving theatre town, so is Beijing. But none of them have our apprentice program, and as you know, there's a problem getting residence in a dome if you're not born there. Once you've won citizenship in Harmony, it's barterable at any of the arts-conscious domes." He looked at me closely. "Why? Are you unhappy here?"

"I am not welcome here."

"A minority opinion. We hope this is being resolved as we speak. When it is, I've little doubt you'll win your citizenship."

I fidgeted in silence.

"There's more to this . . ."

There is an expanse of blue, I thought, and like walls falling away it surrounded me, sucking my breath into its vastness. Always before, some power in Mali's presence had brought this vision, but Mali wasn't here now and the sky was inside me. Blinded by light and blueness, seized by inexplicable longing, I buried my face in my hands to hide the evidence of my madness from Micah's kindly inquiring eye.

"Do you ever feel cheated?" I blurted. "Does it ever bother you that your movements are so circumscribed? Do you ever want to just walk out of Town and over the next hill to see what's there?"

"Always," he replied after a while. "Therefore I invent the other side of the hill in my work, every day."

"It's not the same!" I replied, harsh with frustration, not meaning to be cruel.

"No, but what choice do I have?"

I slid lower in my seat. "The Eye says we have a choice."

"Ah." Micah fit entire volumes of comprehension into that syllable. "Well, I suspect they are right. They are the first truly free-flowing thought current I've dipped into for a long time. They are the future, no doubt, but I hope they are premature. I'm too old for the kind of hard choice and radical change they advocate."

"Oh no," I said. "Mali would want you there with him in the vanguard."

"Old men to the front!" Micah laughed soundlessly. "He might even convince me." He let his attention wander over the audience for a moment. "But we're weren't talking about Mali, were we?"

I looked at my hands. "No."

"The issue of citizenship should be persuasive on the side of staying."

"I know."

"Perhaps he could be convinced to stay here."

I just laughed sourly, and Micah nodded. "Are you asking my advice? In a matter of the heart? You couldn't have picked a less appropriate source."

"There is no appropriate source. I ask the sanest person I know."

He grunted, pleased. "All I can offer without ambivalence is an observation: you have thus far faced the critical decisions in your life with balance and determination. My guess is you'll know what's right when the time comes."

I thanked all the gods I knew of, Chicago's, Harmony's, and Tuatua's, that I had four weeks to ponder this dilemma.

Howie trudged up the aisle, particularly bearlike and melancholy, popping giant red grapes into his mouth in a steady stream. I wasn't sure he even tasted them.

"You heard about the tour?" he asked Micah.

"I heard."

"You heard he wants *Crossroads* instead?"

"I heard."

Howie bent narrowed eyes on the sparsely filled house. "Where the hell is everybody? It's almost curtain."

"At Town Meeting, we hope," said Micah.

"Oh. Christ. Yeah."

Cris sidestepped through the row in front of us and leaned over the lighting console. "I'll tune one of these monitors to Town Hall to give you visual. Gwinn can listen in on the headset now and then."

Mark joined us with his notepad as the lights dipped to half. I slipped on the headset. Around us the rustle of shopping bags and conversation carried well on into the blackout. I've never understood audiences who are restless even before the show begins: if they don't want to be here, why do they come?

The first act was not visibly different from the afternoon. The cast was a little tired, Mali's performance was perhaps a bit darker and less giving. It was nothing you could put your finger on. It just didn't ignite. My attention wandered to the Town Meeting broadcast. I couldn't bring myself to tune my headset away from the show, in case . . . in case anything, but my eye was caught by those soundless images deciding my fate: the mayor pressing her hands against the podium, anonymous SecondGen faces scowling in the speaker's box, Cora Lee's determined profile filling the screen as she rose in protest. During one slow pan of the packed hall, I was sure I saw Sean, yelling with raised fists.

Applause was sparse at intermission, and conversation immediate in the house, the same dull and silly conversations, picked right up as if the first act had never happened.

Howie snatched my headset. "Liz, what was the time on that act? Jeez, really? Only twenty-five seconds longer than this afternoon and we're losing 'em. Tell the cast I'm coming back to talk to them."

"They're angry about the tour," I suggested.

"Reede always had wonderful timing for this sort of thing," remarked Micah acidly.

Cris appeared at my elbow. "I'm watching from the greenroom. Guess who's here."

"Ohh." Again, I'd forgotten about the trap.

"He's in the shop. Just, you know, hanging out with the running crews. They've got Town Meeting on there too, along with a keg of beer. Raucous as shit. Surprised you can't hear the commentary through the loading door."

I shivered. "What's happening at Town Hall?"

"You weren't listening?"

I shrugged, gestured wanly at the stage.

"You better listen," he warned grimly. "There's a new proposal on the floor: immediate expulsion for all apprentices." When my jaw sagged, he laughed skittishly. "Cora Lee took the mike to complain about intimidation tactics and virtually accused the CDL of murdering Jane. I thought she might flush them out, but after that a secret ballot was voted in. The wording's still under discussion."

"*Immediate* expulsion?" Micah repeated.

Nodding, Cris looked at me, showing fear for the first time.

The houselights dipped and rose, signaling Act Two. Cris stroked my arm awkwardly. "I'm back to the greenroom."

I sat back. "What more can you expect when you expected the worst?"

"No premature panic, now," Micah said.

"Think I'll watch from house left again."

Whatever Howie had said to the Eye, their energy picked up in the second act. But the audience didn't. They didn't understand the play or didn't care to. The only things that caught their attention were Sam's sleight of hand and the young lovers' quarrel. The harder Mali wooed them, the stonier they got. It was excruciating. I wanted to leave, to be anywhere that I didn't have to suffer the Eye's humiliation along beside them.

But I couldn't leave. Two, five was approaching and I'd just caught a glimpse of movement at the lobby entrance to my left. It was dark onstage and darker in the house. The black recess of the double doorway could have hidden ten men. I tried to stare into it without seeming to. Whoever was there could see me better than I could see him.

The Matta came out, enveloping Mali in its winding green folds.

The vengeful shadow of the Ancestor lifted its arms.

The flash was blinding. Through the bright sear on my retina, I saw Mali flung aside, twisted in the fabric. He landed facedown on the deck and lay very still as tiny flames chewed the edges of the Matta.

Behind me, an old lady cheered.

They don't even get it. They think it's part of the show.

Sam made it look godlike and effortless as he scooped up Mali's limp weight and swept upstage into darkness. The loose ends of the Matta trailed behind, fluttering greenly. Ule and Cu wheeled after him. Had something gone wrong? Was this what they'd intended? Before I was even aware of moving, I was up and stumbling for the pass door. Onstage, Omea began the final scene as if nothing unusual had occurred. My hands fumbled for the release bar. I shoved the door open and bolted through, heading backstage.

"Hold the door," someone hissed.

In the work-lit connecting corridor, I glanced behind me. Sean.

"Move along," he urged. "I'm just as worried as you are."

Bearing down on me in the dim light, intent and unshaven, he was terrifying.

"Oh, Sean, what have you done?"

"Me? C'mon, it's probably nothing. A lot of harmless sparks." He pulled me along. "You make it sound like I planned it."

"Wasn't Jane enough?"

He slowed. ". . . *What*?"

I sprang away from him down the corridor and pushed through the fire door at the end, freezing as I burst into the stark light of the stage right hallway. Omea's chant filled my ears. People were in frantic motion, Mark looking helpless and stricken, Ule on his knees, Sam tearing at the pile of green silk that had Mali's feet sticking out of it. A monitor on the wall flashed images of Town Meeting: Cam Brigham orated soundlessly from the podium while the speaker broadcasted Omea's mournful chant as the play finished onstage. I struggled to make sense of what I was seeing.

The rest is just good acting.

"He's breathing, let him breathe!" Ule yanked at the Matta.

"Mal, Mal, come on, Mal," Sam pleaded. He peeled back Mali's eyelid, laid an ear to his chest. "Heart, come on, heart."

Sean shoved past me. He grabbed Mark and flung him toward the pass door. "Get a doctor, for chrissakes!"

Mark nodded, sprinted away, then stopped when Sean moved on to Sam and Mali. He caught my eye, shook his head, two sharp jerks. He threw the inside lock on the pass door and slipped around the corner into the stairwell to the trap room.

Sean crouched beside Sam. "What happened? Is he all right?"

Sam turned, snarled, and lunged at him. Sean was too stunned to defend himself. He staggered, twisted away, and went down, scrabbling across the tiles until he could get his feet under him. "Wait a minute! *Wait a minute!*"

"I'll tear your bleeding throat out!" But Sam pulled up just short of leaping at him again as Ule rolled Mali over gently, tossing away the last charred shreds of the Matta.

Mali's face was slack, but I saw his fingers brace against the floor and I relaxed a little.

Sean stood up shakily. "For god's sake, what happened?"

Te-Cucularit bounded up the stairs from the trap room. He dropped a melted twist of fine wire into Sam's outstretched hand. Sam shoved it in Sean's face.

Sean snatched it from him angrily. "What the fuck is this?"

"You ought to know. You put it there."

Ule said, "He's breathing, but barely." He bundled up the torn Matta and placed it under Mali's head.

Sean stared at the wire, then at Sam. "I put nothing there 'cept what I was meant to."

"Yeah? On whose orders?"

Sean looked at me. "What's he talking about?"

In the end, no matter how much my fear had talked me into, I couldn't believe it of him. Sam was wrong this time. Sean hadn't planned this thing. Or even known about it. I glanced around, frightened again. The corridor was empty. Was Peter still somewhere in the building?

"Somebody wired the trap," I told Sean quietly.

Sam glared at me.

"A *bomb*?" Sean glanced at Mali. "Oh, sweet Jesus."

"Spare us the innocent act." Sam pushed close. "One of your crew was down there last night, working late. We saw what he did."

"Who?"

"Peter," I supplied.

"Your man," Sam accused.

Sean dropped the wire and stepped back, palms raised. "None of mine. He's only in 'cause . . ." He stopped, frowning.

"What?" Sam demanded.

"Gwinn, you know this kid, right? Friend of Micah's?"

"No. Never."

"Wait. I remember. It was Cam asked me. Said the kid needed a job, would I put him on?" Sean pressed his hands to his temples as if trying to force comprehension. "Christ. Cora was trying to tell me . . ." He kicked at the wire lying by his foot. "Oh, that motherfucking son of a bitch. Using my theatre for . . . !"

"Now it's coming back to you," prodded Sam nastily.

Sean shoved his hands in his pockets, confounded. "You

think I'd . . . Gwinn, for chrissakes, tell them about me! You know I'd never . . . no, I don't like their ideas but, Christ, innocent people? *Jane?* Gwinny, please, you never thought I . . . ?"

I looked away helplessly.

He jabbed a finger at Brigham's image on the monitor. "It's him, gotta be! He's the one! Look, fella, you get your man looked after. I'm going back to Town Meeting. That bastard's there putting his fuckin' lies on record, and I'm gonna fuckin' put a stop to it!"

Sam moved to intercept. "You're going nowhere."

Sean backed around me. "No, you come along if you want but I'm going!" He shoved me abruptly at Sam, a full body block. Sam threw me aside and grabbed for him. Sean swerved free. "Come on, then! We'll wring his friggin' neck together!" He took off for the stage door, veering like a hurdles runner around scenery and costume racks.

"Go!" Sam hissed. Ule and Cu plunged down the corridor. I grabbed for Sam as he whirled after them.

"No! Sam! Don't go! It's not Sean! I swear!"

He shook me off with a growl and bolted. On the monitor, Cam Brigham raised a clenched fist. Racing feet echoed down the hall. Mali turned on his side, rose onto one elbow.

I smiled at him uncertainly. "I was worried about you when they didn't stop the show."

"No point, when they thought it was all part of it. But we seem to have flushed out the enemy."

I began my denial, but Mali glanced past me, his eyes widening. Movement caught the corner of my vision. I turned to see . . .

Peter. In the doorway to the stage right wing, his face blank with purpose. He raised his arm, pointed it at Mali. Something dull and gray . . .

Mali scrambled to his feet.

I screamed. "Oh no oh no, *Sam*!!"

The muffled cracks were like a blow to my jawbone. *One. Two.* I was unable to look away from the horror of Mali slammed back like a rag doll, splayed against the white wall, a terrible knowledge in his eyes as he slipped toward the floor on a slick of red as bright as a child's fingerpaint.

"Sam!!" I heard pounding in the corridor, returning.

Sam's animal yowl shocked me into motion. As he threw himself across Mali's sinking body, I fumbled for my knife.

Peter's mad calm didn't waver. He aimed for Sam's head. He got off two more shots before I landed on him screeching, with all my weight. I had the advantage of surprise. Terror and rage drove my blade into his neck once, twice, then I lost count before he grabbed hold of me and smashed me against a wall. My head hit first. I had the sensation of bouncing, very hard, and then no sensation at all.

THE CHOICE:

I woke in a bed in a white curtained cubicle. My limbs were heavy and unresponsive, my brain very drifty. I'd always assumed being drugged would feel this way. If I just go with it for a while, I thought, I'll remember where I am, and why.

Then I remembered why. A wail rose from my gut like reflex but it couldn't shut the memory out.

The curtain jerked aside. Hands pushed me to the pillow, patted at me, tried to soothe my struggles. A familiar voice. I opened my eyes, wary little slits.

"Cris!" I grabbed for him and discovered they'd tied me down.

"Easy, easy . . . hey, you're awake!" He seemed flustered. He glanced around. "You okay? You want them to give you something?"

"Who?"

"The nurses, you know, another pill or something?"

"No!" Nurses. That answered the where. Ah, but the why! I fell back, gasping against a new wave of anguish. "Oh god . . . Mali . . ."

"He's okay, Gwinn." Cris spoke slowly, as if I might have trouble understanding him. "Gwinn, listen to me: Mali is okay."

"Mali . . . ?"

"Is okay."

"What?" Eyes wide this time. "He's what?"

"Just shaken up a little, Omea said. It's you everyone's worried about."

Shaken up? "What about Sam?"

He shrugged. "Sam's fine. He wasn't anywhere near the trap when it blew."

"No! I mean *after*!"

"There wasn't any after."

I took a very deep breath. "Cris, don't lie to me."

He spread his hands. "I'm not. Why would I?"

"Cris, I saw . . ." I couldn't bring myself to describe what I'd seen. Remembering was horrible enough.

"I heard what you saw. Everyone did, especially that suspiciously handy Chat reporter who tailed you to the hospital. Damn, and I missed all of it! Mali must have been damn convincing if it blew your circuits that bad, hunh?" Cris grinned. "Does a hell of a death scene, yes indeed! Had Sean coming and going, too."

Was it possible? "And Sam, what about Sam, was he . . . ?"

"I told you, he was right there. Omea says he took care of everything." Crispin's eyelids dipped in resignation. "As usual."

"What does Sam say?"

"Haven't seen him to ask. We don't, you know, talk much."

I lay back, dizzy with peering into the yawning gulf between what I so vividly and achingly remembered and what Cris was telling me. I prayed for a clearer head. Only then would I know if I was going mad. Or if I had already.

"What about Peter?" I asked carefully.

"Oh, he took off. In all the fuss about you, he got away. Security's looking for him. They think he'll make a run for the Outside. I say, let 'im. That's where he'll end up anyway."

Oh god. I closed my eyes. No doubt now. I'd fallen through the Looking Glass. "Cris, do me a favor. Tell me everything that happened after the trap blew. And please . . ." I pulled against the wrist restraints. "Take off this nonsense."

He sat on the bed by my elbow, leaned over, and kissed my nose. "Got to let the doctor decide that. You nearly took out an intern first time you woke up, screeching and flailing like someone were trying to murder you."

"I—I don't remember that."

"Exactly."

"Cris, I'm not crazy!"

"Sorry. No can do." He kissed my nose again.

I turned my head aside on the pillow. I didn't want his grinning, lovely face anywhere near me. I wanted Sam. I'd never wanted him so desperately. Not in bed, just there, whole and well and alive in front of me. "What time is it?"

"Late. Four A.M."

"Tell me what happened."

He sat back. "Jeez, you missed everything important! Micah canceled on Willow Street, he's thinking of canceling on Marin even though the new bids just came back within the ballpark—"

"Cris, please . . . !"

He laughed and got comfortable on the bed. "Thought maybe you needed a little normality. Hey, girl, take it easy. I'm here . . ." He leaned to touch away my sudden tears of frustration. I jerked away from him. "Okay, okay, just relax. Here's the story: the trap blew, you and Sean raced back, convinced Mali was hurt, Sam confronted Sean with the wire, you got hysterical, Sean took off for Town Hall." His mouth twisted. "Ironic that Sean should turn out to be the hero of the evening."

Hero? I shoved this further confusion aside for the moment. "Who says I got hysterical?"

"Omea. Look, there's no shame in it. I'd have been nutso, too, if I thought . . . well, anyway, the crew bundled you off to the hospital. The Eye got Mali back on his feet, took their curtain call, and went home really pissed. Probably plotting revenge right now."

"Took their curtain call? You saw this?" Sam had said even the healing trance took time.

"Nah, I was over left in the greenroom, glued to Video Town Hall. Even missed the trap blowing. The audience thought it was part of the show. Liz wasn't sure herself— after all, we'd only run it once. Nobody'd have known anything about it 'cept Sean got up and announced it to the world when he went after Cam Brigham."

"But after, did you see them after? Did you see Sam or Mali?"

"Hey, what is this, an interrogation?"

"Cris, please! I'm having serious reality problems here. I need to know if you saw them."

"Yeah, I saw them! Everyone saw them! You can see them, if it'll make you feel any better!" He jumped up, pushed aside the curtains at the bottom of the bed. He yanked a portable vid into position. "Here! They were on the news tonight, after what Sean said at Town Meeting." He cranked up the bed and sat next to me with the remote. He called up HarmoNet, scanned the directory, and ran the clip.

The Press had caught the Eye filing out of the stage door. It was pouring rain and very windy. Lamp flare and fog clouded the image. The troupe was still in their curtain-call blacks, hooded and veiled, flirting archly with the vidcams. There was movement around them, raindrops or a lot of birds—in the dark I couldn't tell. I counted heads. Ten. The full complement. Two of them with a third between them, maybe supporting him (her?) a little.

Cris pointed. "Mali."

"Maybe." And Sam? I squinted until my eyes hurt. Damn those black robes for concealing even their differing statures!

"Their usual mystical number, right? Now listen to this."

A figure detached itself from the group and approached the reporters with arms raised in welcome. "Friends! Help spread the word! The Eye invites the citizens of Harmony to a special performance in Town Hall Plaza, nine o'clock tomorrow night! Come celebrate with us!" The reporters surged around as the black-clad figure whirled, laughing, and melted back into the troupe.

"Omea," I noted.

"Yeah. Howie's gonna be insane about giving up a preview, but they've got something big in mind. So. All better now?"

I eased back into my pillow. Physical agonies were beginning to crowd out the psychological ones. "Yes. Thank you."

"Gwinn, let go of it. You imagined it worse than it was. You got the scandalfax all worked up. Everything's fine, and the Eye's gonna do something great at Town Hall tomorrow and we're all going to be there! Okay?"

"Okay." But if Sam was fine, why wasn't he here?

Cris yawned. "So now you can get some real rest, which is what the doc says you need."

"Who is that?"

"Dr. Jaeck. Cora insisted. Only the best for you, kiddo."

He patted my shoulder, kissed my cheek, rather sweet and tentative. "See you tomorrow, okay?"

"Tell me about Sean," I asked weakly.

"In the morning."

I jerked upright, or tried to. My head ached excruciatingly. "The vote! What happened with the vote?"

"I was wondering when you'd ask." Cris smiled. "We won. Tell you about that in the morning, too."

"We won . . ."

"Yeah. In spades."

We won. The nurse bustled in to shoo him out, then took my temperature and fed me pills. I drifted off without complaint.

When I woke next, the clock in the bedstand tried to convince me I'd slept fourteen hours. At least the headache was gone. I lay still, drawing fantasy maps within the minute cracks webbing the white ceiling. Since I didn't know what to think, I didn't want to think about anything at all.

The room outside the white curtains felt large. To my right, a split between the drapes revealed a pale green wall and a mock-antique print of flowers, the kind that sold big to tourists. *Wildflowers*, they were always called. The Eye, I mused bitterly, is the only thing wild in Harmony.

Beyond was a small square window. I heard no one else in the room, no breathing, no stirrings in another bed, no quiet beeps of medical monitors. Outside the window, nothing but the iron gray of the dome and a small bird sheltering on the windowsill, fluffing damp feathers. Still raining. Good. I didn't want to look at blue sky right then, though I couldn't remember why.

A different nurse appeared eventually. He undid the restraints, helped me to the bathroom past the rows of empty beds. He provided soap and towels and let me clean up a little, then fed me a meal, all without a word other than his gently phrased instructions.

I thought, He's treating me like we treated Jane after her crack-up.

He watched carefully while I ate and when I was done, he buckled up the restraints, looser this time but one hand still could not touch the other.

"How long?" I demanded, rattling my chains.

"Oh, not long. Be glad you're inside. The weather's terrible out." He smiled encouragingly and left.

I checked the clock. Six-thirty. Nearly a day had passed and no word from Sam. What could I have done or said in my madness that would keep him away, if he was well enough to come to me? Despair replaced the phantom grief I hadn't yet been able to shake despite all of Crispin's reassurances.

The evening nurse came in and found me weeping.

"There, there, straighten yourself up. You have visitors." She wiped my eyes and cranked up the bed. Through my little window I saw dusk-colored mist. I waited with my heart in my throat, but my "visitors" were Micah. I tried not to look desolate, because in truth I was overjoyed to see him.

He was bundled in a thick sweater beaded with rain, and it struck me again that he was looking old. He sat on the foot of the bed, repressing shivers and studying me with grave concern. Beyond the weary relief in his eyes was something darker and more complex.

"Why bother with a dome if the weather's going to act like this?" he grumbled, then paused and looked down. "Dr. Jaeck tells me I've been working you too hard."

I smiled. "Not you. Speaking of which, it's nearly eight. Aren't you going to Town Hall?"

"Wanted to check on you first."

"What's it all about?"

"The Eye says to celebrate the end of curfew, but I think it's mostly to clear the air and give us some space from last night. The media are having a field day. Howie needs the time to stomp out the resulting brushfires. The shop needs to put the stage back in working order, and the cast needs a rest. Not to mention the design staff. It's a good idea. First preview tomorrow."

"Have you seen them, Micah? How are they?"

He looked down at the bed cover, brushed away crumbs left from my dinner. "They've been in seclusion at Cora's, but Omea assures us everyone's fine. Preparing for the big event." He dipped into the stretched-out pocket of his damp cardigan. "I have something for you."

He held out an oversized square envelope.

"Sorry. I can't." I indicated my wrist restraints.

"What utter nonsense," he growled and unfastened them immediately.

"They think I'm crazy. Even Cris."

"Are you?"

"I . . . don't know."

He grunted and placed the envelope on my palm. "This may color your thinking about certain matters that have been weighing on your mind."

It was crisp creamy parchment, hand-pressed, with my name in fine, bold calligraphy on the face and the town seal embossed on the flap. I shook life back into my wrists and opened it. The fancy document inside appeared to be my citizenship.

"Micah, is this for real?"

"Yes, and hard won at some cost to a friend of yours."

"How did . . . ?"

"Wait. Let him tell it." He turned. "Sean?"

Sean stepped around the curtain at the foot of the bed. He returned my astonished stare with a weary, bitter grin. "She was sure she'd never see you 'n me in the same room ever again."

"How come you are?" I blurted. I grabbed at this excuse for joy, seeing these two who meant so much to me, side by side again, even if distanced still by the awkwardness of a reconciliation that comes after too much has already been said.

Sean waved a dismissive hand. "Aah, I apologized."

"You did a bit more than that," Micah replied.

"Yeah, first I yelled at him, then I apologized."

"I wish it had been that easy."

"I wanted to rip your friggin' head off! Jesus!" Sean shook his head, then laughed. "And you thought I was gonna for a minute there, didn't ya?"

It appeared an uneasy peace but a willing one. With some regret I realized I'd never get the real blow-by-blow of their confrontation, not from either of them. Kept between them, it would cement their rebonding. Made public, it would embarrass them both.

Micah nudged him. "Town Meeting."

"Yeah." Sean dragged a chair from behind the drapes, then just leaned on it heavily. "Well, you were there for the start of it. That wire put it all together for me and I took off. Brigham was there spouting off the same crap he'd been filling our ears with, crap he had me partway believing, about the apprentice conspiracy with the Open

Sky to take over Harmony, when all the time it was him conspiring for power and using us to do it."

"Us . . . the CDL?"

His eyes flared defensively. "Yeah, the CDL. Us. Me. When I got there, one of our guys had just jumped up to beg Cam to run for mayor, like we'd planned, like *he'd* planned—he wanted it to look like a response to overwhelming public demand for a new leader who'd be tougher on immigration and such."

"Who'd throw all the apprentices out."

"That wasn't in the plan at first."

I shuddered. "What'd you do?"

"Grabbed the floor mike and told everyone Cam was killing people. Then Cora Lee had all this information handy, enough to get Cam under house arrest and his passport revoked."

"Oh, Sean, bravo!"

"I watched it on the shop monitor," said Micah. "After the show came down. He was brilliant. Turned the vote right around. Even in the shop, where they'd been just about ready to throw me to the wolves along with everyone else."

Sean eyed him ruefully. "Yeah. Some performance. But most of the Door were so pissed at Cam, they rose up in support. No matter how bad we want changes in Harmony, that ain't the way we're going to make them."

Micah was looking proud, but he hadn't been chased and terrorized and bashed around—unless I'd imagined that, too. I felt something further needed to be said. "What's the difference, Sean, murder or expulsion? They're the same thing in the long run."

Micah shifted protectively, made a sound of denial.

"No, she's right," Sean allowed. "That's why the agreement we finally hammered out."

I jiggled the citizenship paper. "This?"

He nodded. "Full citizenship for all current apprentices and a five-year moratorium on new admissions while we take a long, hard look at the OAP. That's all the Door was at first, concerned like-minded folks getting together to study the problem."

"Then why all the secrecy?"

Sean's strong, stubby fingers drummed the side of his thigh. "Well, it was a damn delicate issue, when you're talking about people you know and work with. People you're fond of."

"I'll bet," I said ungracefully.

"Okay, yeah, things got out of hand! Shit, Cam was whipping us up with his Open Sky horror stories—one night he brings this Deeland fella from Tuatua and he's so convincing about someone in the Eye being this terrorist Conch guy, it friggin' scared us, and Cam sees an issue he can use to seize control. He ferreted out the ones who'd listen to him closest. I'd suspected the e-mails were coming from inside the Door, but it didn't seem such a bad idea and I was up to my ass at the theatre and getting a lot of pressure from Bill Rand and . . ." Sean's hold on the back of his chair had tightened into a death grip. He took a breath and let go. "I got myself so deep in a hole, I couldn't see out! By then Cam had veered off on his own when he saw we weren't going to be as radical as he wanted. Believe me, Gwinny, I didn't know about the soccer teams 'til Cora told us."

"I believe you." I knew Cora had been circumspect about what she'd told. "What does Brigham say about all this?"

"Ha," replied Sean lightly, "not much."

Micah's expression was as neutral as I'd ever seen it. "Cam was found dead at his home this morning."

"Yep." Sean bared his teeth unconsciously. "Slipped right through the Security cordon, someone did. Sliced him from ear to ear. Couldn't happen to a nicer guy."

"Oh lord," I said inadequately. "Who . . . ?"

"No one knows."

I had my suspicions and Micah's careful silence suggested that he did, too. I remembered my own knife and wondered where it was.

"Lot of blood on the sand the past few weeks," Sean noted. "I feel the worst for Jane, who'd have her papers now if she'd just goddamn stayed alive." His chair rocked and slammed against the floor. He jerked his hands away from it. "Sorry. Well, I'm off."

"Going to Town Hall?"

Again the crooked, bitter smile. "Nah, I'll let them celebrate on their own. I've had enough of Town Hall for the time. 'Sides, we're still cleaning up at the theatre. Close call for your guy Mali—you should see the stuff that *didn't* go off. Anyway, you rest up, hear? Micah can't get fuck-all done without you."

"Sean . . ." I reached for his hands.

He folded them in front of him and stood back. When I stared at him, he said, I can't believe you really thought I'd . . ."

I let my own hands fall to the bedclothes. "I seem to be thinking a lot of weird things lately. I'm sorry."

"Me too."

When he was gone, Micah waited while I blotted my eyes with the sheet, then said, "What he conveniently forgot to tell you is that he quit this morning."

"Quit?"

"His job. At the Arkadie."

"Sean?"

Micah nodded, somewhat enviously. "He said—and I quote—'A man's gotta know when he's hit burnout.' Howard's trying very hard to figure out some way to blame it on me."

"Quitting's a brave move, but it's true, he could use a rest."

"Rest? Not Sean. He's decided to run for his village's vacating Town Council seat in November. Says he's doing his politicking in public from now on. After last night I'd be very surprised if there wasn't a landslide in his favor."

Micah paced a little, enlivened by the memory. "You should have seen him up there! He really was magnificent: outraged, emotional, personal, obscene, funny, everything you could want in a politician!" He sighed. "Except the right politics. Sean's a Harmony-firster, dyed in the wool. I don't understand how I can like and admire him so much, given how differently we view the world . . . as it turns out. But it won't hurt to have someone official raging against overpopulation and excess development. Tourists are population, after all. Cora Lee thinks Cam Brigham wasn't worried about the OAP at all, but was just using the issue to distract the CDL from his big plans with Francotel."

"And using Jane." I toyed with the precious paper in my hand.

"Yes. But even she would applaud the result, which is: welcome to Harmony, Citizen Rhys." Micah held out his hand.

I shook it. "Now I'm a citizen, will they let me out of here?"

"Are you sure you feel up to it?"

"I think so. Why? What's all the fuss? What do they think's wrong with me?"

"The official story is nervous collapse brought on by over-exhaustion and stress. That's what Jaeck told the Chat."

I peered at him. He was trying to tell me something. "And unofficially?"

"Concussion."

The room lurched. I saw myself again flying through the air, the white wall rushing at me. I covered my eyes, moaning in horror.

He came over and put his arms around me.

"Oh, Micah . . . I'm so afraid."

"Tell me exactly what you saw."

I told him what I'd seen, and what I thought I'd done. He held me, smoothing my temples like a mother while I forced the words out. When I was finished, he let me go and slumped aside, organizing his own apprehension into coherent form. "The worst of it is, it could be true. In all the chaos—you, Sean, Town Meeting . . . Omea said everyone was fine and we were too distracted to question."

"Cris said everybody saw them. I saw them, on the vid!" Now I didn't want to credit it. "Two bodies, Micah?"

"Three, if your aim was true."

"Has anyone searched the theatre?"

"Thoroughly. Looking for Peter."

"Oh! Mark! Talk to Mark! He was there!"

Micah chewed his mustache. "Mark wasn't at the theatre today. Songh was looking for him. We're also looking for the Matta. You don't know where that ended up, do you?"

"The Matta! Oh god!" I wrapped my arms around my chest, rocking miserably. "It's gone, of course it's gone! It had blood all over it! Micah, where are they? Why isn't he here? Why are they doing this to me?"

Why the charade? If it was one.

Micah fidgeted, trying to set an example of calm. "I expect there'll be some answers at their big event tonight."

"Not soon enough!" Urgency seized me. "Micah, please get me out of here. I've got to go to Cora's. I've got to know!"

"Gwinn. Wait." He captured my flying hands. "Before

you go. I'm . . . going to betray a confidence. I just came from Cora's. Omea received me alone, looking exhausted. She offered the rest of the troupe's excuses and thanked me for my work and my concern. Then she swore me to secrecy, saying she wanted to be sure I understood why they had decided not to finish out their run in Harmony, that in fact, they would not be playing the first preview."

"They're leaving? They're leaving!"

He nodded. "A gesture of protest, the safety of the troupe, many other reasons which we went into at length. I even agreed with a few of them. But listening to you now, I fear the real one is that they *can't* play that preview."

"Without Mali."

"Or . . ."

I whispered, "Without Sam."

"Without both of them."

"No!" I flung the bed covers aside so violently they fell in a pile in Micah's lap. "No!" I lunged out of bed, tottering, searching for my clothing, muttering. "If they're not going to play the preview, they'll leave before tomorrow night!"

"She wouldn't say. At least it can't be tonight. It's past six. The Gates are closed and they have their Town Hall event at nine."

I pushed the plastic curtains aside, felt around wildly under the bed. "I've got to get to Cora's."

Micah bent to the bedstand. "Here."

I took the folded coverall from him It wasn't mine. "What's this?"

"What you were wearing when we brought you in."

Chilled, I shook it open, checked the label inside the neck: MARK BENEDICT.

Of course. Mine would have had Peter's blood all over it.

I pulled the coverall over my hospital gown, clumsy with dread. It fit well enough, not that it mattered. I stuck my hands in the pockets and my fingers closed around a small, rough-surfaced sphere on a leather thong. My necklace. The thong had been broken, perhaps torn. I knotted it crudely and put it on. "It's true, it's all true," I muttered. Piece by piece, the evidence mounted. In the other pocket, a scrap of paper: "Come if you will. You are needed. M."

I showed it to Micah. "Mark's with them. That's why you haven't seen him."

"All right," he said. "Let's get you out of here."

He had to pull rank to do it, a complex process of subtle intimidation in Harmony, where the only rank is citizen or non-citizen. But Micah was very good at it and the night staff a little lax. We prevailed. The hospital was in Underhill, north across Founders' Park from Cora's house in Lorien. We avoided a Chat reporter dozing in the lobby and sprinted through the rain for the Tube. I stopped at a public newsbox to grab the latest edition. Under a color pix of the Eye in rehearsal, the headline, IS HE OR ISN'T HE? I crushed it in frustration but shoved it in my pocket. Sam's face was clearly visible in the background. As we hurried for the Tube, I heard a low rumbling overhead. I slowed, glanced upward.

"No," said Micah. "Don't suppose you would have heard thunder before, would you?"

"In the vids. Thunder?"

"There's been talk that the weather program's developed a serious glitch."

Or the Preacher's stormsongs. I found myself grinning unaccountably. How could they be dead? They were magic, weren't they?

At the station Micah stopped at the Silvertree-BardClyffe line.

"You're not coming with me?"

"I think," he said gravely, "that this journey you are meant to make on your own."

"Micah, I meant to Cora's."

"Even that far. When you know what's happened, you'll tell me."

I hugged him tightly, kissed his cheek. "Thank you for believing I'm not a crazy person."

"Pray God you don't end up wishing you were."

"Yes. Micah, are you really going to cancel Marin?"

"Yes. Now be off. Here comes a southbound."

"Tomorrow!" I called as the doors slid shut between us.

The ride felt like forever. I wanted instantaneous transport. Though it was after six, there were a lot of tourists in my car. Lately, with the new hotels opening, there seemed to be tourists everywhere, all the time. These were wet and anxious, complaining about the rain and chill while debating the events at the Arkadie. Sean's Town Hall speech was even being quoted.

I was startled from my eavesdropping when a party of apprentices I didn't recognize gave me a hearty thumbs-up sign. Was the Chat spreading my face around Town as well? No, rain-drenched as they were, they were exchanging victory acknowledgments with every apprentice in the car. The reality of the Town Meeting began to penetrate. Even more convincing than the fancy parchment folded away in my breast pocket was an older woman offering her hand as we rode the escalator to the surface. "Welcome, citizen!"

I smiled a proper thank-you, seething inside for Jane's sake. *People had to die to make you willing to say that!* And then I knew I didn't belong in Harmony anymore. I shivered in my borrowed apprentice coverall. Ah, Micah, I risked everything to come to Harmony, to learn to make Art . . . but I can't do it here, not now, not anymore.

The dome was deep lavender when I came out of Lorien station. The crowds had thinned. From the village to Cora's was a ten-minute walk: I ran it in five, down the smooth wet tree-lined streets, so seemingly benign, past sugarplum bungalows becoming houses becoming august mansions set far back on misty velvet lawns.

It was night in the empty aspen grove and Cora's gate was shut. The ground was damp, but here it did not seem to be raining. I peered through the ironwork and rang the bell. The tall, arched windows of the great-hall were dark. The only light visible was in an upper room. I walked the ground plan in my head: Cora's sitting room. I rang again.

Cora had no entry monitor at her gate, no intercom. Just the old brass bell plate and silence. People always called ahead before they came to Cora's. I rang a third time, many desperate presses of that ungiving antique, then I stood back and shouted.

I shouted Cora's name, I shouted Sam's. I was sure Security would be down on me in a minute for disturbing the rich folks' rest, but I paced back and forth before the gate and shouted all their names, one by one, and when I got to Mali's last of all, it came out in a choked cry of pain. I'd remembered the Station Clans' mourning chant and could not bear the implacable silence that answered my every call.

Light appeared in the great-hall windows, a slim golden crack between the tapestry drapes. Cora Lee hurried down the entry steps. Her small slippered feet clicked across the drawbridge. Without makeup, she was as pale as the porcelain of her ancestors.

"Cora . . .?" I hardly knew where to begin. "Are they all right?"

"Of course, dear." Her face was closed. She was not going to tell me anything. "They're preparing for tonight."

"Can't I come in? Doesn't he . . . don't they . . . Cora, won't you tell me what happened? Mark said I should come!"

Pity was softening the mask. "Gwinn, I know this has been hard on you."

"Hard? I don't know if they're dead or alive. I don't know what's real anymore! You've got to let me in!"

"Gwinn, dear, they're not here. They've gone already."

"Gone?" I said stupidly. "All of them?"

"Of course . . . to Town Hall Plaza. It's nearly nine."

Her hesitation was like an alarm going off. She said all of them, but her eyes said otherwise. They wouldn't do a performance without . . . would they? And why had they chosen nine o'clock? Because the curfew had been nine o'clock, but also . . . then I remembered it was Friday. The Gates were open until nine and thronged with tourists. The perfect crowd for adepts at disguise to lose themselves in. No ceremonious leave-taking for the Eye. No funerals or celebrations. They were simply going to vanish, and leave the entire Town of Harmony in Town Hall Plaza waiting for them.

Misdirection. Why? What elephant were they trying to make disappear this time? *Themselves.*

"When, Cora? When did they leave? For the love of god, *when*?"

A glimmer of secret light showed in her dark eyes. "Already twenty minutes ago. You're too late, really."

"No!" I whirled away from her and bolted.

I thought hard as I ran, through the silent aspen grove, past the glowing mansions. Settling my body into a steady automatic pace as Sam had taught me, I calculated times and distances. I decided they wouldn't take the Tube. Not because Ule had such a horror of the underground or even because of the occasional breakdown that stalled you in the tunnel for minutes at a time. In the Tube you had to remain too still for too long for successful disguise, and there'd be no escape if one of them were recognized by some citizen as eager for the truth as I was.

But if I took the Tube, I might beat them to Gateway Plaza.

What was I going to do if I found them? At least then I'd have the truth. If Sam was with them, I knew I'd have no pride, but what if he wasn't? I realized I'd taken Mark's note very much at face value.

At Lorien station, I blessed the westbound when it arrived quickly and was a Closing Time express. I had to wedge myself in viciously to get on. I was panting and heated from my run, and wet from the rain that had begun again as soon as I left Cora's grove. A citizen behind me muttered about rude apprentices. I didn't care. I didn't even remind him I was now a citizen because I'd forgotten it myself already. When we slid into Plaza station, I exploded through the doors, propelled by the pressure of the crowd and my own single-minded urgency, up the escalator into stinging cold rain.

My heart sank when I reached the crowded plaza. It must have been winter holidays in one of the African domes. Dark, nervous faces and bright colors everywhere, distorted by the deepening dusk and the dancing reflections of the lighted cafés in the puddles dotting the pavement. The damp chill encouraged extra layers of clothing, and the shadows under an awning or a hat brim were impenetrable. I was going to need luck to find them if they didn't want to be found, and right then I wasn't feeling very lucky.

If they were here, they'd surely split up and find their way to the Gates separately. I made myself be cold-blooded long enough to decide which one of them to look for. The women were hopeless, given the oddities of current fashion. Mali was the hardest to hide, but if he wasn't there, I'd lose the rest while looking for him. Sam I'd never find even if he was there, no matter that I knew his every gesture and movement, every color and measurement that would describe him. He could change them all at will, and would elude me.

Cu or Moussa, I decided, as I raced up the steps to the observation deck above the Gates. Finally I settled on Cu. His beauty he could disguise, but in his ramrod back was a pride so ingrained, he'd never think to alter it.

I gained the railed platform as the Voice of Harmony

began to hurry the tourists along in earnest. It was quarter to nine. Out on the busy tarmac, the field lights glared. No rain Out There. A dry, hot dusk. The ranks of hovercraft were filling fast, the usual commercial airlines, a few private or executive hovers scattered among them. A dark green one without a company logo caught my eye. It was parked a bit apart, unusually close to the edge of the field where the Outsiders pushed up against a recently installed white picket fence. It was a good two meters high but so cutely picturesque, it made my gorge rise. It was stronger than it looked, holding back the weight of the mob without giving an inch. Still, that's a reckless pilot, I thought, parking so close when the Outsiders are obviously interested in his hover.

Two women detached themselves from the stream of boarding tourists and walked toward the dark green craft. They carried fancy shopping bags and tottered gracefully on too-high heels. They leaned into each other like laughing girlfriends, but they moved in sync like twins. *Like dancers!* By god, I'd guessed right! I screamed at them, a useless gesture behind the shell of the dome, and stupidly conspicuous if the Eye actually wanted to avoid me.

A visible shudder ran through the Outsider mob as the women passed. There was a silent massing closer to the fence. I thought those in front would be crushed, but the mob was surprisingly orderly. Children were lifted to their parents' shoulders so they could see through the palings of the fence.

What are they looking at? The stylish, well-fed domers going home to their well-fed domes? A masochistic pastime.

I dropped out of direct view, among some SecondGen kids playing umbrella tag on the stairs. They giggled at my blue coveralls and whispered among themselves. I stared at the plaza, praying that Lucienne and Tuli hadn't been the last through the Gates. I was doing the biggest and most important room scan of my life. To my utter amazement, I spotted Te-Cucularit almost immediately. Leaning against the wall by the westernmost Gate, wearing a broad, curled-brim hat tilted against the rain and reading a glossy brochure in the glare of the Gate light. Waiting. For the others? For me?

I saw a superior hand in this, someone who knew who I'd look for, someone who always seemed to guess my thoughts, which as much as I loved him had never been Sam. But Mali alive might well mean Sam wasn't.

Joy and terror ran with me down the rain-slick stairs. The final alarms were sounding, harsh blares that said, *"Get your ass out of here!"* The visitors most reluctant to forsake their Campari and soda in the shelter of the café awnings became the ones who shoved hardest in the lines at the air locks. I shoved back, moving crosswise to the traffic. I lost sight of Cu several times as anxious people with wet luggage surged around me, throwing me off course. Once when the crowd cleared a bit, I saw him nod to a woman entering a lock who, underneath her flowered hat, might have been Omea. No Sam, no Mali. The Voice now reminded everyone that all the hotel rooms in Town were booked for the evening and Harmony did not allow sleeping in the streets.

I'd almost reached him when someone grabbed my arm. A total stranger, some flush-faced damp young man whose eager grin reminded me sickeningly of Peter. "Hey," he burbled drunkenly. "Congratulations, *citizen!*"

"Thanks!" I yanked free, but when I turned back, Cu had vanished. The alarms rang insistently. I broke through the last ranks of the crowd and threw myself against the wall in despair. Backing against it, I searched frantically, then at the last moment ran for the Gate. The Greens were preparing to close up. Cu's brimmed hat bobbed at the entrance to the airlock.

"TeCu!" I screamed.

His head went up. He turned against the human traffic and saw me. He gave me a strange, bright look of warning and challenge, then let the traffic carry him into the lock. A final tourist hurried through behind him.

TeCu was the last to leave, I knew he was. The Green on duty lifted an eyebrow at me as I danced at the barrier. "The Gates are closing, citizen."

"TeCu!"

Through the clear wall of the lock, I spotted Tua ahead of him, Ule and Moussa just beyond. Still no sign of Sam or Mali or anyone who could be them, but all along the boulevard, the Outsiders pressed close to the rail as the Tuatuans drifted toward the far edge of the throng. Feral eyes followed them, gray lips muttered, scrawny hands stretched between the pickets, begging for a handout. Within an arm's length of the fence, Cu did not look at them, but hidden by the crowd to most eyes but mine, he reached out to them, his fingers grazing theirs, his clean brown hand slipping from one grimy outstretched paw to the next. They did not snatch at him. It was his touch they demanded, and Tua's and Moussa's and Ule's ahead of him. A mere touch of their fingertips and the grimy paw was withdrawn in gratitude. In reverence. Worshiping eyes followed after them, lips moved in soundless longing, shaping over and over a name I recognized: *Latooea. Latooea. Latooea.*

Latooea! There!

Caught in a sudden haze of blue, I shoved the astonished Green aside as she unlatched the safety barrier and let it slide home. I skinned through the narrowing slit and pounded after Te-Cucularit, not caring whose shoulder I rammed into or how many toes I bruised. Cu did not look at me when I caught up with him, breathless. He gripped my wrist tightly and guided me toward the hover.

He was angry, but I wasn't sure it was at me. Wonder and apprehension kept me mute. *Latooea!* the Outsiders breathed, hardly a name at all but a round and rolling murmur like oceans. The Outside summer heat hit me like a blow to the chest. The air was thick and moist and dirty, the tarmac soft and hot and very black. The floodlights glared brighter than the sun glowering above the mountains.

Oh, Micah, what have I done? Thrown away my citizenship on the very day I acquired it! For Latooea? For a patch of sky?

I followed Te-Cucularit toward the green hover, refusing to think about being Outside, or about who had lived and who had died. I let time slow and relished the few moments left when I didn't know the truth.

At the gangway, Cu stood aside for me to ascend. Tua held back and surprised me with a quick hug. "Good work," she said, mystifying me. At the top of the ramp, Omea met me with a maternal embrace. "Gwinn, thank the good powers. Are you all right?" Her eyes searched me as she urged me inside. My grace time was over.

The hover's interior glowed with a softer light, cool spring greens in the carpet, richer leaf greens on the fabric-lined walls, in the velvet seats, in the silk window shades. Cora Lee's private craft, I was sure. The ceiling was recessed and lit around the rim. It was blue, a profound and endless sky blue. I stared up into it, transfixed. For a moment I forgot why I was there.

The rest waited inside, their silly tourist outfits in rude contrast with the serene decor. Ule was already stripping off his shirt, flinging it to the floor as if to punish it. I began counting immediately. Including the three outside, nine, and the ninth was Mark. Mark, in tourist garb like the others. No Mali. No Sam. Behind me, Omea told the pilot he could retract the gangway.

Nine, plus me. The tenth? Me? Oh no, that couldn't be. Not Sam. Not Sam too. He'd promised *I'd* be safe. I'd never thought to worry about him.

Mark put his arms around me, rocking me gently. "Gwinn, Gwinn. We were afraid you weren't coming."

We. Already it was we. "He's dead, isn't he? They're both—"

Mark touched a finger to my lips. "Everything in good time." He took my hand and led me to the rear of the craft. Through a green-curtained doorway was a little tassel-and-tufted-velvet observation lounge. There with his back to us, staring out the dome-side port, was Sam.

I pressed my fist to my mouth to keep from crying out. Mark squeezed my hand and left, letting the drapes fall shut behind him. I stayed where I was, just looking. Sam. Alive at least. As for well, I couldn't say. He was in a black T-shirt and jeans. Bandages wrapped his chest and right shoulder, immobilizing his arm in a sling. A brightly patterned jacket and scarf lay shucked in a corner.

When I could trust myself to show some dignity, I went over and stood beside him, looking where he was looking, silent, not touching him for fear my crazy joy would fracture against his hard transparent shell.

Out on the tarmac, the last tourists shoved on board. The hovers retracted and closed up, taking off one by one. The field lights dimmed. The floods illuminating the stone Muses carved above the Gates flicked off. The dome was a shimmering liquid darkness swimming with stars. Along the boulevard, the Outsider mob eased away from the fence and straggled off to their shacks and smoky lean-tos. A few remained, young mostly, gazing steadfastly at the green hover with distant fire in their eyes.

"Good work, Rhys," said Sam. "You made it. You listened better than I knew." He reached into his back pocket and pulled out my little knife, safe in its sheath. He handed it to me without looking. "You'll need this where we're going."

I took it, drew the blade slowly from the dark tooled leather.

"I cleaned it for you," he said, and that told me everything I didn't want to know. To steady myself, I rolled up the leg of my borrowed coverall and strapped the knife in place. I'd missed it while it wasn't there.

"I thought you were dead."

"And you came anyway? Better and better, Rhys."

"Then I did right, coming? He said you'd never ask."

"Mali?" he whispered.

"Mali," I said, and felt my heart crack wide open.

He exhaled, as if he'd been holding his breath for hours, then curled his good arm around me, and held me tight to his bandaged chest while I wept for the lack of real magic in the world to bring back the dead.

EPILOGUE

THE OUTSIDE:

"Sam?" Omea stood in the curtained archway. "Tua's got the Town Hall tap on the vid, if you want. It's nine."

He didn't answer at first but must have felt curiosity stirring beneath my tears. He let me go and turned away from the port. "Come on, then. The farewell performance."

In the forestgreen room, the others hunkered in front of the big wall vid like eager, vengeful children. I started at seeing Harmony so clearly again, as through an open window, as if I'd never left it: Town Hall Plaza, the rain, and the growing throng sheltering under scattered umbrellas or jackets pulled up over heads.

". . . *and though we can see from our third-floor vantage,*" the vid commentator was saying, "*that the nasty weather has discouraged many from accepting this peculiar invitation in person, the crowd is still enormous, and we know you're there at home watching . . .*"

I sank to the rug beside Moussa. Sam stood by, unwilling to settle. Moussa folded me into the circle of his arm. "Welcome."

"*. . . you can see the rain is still coming down hard and the wind has been picking up all afternoon, but Mayor von Hirsch has asked us to announce that Maintenance is hard at work searching out these temporary glitches. Also, those citizens concerned about the strange restlessness among Harmony's bird population should understand that this is a natural response to an abrupt change of climate and is also temporary . . .*"

Beside me, Moussa shook with deep private laughter. The soft whoosh across the carpet was Sam pacing, ranging the edges of the room as Mali would have done.

"*Now, at twenty seconds to nine o'clock, the silence out there is deafening . . . fifteen . . . ten . . .*"

In the plaza, the gusting winds beat up to a sudden gale. Rain-swept foliage heaved and swayed along the edge of Founders' Park, waves of green lashing the wet shore of pavement. Umbrellas and jackets tore free and rose like a flock of frightened birds, red and yellow and orange, fleeing toward the zenith.

"Five seconds, citizens, and are we ever glad we're inside!"

Exactly at nine, the wind died and all the artificials blinked out. Umbrellas and jackets and hats spiraled gently through the slackening rain onto the heads of the crowd. Under the gathering of cloud at its apex, the vast curve of the dome was as transparent as fine crystal, as if it weren't there at all. The hard line between In and Out melted into clear, bright air. Rays of amber and pink shot lengthwise across the white plaza as Outside, the sun slid along the dark edge of mountains.

"They could have it that way all the time," Omea sighed.

A rainbow misted into view above the twin towers of Town Hall.

Ule cheered and whalloped Tua on the back. "What finesse!" Tua coughed, then nodded graciously.

The rainbow faded as the rain stopped and the cloud dispersed. The plaza shimmered gold and pink. The dying sun picked out damp jewels in the flowerboxes and etched the faces of the citizenry, who lowered their umbrellas and gazed about, taking great breaths of relief and bewilderment.

"A whiff of jasmine, a tang of orange and ginger," offered Tua.

"Like home," Omea smiled. "Well done."

"Home!" Pen echoed fervently.

"Hullo! What now?" demanded the commentator. Cries rang out from the plaza. Pointing arms surged skyward like a legion of bayonets. The vidcam panned up sharply. In the furthest heights of the dome, a cloud of darkness circled, now sinking like smoke through the misty golden air. Moussa leaned forward eagerly as the darkness resolved into separate inky specks, wheeling in formation.

Birds. Thousands of birds. Different kinds but all black, flying together, the loon side by side with the raven, the toucan with the crow. They circled above the marble steps, around and around in an edgy symphony of wings, until the crowd backed away and left them room. On the spot where we'd presented our petition, the spot where Jane had lain, the flock landed, turning the white marble to mobile ebony.

I turned to Sam. "How did you . . . ?"

"Not me. That's Moussa's crowd."

I leaned away from the big African beside me, eyes wide. "Akeua," he nodded.

Ule cackled. "And a shitload of bird food."

The vid commentator's vocabulary was being sorely tried. *"What a sight! This is unbelievable! This is the most extraordinary . . . !"*

The screen blanked abruptly, then flashed bright blue. The message built letter by letter: HARMONY NEEDS DISCORD, white like clouds in . . .

. . . *sky!* Yes! The blueness seized me, filled me with the joy of Mali's gift: the courage to embrace freedom. His gift to me.

Sam mistook my intake of breath. "I know. Mali would have written it better."

Cora's hover lifted of at nine-fifteen, joining the end of the caravan gliding toward the Albany–Springfield airport. I stood with Sam at the observation port as the geometric glitter of the landing lights and the red safety beacons atop the Gates and finally the fitful glimmer of the dome itself shrank into darkness.

Leaving Harmony.

"Where are we going?"

"I can't tell you that. Later, everything."

"Is this a test?" I asked lightly.

He shifted, eyeing the green-draped walls.

"Even here?" I whispered.

Sam only shrugged.

Leaving Harmony. But not the Harmony of my childhood dreams. That had been taken from me before I left.

My only regret was not saying good-bye to Micah. I hoped he'd understand as he always seemed to, that Cris and Songh could keep the studio running properly without me, without Jane, with the SecondGens who were to be Micah's new help. That was the agenda, after all. Train the home folk, see if they can do the job. See if all that foreign talent can be done without.

They'd manage. Competently, earnestly, mostly without inspiration but always adequately enough to satisfy those to whom Art was a foolish luxury. No matter what Sean said about reviewing the OAP, I knew my generation of apprentices was Harmony's last. Oh, Crispin would be famous very soon, I was sure of that, but from now on, Harmony's younger artists would know nothing but Harmony. At least the adoptees knew their birth-domes. We had all been, at least once, Outside. In time, the work coming out of Harmony would have reference only to itself. It would be rarefied and insular. I did not weep for three years wasted as the lights of the dome were swallowed by the night. I was grateful to get out with my creativity intact.

Ahead of us, the slow-moving curl of red and blue running lights banked toward the south. When our craft slowed and quietly dropped off the end of the caravan, I realized we weren't going to the airport. We veered off into the void without beacons to guide us. I glanced at Sam but held my tongue. He was absorbed in the darkness beyond the port. Now that I was there beside him, he'd put me from his mind entirely.

He wouldn't sit. Between long vigils at the port, he paced the little lounge as if struggling with a particularly thorny problem, which I interpreted as how he should negotiate the chasm of grief that confronted him no matter how hard he tried to avoid it through withdrawal or outrun it by endless circling of the room. Finally Omea wheeled in the onboard first-aid module and made him sit long enough to have his bandages changed.

The shoulder wound was a nasty laser tear-and-burn. Omea probed and swabbed, and it hurt to watch Sam lean eagerly into the pain, welcoming the distraction of a bodily agony. He seemed disappointed when she finished quickly, and refused the painkiller she offered.

"You're worrying too hard," she soothed.

Sam grunted.

"Should have given Jaeck time to work you over more thoroughly."

"I was busy."

"Moussa's putting food together in the galley," she said as she repacked the module. I doubted Sam could be convinced to eat, but I'd had only a meager hospital meal since the night before. I thought of Jane and her pragmatic refusal ever to miss a meal, just in case. I took Omea's hint and went forward.

The galley was tiny, silvery, and compact. Moussa filled it entirely. He had every cabinet open and all four cookers going. With severely limited counter space, he was creating an elaborate casserole of eggplant, tomatoes, cheese, and spices. He laid out each vegetable as if preparing it for ritual sacrifice, slicing and dicing and setting the pieces aside with slow, frowning concentration. Filling the unfillable emptiness, I thought as I watched from the doorway.

"How is he?" Moussa asked after a while.

"Oh, very bad, I think. How's everyone else?"

He laid out a fat, ripe tomato and quartered it precisely. "This is . . . is . . ."

"Difficult." Ule squeezed in to snatch away a whole tomato, biting into it as if it were an apple. "You going to cook up everything in the kitchen?"

Moussa shrugged.

"You think that's what he'd want?" Ule growled in disgust. "Us moping about meanwhile?" He hooked my elbow and hauled me into the main cabin, where the deep-cushioned seats were arrayed in neat rectangles around low teak tables, more like a fancy waiting room than an aircraft. The seats reclined into beds. Pen was stretched out flat, Tuli cradled in his arms. Tua dozed, curled into a feline ball. Lucienne and Te-Cucularit talked quietly in a corner. Cu looked up, frowned, and looked away. Maybe it was me he was angry with. For coming? For being here when Mali wasn't?

Ule shook me gruffly. "Proud of you, ladykins. You used it when you had to."

Mark was sitting by himself, staring into space. Mark, the tenth. Mali's chosen heir. I dropped into the chair next to him. "Yeah, great. I lasted about six seconds."

"Long enough. Would've been two down, otherwise."

Ah. Could I have saved Mali, then, if I'd moved faster, if I'd seen Peter sooner? If? If? I glanced toward the curtained doorway with new understanding of at least one of the tortures Sam was putting himself through in there.

"What happened after I . . . went out?"

Ule perched on the edge of the chair opposite me, his bony knees up around his ears. "Well, you slowed the kid down real well but you didn't exactly stop him, and we already had enough cleanup to do and Sam was moving a little slow, so Cu finished the job with those good hands of his, then dumped him while Sam and I made Mali invisible and wiped up the gore."

"I used you to distract the stage crew," murmured Mark.

"And then took Mali's call with the rest of us." Ule

clicked his teeth appreciatively. "Mali was right under their noses all the while they were fussing over you."

And the elephant vanishes. I rubbed my eyes. "Dumped him?"

A malicious mischief glimmered in Ule's dark eyes. "The protein tanks out at the recycling station may smell a little peculiar for a few days."

My stomach knotted, turned over. The hover shivered in a gust, dropped, and settled. "And Mali?" I whispered hoarsely.

"You'll see soon enough."

I didn't understand. "But why, Ule? Why the cover-up? Why not tell the world what happened? They suspect it anyway." I pulled the damp and crumpled newsfax from my pocket and pushed it at him miserably. "Why not wipe their noses in it? Jane's murder was useful but Mali's isn't?"

They were both staring at me, Ule's eyes narrowing as if I'd confirmed some suspicion. He took the fax and spread it out on the tabletop. The polished teak was inlaid with colored woods in an elaborate pattern of leaves and flowers.

"Is he or isn't he?" A cold grin curled Ule's lips. "A very excellent question."

Mark glanced away. "Ule—"

"Hush, boy. He'll have his reasons." Ule turned back, crushing the fax under my nose. "You see how the media can tame a man? Dead or even wounded, he's mortal, measurable, a mere witty headline, his cause made trivial by gossip and the gory details. But alive, alive despite all, he's a mystery and a miracle."

He leaned forward, fierce and dark and quiet, his arms braced on the low table as if to hold himself back. "Understand, ladykins. The Eye must seem always to walk through the fire unscathed. That is more important for those who hold faith in us than any amount of useless raging at a world seeking to kill us off. For them, Mali will live, must live."

I saw again the scrawny Outsider arms stretching to the touch of Te-Cucularit's fingertips, sooty lips mouthing a soundless litany.

"Latooea," I murmured. It was suddenly so obvious. Why must a hero be one when ten could do it so much better?

"Aye, ladykins. Walking the Stations of the World, to save its life." He touched the carved bead at my throat, grinning. "Latooea's totem. You've been wearing it all along."

"But they keep your secret, the Outsiders?"

"It's their secret. Besides, who in the world of domes cares what an Outsider knows? Only gets sticky on Tuatua, where the two worlds interface."

"Somebody knew enough to come after you in Harmony."

"The Planters' Association has tribal informants. But if they knew the full truth, they wouldn't be trying to pick us off one by one. You see, they can't imagine a leader that isn't the one they'd like themselves to be, a single all-powerful individual. And then there's the suspicion that nags even the coolest heads among them: that the Conch *is* magic. That is their nightmare, for if the Conch is magic, how shall they prevail? Thus we steal their hope, eat at their confidence, leave them sleepless in a cold sweat, wondering as you wondered when we danced into your life: *Is it really magic? Could it really be?* A knife is a fine weapon, yes, but our fists around their very hearts, that is power." Ule glanced at the silent, brooding Mark, then peered at me as if to be sure I was listening. "We do anything to nourish the magic. *Anything*. Remember that, ladykins.

Hovers are slow, and ours flew a lazy, random pattern of evasion before it finally began its descent. I knew we could have been at our destination hours before were it not so important to keep its location secret. If even Cora's hover was bugged, as Sam seemed to fear, couldn't they find us anyway?

There was no baggage to gather. I'd come empty-handed, without even my own coverall. The Eye had brought nothing, either, except their tourist outfits and whatever they had on under, and there was no hidden baggage compartment in Cora's elegant craft, where extra hydrogen tanks must be taking up the entire space below decks. This hover only looked like a lady's airport shuttlecar: it was built for long distances and its galley was stocked to feed a small army. Cora Lee was a lady of power and surprises. I considered her public association with Outsider charities and wondered what other activities her philanthropy hid.

We came down in darkness, floating out of black sky to be swallowed up in blacker land. Sam was at the front hatch before the rotors cut out, leaning into the blue-lit cockpit. "Contact?"

"On the mark," the pilot replied. "Ready and waiting."

"Let's make it fast." Sam palmed a wall plate and the cabin lights dimmed. The Eye became mere shadows clustering in the close, warm darkness as the whine of the fans died into silence and the faint vibration of the floor stilled. The hatch swung open and upward. The Outside night came rushing in.

It was the sound at first. Not just the occasional night-calling bird and an insect or two, but a bewildering variety, all of them screaming at the top of their lungs. Uncontrolled populations of who-knew-what kind of mutated owl or cricket or frog.

And the smell. I shrank against Mark as we both stared into the singing, odoriferous void on the other side of the hatch, asking ourselves, *Is it really safe to breathe?*

"There's the signal." Sam moved instantly down the ramp, homing in on an invisible point in the blackness. The others filed past quickly while Mark and I waited to be felled by this air that smelled so dangerous and yet so alive, so surprisingly cool, so thick with dampness and vegetation. It smelled active, the metallic tang of ozone warring with the rich green scent of pine, as if great battles were being waged for possession of our lungs. I forced myself to breathe deeper, more slowly.

The last passing shadow paused in the hatch. "Think of your grandfather, Gwinn-Rhys. How he wanted to be where you are going."

"I will, TeCu. Thank you."

"Then hurry."

The ramp retracted as soon as we cleared the bottom, stealing away the last vestige of visibility. Te-Cucularit drew us quickly out of range. The pilot kicked his fans into spin. The hover rose without running lights, a black cloud moving against the . . . stars!

I jerked at Mark's sleeve. "Look!"

"Hush!" someone scolded.

"Omigod," whispered Mark, craning his neck as I did to this new wonder. Mali had shown me the blue but not this dizzying whirl of naked fire through velvet, incomprehensible vastness.

"Domers," muttered Pen.

"Stars later," growled Ule, pulling us along. I stumbled after him blindly. The ground was soft underfoot, with the crisp surface crackle of dry pine needles. Overhead, the stars disappeared. I heard the sigh of wind through heavy branches, and up ahead, a woman's voice, flat and authoritative.

"That one," Ule said quietly. "And this one." New hands grasped me, gentle but firm, a touch I didn't recognize.

"Apologies, ma'am." A boy's voice. A blindfold was wrapped around my eyes, a gag pressed to my mouth. "Just for a time. You breathe okay?"

I nodded, doubting and suddenly terrified. The gag tasted dirty and the boy smelled of sweat and onions. Had the Eye led us this far to give us up into the hands of Outsiders? But then, where did I think I'd been every time I went to bed with Sam?

"Bit of a walk now." The Outsider boy gripped my arm above the elbow, whispering, "A big root there to your right, ma'am," and so on, as we climbed through the trees. Invisible things snatched at my pant legs. Wings that sounded too big and too chitinous to be healthy buzzed past my ears. Branches whipped my face. I felt like a captive enemy, and wondered how long it would be before they decided to trust me.

After a while, the tree sound was thinner, the soft rattle of leaf against leaf. There were roots, slippery ledges that crumbled underfoot. Still we climbed, up and then down. Exhausting, this walking blind. The boy was strong and bone-thin. His breathing came easily long after mine labored. I tried to guess how old he was. Nobody had ever called me ma'am before. When we stumbled down off the rocks, I was grateful for secure footing and let it calm the panic rising in my soul. We waded through thick, damp grass as tall as my thighs. The insect roar was deafening.

Among trees again, we stopped. A murmur of voices broke the quiet, and a low arrhythmic growl. The boy untied my gag and blindfold and left me blinking in two parallel shafts of light that roiled with smoke. I inhaled cautiously. Smoke and steam. And people, four or five, hurrying back and forth in front of the light. I squinted after my guide, caught only a ragged thatch of blond hair melting into the night.

The shafts lit up a strange sort of clearing. A broken road

ran the length of a narrow break in thick, scrubby trees. Along one side a cluster of two-story concrete buildings grew out of riotous underbrush. A fainter golden light shone through an open doorway, which just as I noticed it, was extinguished. A door squealed on rusted hinges, thudded shut. Voices called to each other, low and urgent. The shadowy people hurrying in the light were laden with boxes and crates and holdalls.

"Some trip, huh?" Mark joined me in the odd double beams, untying his own blindfold from around his neck. His eyes were bright, worried, excited. "See where we are?"

"Do you?"

"Oh, somewhere north. Maybe Canada. I mean, over there." He pointed at the darkened buildings. "It's a decommissioned maintenance station for the vacuum tubes. Can you believe it? They've found a way to intercept tube shipments."

"Between the domes?"

"Remember in the news, all those goods vanishing mid-shipment?"

It made me smile. Another of Sam's "leaks" in the closed system.

Two short, thick men trotted through the beams in front of us. They wore stained leather tunics and long beards trimmed with glittery beads, and carried a crate stamped with the Arkadie logo. I recognized one of Hickey's prop boxes.

"From Harmony?"

Mark nodded eagerly. "Couldn't get the uh, baggage out of town otherwise, without people noticing."

Now I was glad for the gag and the blindfold, and Sam's uneasy silence. I didn't want to know the location of such a secret. I followed Mark into the beams of light, toward the growl and the billowing steam, which resolved into a square, hulking groundcar with twin headlights and oversized wheels, a narrow driver's cab beside a glowing firebox in front of a big, boxy trailer with high window openings along the sides. It looked cobbed together out of mismatched parts, some domer child's idea of a ground vehicle, shuddering and hissing like a living creature, coughing white steam from its funnel-shaped stack. I thought of Micah's dragons for Marin as Mark led me around the back. Double doors spread wide. A lantern swayed from a ceiling hook, shooting flickering light and shadow across the ancient, scarred sheet metal of the walls.

The Eye's wardrobe trunks and prop crates were stacked inside, blocking the small window between trailer and cab. Sam paced the lowered tailgate, urging the loaders to hurry. His wounded arm hung free of its sling. He'd been working it and the bandages were thick with new blood. His face shone ashen in the dim light, sweated with pain and worry. Below him, a thin, dark woman in a red turban and leather breeches leaned against the tailgate, sucking on a smoking twig.

"Weah's yer tall un?" she demanded idly.

"He'll be joining us," Sam replied. "He had work to do."

"Nevah tried movin' tis mush tru heah befoah," she muttered. Her weathered skin was oddly stretched across her face. Her jaw seemed overlarge, too stuttery and angular. Tales of mutant Outsiders boiled up in my brain.

"Easy, Red Momma," growled Sam. "You never had anything this precious through here before."

"Ay-yuh," she agreed amiably, frowning at his bleeding shoulder. "Getsher sel' fished up, willyuh?"

"Yeah. When we're loaded. You get us going, ha?"

The woman helped Tua swing two heavy wicker baskets into the truck, then stalked away toward the front. I saw she moved with a faint rolling limp that slowed her down not a bit. For no reason and every reason, she made me think of Sean, and I felt a surge of panic and homesickness. What in Cora's luxurious little hover was still an adventure scenario became in this black wilderness a terrifying reality.

Oh god, what have I done?

Sam was watching me, must have seen the panic race like bird shadow across my face. "So why *did* you come?"

I stared up at him as if at a stranger. None of the answers I had right at hand seemed worthy of so all-encompassing a question. "Mali's visions."

He frowned. "What visions?"

I scribed the arc with my arms as Mali had done. "The sky. The blue open sky."

Sam studied me, said nothing.

"And to work where it will mean something," I added finally.

He shook his head, then let it loll wearily against the side of the truck. "Sonofabitch is always right," he muttered. "Well, I wouldn't want to think it was just for me."

The two bearded and beaded men hauled in a final crate, slid it into place, and came forward, extending grimy paws to hoist Mark and myself aboard. The rest of the Eye waited inside, clustered silently around a long crate shoved against the wall, Tua's baskets piled casually on top. Ule nestled among them swinging his legs, looking more gnomelike than usual in the lantern's unreliable glow. Moussa crouched with one arm thrown protectively across the box. Omea stood at its head, as if it were an egg she was hatching. I was distracted enough not to notice except they were all as nervous as cats, and I didn't understand what was going on.

The moment the doors clanged shut, the Eye went into action, clearing the top of the crate, dragging it to the clear space by the doors. Moussa grabbed the lantern from its hook and held it close while TeCu and Omea worked at the metal latches on the sides. Up front, the throaty spit-and-growl accelerated into a chuff-chuff. The truck shuddered and began to move. I almost missed the faint hiss that escaped from the crate as the latches clicked open. The lid rose as if taking a breath, and I did not miss the quiet repetitive beep that seemed to be coming from inside. Pen and Cu grasped the edges of the lid and pulled it free.

A man-sized box full of blood-spattered green silk and Mali's dead face lying among the folds.

Tears sprang hot to my eyes. I had thought never to see that face again. I was amazed that a dead man could look so alive, so still but serene, as if he were only sleeping. Then I noticed the thin tube snaked into Mali's nose.

The crate was lined with a heavy mil plastic. The beeping came from a flat gray box that Omea was lifting from under the layers of fabric. I recognized it. I'd just been in a hospital. It was a life-support monitor.

"Still stable," she announced. "Like a rock."

Tuli began to weep. Tua's hands flew to her face to quiet her unbelieving grin. I backed against the rusted metal doors and slid to the floor with a hard, dumbfounded thud.

Sam knelt, laid two fingers under Mali's jaw as if the monitor wasn't proof enough, then dropped his head to his arm in a spasm of inarticulate relief.

"Can you wake him?" Ule asked. "Can you chance it yet?"

Omea considered. "Mali's good in trance. He may refuse the wake-up if the healing's not gone far enough."

"Only an hour or so to the village," Moussa said.

"Have to convince him," said Ule. "He's got to walk in."

"Or give Ideela too much explaining to do," agreed Tua.

"Let me look him over." Omea reached in to fold back the shimmering green of the Matta. The wounds were there as I remembered them, one just below his collarbone, the other to the far left side of his chest. They were neatly sealed with suture tape. The surrounding skin looked healthy. Well worked over by Dr. Jaeck, deep inside Omea's trance, his heartbeat so slow and faint the monitor barely registered it. Mali was hard at work healing himself.

Healing!

Omea uncovered Mali's arm, untaped the drip in the crook of his elbow, then unclipped a hypo from the side of the monitor, and pressed it to his bicep. She adjusted the flow from the oxygen cylinder buried under the folds at Mali's side. "Let's see what he wants to do."

I looked for Mark to share this miracle. He sat beside the crate, smiling moistly, and I realized he'd known about it all along. It was only me they didn't tell. And now no one remarked on my astonishment or paid me any heed. Only Te-Cucularit, who across the bent bow of Ule's back offered sympathetic disapproval. Not angry with me after all, but for me, after all I'd done.

Even wept my heart out for a man who wasn't dead.

The truck lurched across a particularly broken stretch of road, perhaps no road at all beneath its rotting tires. The crate shuddered and slid sideways. Ule and Moussa steadied it.

We watched the vital-signs monitor for the slightest quiver. Then Omea said, "Heart rate's increasing." She put her hand gently to Mali's chest. "He's engaged. He's going to give it a try."

' Sam slapped the side of the crate. "Yes!"

Tuli let out another rapturous sob.

Omea sat back on her heels on the jolting floor. "It might take him awhile to climb back to us. He'll be sensible about it. Not like you, Sammy, crazy to get back to the battle at any cost."

Sam grunted. He flattened his palm across Mali's forehead, the slightest caress, then rose and glanced around. When our eyes met, I backed away, out of the lantern light.

Sam came after me. "Rhys? You all right?"

"You promised me the truth!"

He was taken aback. "If I'd known it, you would have had it."

"You could have told me!"

"We didn't know if he'd make it." The truck lurched. Sam snatched me with his bad arm, gripping me hard though it must have been agony. "Would you have wanted to see him die twice, if he hadn't?"

It was arrant emotional manipulation, but it stopped me cold. I squeezed my eyes shut at the memory, and the wonder of Mali alive overtook me again. "Oh, but through the vacuum tubes?"

"He was too far gone to walk out. We had to vanish him before anyone knew he was down."

Through the fire unscathed. And now excited whispers rose from around the crate. Mali's chest moved to a living rhythm.

Sam pivoted away. "Is he . . . ?"

"Coming back to us already," Omea exclaimed.

"He wants to know, did he make it out alive?" Ule grinned.

The others laughed, the light, eager sound of heartfelt relief. It was a visible battle, Mali working his way up through the levels of trance, a diver surfacing from the deep: stroke, stroke upward, then rest to decompress, rising layer by layer, a battle played out only in the flickering of his eyelids. His body lay inert, his jaw slack. Nothing living but his lidded, tremulous eyes.

And then he opened them. Slowly. No confusion, no struggle for consciousness. It was there already. He took in the shadowed roof of the truck, the faces of his troupe leaning over him in concern, the high sides of the plastic-lined crate cutting off his peripheral vision. He didn't stir. "Where?" he croaked.

Omea giggled happily. "On the way to Ideela's village. Welcome back to life, oh, my brother!"

"Yah." His eyes slid shut.

Sam dropped beside him. "No, Mal. Stay with us. This is your half-hour call."

Mali groaned. "Sleep."

"Not now."

"Ah. Hurts."

"Gotta get up. For Ideela."

"How can you ask him to?" I burst out.

They all stared at me.

"Because he must," said Te-Cucularit gently.

And he did. When the truck finally lurched to a stop, Mali was sitting upright on the closed crate, draped in a concealing robe from Tua's baskets, supported by Moussa's solid bulk. His eyes were crazed with pain and determination, but when the double doors flew open, he stood up. His eyes cleared. He walked to the tailgate and surveyed the busy, torchlit clearing, people cooking and sewing and debating around fire pits, people coming and going with children and food and stacks of paper. He smiled at Moussa and arced his free arm at the soft glow spreading behind a sawtoothed horizon of trees, a pinkish glow, the color of orchids or the inside of shells. It touched the crisp dark leaves of the shrubbery, warmed the ragged bark of the pines, and softened the sudden twist of Mali's jaw as he forgot himself and laughed for joy.

Ule shrieked with mad release and leaped off the truck. Lucienne and Tuli followed and were immediately surrounded with greetings and hugs, with demands for news. TeCu handed Omea down from the tailgate. A dark-haired boy hurried up. One arm was shorter than the other and terribly scarred. "Can you make a debriefing by nine or do you want to rest up first?"

Omea smiled. "Rest first. How about three?"

"I'll spread the word." The boy charged off.

Mali stood free of Moussa's arm. He greeted the red-turbaned woman as she gaped at him in astonishment, then crouched and vaulted to the hard-packed dirt into the embrace of a tall woman with braided hair whose brilliant smile was the mirror of his own.

My jewelry peddler, from the day I'd arrived in Harmony. I clutched at my necklace and stared.

Sam said, "Ideela, Mali's sister. She runs this training center. I believe you've met before."

"Yes," I murmured, astonished to learn just how long I'd been manipulated, "we have."

He grasped the back of my neck and shook me gently,

possessively. You think you're here just to keep me company?"

"The Eye has a training center?"

"Open Sky does. Several of them. You want to work where there's meaning to it?" He gestured proudly. "Your new home, Rhys, and welcome to it."

The Outsider woman was muttering with her bearded companions, nodding at Mali with awe-muted glances. Sam grinned. "Don't look so surprised, Red Momma. I told you he'd be joining us."

I moved to jump down from the truck.

"Hey, Rhys," Sam called softly. His hand flicked, came up presenting a perfect white rose. "I'm glad you came."

I stared at it, at him, said nothing.

"Almost as hard to keep this alive as it was Mali." He waited for a smile, then tossed the rose aside abruptly. "Why do I get the feeling I'm gonna have to start all over with you?"

"Something about the issue of trust," I mumbled.

"No." He caught my head in his hands and kissed me until it only made sense to put this anger away for another day. "That's better," he said, when he felt me let go of it. You asked me once if I believed the world would end if the Clans couldn't walk the Stations. Look out there! That's what would end: unshielded dawns and winds and weather, wildlife that's actually wild, thirty-mile hikes without running into a force field! Is it worth it? Worth the risk, worth nearly killing Mali, worth what I put you through? Worth the lies we tell and the charades we play, every day, even the lives we take, the lives I've taken when I've had to, with my own hands, to keep *our* lives long enough to tell that truth, out there: Father Rock, Mother Wind, Laukule-lemelea the Water, Wurimutonutonu the Sun. The noblest Art, the most awe-inspiring magic: the living world. Undiminished, uncaptive, undomed." He swept his good arm at the flush brightening into orange behind the trees. With the abrupt movement, fresh red stained his bandages. "Nothing else in life *is* worth it!"

Past the glistening bloody profile of his shoulder, orange slid into yellow into pale green into blue. The deep blue bowl of the sky that Mali had shown me long before I knew it was what I wanted.

"No," I said faintly, "nothing is." And I lifted my eyes

hungrily to the gilded warmth of the sun as it edged above the dark tree line.

Sam laughed. "Don't stare at it, Rhys, you'll go blind. Don't you domers know anything?"

About the Author

Marjorie Bradley Kellogg lives in New York City and designs scenery for the theater. She is the author of *A Rumor of Angels*, *The Wave and the Flame*, part I of Lear's Daughters, and *Reign of Fire*, part II of Lear's Daughters, all published by Signet. *Harmony* is her first novel since 1986.

WORLDS OF IMAGINATION

☐ **HAWAIIAN U.F.O. ALIENS by Mel Gilden.** A four-foot alien with a two-foot nose is sleuthing out a Malibu mystery. But it seems even a Philip Marlowe imitator might find himself and his duck-billed robot sidekick headed for disaster when he takes on spiritualists, thugs, and a Surfing Samurai Robot reporter. (450752—$3.99)

☐ **STRANDS OF STARLIGHT by Gael Baudino.** A stunning, mystical fantasy of a young woman's quest for revenge against her inquisitors, and her journey through the complex web of interrelated patterns and events that lead to inner peace. (163710—$4.50)

☐ **THE MAGIC BOOKS by Andre Norton.** Three magical excursions into spells cast and enchantments broken, by a wizard of science fiction and fantasy: *Steel Magic*, three children's journey to an Avalon whose dark powers they alone can withstand. *Octagon Magic*, a young girl's voyage into times and places long gone, and *Fur Magic*, where a boy must master the magic of the ancient gods to survive. (166388—$4.95)

☐ **BLUE MOON RISING by Simon Green.** The dragon that Prince Rupert was sent out to slay turned out to be a better friend than anyone at the castle. And with the Darkwood suddenly spreading its evil, with the blue moon rising and the Wild Magic along with it, Rupert was going to need all the friends he could get.... (450957—$4.99)

Prices slightly higher in Canada.

**Buy them at your local
bookstore or use coupon
on next page for ordering.**

If you and/or a friend would like to receive the *ROC Advance*, a bimonthly newsletter featuring all the newest and hottest ROC books and authors, on a complimentary basis, please fill out this form and return it to:

ROC Books/Penguin USA
375 Hudson Street
New York, NY 10014

Your Address
Name _____
Street _____ Apt. # _____
City _____ State _____ Zip _____

Friend's Address
Name _____
Street _____ Apt. # _____
City _____ State _____ Zip _____